FALLEN ANGEL

WITHDRAWN

MAJOR **JEFF STRUECKER** AND **ALTON GANSKY**

PUBLISHING GROUP

NASHVILLE, TENNESSEE

Published B&H Publishing Group
Nashville, Tennessee

Dewey Decimal Classification: F
Subject Heading: ADVENTURE FICTION \ ARTIFICIAL
SATELLITES—FICTION \ MILITARY INTELLIGENCE—FICTION

Jeff Struecker is represented by Wheelhouse Literary Group
1007 Loxley Drive, Nashville, TN 37211
www.WheelhouseLiteraryGroup.com

FALLEN ANGEL

For Joseph:
I am glad to call you son.

ACKNOWLEDGMENTS

FOREMOST THANKS TO MY King, Jesus Christ. Next I would like to thank my best friend, Dawn. Thanks also to Jonathan and DonnaJune for keeping me on track and on time. I would also like to especially thank Spud, Jesse, Blitz, and the rest of 4D. You guys are awesome. Finally, I want to thank my pastor, Don Wilhite, and the rest of my church family at Calvary Baptist Church in Columbus, Georgia. I am glad God brought us together.

*All that is necessary for the triumph of evil
is that good men do nothing.*
—EDMUND BURKE

*No one has greater love than this, that someone would lay
down his life for his friends.*
(JOHN 15:13 HCSB)

MILITARY ACRONYMS/ ABBREVIATIONS

ABU—Airman Battle Uniform
CID—Criminal Investigations Division
CRRC—Combat Rubber Raiding Craft
ICBM—Intercontinental Ballistic Missile
IED— Improvised Explosive Device
KIA—Killed In Action
NORAD—North American Air Defense Command
NVG—Night Vision Goggles
PLA—People's Liberation Army
POTUS—President of the United States
PT—Physical Training
RHIB—Rubber Hull Inflatable Boat
SAAM—Special Assignment Airlift Mission
SECDEF—Secretary of Defense
SMDC—U.S. Space and Missile Defense Command
STRATCOM—Strategic Command
UAV—Unmanned Aerial Vehicle
USACIC—United States of America Criminal Investigation
    Command
XO—Executive Officer

THE TEAM

Sergeant Major Eric "Boss" Moyer, team leader.
Master Sergeant Rich "Shaq" Harbison, assistant team leader.
Staff Sergeant Pete "Junior" Rasor, communications.
Sergeant First Class J. J. "Colt" Bartley, weapons and explosives.
Sergeant First Class Jose "Doc" Medina, team medic.
Sergeant First Class Crispin "Hawkeye" Collins, surveillance.

PROLOGUE

Space Command, STRATCOM
Offutt Air Force Base
Omaha, Nebraska
May 27

MAJOR BRUCE SCALON'S MIND was elsewhere, someplace with sunshine, cool breezes, and warm ocean waves. The where didn't matter as long as it was someplace other than the windowless buildings where he spent the bulk of his days.

It wasn't that he didn't love his job. It had everything he wanted: a challenging mission blended with high-tech electronics. But a man needed to bask in more than the cold light given off by computer monitors.

As a kid he saw photos of the early days of NORAD, the North American Air Defense Command, tucked away in Cheyenne Mountain, Colorado. From that day on he wanted to be one of those people who monitored the skies over the United States, tracking space objects and missiles launched by any country seeking self-immolation.

One of his favorite childhood games was to draw dials and gauges on cardboard boxes and pretend they were advanced computers. He spent hours creating new and challenging scenarios to occupy his mind. *One day, I will sit behind a desk and know everything that goes on in space.*

But Scalon had a problem. He wanted to be Air Force, yet his Army father wouldn't hear of it. His father thought the Air Force was a second, lesser choice, something a man did because he couldn't hack it in a real military service. Scalon followed his father into the Army. First came West Point, then Officer Training School. His superior officers took note of his skill with all things technical and before long he was living his dream, just doing so in a different uniform than he imagined.

Places like NORAD got all the attention, but many other such facilities existed, each with its specialized mission. On April 7, 1988, U.S. Space Command came to life, its three battalions providing satellite control, communications, and early missile detection. He was proud to be part of the joint military effort to monitor and control space, even if very few citizens knew of the work.

Despite the pride and fulfillment his work gave him, it had one drawback. His was strictly an indoor job. While other soldiers logged time on the ground or in aircraft, he piloted a gray, padded swivel chair. Most days he was fine with that, but at times, like now, he longed to feel the sun on his cheeks and inhale something other than mechanically treated air.

The phone on his desk rang. He picked up. "Major Scalon."

"Major, this is Lieutenant Colonel Amy Moen, Vandenberg."

Joint Space Operations Center in California. Scalon had dealt with them many times. They used optical and radar equipment to monitor space junk. They had more than fifteen thousand pieces to keep track of. Moen was one of the commanding officers of the Space Surveillance Network.

"Yes, ma'am. Is the sun shining in California?"

"The sun is always shining in California. It's the law. Rain has to get a permit to fall. Gray and bleak in Nebraska?"

"Who knows?" Scalon sighed.

"I hear that. We probably have the same view. Listen, we have a situation. A dead Chinese satellite is headed at one of your birds."

"Close?" He leaned back in his chair and gazed at the ceiling. He had heard this before. Space was so littered with rocket boosters, lifeless communication satellites, and other debris that "near misses" were common. Part of his job was moving GPS and communications satellites out of harm's way. In recent years, the crew of the International Space Station had to take refuge in the station's life raft because debris came within a mile of threatening the lives of the men on board.

"Too close. In fact, if you don't act quickly, we think impact is certain."

That got his attention. He straightened in his chair and placed his fingers over his computer's keyboard. "Which bird?"

"Angel-12."

Scalon prided himself on his cool demeanor and controlled emotions. Both shattered like a crystal vase on concrete. He swore hard and loud, then caught himself. "Sorry, ma'am."

"I haven't been read in on that one, but I'm guessing it's important."

"They're all important, Colonel, but you're right. How much time do I have?"

"You should be able to move it with time to spare—"

Scalon heard another voice over the secure line. Someone was talking to Moen.

She came back on. "Hold one, Major."

A sound told him she placed a hand over the mouthpiece. Although it was muffled he could tell an argument was going on. Then swearing. Apparently it was contagious.

The voices cleared. "Now, Sergeant. I want verification, *now*. You got sixty seconds. Do you read me?"

A young voice snapped, "Yes, ma'am."

"Sorry, Major."

"Problem?"

"More like an impossibility."

"I've been known to believe in six impossible things before breakfast."

The colonel chuckled. "*Alice in Wonderland.* Nice reference. I loved that book when I was—Hold." Again muffled voices. When Moen spoke again, Scalon could hear the stress in her voice. "You need to move Angel-12 and move it now."

"Why? What's happened?"

"The object headed for the bird has picked up speed. It's not stumbling across Angel-12's path; it's targeting it."

CHAPTER 1

"EXCUSE ME, ARE YOU Mr. Moyer?"

Eric Moyer didn't open his eyes. He was dead tired and wanted to sleep enough that he didn't care who he offended to get it. If he ignored the questioner, she might go away.

"Sir?"

She was insistent.

"Sir. Excuse me? Are you Mr. Moyer?" The flight attendant took on the "don't-mess-with-me" tone the airlines taught them in whatever school flight attendants attended.

Now it was a contest of wills. Moyer countered by turning his head away and pretending to snore.

"Here, let me try, miss."

Pain shot up his shoulder. "Do that again, Rich, and you'll be pulling back a bloody stump."

"Sorry, man, but this young lady wants to talk to you."

"Is she pretty?" He heard several chuckles.

"Almost as pretty as your wife."

1

Moyer brought his seat back forward and directed his eyes to a petite brunette in a United Airlines uniform—a pilot's uniform. The three gold bars on the shoulder epaulets told him she was the first officer. Members of the flight crew seldom left the cockpit except to use the latrine and that was in first class, not coach where he was seated. Something was up.

"Yes, ma'am. I'm Eric Moyer, but you should know that my wife frowns on me dating other women." Moyer, approaching forty, scratched at his goatee, which had just enough gray to make him wonder if he'd be one of those men who bought product to hide unwanted reminders he was no longer young. He wasn't ashamed of a few gray hairs, but if they started appearing in his longish, brown hair, then he might reconsider.

"I can't imagine why." She seemed put out.

"How can I help you?"

She held out a piece of paper. "I'm delivering a message."

"Someone sent me a message via the cockpit?"

"Yes, sir." She pushed the note forward.

Moyer took it and waited for the woman to return to the front of the aircraft. He glanced at Rich Harbison, a giant of a man with ebony skin. His linebacker build concealed a keen mind and an unexpected love for Broadway musicals. To look at him or any other member of the team, a person would be hard-pressed to identify them as one of the Army's elite Special Ops unit. Unlike most military personnel flying commercial, they wore no uniforms, their hair was longer than Army regs allowed—except Rich "Shaq" Harbison, whose head made a billiard ball look hairy—and wore casual clothing.

Rich cocked his head and flashed a "what-are-you-waiting-for" look.

Moyer unfolded the paper, read it, then closed his eyes again. "I so wanted to sleep in my own bed."

Seated around him, the other men on his team spoke no words, but their expressions said everything.

THE PLANE LANDED IN Los Angeles. Ten minutes after the cabin door opened, Moyer and the five members of his team were on another flight, one held over for them. They were greeted with angry expressions. The passengers didn't like waiting.

One man in first class looked up as Moyer and the others streamed in. "You know, if you'd buy a watch—"

Rich laid his large hand on the man's shoulder. "Rethink it, pal. Seriously. Rethink it."

Moyer led the group through the cabin, each taking a seat wherever they could find one. Rich and Moyer found seats together in the last row of the Boeing 757.

"Omaha?" Rich said.

"Yes." Moyer snapped his lap belt.

"Nebraska?"

"Yes."

"Omaha, Nebraska?"

"See, you got it. And people say you're slow."

"Who says that?"

Moyer shrugged. "Everybody."

"It's a good thing you do what you do because you'd make a lousy diplomat, Boss."

Moyer pushed up in his seat and made a mental note of where each of his soldiers sat.

"So what's in Omaha, Nebraska?"

"Offutt Air Force Base."

Rich rubbed his face. "Air Force! Can I get off the plane now?"

THREE HOURS LATER, MOYER stepped from the aircraft and entered the Omaha terminal. A man dressed in jeans and a white dress shirt stood near the baggage-claim area holding a handmade sign that read: MR. ERIC MOYER, TECHNIC WORKS.

Rich leaned close to Moyer's ear. "Technic Works? Really? Do you know how to turn on a computer?"

"That's what I hired help like you for."

"Oh, so that's how it is? Hired help?"

Moyer walked to the man, his crew nearby but not in a group. Several of the team took places a dozen feet away. Only one followed Moyer and Rich to the sign holder. He was in his twenties, five ten in his combat boots, well muscled, short red hair, and a face that fought a long battle with acne. Of the group, Crispin Collins looked the most military.

Moyer glanced at him, seeing the ever-present iPod earbuds jammed into the man's ears. He tried not to frown but failed. Crispin saw it and immediately removed the tiny speakers.

"You're Mr. Moyer?" The man in the white shirt lowered the sign.

"I'm Moyer."

The man held out his hand. "I'm Tim, your driver."

"I hope it's a big car," Rich said.

Moyer watched the driver's eyes trace Rich's large form. "I think we can fit you in."

"I mean there are six of us."

The man flushed. "Oh. Sorry. We have two large SUVs. We can handle all of you." He cleared his throat and focused on Moyer. "My understanding is your luggage will be arriving late since you changed planes so quickly."

"Our luggage will be home long before we are. Is that right, Tim?" Moyer gauged the man's reaction. He showed no sign of being in the loop.

"I wouldn't know, sir." Tim turned sharply and started for the glass doors.

At the curb outside were two white Ford Expeditions. A young woman in black pants and a pale blue shirt stood by the rear vehicle. The moment Moyer emerged, she opened the front and back doors. Moyer, Rich, and Crispin stayed with Tim. J. J., Jose, and Pete slid into the woman's car.

Moyer sat in silence trying to stuff down his disappointment at being diverted from his home near Fort Jackson, South Carolina. He and his team spent the previous two weeks at Fort Lewis in Washington state working with the 1st Special Forces unit and picking up some specialized and experimental field equipment from the 201st Battlefield Surveillance Brigade. They also picked up young Sergeant First Class Crispin Collins.

Tim pulled onto I-29 and headed south, situating the car in the number two lane.

"So, if I'm not violating some kinda security, where did you guys fly in from?" Tim kept his eyes on the road.

"Fort Lewis."

He nodded, then furrowed his brow. "Fort Lewis, isn't that the new joint base? Lewis-McChord?"

"It is." Moyer smiled and glanced back at Rich. Rich was a purist and believed the branches of the military should be kept separate. It was a pride thing. "One of twelve such bases."

"I suppose that's apropos."

"Oh yeah?" Rich leaned forward. "And why is that—Tim?"

"The Army gave birth to the Air Force. Long before our time, the Air Force used to be the Army Air Corps. Let's see if I can recall my Academy history class."

"Academy. Air Force Academy?" Rich said.

"Yup. Best years of my life. Well, except the first year. That was a little rough."

"Rough?" Rich laughed. "What'd they do, make you wash your own laundry?"

"It was a little tougher than that. I did a lot of marching in the rain."

"Doesn't sound so bad," Moyer said.

"In February? In Colorado? Yeah, it can be bad."

"That was part of your training?" Rich didn't bother to hide his disdain.

"Just at the Academy. The commandant apparently didn't like practical jokes. Anyway, as I was saying, it was in September of 1947 that the Air Force left the Army behind."

"Left the Army behind?" Rich leaned closer to the front seat. Moyer could smell his breath.

"My bad," Tim said. "Poor choice of words."

"Don't let Rich get to you. He is a man of strong opinions."

"And I'm always right too."

Moyer let the quip pass. "Just what do you do, Tim? If I'm not violating some kinda security."

Tim grinned at hearing his words repeated. "I am assigned to Space Command. The same unit the Army leads. It's a joint operation. I work under Major Bruce Scalon. I suppose I should give you my full moniker: It's Captain Tim Bryan, formerly with Air Force Special Operations, now with STRATCOM."

"Didn't like field work?" Moyer kept all sarcasm from his voice.

"Loved it. Love the smell of gun oil. If they made an aftershave that smelled like that, I'd wear it. Got busted up while on mission. Two back surgeries and another Purple Heart later, the Air Force, in its infinite wisdom, decided a desk job might be better for the health of my team. So much for military intelligence." The last words had a chill to them.

"Sorry to hear that." Moyer saw many men who spent years training to do Special Ops work only to be injured and have their lives turned upside down. Those were the lucky ones. They got a second chance.

"I saw plenty of action. So did my dad. Vietnam. Green Beret. KIA."

"I'm sorry to hear that, Captain."

"A lot of soldiers left their all over there." Tim's voice grew soft. "Most people won't understand this, but you guys will. You've been to the Vietnam Veterans Memorial?"

"Yeah," Moyer said. "Several times. Your dad's name must be there."

Tim shook his head. "It's not. Over fifty-eight thousand names on that wall but not my father's."

Moyer didn't ask and Tim didn't offer to explain. He didn't need to. Moyer had no doubt the man's father died while on a secret mission, one that couldn't be talked about even four decades after the war ended. That's the way it was for people like Moyer and his team.

He glanced at Rich in the backseat. The man's expression spoke so clearly words were not needed. Although, seated as he was behind Moyer, Crispin was harder to see, Moyer caught enough of the young man to know that, despite the always present earbuds, he heard everything. Crispin stared out the window, his face drawn.

Every Special Ops—whether Army Rangers, Green Berets, Marine Special Operations Command, Navy SEALs, or Air Force Special Tactics Squadrons—held the same fear. Not dying. They were prepared for that. But dying while on a covert operation, leaving their families without the closure of knowing how or why their loved ones would never come home. In the end, they would receive a neatly folded flag and the thanks of a grateful nation. But they would go home and forever wonder what happened.

Moyer decided to lighten the moment. "What can you tell us about Offutt?"

"I can give you the basics. We have about ten thousand military and federal employees. We're home to the 55th Wing, the Fightin' Fifty-Fifth, and a handful of tenant units including STRATCOM. Oh, and we have a great golf course."

"I doubt we have time to do any golfing," Moyer said.

"So you're responsible for satellite operations," Rich said.

"Yes and no. There are several such units working under U.S. Strategic Command—USSTRATCOM. For example, there is the U.S. Space and Missile Defense Command: SMDC. SMDC provides command and control to the 1st Space Brigade and the 100th Missile Defense Brigade. They also provided space-based tracking.

"There is also the 193rd Space Battalion run by the Colorado Army National Guard. They provide space-based support to ground-force commanders. Working alongside them is the 100th Missile Defense Brigade that oversees our missile-defense system.

"The 49th Missile Defense Battalion is run by the Alaska Army National Guard at Fort Greely, Alaska."

"Why do I think it's all more complicated than that?" Rich said.

"Because you are a smart man." Tim glanced in the rearview mirror. "You've been military long enough to know that everything is more complicated than it seems."

"Can you talk about why we're here, sir?" Crispin had come out of his trance.

"No," Tim said. "Major Scalon will read you in when we arrive."

"Understood, sir."

"Do they eat at Offutt?" Rich said. "I could use some vittles."

"Don't mind him," Moyer said. "He's always hungry."

"Hey, I was gonna barbecue some pork chops tonight."

Tim glanced at the mirror. "I'm afraid those chops are going to have to stay in the freezer."

"I don't like the sound of that." Moyer leaned his head back on the rest and closed his eyes.

"I didn't think you would." Tim pressed the accelerator a little closer to the floor.

CHAPTER 2

CAPTAIN SCOTT MASTERS OPENED his eyes and tried to focus the blurry image playing on his brain. Something was wrong, but he couldn't put his finger on it.

He was afraid.

Terrified, but he couldn't remember why.

His heart alternated between fluttering and smashing the inside of his rib cage like a jackhammer.

He blinked, then squeezed his eyes shut. A second later he opened them again. The fog in his mind cleared and his vision sharpened. He was on his back, staring at a water-stained ceiling. Dark patches dotted with black mold hovered over his head.

He tried to swallow but couldn't muster enough saliva to make the effort worthwhile. He ran a dry tongue over even drier lips.

Where was he? His sluggish mind tried to piece together the jigsaw puzzle of memory, but it was like catching houseflies with his bare hands.

Think. Remember. He was good at giving orders. It was one of his strengths. Still, his confused brain refused to obey.

He turned his head to a dirty plaster wall and a row of small windows set just below the ceiling. Each window harbored milky-white, translucent glass letting light in but not allowing a view of the outside world.

A dripping sound drew his attention to his right. Water fell, drop by drop, to a puddle in the corner of the bare, cracked concrete floor.

With most of his brain cells firing, Masters took inventory. He was on a metal-framed bed. The mattress was lumpy and smelled of urine. He could see a 1950s-style metal chair with torn upholstery on the seat and backrest. The rest of the room was empty. On the far wall was a wide door with peeling white paint.

Wait. That's what he had to do. Wait for his mind to clear more, then he'd know what to do next. Overhead hung a row of pendant lights with glass diffusers. Countless dead bugs inside the glass shades.

As his brain grew more aware, so did his body. Pain, both sharp and dull throbbing, radiated from his right shoulder, the fleshy part of his right waist, and from the right side of his face.

Injured. *I'm injured—wounded.*

The pain grew and Masters began to wish the brain fog would return.

He tried to rise from the bed but couldn't. Something held him down. He willed his right arm to rise, but it refused. A few moments later, he felt the leather straps confining him to the bed.

Tugging, pulling, wiggling, Masters tried to free himself, but he lacked the strength. Weak. He was so weak, something he attributed to blood loss when—

It came back, striking his consciousness like a cruise missile. The sound of automatic gunfire, the *thud, thud, thud* of 7.62mm rounds striking him. At first there was no pain, just the sense someone slugged him several times. Then the pain came: hot, piercing. His first thought was to wonder how the rounds got past his body armor; his second thought was to scream at the top of his lungs.

He remembered falling. "I'm hit! I'M HIT."

The ground was hard and cold. He rolled onto his back. The sky was a washed-out blue. He saw a face: Tech Sergeant Eddie Glassman. "Take it easy, Cap. I gotcha. You're gonna be all right." Glassman's face said otherwise.

Masters heard another shot and Glassman disappeared. A moment later, everything vanished.

The door to the room opened. Masters turned to see a short but thick man stroll in. He wore old-style fatigues, definitely not U.S. issue. On his side he wore a GSh-18 9mm sidearm. Russian.

"Greetings, my friend." The man spoke in a higher pitch than Masters expected. Although his accent was thick, he spoke English well. "I hope you are feeling better. You've had a rough time of it."

"Who are you?" Masters could barely recognize his own voice.

"I am Podpolkovnik Vitaly Ivanovich Egonov, your host."

"Pop . . . pod . . ."

Egonov chuckled. "You Americans have such trouble with the Russian tongue. Podpolkovnik. It is my military rank. Very much like your lieutenant colonel. You may call me Vitaly Ivanovich unless you are opposed to using the patronymic, in which case you may call me Colonel."

"Where am I? Why am I strapped down?"

"You are in a hospital not far from where you invaded our land with your soldiers. You have been wounded. We have saved your life."

"Are you the one who endangered it?"

Another chuckle from the Russian. "As a matter of fact, I and my team are responsible. We shot you just as you would have shot us had we snuck across your borders armed with military weapons. You must admit, you were asking for it."

"We were just sightseeing."

"In Siberia? No one goes sightseeing in Siberia, not carrying automatic weapons and high-tech military communications." Egonov pulled the worn chair next to Masters's bed and sat. From the right pocket of his pants he removed a pack of cigarettes and a lighter. A moment later he blew gray smoke in Masters's face. "Now, why don't you tell me who you are?"

"Just a guy passing through town."

"What? No name, rank, and serial number?"

"You watch too many movies." According to the military Code of Conduct, Masters was required to give his name, rank, and serial number. Information might keep him alive. He was taught to give only enough information to keep himself alive without compromising the mission. He didn't feel like providing that much information.

"Perhaps you are angry with me for having you shot. I can understand that, but you must remember you shot back. Some would argue you shot first."

"They would be wrong." Masters's voice grew stronger with each phrase he uttered. So did the pain.

"Perhaps." Egonov took a long draw on the cigarette, then blew a long stream of smoke into the room. "What is your name?"

"Puddin' Tame, ask me again, and—"

"—and I'll tell you the same. Yes, I'm familiar with the term and poem. Very well, let's go about this another way. Your name is Scott Masters and you are a captain in the United States Air Force assigned to the Air Force Special Tactics Squadron."

"If you know all that, then why bother asking me?"

Egonov rolled the cigarette between his index finger and thumb, staring at it as if it held secrets of its own. "Verification and to see how cooperative you are. I'm disappointed in the last matter."

"Gee, it hurts me to hear that." A bolt of pain ripped down his back. "Where are my men?"

"They are being taken care of. The ones who are alive, I mean."

A shot of adrenaline ratcheted up his heart rate. "I demand to see them."

"Demand? Demand! You're in no position to demand anything. You are my prisoner."

"Our countries are not enemies."

Egonov stood. "Nor are we friends. I don't know what they teach you in the United States, but Mother Russia is not as cohesive as you imagine. Much of the economy is in the hands of gangsters, and our leaders are impotent oafs, poisoned by the West. We are a fragmented country, Captain. The one hand doesn't know what the other hand is doing. Some of us have different ideas about the future of this great land."

"I'm not into politics."

Egonov slipped a hand into his pocket and retrieved a piece of paper. "I've been doing a little research. Even now, I have a great many people learning as much about you as possible. I found this on the Internet." He raised the paper and waved it in the air. "I'm not as familiar with your Air Force as I should be. My focus has always been on troop movements. You should know this well." Egonov sat again and brought the paper in front of his face.

I am an American Airman.
I am a Warrior.
I have answered my nation's call.

I am an American Airman.
My mission is to fly, fight, and win.
I am faithful to a proud heritage,
a tradition of honor,
and a legacy of valor.

I am an American Airman.
Guardian of freedom and justice,
My nation's sword and shield,
Its sentry and avenger.
I defend my country with my life.

I am an American Airman:
Wingman, Leader, Warrior.
I will never leave an Airman behind,
I will never falter,
And I will not fail.

"Sound familiar?"

Masters turned his face away. "I may have heard it before. What about it?"

"May have?" Egonov chuckled. "I bring it up because you need to know, if you haven't already figured it out, that you have *faltered*, you have *failed*, and you did *leave* men behind."

A sledgehammer to the gut would have hurt less, but Masters showed no emotion. Instead he stared at the water stains on the ceiling.

Egonov waited in silence, then sighed. He stood and shouted something in Russian. The door opened and a thin man in a white lab coated entered, pushing a medical device similar to what

Masters saw while visiting his brother in the hospital. A burst appendix landed his brother in a hospital bed attached to several IV lines.

Egonov tossed the still-burning cigarette stub to the concrete floor and let it simmer. A moment later, he lit up another.

"Those things are bad for your health, you know." Masters was glad his fear hadn't yet affected his voice.

"You might be surprised at the number of things bad for a man's health." Egonov inhaled deeply showing his defiance. "Cigarettes, bad food, bad vodka, an angry captor: all things that could be harmful to a person."

The skinny man pushed the device to the middle of the room and stopped when Egonov raised a hand. Masters studied the device. It was an IV pump mounted to a chrome pole with wheels at the base. Several plastic IV bags swung from the hooks at the top of the pole. Masters's heart revved up.

"Some information for you, Captain Masters." Egonov motioned to the man with the IV stand.

"The captain has several wounds, all caused by bullets." He spoke as if he had a pair of hardboiled eggs in his mouth. "The first is just above the belt on the right side. The bullet passed through the flesh cleanly and missed all vital organs. Unfortunately, it has grown infected. I imagine it is quite painful."

Masters said nothing.

The man shrugged then continued. "Another round grazed the right zygomatic arch—the cheekbone—and passed through the right ear. The resulting damage will require substantial plastic surgery. It, too, is infected."

A grotesque image played on Masters's mind. Would his wife and daughter still love him if he returned home looking like a man who tried to shave with a lawn mower?

"The patient's third wound is to the right shoulder. The round entered at roughly a forty-five degree angle relative to the medial line of the torso and the shattered proximal humerus bone and the great tubercle. The glenohumeral joint is, well, it is quite the mess. Like the other wounds, this one is also deeply infected. Without treatment the best-case prognosis is complete loss of the arm's usefulness; worst-case scenario, well, let us just say it is grim."

Masters's stomach twisted and fought the urge to vomit.

Egonov stared at him for a full minute. "Do you understand what the doctor is saying?"

Masters nodded. "He said, I'm busted up."

"A nice American colloquialism. Yes, you're busted up and each of your three wounds is infected." He motioned to the IV stand. "You need at least twenty-four hours of intravenous antibiotic treatment. Probably forty-eight hours." He looked at the doctor who nodded.

"We should begin soon." The doctor unwound the power cord, and pushed the IV stand to the head of the bed. A moment later, the IV pump powered up. Although he couldn't see it, Masters assumed the doctor plugged the device in. It emitted a sharp beep.

"Not just yet, Doctor." Egonov moved to the foot of the bed and exhaled a lungful of smoke that circled his head. "Have you ever seen gangrene, Captain? It's a horrible sight. Those who have had it tell me it's extremely painful. I have seen men beg for death, but that's not the worst. Do you know what the worst part is?"

"I've got a feeling you're going to tell me." He shifted on the bed and pain rifled through his body. Even his toes hurt.

"The worst part of all, Captain Masters, is the smell. It turns the stomachs of the strongest men. Without the proper antibiotics, your wounds will grow worse, and you will die a horrible death from infection."

"And if I talk, you'll give me the drugs?"

Egonov nodded. "You are a smart man. As a special gift, I'll let the doctor administer pain medications. You'd like some pain medication, wouldn't you? It will help you sleep."

Masters gave a graphic description of where Egonov could stick his meds. It made the man laugh.

Egonov rounded the bed to Masters's side. "I know we've only known each other for a few moments, so let me tell you something about myself: I am a patient man and a man of good humor, but I have my limits when it comes to my work. You do not want to cross the line with me. I am giving you an opportunity to be returned to health."

"All I have to do is sell out my country."

"Such a harsh way to put it. Your country has sold you out. Did I get that phrase correct? I know how your military works. You are part of a Special Operations team. You've entered my country like a thief. You wear no insignias, no patches, nothing to identify you. That way if you are captured, just as you have been, your country can deny your existence—which they are about to do. I don't ask much. I want to know why you're here. It is that simple."

"I'm a tourist."

"A tourist. Really? You will talk and I will have to do nothing more than watch."

Masters wished he could muster enough saliva to spit, but his mouth was desert dry.

Egonov drew deeply on the cigarette until its end glowed a bright red. He exhaled into Masters's face. "Let me say it again. I am not a man to trifle with." Egonov straightened, removed the cigarette from his mouth, and slowly snubbed it out—in Masters's facial wound.

The pain was so great he thought he'd lose consciousness. He wasn't so lucky.

Egonov and the doctor moved to the door. "Think about my offer, Captain. And, just so that you know, you are not the only American here facing death by infection." Egonov smiled, gave a two-finger salute, and left.

Masters fought back tears.

He thought of his situation. He thought of his men. He thought of his father and mother. If they knew—and surely his father knew—they would be devastated.

He prayed his capture had not compromised his father.

CHAPTER 3

TIM BRYAN PULLED TO a stop at the main entrance to Offutt Air Force Base. A purple sign identified the entrance as "Kenney Gate." Although Tim was not in uniform, the armed guard gave him a snappy salute and motioned the vehicle through.

"Welcome to the home of the 55th Wing, the largest wing within the Air Force's Air Combat Command." Tim motioned to the buildings populating the base. "We have four thousand acres of prime Nebraska property."

"Does Nebraska have prime property?" Rich chuckled at his own joke.

"You bet it does, big guy. We are also home to such units as the U.S. Strategic Command Headquarters, the Air Force Weather Agency, and the Defense Finance and Accounting Service."

"Now you got me," Rich said. "I always was a pushover for accounting."

"Aren't we all?"

Moyer weighed in. "I take it you do other things here you can't talk about."

"Affirmative. The Strategic Air Command Museum is here. You really should see that."

Moyer looked at the driver. "You think we'll have time?"

Tim shook his head. "You'll be lucky to have time to catch a sandwich."

"Swell," Rich said.

"You will get to see something very few see."

"Like what?" Moyer turned his attention to the road ahead. They were approaching a modern-looking, boxy, reddish building. It reminded Moyer of a large post office near his home. The structure was surrounded by a well manicured lawn. Tim parked in front of the building. Moyer and the others exited the vehicle and walked across a wide concrete patio leading to a metal roofed lobby. To one side of the building stood a tall flagpole with the Stars and Stripes flapping in a gentle breeze. The sight of the flag warmed him. Some would think the sentiment was sappy. Maybe it was, but he didn't care. He and his men pledged to protect all the flag stood for—sappy or not.

Footsteps behind him let him know the rest of the team had closed the gap between them. A glance told him all his men and their two escorts were accounted for. It was a habit Moyer picked up on the first mission he led: count your crew. Always get a head count.

"This way, gentlemen." Tim opened the wide glass door and waited for everyone to enter the foyer before following them in.

Several armed security men met them in the lobby. IDs were checked, and portable, digital fingerprint readers were used to log their identities.

"That was quick."

Moyer turned to see twenty-eight-year-old J. J. Bartley standing near Tim.

"That's because you were expected." Tim smiled. "You've already been photographed and run through a face-recognition program. That, your fingerprints, which were just compared to the military database, and a few other identification techniques, tell us you are who you say you are."

"Who else would we be?" Rich gave a cheesy grin.

Tim nodded. "Yeah, I know it's overkill, but would you want to be the guy who let in someone he shouldn't just because he was sure he had the right guy? That's not a screwup I'm willing to chance."

"Makes sense to me." Moyer looked around. "Where's your partner? The one who drove the other SUV."

"This is as far as she's allowed to go. She's gone back to work."

"So she doesn't have clearance?"

"Nope."

"What does she do?"

"To the elevators, please."

Rich stepped next to Moyer and J. J. "I don't think he's going to answer your question."

"I got that impression."

J. J. spoke just above a whisper. "I asked the same question in the car. She wasn't real talkative. My guess is she does some kinda secret work."

Rich placed a hand on J. J.'s shoulder. "That or she just doesn't like you, buddy. It's hard to hear, but you gotta hear it: You ain't no ladies' man."

"That's good." J. J. shook off the hand. "My new wife is the jealous type."

"Gentlemen." Tim's voice carried a hint of impatience.

Moyer and the others followed Tim down a wide hall to a small alcove where two pairs of elevator doors awaited them.

Moyer looked for the call buttons but saw none. Then he realized something. The building was a single-story affair. Who needed elevators in a single-story building?

Tim removed a key card from his shirt pocket and held it next to a small, dark glass panel. He then held the back of his hand next to the glass. A moment later, one set of doors opened. They entered a cab twice the size Moyer expected. The doors closed and Tim spoke. "Captain Tim Bryan."

The elevator moved at the sound of his voice.

"Coolness."

Moyer looked at Crispin. "What's so cool?"

"The security: card reader and security card with a smart chip, back of the hand biometric reader, and voice recognition." He turned to Tim. "I bet there are multiple cameras in here."

"You'd be right. You must be the security specialist for the team."

"Intel mostly, but I double up on security, yeah."

"What else do you do?"

Crispin smiled but said nothing. Moyer was starting to like the newest member of the team.

The elevator picked up speed and Moyer expected the pit of his stomach to drop. It didn't. It rose. Of course. There was no place to go but down.

"If I asked how far below grade we're going, would you tell me?" Moyer had his doubts.

"You may ask whatever you like."

"But you promise no answers. At least no details."

Tim shrugged. "I do as I'm told."

"Understood." Moyer couldn't fault the man.

The elevator slowed and settled to a stop.

The doors parted.

Moyer had been in many high-tech facilities, but this one looked straight from the Syfy channel. For a moment, he thought he was stepping into NASA's Houston Control, or at least what he imagined it would be. He saw photos of the control center during its Apollo days: a big room filled with people sitting at consoles gazing at computer monitors and clacking away on keyboards. Except this place was more streamlined. The computer monitors were thin, flat screens and the people who sat at them wore uniforms. Most wore the new Army Service Uniform of white belted trousers, black pullover sweater, and jump boots. Half of the workers were women.

On the opposite wall a massive series of monitors covered two-thirds of the wall and reached to the ceiling. Moyer estimated the monitors covered sixty feet of wall. Above the monitors ran several rows of digital numbers in yellow and red lights. He couldn't make sense of most of them but did notice a few coordinates and dates. The rest read like code.

"Wow," Crispin said.

"Amen to that," J. J. added.

Moyer scanned the images on the giant display. Several were present: In one he saw what looked like a U.S. fast-attack submarine skimming the surface of some ocean; in another he recognized the barren terrain of Afghanistan, territory he was all too familiar with; another monitor showed a view of a wide, meandering river. If Moyer's geography was right, he was looking at the Yangtze River in Qinghai Province in China. "Is that—?"

"This way please, gentlemen." Tim led them along a raised walkway to a pair of double doors. A shiny metal sign bore the words: TELECOM. Tim opened the door, which swung inward, then stood to the side. Moyer was second in, followed by his crew.

This room was small by comparison but similar in that it had a console along one side and six large monitors mounted to the wall. Soundproof batting covered the walls. No art. It was Spartan, just like the military liked it. Several rows of padded chairs, like theater seats, faced the monitors.

"Have a seat, gentlemen." Tim motioned to the chairs. Moyer and the others sat.

"What's the movie?" Rich lowered his bulk into the front-row seat next to Moyer. The others sat in the second row. "And where's the popcorn?"

Moyer glanced at his second in command. Rich Harbison was always a font of jokes, quips, and digs, but he knew when to be serious.

The door opened and an Army major walked in. Moyer and the others were on their feet a half second later.

"As you were." The man was tall, sported short brown hair, and eyebrows a half-size too large for his face. His thin lips were pulled tight.

Moyer and his team sat.

"I am Major Bruce Scalon, one of the officers in charge of STRATCOM here at Offutt." He exchanged glances with Moyer. "You the team leader?"

"Yes, sir." Moyer gave a nod. "Sergeant Major Eric Moyer."

"Introduce your team, Sergeant Major."

"Yes, sir." Again Moyer stood. He pointed to Rich. "This is my second, Master Sergeant Rich Harbison. On mission he goes by 'Shaq.'"

"I can see why," Scalon said.

"Staff Sergeant Pete 'Junior' Rasor, communications. He's the baby of the group, well, *was* the baby of the group. Next to him is Sergeant First Class J. J. 'Colt' Bartley, weapons and explosives. He's also the team sniper."

"Bartley?" The major furrowed his brow. "Do you have a brother in the Army?"

"Yes, sir. Paul Bartley."

"The chaplain?"

"Yes, sir. Do you know him?"

"I do, but not well. Bumped into him once or twice." Scalon returned his attention to Moyer. "Carry on."

Moyer pointed to a dark-haired man. "Sergeant First Class Jose 'Doc' Medina, team medic. Last, and probably least, Sergeant First Class Crispin Collins, surveillance."

Scalon looked puzzled. "No nick?"

"He's new to the team. We haven't given him a nickname yet. He's the newest and youngest."

"Do any fieldwork before?" Scalon asked.

"Just training, sir, but I'm ready for whatever the Army has planned for me."

Scalon chuckled. "It's not my place to judge your readiness, Sergeant. I'm an overweight desk jockey. I do my fighting from behind a computer monitor." No one commented. "I suppose they call you, 'Boss,' Sergeant Major. Is that correct?"

"Yes, sir. They do."

"It helps with his low self-esteem." Rich grinned, then quickly added, "Sir."

"It's my understanding most teams like yours have a designated class clown. You it, Harbison?"

Rich puffed out his chest. "I am, sir."

"Well, keep the funnies in check for now." He put his hands behind his back. "Do you know where you are?"

Moyer answered. "Captain Bryan gave us some information about the base and your mission, but nothing beyond that."

"September 11, 2001. It's a date none of us will forget. Then President Bush, as is required by Secret Service and military protocol, left Washington, D.C. One of the places he flew to was here. He held video meetings here with his secretary of state, chief of staff, the head of the Joint Chiefs, and others. Of course things have changed since then." He sat at a small table and looked at a simple monitor system. "We're over a decade past that now and the technology has improved."

An airman seated behind the electronics console at the side of the room turned in his chair. "Sir, we're ready."

"Go ahead." Scalon stepped to the side and stood by the first row of chairs. The large monitor blinked to life and the image of a well-muscled man in his fifties appeared. His hair was Army short, his skin tanned, and his face chiseled. Moyer knew he wasn't a dour man; he'd seen him smile twice in the years he had known him.

"Do we have a clear connection?" Colonel MacGregor looked to his side, apparently to whoever was twisting knobs and flipping switches. Moyer heard, "Affirmative."

"We're good on our end," Major Scalon said.

"Good." Colonel Mac looked into the camera. "Gentlemen. Sorry to change your itinerary, and I'm even sorrier to tell you you won't be coming home right away."

J. J. sighed. Moyer couldn't blame him. J. J. had a new wife at home. Moyer had a wife and two kids he was dying to see. "No problem, sir." It was a lie.

"Down to brass tacks. Three days ago one of the Army's satellites was knocked from orbit. As you know, we and the other branches of the military have come to depend on satellites for GPS, communications, real-time observation, and battlefield control.

I don't need to tell you there are a hundred other things these birds do for us. Angel-12 is one of the latest intel and recon satellites. I hear Sec Army has a personal stake in this device. He pulled a lot of strings and shook the hands of a lot of senators and representatives to get the funding. That being said, this has nothing to do with the secretary of the Army's pride."

Mac took a deep breath. "The bird has sensitive optics and communications, things we'd like to keep to ourselves if you follow my drift. And that's just the stuff I know about. I'm pretty sure there's more to it than that, something a few thousand feet above my security clearance. I can't prove that, but I wouldn't bet against me."

"I'd never bet against you, sir." Moyer understood the unspoken words. Much of contemporary military operations were based in technology. The army with the best tech always had an advantage.

"Where did it come down, Colonel?" Rich put all the jokes aside.

"It hasn't. Not yet, but we know the general area. I will reveal that in a moment. First, Major Scalon will fill in the basics for me."

"Yes, sir." Scalon moved two steps forward, not in front of the monitors, but just far enough so the team could see him. "Part of the Joint Space Operations Center at Vandenberg Air Force Base in California's mission is to monitor everything of importance in space. Space has become more crowded than most people know. They keep an eye on more than one thousand active satellites and nearly four thousand inactive satellites or rocket debris. All told, they watch close to sixteen thousand objects; most moving at five miles per second."

Crispin whistled. "That's . . . what? About eighteen thousand miles an hour?"

"That's right, Sergeant. If we count smaller objects, there are close to half-a-million bits of debris over our heads. An aluminum object the size of your fist carries the same kinetic energy of fifteen pounds of TNT. Imagine the kind of damage something the size of a Buick could do." Scalon rocked on his heels for a moment. "On average, there are seventy-five possible collisions every day. When a collision occurs, the satellite usually bursts into pieces. To give you an example, on February 10, 2009, a busted-down Russian communications outpost called Cosmos 2251 collided with one of our Iridium 33 communication birds. It knocked out some phone calls and left more than two thousand pieces of debris."

"So this happened to Angel-12?" J. J. asked.

Scalon shook his head. "There are similarities. It was a deactivated Chinese satellite that did the deed, but this time it was no accident."

"They intentionally rammed us?" The idea infuriated Moyer.

"We think so. There's been no public discussion of this, of course, but behind-the-scene talks have been revealing. The Chinese claimed they were attempting to park their satellite in a graveyard orbit."

"A what?" Rich said.

"Most satellites orbit in geosynchronous paths 22,400 miles above the earth. Dead or out-of-date devices are pushed to a slightly higher orbit where they won't present a danger to other satellites."

Moyer spoke. "But you suspect the Chinese are lying."

Scalon nodded. "Their satellite was inactive for more than two years. Why the sudden concern about its location? I suppose we'd buy the story if the thing hadn't changed course. It didn't bump into our equipment; it targeted it."

"So we're out a bird?" Rich said. "Won't it just burn up in the atmosphere?"

"Good question. With almost any other satellite, the answer would be yes, but Angel-12 has been hardened."

"Hardened?" Moyer said.

"On January 11, 2007, the Chinese shot down a defunct Fengyun-1C satellite using a 'kinetic-kill vehicle,' an unpowered projectile. They scored a direct hit, shattering the satellite into three thousand traceable pieces. One of the things that keep guys like me and my superior officers awake at night is facing an enemy who can shoot down our satellites. Imagine a war in which only one country has eyes in the sky. We'd be fighting like we did in World War II while facing a twenty-first-century enemy."

"So by 'hardened' you mean Angel-12 is up-armored." Moyer kept his gaze on Scalon.

"Yes. It's a new, lightweight armor you don't need to know about." Scalon inhaled deeply. "Pieces of space junk have made earth-fall before. In 1997, a Delta II fuel tank landed in the yard of a home in Georgetown, Texas. In 2001, a titanium motor casing from a Delta II came to rest in Saudi Arabia. Fortunately, it hit the desert and not a city. Most objects that fall from space burn to ashes; those that don't, land in the ocean or in unpopulated areas. Angel-12 will do the same."

J. J. shifted in his seat. "Do we want to know where?"

"These things can't be predicted with absolute accuracy, but we can get close . . ."

"You're killing us here, Major," Moyer said.

"Siberia."

Rich swore.

"Siberia. As in the Russian wasteland?"

"Some people call Siberia home," Scalon said.

"No one I know," Rich whispered.

"In June of 2010, the Japanese Space Agency guided the Hayabusa spacecraft—the one that landed on an asteroid and returned to earth—to the Australian outback. Unlike them, however, we have lost all control of what's left of our bird; otherwise, we'd direct it into some deep ocean. The best we can do is crunch the numbers and watch it fall."

"To Siberia," Rich mumbled. "First Nebraska, now Siberia."

"Yes, to Siberia."

"There's more." Colonel Mac's voice rolled from overhead speakers. "In fact, it's why you're the ones going and not someone closer. The Air Force sent in one of their Special Ops units. They were captured and we believe they are being held near the area where Angel-12 will impact. Your mission is twofold. First, be the first to the satellite, secure its nuclear power source, and then destroy its sensitive communications and optics. Second, if possible, get the flyboys home. Is that understood?"

"Understood, sir." Moyer paused, then added, "How do we insert into Siberia?"

Mac smiled. "You like fishing?"

CHAPTER 4

"YOU GOT TEN MINUTES," Captain Tim Bryan said. "I wish it could be more."

"Not your fault." Moyer's mind believed the words, but his heart was not so agreeable.

"Follow me." Tim led them from the elevator and down a long, wide corridor with a floor polished like a mirror. The footfalls of seven men echoed off the hard surfaces. Tim stopped at a door marked Accounting 105, turned the knob, and swung it open. Inside, two airmen and one lieutenant sat at computers. Were they really doing accounting work or something more covert?

The three came to their feet the moment Tim stepped into the room. "At ease, gentlemen." Tim faced the officer. "I need the room, Lieutenant."

"Excuse me, sir?"

"Lock down your stations and then go get a cup of coffee."

"Um, yes sir." The officer turned to the airmen in the room. "You heard the captain. Secure your computers and desks."

The man's puzzled look brought a smile to Moyer's face. He did his best to hide it.

As the three accountants filed from the room, Tim stopped the officer. "I need five more rooms with phones."

"Sir?"

"In about ten minutes, these men are about to take a long trip. I want them to have a few minutes to make a phone call."

"But, sir—"

"You ever been in Minot, North Dakota, in January, Lieutenant?"

"Five rooms empty and with phones, sir. Got it."

Tim turned to Moyer's men. "The lieutenant will escort you to offices where you can make your calls. He'll show you how to get an outside line."

Moyer looked at the former Air Force Spec Ops warrior. "Are you going to get in trouble for this, Captain?"

Tim shrugged. "I don't know what you're talking about." He slapped Moyer on the shoulder. "For me, this was always the most difficult part of any mission." He chuckled. "When I was wounded, my first thought wasn't if I'd live or die. I was worried about explaining it to my wife."

"I got one of those wives too. My men and I appreciate this." Moyer held out his hand and Tim gave it a man-to-man shake, the kind of handshake that says more than words.

"Come on, Sergeant Major. Let me see if I can't get you an outside line."

Sixty seconds later, Moyer stood at the lieutenant's desk, phone in hand. He was having trouble drawing a deep breath.

"Hello." The voice was like silk: smooth, cool, and soft. It also carried a hint of suspicion. The voice cut Moyer's heart like a sharp knife. He had been through this before. The caller ID at his home read: UNKNOWN.

"Hi, babe." The image of his wife, shoulder-length strawberry-blond hair, sparkling eyes, and million-dollar smile, flashed on his brain.

"Eric? I thought you . . . oh."

"Yeah, my business trip has been extended. I have to make another stop or two before I can make it home."

Stacy had been a Spec Ops wife for years, but it wasn't something a woman could get used to. Eric knew this because she made it clear several times. Never in anger; never in an accusatory tone. Her love bathed her words the few times they discussed the work he did.

Such discussions were always vague, something required by security, not just for Moyer and his team, but also for his family. Truth was, only a handful of people knew about any mission his team undertook. Not even the president knew when a mission began or ended unless he was the one who called for the action. The military survived on invisible compartments. Captain Tim wasn't being snide when he refused to say what operation he was on when he was wounded. Moyer knew a lot about Spec Ops activities, but the fact he was a team leader didn't give him access to what other teams were doing.

Most men could discuss work with their families: the good, the bad, the frustrating, the layoffs, the awards, the contracts. Moyer and men like him could say nothing to family or friends. Those who know what he did—and they were few—could only watch the news and guess if their son, husband, or father was somehow behind the story.

Moyer didn't want to count the number of times he was called up with just enough time to kiss his wife good-bye and wonder if it would be the last time he ever did so.

"I see. Should I push Gina's birthday party back a week or so?"

Moyer could hear the sadness in Stacy's voice; he could also feel the red-hot emotional knife the question plunged into his gut. "That's a week away. I'll try to be back by then." He paused. He had no idea when he'd be back. "Let her decide. If I can't make it back in time for the party, then we'll do something special when I get back in town." He lowered his head. "Is she there now?"

"She's about to leave for the library."

"Put her on."

"Hang on."

A moment later a familiar, chipper voice poured over the phone. "Daddy!"

"Hey, kid. You doin' okay?"

She put on a Jersey accent. "I do fine. How you doin'?"

Moyer had to laugh. "Listen, munchkin, I'm being called to a special meeting so I won't be home tonight."

"Oh. Okay. I understand."

"I'm still going to try to make your birthday party." His stomach tightened into a knot. "If I miss it, we'll do something special. I know, we'll go to your favorite restaurant." Another second-rate offer to compensate for missing another important date in his family's life.

"Can I bring a boy?"

"Do you mean to be dinner or join us for dinner?"

"You know what I mean."

"Only if I can call you baby names through the whole meal—in front of him."

"Never mind." She sounded pouty and loosened Moyer's heart.

"I'm just kidding."

"I know. Me too. Be safe, Daddy. I miss you. Gotta run. My ride to the library is here."

"I miss you too. See you soon."

Stacy returned to the phone. "You made her day."

"She made mine." Moyer chuckled. "You know, I think she's the only person her age who goes to the library voluntarily."

"She loves it. You know her, books are everything."

"You'll have to cover for me if I miss the party. How many times have I had to do that?"

"Stop it, Eric. Your . . . business is important. Don't beat yourself up." She paused. "Leave that to me."

"You could probably do it."

"Probably? Probably? No probably about it, bub."

Moyer laughed, but it was mirth mixed with regret. "Rob behaving?"

"Yes. Oh, he got that job."

"Flipping burgers?"

Stacy said yes. "He thinks he can earn enough money over the summer to buy an iPhone before he starts college."

"When did I get old enough to have a college-aged kid?"

"Many years ago."

"Watch it." The image of his tall, lanky son played in his mind. Just two years ago he and Rob were at each other's throats, but events changed him; that and some wise counsel from J. J.'s chaplain brother.

"It's good to know he's there for you. I don't suppose he's there."

"No. They're at that age, Eric: always gone; always doing something. Do you remember when we were that way?"

"I remember everything about you."

The conversation fell silent. "Yeah. What you said. Me too."

Moyer chortled. "You are a romantic."

"You know how I get when you make these kinds of calls."

He did know. Two years earlier, Stacy started having nightmares when his work separated them. It began while he was on mission in Venezuela. The dreams returned while he and his team were in Europe and then in Mexico. Stacy kept the last set of dreams from him for three months after his return.

"Yeah, I know. I'm sorry."

She sniffed and he could imagine tears welling in her eyes. His eyes began to burn. He looked at the far wall, as if doing that would take the sting out of his heart.

"Don't be sorry. It is what it is. You were in the Army when I married you. At our wedding I got a husband and a large branch of the military. I'm proud of you and what you do. What you do isn't easy."

"What *you* do may be more difficult."

"Of course it is, but I'm a woman. I can take it."

"There is not a doubt in my mind."

Another pause passed without words but heavy with meaning.

"You know I love you, right?" Her voice was a decibel above a whisper.

"It's my reason to get up in the morning. Well, that and scrambled eggs."

"And the kids?"

"Let them get their own eggs."

She laughed. "Hug yourself for me."

"You too."

Moyer hung up, then spent a minute stuffing his emotions into the basement of his mind. The conversation was tough, but something tougher was coming. He had to get control of his emotions before he stepped back into the hallway to meet the rest of his team. In order to keep his emotions in check, Moyer practiced a trick he learned years ago—stop thinking about his family and start thinking about everything he needed to do to keep himself and his men alive for the next mission.

A dozen deep breaths later, he emerged from the office. His team waited in silence. Rich stood the farthest down the hall. J. J., who had been married less than a year, had his hands in his pocket and his face turned to avoid eye contact. Jose Medina, who was doing his best to bring up his own basketball team, gazed at his smartphone looking at pictures of his children. Pete, like J. J., had been married a short time. Crispin was unmarried, but he showed the good sense to give the others whatever time they needed.

A few steps away, standing at the mouth of the corridor, Tim waited, his hands clasped in front of him. In the lobby, the displaced office workers stood in a group and off to themselves.

Moyer and Tim made eye contact.

"You good to go?" Tim asked.

Moyer inhaled deeply and faced his men. "We ready to rock?"

"Hooah!"

Moyer turned back to Tim. "All right, Captain. Let's catch the first thing smokin' out of here."

TESS RAND-BARTLEY CONTINUED TO stare at the phone as if she expected it to come to life, or better yet, ring again with her husband's voice saying, "Just kiddin', kiddo. Turns out I'll be home tonight after all."

But she knew it wouldn't. She might be a new Army wife, but she had been around the military enough to know she wouldn't hear from J. J. until he was off mission. Unlike other Army wives, she was often "in-the-know." Her basic work didn't require keeping secret her identity or function. Those who saw the petite, auburn-haired twenty-something woman would not suspect she was an expert in terrorism, female suicide bombers, and international affairs. Although younger than most of her peers, none doubted her right to teach at the War College in Carlisle Barracks, Pennsylvania.

Her exceptional expertise brought her to the attention of the military where she often served as a military consultant to Spec Ops. Although the material she had to deal with was emotionally distasteful, what she did often helped to save lives—including that of her new husband.

Next to the phone was a military mug shot of J. J. in his dress uniform, colorful ribbons across his chest. It was a new photo and among the medals on his uniform was a Purple Heart. The wound that almost took his life left him with a slight limp. Doctors saved both life and leg, but if you asked J. J. what they really saved was his career.

The phone rang again, and for a moment Tess's heart skipped with hope. "Hello?"

"Tess, it's Mac."

Always first names and informal on the phone. "Yes, Mac."

"You probably haven't heard—"

"He called a short time ago. No details of course, just that his trip was extended."

"Right. I need you on this. Can you handle that?"

He was being obtuse, but she got the meaning. He wanted to know if she could consult on a mission that involved her husband. Bad form. Bad policy. But sometimes necessary.

"Yes. I'll have to check with the dean—"

"Already done."

She smiled. "Did you ask him or inform him?"

"Is there a difference?"

"Not in your world, Mac. Not in your world."

"YOUR SOURCE IS GOOD?" The thickly padded leather chair made no noise as the man seated in it leaned back and formed a steeple with his fingers.

"It's good." The man who spoke wore a suit and a yellow power tie.

"What's being done?"

"A team is being sent. They should arrive before the satellite makes earth-fall."

"That's unfortunate."

"For us?"

The man leaned over the desk. "For them."

CHAPTER 5

THE TEAM HAD HABITS. All Spec Ops teams did. One such practice was to sleep as much as possible before a mission. If they weren't planning, they were snoozing. It only took a couple of missions to know sleep was as rare as emeralds. Moyer learned to sleep anywhere and at anytime. The rumor was he could sleep through a flash flood. This evening, despite his best efforts, he proved the rumors wrong. The phone call with his wife unsettled him more than usual. He had no idea why. He had such conversations before, and while they left him sad, he was always able to focus on the upcoming mission. Now all he could do was think of his family.

He rose from his seat in the C-20 Gulfstream IV and walked the narrow aisle, doing his best not to disturb his sleeping men. He had been seated at the front of the aircraft. It was the second time he and the unit were transported in the customized corporate jet. This plane, like a handful of others, was SAAM designated: Special Assignment Airlift Missions. The Navy, Coast Guard, and

Air Force used them for special transport. Usually the passengers included people with stars on their shoulders.

"Can't sleep?"

Moyer looked at Rich, his large body pressed into one of the rear seats. "Sorry, didn't mean to wake you."

"Who said you woke me? An active mind like mine runs all the time."

"Hmm, that explains why your mouth runs all the time."

"Hey now, Boss. That was unkind. Accurate, but unkind. If you're not careful, you'll hurt my little feelings."

Moyer smiled. He was not a man who gave his trust away easily. Those new to the unit knew his trust and admiration had to be earned, repeatedly. Not only did Moyer trust Rich with his life, but that of every member of the team, his family, and the key to his liquor cabinet.

Rich pushed himself up in the seat. "Care to join me? I'm not doing anything and I'm planning on doing more of it."

"Thanks." Moyer sat in a port-side leather seat and faced his friend across the aisle.

Rich stretched. "You know, I could get used to traveling like this. It beats sitting in the back end of a cargo plane."

"Last year we rode on TP-01 and Air Force One. I think you're getting spoiled." While on mission the previous year, the team traveled on the Mexican equivalent of Air Force One.

"Some folk just deserve to be spoiled. I'm one of them."

"Probably."

"Uh-oh."

"What?"

Rich leaned forward. "When you start letting me get away with quips like that, I know something is buggin' you. What is it?"

"You don't know me as well as you think."

"Of course I do. Your wife tells me everything."

"Does she now? I'll have to talk to her about that."

"Come on, Boss. Spill it."

Moyer looked away. "I can't put my finger on it. I feel out of sorts. I don't know why. It's not like this is my first mission."

"When did it begin?"

Moyer shrugged. "Can't be sure."

"I bet you can. I'll bet the new guy's paycheck it started when you called your wife."

"Something I've done many times before."

"Uh-huh."

"What? You made the same kinda call."

Rich nodded his big head. "Do you see me sleeping?"

Moyer sighed. "So why is this time different?"

"I don't know. That's something for the shrinks to figure out, but I got a guess."

Moyer raised an eyebrow. "Which is what?"

"Age and odds, Boss. Age and odds."

"How do you mean?"

Rich leaned forward. "I know I'm preaching to the choir here, but you and I are the old guys in the unit. That means we have more training and experience. It's why you're boss and I'm your better-looking backup."

He pressed his lips together for a moment, as if waiting for the words to ride down a slow-moving escalator from his brain. "Every time we go out, we increase the risk we won't be coming back in a vertical position. I'm sure some statistician could punch holes in my theory, but I don't care. We both know we have the riskiest job on the planet. We do it because it matters and because we're unusually good at it. But . . ." Rich looked at his feet. "But we know every new mission stacks the deck against us."

"We can't think like that, Shaq."

"But we do, Boss. I'd never say this to anyone but you, but with every new mission I wonder if I'll make it back the same stunningly handsome guy I am." His tone softened. "I wonder if I'll have kids. I wonder if I'll make Robyn a widow."

"Are you looking for a transfer?" Moyer already knew the answer. Rich's face hardened to stone.

"No, and with all due respect, Boss, I hope to never hear that question again. I haven't lost a step. Not physically; not mentally."

Moyer raised a hand. "Easy, pal. I had to ask. You know that. I have no doubts about your abilities."

Rich leaned even closer and whispered. "Look, we almost lost J. J. He should be a cripple, hobbling around his apartment on one leg. Call it a miracle, call it whatever you like, but the kid almost checked out on us in Mexico. So did Data."

Jerry Zinsser, "Data," replaced a team member killed in Venezuela. He was a problem from the get-go but came through when it counted. It nearly killed him. Jose, the team medic, had to do an emergency blood transfusion using Rich's blood.

"I get what you're saying." Moyer also leaned forward. "Okay, I'll admit that I can't get my family off my mind. I keep thinking of the kids. They're at important transitions in their lives and I wonder how they will deal with life without me there to ride them about what's right and wrong."

"That's my point, Eric. We're getting older, the missions are getting more dangerous, and because of our success rate, we're pulling the impossible duty. We're the best so we get the worst."

Eric? Rich seldom called Moyer by his first name. "We've beat the odds before and we're not that old yet."

"I know. I don't want you to think I'm whining here. I'm just trying to explain what's bugging you and me." He sat back. "If you think it's bad now, wait until the next mission. I have a theory; worry is like mercury poisoning: it builds up over time."

Moyer considered Rich's comments. He couldn't deny the truth in them no matter how much he wanted to. "So what's the answer, Shaq?"

"We do what we do, we do it better than anybody else, and then we keep doing it until we become anchors to the team."

"Then what?"

"Then we go fishing and spend our evenings at the barbecue."

Moyer smiled. The image of standing in his backyard burning pork chops drove away the emotional shadows. "Man, that sounds good."

"Don't it though?"

THE GULFSTREAM LANDED AT Elmendorf Air Force Base just outside Anchorage, Alaska, and taxied from the concrete runway onto the tarmac. Through the small window by his seat, Moyer saw a canvas-topped truck—an old Army "Deuce and a Half."

"So much for the first-class treatment," Rich said.

"You were letting the good life go to your head anyway." Moyer released his safety belt before the corporate-style jet came to a full stop.

"That's an unsafe thing to do, you know?" Rich had a cheesy grin pasted to his face.

"You didn't even fasten yours." Moyer stood.

"You know me. I like to live on the edge. Besides, I'm pretty sure it won't be an unlatched seat belt that gets me."

J. J. stepped to Moyer but faced Rich. "It's all that pizza you eat. Now that'll kill you sooner or later."

Rich's grin faded. "Listen, little man, I've seen you down a few pounds of pizza."

J. J. shrugged. "Danger is my middle name." He turned to Moyer. "Speaking of pizza . . ."

"Sorry, kid, they didn't give us enough time to follow tradition."

Whenever possible, the team met for pizza the night before deploying on mission. It had become a custom. Pizza before; pizza after.

"Doesn't seem right." J. J. leaned and peered through a window. "Are they kidding us? Black Jack Pershing rode in that, didn't he?"

"You were expecting a limo?" Shaq took to his feet. "Man up, Colt."

"What? Didn't I just hear you complaining about the same thing?"

Rich gave the weapons expert a punch in the shoulder. "The extra stripes on my uniform give me the right to be capricious."

"You're not wearing your uniform—capricious? Did you just use the word *capricious?*"

"Leave it alone, J. J., Rich has a right to be inconstant if he wants."

"Inconstant? Who are you guys and what did you do with my team leaders?" J. J. turned and started forward. "Heads up, guys, we have crossed over into the twilight zone."

The Gulf Stream came to a gentle stop and a few moments later the second officer emerged from the cockpit and opened the door. Although it was May and summer was just a few weeks away, cold air rushed into the cabin. A man in an Air Force ABU jogged up the stairs. Moyer guessed he was only a couple of years out of high school. The moment he entered the confined space of the aircraft, he removed his blue garrison cap.

"I'm looking for Sergeant Major Moyer." His voice had a nasal twang.

"Clear the aisle." Moyer pushed past the men of his unit. "I'm Moyer."

The young man held out his hand. "It's good to meet you, Sergeant Major. I'm Airman First Class Quentin Allison."

"Quentin? You take much of a ribbing for that name?"

"You have no idea, sir." He had an innocent smile. "I'm your driver, although it won't be much of a drive. You'll be airborne again in a few minutes. If you'll follow me, please."

Airman Quentin didn't wait for a response. He donned his cap and headed down the retractable stairs.

"Let's not keep the man waiting." Moyer stepped into the cold Alaskan breeze.

Quentin stood at the back of the vintage truck and opened the fold-down rear gate.

"I gotta ask," Rich said. "I know times are hard all over, but is the Air Force so strapped it can't afford something a little newer?"

"What, you don't like Betty?"

"You named the truck?"

"Of course. She's a beauty, isn't she? A group of us got her from a military surplus store. The guy who sold it to us said she was used on one of the Pacific islands during the war."

"And you believed him," Shaq said.

"No, sir. Not for a minute. We've been restoring her for the last two years. Parts are a tad hard to come by."

"I imagine so." Moyer took in the box lines of the old truck. "You've done a good job with her."

"Thank you, sir. You'll be happy to know she's Army." The airman motioned to the back. "If you wouldn't mind. Your kit arrived about an hour ago. I'm told someone named Colonel Mac had them prepared in Yakima and flown here. I'm supposed to tell you to check your gear before liftoff. I imagine you already planned to do that."

Shaq nodded. "You got that straight." He turned to his team. "Mount up."

As promised, the field kit rested in front of the wood benches lining the inside of the personnel carrier's bed. Name tags attached by hook-and-loop strips identified each kit. Six small duffle bags sat next to the rucksacks. Strapped to the kits were fresh weapons.

Crispin was the last in the truck before Quentin slammed the truck gate closed and inserted metal pins into the lock brackets.

The diesel engine coughed to life and Moyer could smell the oily exhaust. He didn't want to admit it aloud, but he was enjoying the experience. How many soldiers had ridden in this old beast? Most outdated military equipment was sold to third-world countries, scrapped, or sold through surplus stores. He admired those who gave their free time to keep representatives of former technology running.

A UH-1N Twin Huey rested on a helipad at the end of the tarmac, its rotors already slicing the air as the pilot warmed the engine.

The truck pulled to a stop. Quentin appeared five seconds later and released the gate so Moyer and the team could exit. "There's your ride, Sergeant Major. First Lieutenant Dan Blain is your pilot. There are three other crewmen, but I'll let him make those introductions if he wants."

Moyer shook hands with the man again and lowered his head to avoid the rotor blast. The unit followed him. As he neared the side door, a voice shouted over the sound of the engine and wind blast. "Let me take that."

Moyer looked up at a short man in a flight suit extending a hand. Moyer lifted his kit and duffle and handed it to the crewman. The man then helped Moyer aboard. The movement was repeated for each team member. Moments later, everyone was strapped into the jump seats.

The stout man leaned close to Moyer's ear. "Welcome aboard, Sergeant Major. I'm the crew chief for this little jaunt. Please confirm all your team is aboard."

Moyer gave a thumbs-up. "Affirmative. We're good."

"Very good." The man pulled a plastic bag from one of the pockets of his jumpsuit. The bag held soft, orange earplugs. "I think you might appreciate these." He passed the bag around, then moved the microphone close to his lips. "We're good to go, Lieutenant."

The craft lifted off before the crew chief finished the last syllable.

NINETY MINUTES PASSED WITH little discussion. Talking above the noise was too difficult. Moyer sat with his eyes closed, trying to think about the mission ahead. The most difficult moments of any mission were being shot at and waiting for the mission to start. Both could get on a man's nerves.

The crew chief approached. Moyer pulled the earplug from his right ear. "Have you been briefed about the next stage?"

"You're to drop us off on a Navy ship."

"Correct, but there's a catch. It's not just any Navy ship."

"What's that mean?"

"We'll be dropping you on a DDG-1000, Zumwalt-class destroyer."

"And that's a problem?"

"Unlike most surface ships, the DDG-1000 has a special hull design. You'll see what I mean in a minute. The problem is this: There's no landing pad."

"Then how do we get aboard?" Moyer didn't like where this was going. He had made many high-altitude-low-open and high-altitude-high-open parachute jumps, so leaving a perfectly good aircraft was nothing new, but he had an idea there was a twist in this.

"You're going to have to rappel to the deck."

"No problem. We've done plenty of rappelling."

The crew chief grinned. "Onto a pitching, rolling ship?"

"Um, you got me there. It's okay. We've been bumped around before."

"Well, there's another itty-bitty problem."

"And that is?"

"We are in the North Pacific. The waaaaay North Pacific. That means the water is cold. You don't want to fall in."

"And if I do?"

"You got maybe ten minutes before you go to the great, big Army base in the sky."

"Ten minutes?"

"Maybe ten minutes. Probably less since you won't be wearing a survival suit."

Moyer frowned. "Aren't you a ray of sunshine."

"I try." He motioned to the other men. "I'll pass the message. We're ten minutes out, so it's time to suit up. I'm afraid we will have to do this quickly. If we linger we'll go bingo fuel, and as good as this baby is, it floats like a brick."

"Understood, but I'll tell the men."

"If you want, we can lower you in a basket."

"Ain't gonna happen." Moyer popped his safety harness, made sure his men were looking at him, and pantomimed unbuckling a seat belt.

His team understood. The men released their restraints and reached for the duffle bags. Five minutes later they were garbed in their uniform MultiCam designed to blend anywhere; no emblems, no patches, no name tags.

He motioned for the men to huddle. Each removed one earplug. "We're going to rappel in."

"Nice," J. J. said.

"Our landing zone is a moving deck on a new destroyer. That's the good news."

"What's the bad?" Shaq furrowed his brow.

"The water. Fall in and you're a soldier-sicle."

"I take back my 'Nice.'"

"Shaq, you take lead. Colt, you follow."

J. J. nodded.

"I'm sure we'll have help on the deck, but we may need you two to help when we winch down our gear."

"Why not just rappel with our kit?" J. J. asked.

Moyer studied his weapons expert. "Um, because they don't float so well, and if you're wearing them—"

"Understood, Boss."

"Doc, you follow Colt; Junior, you follow Doc."

"Got it, Boss," Pete Rasor said.

Moyer turned to the newest member of the team. "I'll push Crispin out the door."

"New Guy needs a nick, Boss," Rich said. "It's tradition."

Crispin crossed his fingers and chanted, "Please let it be a cool name, please, please, please."

"Make it quick," Moyer said. "Suggestions?"

"Punch."

"Judy."

"Punch and Judy."

"Shep."

"Momma's Boy."

"Peach Fuzz."

"Come on, guys, I'm going to be shackled with this nick for a long time." Crispin looked worried.

J. J. put a hand on the man's shoulder. "He's right. How about Lassie?"

The crew chief patted Moyer on the shoulder. "Sixty seconds out."

"Understood." Moyer turned to Crispin. "Since you're our go-to surveillance guy, I hereby dub you . . ." Several moments passed.

"Come on, Boss. You're killing me here."

"Hawkeye."

"*Yes.*" Hawkeye pumped a fist.

"I don't know, Boss." Shaq attempted to look serious. "What's it mean when a man is more worried about his nickname than swinging from a rope over frigid water?"

"It means he has his priorities straight." Moyer stepped to the side. "Line up, gentlemen. It's time to get some fresh air."

"Do you think the rope will hold Shaq?" Hawkeye flashed a wide grin.

Shaq grinned too, then seized the front of the man's vest so fast Moyer barely saw it. A half second later, Hawkeye was nose to nose with Shaq.

"I'm sorry, young man, I'm having trouble hearing over all the noise. What did you say?"

"I . . . I said that watching you work will be the pinnacle of my training."

"I guess I did hear it correctly." Shaq let go.

Not even the engine noise could drown out the laughter.

The crew chief opened the side hatch and double-checked Shaq's carabiner. Moyer stood to the side and peered out the hatch. Below, a pale gray, angular ship sat low in the water, rolling in large swells. "It looks like a Civil War iron side."

"That she does, Sergeant Major. She's a beauty. You are lucky men."

"Yeah." Shaq moved to the open door. "That's me. Lucky." He looked down, flashed a cheesy grin, shouted, "Tallyho!" and stepped into the air.

THE COLD BREEZE OF the North Pacific, heightened by the pounding rotors of the helicopter, slapped at Moyer's face, making his skin feel as if he were staring into an open oven. The irony of cold making his skin feel burned wasn't wasted on him.

He slowed his descent as he neared the rolling deck of the strange-looking destroyer. On deck were four sailors and one soldier. Shaq stood out of the way, but Moyer had no doubts the man could reach him in seconds. From his perch in the helicopter, Moyer watched Shaq help each team member to the deck safely.

The wind was a problem. The same gusts whipping up the waves were pushing Moyer around like a tiny spider on a thin

strand of web. Moyer could control the speed of his descent but not
what the wind did to him.

He began to swing perpendicular to the ship's beam. The swing
turned into a wide circle. Moyer spread his legs to slow the motion,
but it did little to help. He looked up at the helo. It was bouncing,
buffeted by the increasing wind.

Continuing his descent, Moyer tried to focus on the ship's
deck. The sailors wore survival suits and life vests, each was
tethered by a line to the deck. Shaq moved a few steps closer to the
designated landing spot marked off by the position of the sailors.
One of the crewmen motioned for Shaq, who wore no safety
line, to move back. Moyer assumed the man was telling him to
get inside. Shaq shook his head. The sailor stepped close and got
in Shaq's face. Even thirty feet above the deck, Moyer could tell
the sailor was shouting, perhaps to be heard above the sound of
rotors and screeching wind. Most likely he was trying to intimidate
Shaq.

"Don't do it." Moyer couldn't hear his own voice.

Shaq pointed to the landing spot and said something. The
sailor moved back to his spot; Shaq held his.

As Moyer approached the deck, the circle his body was
inscribing in the air widened, a function of the ever-lengthening
line that tethered him to the helicopter above.

Twenty-five feet.

Twenty.

Fifteen.

This is going to hurt.

Ten.

Five.

Moyer swung over the frigid green waters, circled in front of the
bow, and careened toward the port side.

A sailor stepped forward and extended his arms in an attempt to take hold of the human pendulum. Moyer's momentum knocked the man backward onto the deck. The man slid several feet along the wet surface until he reached the edge of the deck, his feet hanging above churning water, saved only by his tether.

A second sailor attempted the same move and received the same punishment.

Again Moyer swung over the churning ocean, around the bow, and back to the deck. The first sailor was on his feet again, arms spread. His face told Moyer all he needed to know: He was looking for another knockdown.

The man closed his eyes.

Great.

Shaq took two steps into the arena, pushed the sailor aside, and stood in Moyer's path. The sight sickened him. Shaq wasn't tethered. Moyer's impact could send the big man over the edge.

Moyer waved him off.

Shaq shook his head.

The impact felt like running into a brick wall. Arms clamped around Moyer with rib-breaking force, but Moyer's forward motion continued, driving Shaq backward, his feet sliding along the deck.

Six feet along the deck later, Moyer's feet were down. In seconds, Shaq had freed him from the line and was moving him to the superstructure near the middle of the ship. They ducked through a hatch and into the warmth of the destroyer.

A sailor led them toward the bridge.

The adrenaline in Moyer's body acted like jet fuel on a fire. "Of all the stupid, boneheaded, irresponsible things to do. Were you trying to get both of us killed?"

A voice came from behind them. "That was the dumbest, most unprofessional thing I've ever seen anyone do." Racially laced curses filled the air. Moyer turned his head to see the sailor he unintentionally knocked to the deck.

Moyer stopped midstep, turned, and raised a finger. "Last time I knocked you down it was an accident. I hear one more bigoted word from your yap and I'll put you on the deck and make sure you never get up. You read me?"

The sailor's face reddened but he said nothing more. Moyer returned his attention to Shaq. "Where was I?"

"Irresponsible."

"That's right. What kind of knucklehead does that? You let the sailors do their job and we do ours. Is that clear?"

"Yes. And you're welcome."

Moyer did his best to stoke the coals of his outrage, but the fire went cold. "That was pretty cool. By the way, your nose is bleeding."

"A small price to pay to be the hero in your life."

"Get Doc to look at that. I don't want to explain to your wife that I brought you home uglier than you left."

"Will do, Boss."

The mouthy sailor moved past them. "If it's not too much bother, gentlemen, the captain hates to be kept waiting."

"To the bridge?" Moyer asked.

"Not a chance. You're not cleared to see what's up there. He'll meet you in the chow hall."

CHAPTER 6

THE TEAM SAT AROUND a set of tables in the corner of the ship's enlisted dining area. Men dressed in blue coveralls joked over the evening meal. Moyer and his men wore MultiCams, which made them stand out. They received a few courteous nods and many more stares. Moyer doubted this was the first time the crew saw non-Navy personnel. The Navy often provided transportation for ground forces. Moyer knew several Marines who, although strictly speaking were under the Department of the Navy, often distanced themselves from the sailors whom they considered chauffeurs.

Moyer took a sip of coffee. It was the only thing in front of him and his men. They had not been offered anything but this corner of the room in which to wait for the skipper.

A tall, narrow man slipped from the passageway on the other side of the hatch and entered the mess. Immediately every sailor in the compartment was on his feet. A man built like a barrel followed.

"As you were, gentlemen." The tall man, dressed in blue coveralls, moved toward Moyer and his men. Moyer eyed the eagle image on his collar. In Moyer's world that would mean the man was a colonel; in the Navy it meant he was looking at the ship's captain. Moyer stood and his men followed.

"Who is the team leader?" The man's voice was smooth and loaded with authority.

"That would be me, Captain. I'm Sergeant Major Eric Moyer."

"Moyer, eh?" The captain's eyes shifted to Shaq. "I don't know whether to toss you in the brig or shake your hand, soldier."

Shaq gave a polite nod. "The latter would be the greater honor, sir."

The captain studied Shaq for a moment, then smiled. To Moyer he said, "Is he always this smooth?"

"You have no idea, sir. If I may present Master Sergeant Rich Harbison, assistant team leader." Moyer introduced the other men in his unit.

"I'm Captain Glencoe. With me is Commander James Spencer, my executive officer. Welcome to the USS *Michael A. Monsoor.* Come with me. We'll be able to talk better in officer country." He didn't wait for a reply.

Moyer and the others scrambled to keep up with the captain. Clearly he was a man who didn't like to waste time. A few moments later Glencoe led the line of men into the officer's mess, a wide room occupied by two lines of tables placed end-to-end. Several off-duty officers were playing cards and drinking sodas.

"I need the room, gentlemen. Last man out secure the room." The officers vacated without a word, closing the door to the space. "Pull up a chair, men."

Moyer and his crew did. As they sat, Glencoe moved to the head of the table but didn't sit. Spencer went to a wall-mounted phone and picked up the receiver. He punched one button and uttered one word: "Report." A few moments later he put the handset back in place and turned.

"XO?"

"Sir, bridge reports we are on heading making best possible speed. Weather states the seas will settle in a few hours and we will make time."

"Very well."

"Wait," J. J. said. "We've increased speed? I'd think I would have heard the engines revving up."

Glencoe crossed his arms. "The *Michael A. Monsoor* is one of the pilot ships of the new DDG-1000 class of destroyers. Our propulsion is electric. That means we are fast and quiet. It also gives a few other advantages."

"Like what?" Shaq asked.

"I guess I can give you the Internet version." Glencoe's smile carried a lot of pride.

"Internet version?" Crispin said. "You mean the kind of intel we can get from the Internet."

"That's right, soldier. You may have noticed we don't look like other destroyers."

"You look more like the old *Merrimack*—the ship, I mean," J. J. corrected himself.

"I know what you meant. Those old warships had the right idea. The new Navy emphasizes stealth. We are six hundred feet in length and eighty feet across the beam, but on radar we look like a small fishing vessel. Also, being electric, we can reallocate our energy to fit our needs—like our rail gun."

"What's a rail gun?" Shaq asked.

Crispin answered before the captain could speak. "It's a gun that launches its projectile by magnetism. The projectile is conductive so it rides the rails at great speed."

"I take it you read a book or something," Shaq said.

"I do that from time to time."

"You're right, soldier. That and many things I can't describe come to you for a mere three billion of taxpayers' dollars. It's one reason I was not happy to reduce speed in rough seas."

"With all due respect, sir," Moyer said, "we don't especially like boarding a ship in heavy seas."

"I can respect that. Okay, enough chitchat. I've got you for six hours. After that I'll hand you off to your next ride. Is there anything you need?"

"Some chow would be good, sir." Moyer studied his men for a moment. "And maybe a place to stretch out."

"XO, get them what they need."

"Sir?" J. J. raised a finger. "I have to ask. I've heard a lot of ship names, but not the *Michael Monsoor*. Who was he?"

The captain's face darkened. "Master-at-Arms Second Class Michael A. Monsoor was a Navy SEAL, Delta Platoon, SEAL Team Three. He enlisted in the Navy in 2001. Five years later he was dead. On September 29, 2006, he and his team were engaged against insurgents in Ramadi, Iraq. One of the enemy tossed a grenade onto the roof where he and his comrades were positioned. Monsoor smothered the grenade with his body, saving the others from injury and death. He was posthumously awarded the Medal of Honor. The ship is named after him."

The air in the room grew heavy, then Moyer rose from his chair. The others followed. They stood in silence until Captain Glencoe said, "I wish you better luck in whatever it is you're about to do."

TESS AND COLONEL MAC moved around a small group of tourists and down the corridor. Ivory walls and a light brown carpet made the hallway seem larger than it was. Overhead lights pushed the darkness of evening away. In front of them walked a woman with the bearing of an Abrams M1 tank. Helen Brown was more than the president's chief of staff; she was the engine that kept the administration running. Her no-nonsense demeanor was legendary. One Washington insider said the COS had the personality of a meat grinder. Tess had no desire to test that assessment.

Tess had been to the White House before. In fact, she was here just a few months earlier. Because of J. J.'s heroics at the G-20 meeting in Italy that saved the life of not only the president but a dozen heads-of-state and their spouses, the president made the Rose Garden available for their wedding. Now her new husband was on another mission and Tess was meeting the president again—this time on official business.

The corridor emptied into a small waiting area just outside the Oval Office. A marble bust of George Washington sat on a short Greek-style column. A similar bust of Thomas Jefferson rested on the opposite side of the alcove, as if scrutinizing all who passed by.

"One moment, please." Helen Brown slipped into the outer office and spoke to the president's personal secretary.

Tess couldn't hear the exchange, but the body language indicated Brown was informing not requesting. A few seconds later she turned and motioned for Tess and Colonel Mac to follow. Butterflies zoomed through Tess's stomach like jet fighters. Colonel Mac looked unfazed.

Brown opened the door between the outer office and the Oval Office, then closed it behind her as they entered.

President Ted Huffington was seated on one of the sofas at the center of the room. A matching sofa framed a wide, sturdy coffee table. On the table rested a pitcher of water and a carafe of what, based on the cups next to it, Tess assumed was coffee. The president looked unchanged since she last saw him. However, his brown hair sported a little more gray. The result of dealing with the unyielding problems of running a troubled and divided country, or was he just tired of hiding his sixty-one years with hair dye? It didn't matter. The man always looked dapper and scholarly.

Seated with him was a thinner, taller, older man who looked as if he had gone without sleep for the last week: puffy, red eyes; hunched shoulders; pallid skin. The vice president's appearance stunned Tess. She glanced at Mac and caught a glimpse of confusion.

"Tess, my dear." Huffington moved from the sofa and embraced her. His arms were firm and powerful, like anacondas circling her small frame. "Married life has made you even more beautiful."

"Thank you, Mr. President. You're looking well."

He shrugged. "I feel pretty good. I'm getting a little arthritis in my back, but nothing a couple of pain relievers can't handle."

"I'm sorry to hear that, sir."

He waved her off. "Nothing to worry about. When you reach sixty, you're required to make some kind of complaint about your health. I think it's hardwired into our genes."

"I had no idea. I'll keep an eye out for that."

The president smiled broadly, then turned to Colonel Mac. "Mac, how are you? You look good for an old man."

"I'm fine, Mr. President. Thank you for asking."

Huffington turned back to Tess. "This is the advantage of being president: I can insult powerful men and women and get away with it."

"For now," Mac deadpanned.

Huffington laughed but it lasted only a moment. "I'm sure you know Vice President Andrew Bacliff."

Bacliff moved close and extended his hand. "Pleased to meet you, Dr. Rand. I'm sorry I missed your wedding. I was out of country."

"No need to apologize, Mr. Vice President."

"That doesn't mean I don't know about you. Our country owes you a large measure of gratitude." His voice was smooth, that of a well-practiced speaker. If the rumors were correct, Tess was shaking hands with the next man to call the White House home.

"Let's be seated." Huffington motioned to the sofas. Instead of returning to where he was sitting a few moments before, he settled into a dark, thickly padded leather chair. Tess recalled her father calling the style a "cigar chair." She assumed he was taking the position of authority for the meeting, something he didn't have to do while alone with the VP. Helen Brown sat where the president was earlier.

"Mac, my latest intel says the boys are safely aboard the *Michael Monsoor* and they're underway at best possible speed."

"That's the latest report I have as well, Mr. President."

Huffington nodded. "There's something you don't know, Mac." He paused. "Actually, there are three things. I want to bring you in on the loop on two of those items. Depending how the mission unfolds, I will bring you in on the other. Right now, it's need-to-know only. Understood?"

"Yes, sir. Understood."

Huffington looked at his vice president, then nodded. Bacliff removed an envelope from the inside, front breast pocket and pushed it across the coffee table. Mac took it and started to open it.

"Before you read that, Mac, I want to make this official for you and Dr. Rand: Nothing we discuss here is to be repeated."

"I assumed that, Mr. President."

"I know you did, but I'm making it an order from your commander in chief."

"Yes, sir. Fully understood."

"Carry on."

Mac pulled a letter from the envelope. Tess could see a seal at the top of the letterhead but couldn't tell if it was from the office of the president or vice president. She turned her gaze to the coffee carafe, not from desire but to avoid reading what might not be meant for her eyes. Mac lowered the letter.

"Please share it with Dr. Rand." Huffington slipped forward in his chair, took the carafe, and poured coffee in four china cups on the table. Each cup bore the presidential emblem.

Without comment, Mac handed the letter to Tess. It bore today's date. She read:

> *To President Ted Huffington.*
>
> *Dear Mr. President,*
>
> *Certain family concerns compel me to resign as vice president of these United States of America effective on any day you see fit.*
>
> *It has been my honor to be of service to you and to our great country.*
>
> *Respectfully,*
> *Andrew Bacliff*
> *Private citizen*

"I don't understand." Tess lowered the letter.

"I do." Mac looked at the president.

"Go on."

Mac turned his gaze to the VP. "The Air Force Spec Ops team?"

Bacliff nodded and although he tried to show no emotion, fear seeped through his expression.

Tess cocked her head. "I've been briefed on the team, and I don't recall reading about any of your family members, sir."

"That's the way it's supposed to be, Dr. Rand. My son and I thought it best to keep his identity a secret. When he entered the military, he changed his last name—well, he didn't really change his name, he just used his mother's maiden name as his last name. Of course, the military knows this. At the time, I was a ranking member of the Armed Services Committee in the Senate. I asked for a favor and received it. Considering the present state of the media in our country, you can understand why I would like to keep that under wraps."

"Yes, sir." Tess understood. Bacliff was one of those politicians who ran for office because he cared so much for his country. The man could have made millions in business, but he chose a life of public service. Such men often brought up children who shared the same level of patriotism.

"My son wanted to be a military man ever since he was eight years old. I figured it would pass, but it didn't. I chose a life of public service, which created problems for him. He didn't want to be just another senator's child in the service, passing time in the States. He wanted to do real military work. You can imagine the problems being my son might present."

Bacliff inhaled deeply. "He wanted no special treatment or protection. He just wanted to serve." Tears welled in his eyes and Tess caught herself looking away.

"He sounds like a brave man." Mac didn't break his gaze.

"He is, Colonel. He is. His mother is in a terrible state."

"I can't even imagine," Tess said.

"You see the problem." Bacliff dabbed at his eyes, unembarrassed by the show of emotion. "If his captors learn of his connection to me, then it will make things even more difficult for all involved. It is reasonable to assume they might use him to get to me. I can't allow that. All I can do is resign. That way, I'm out of the picture."

"I don't think you'd use your influence to try to gain his release," Tess said.

"Yes, I would, Dr. Rand. You would too. When you have children, you will understand."

The phrase knifed through her, but she said nothing.

Tess turned to Mac. The man pressed his lips into a line. "May I ask his name?"

The vice president was quiet for a moment. "Captain Scott Masters—Captain Scott Masters Bacliff."

Mac swore softly, then caught himself. "Excuse me, sirs."

Huffington waved a dismissive hand. "You should have heard what I said."

"This is horrible." Tess struggled to sort her emotions.

"It's horrible when any of our troops are captured." Bacliff's words were soft. "The fact that one of them is my son doesn't make a difference except to me and my family."

"Yes, sir. Of course, sir."

Huffington raised the cup of coffee to his lips, sipped, then set it back on the table. The other cups remained untouched. "Colonel, I need to make this clear. I've already discussed this with the vice president. Your primary mission is the satellite. That must come before rescue."

Tess couldn't believe what she heard, and her face must have telegraphed the fact.

"Dr. Rand, I know how that sounds. How can I put a machine over men? Well, I don't do it lightly and I have my reasons. Military leaders know what it is to send men and women to their deaths, sometimes for something as seemingly unimportant as a strategic hill. If history gets hold of my decision, then I'll be portrayed as a heartless man. I'm not."

"Of course not, sir. I didn't mean to imply you were."

Huffington faced Mac. "At the moment, only five people know about this; six if you count Captain Masters. That will change by the end of the day. Thirty minutes from now, I'll brief the speaker of the house and the Senate's president pro tem. I will bring in the chairman of the JCS. I will ask him to keep the information to himself. The other members of the Joint Chiefs of Staff don't need to know, at least not at the moment. The fewer people who know about this, the better." The president drummed his fingers on the arm of the chair. "While what I'm about to say isn't mission crucial, I'm going to bring you in on this. I do so because I want you and your team focused on the mission. Clear?"

"Clear, sir."

"Brownie here will be our new VP. I know she can pass a Senate review. She has something on everyone in Congress. No one's going to give her grief. We have too many things going on to miss a beat. Appointing Brownie VP will make sure things flow smoothly."

"If only I can get him to stop calling me Brownie." The woman smiled, and for a moment Tess thought she saw skin crack. The group gave a polite laugh; everyone except Bacliff.

Mac said, "You said there were three items, Mr. President."

"All I can say about the second item is this: There is more to that satellite than you know or can imagine. I can't tell you more. Not yet."

"Does it impact my team's mission?"

"No, their task remains the same. Just know that it is extremely important that your team succeeds."

"Yes, sir."

Tess wanted to pump the man for more information. Information was her specialty, being deprived of it made her uncomfortable, especially since her husband was one of the men tasked with finding and destroying Angel-12. She reined in her curiosity. Such protocol existed for a reason.

"Third and final item for this meeting: We've received intel that confirms one of our fears. Your team is racing three enemy factors. First is the Russian government. They monitor our satellites just as we monitor theirs. That isn't new. This is: We know a Chinese Spec Ops team is headed to the same area."

"Chinese?" Tess let her surprise slip.

"As you know, it was a defunct Chinese satellite that started all this, except our intel groups believe the satellite wasn't defunct at all: it was a sleeper."

"A sleeper?" Tess raised an eyebrow.

"A satellite in orbit that appears to be nonoperational but can be reactivated for a purpose. In this case, to knock our bird out of the sky."

"Has this happened before?"

"There have been collisions, but this seems to have a different purpose. We now suspect the Chinese waited until just the right time to knock down Angel-12. If our space warriors hadn't tried to move the bird before impact, it would have landed in the heart of China. The last-minute maneuver changed its impact area. Which means—"

"The Chinese targeted that particular bird." Mac rubbed the back of his neck, the closest the man ever came to showing emotion. "But why?"

"They couldn't know." Helen Brown looked at the president. "Could they?"

CHAPTER 7

CAPTAIN SCOTT MASTERS FOUGHT the urge to writhe. Throughout his life he had experienced pain: a broken leg acquired on a ski slope, cracked ribs from a fall during basic training, and scorching agony from an abscess in his jaw. The moment made all of those events seem like mere annoyances.

Tears leaked from the corners of his eyes and wetted the side of his face. On his back and strapped to his bed, he could do little more than shift from side to side. He was being observed and his captors would consider every groan a victory.

Behind him he could hear the gentle beep of the IV stand and, if he turned his head enough, he could see the still-full bags of antibiotics and the limp, clear line that should be connected to his arm. Bags of life hanging just out of reach, just close enough to provide mental torture.

The pain in his side seemed to be expanding. The skin around his wounds, especially the facial injury his captor used as an ashtray, grew warmer by the hour. Masters had no doubt the seeping injuries were infected.

How long before the infection spread to his blood and to his organs? Would it reach his brain? Infect his heart or liver?

He thought about Egonov's threat of gangrene. Masters saw gangrene during a tour in Afghanistan. A boy, no more than eight, was wounded by shrapnel from a suicide bomber. The wound wasn't life threatening, just a deep cut to the right forearm. His parents decided to nurse him themselves. Medications were in short supply and the injury festered. When the boy's parents approached Masters and his team as they swept a village, the wound was gangrenous. Masters's team transported the boy to the nearest functioning medical facility. The last time Masters saw the boy, he had only one arm.

What would need to be cut away from his body to save his life?

He heard a scream. Distant. Muted. Familiar. He had been hearing such agony-laced cries every few minutes. Hearing another human beg for mercy was soul crushing; it was worse when the voice was recognizable.

Stu. A young sergeant. Tough as nails and fearless in a firefight. Funny. Always ready with a joke, especially off-color jabs. Masters never met a man who liked to laugh more.

The laughter was gone. Just wails and screams and weeping.

It came from the room next door. Masters could hear the door open and close. It would open and a few moments later the pleading would begin. Later the door would open and close again and all would go silent. He knew what they were doing and he hated them for it. They were bringing his men into the adjoining room so Masters could hear them being tormented.

He understood the plan. They would let pain and infection torture his body and let the cries of his men fry his brain.

Masters wanted to pray for release, for rescue, for miraculous intervention, but his prayers ran a different direction. "Five minutes, God. Just give me five minutes alone with Egonov; just five minutes to make my point."

MOYER AND HIS TEAM stood on the pitching deck of the destroyer looking at the thirty-three-foot-long, rigid-hull inflatable boat rising and falling in the swells of the discontent North Pacific. He raised his gaze and looked across a quarter mile of churning sea to see a rolling Japanese fishing boat.

J. J. said what Moyer was thinking. "I thought the skipper said the seas were calm."

A narrow chief with a square jaw looked puzzled. "These are calm seas."

"Be honest," Rich said. "You're just trying to have some fun with the Army boys, right?"

The chief shrugged. "The SEALs don't seem to mind. By the way, that's their boat, so don't do anything stupid like shoot the rubber hull. Those boys are a tad sensitive about their equipment."

"We won't hurt their little toys, Chief." Rich took another look at the boat.

"Toy, eh." The chief huffed. "You would perhaps like to swim?"

"We wouldn't dream of hurting your feelings." J. J. exchanged glances with Rich. "You look a little green around the gills, Shaq."

Rich frowned. "Black men don't get green around the gills."

"If you say so, big man, but I know green when I see it."

"Yeah? Well, I feel good enough to throw you all the way to the fishing boat."

"Stow it, gentlemen." The chief moved to the edge of his ship. "We don't want to spend any more time here than we have to. It's dark, but not dark enough for my liking." He pointed skyward. "Who knows who's watching."

"God?" Crispin said.

"I think he means spy satellites, Hawkeye."

"Oh. I knew that."

"Sure you did, kid." Rich put a hand on the shoulder of the newest member of the team. "You know, the new guy goes first, right? It's tradition and this unit is big on tradition."

"But just think of how much I can learn from watching a professional like you."

"Hawkeye?" Moyer said.

"Yeah, Boss?"

"Get your butt in the boat."

"Yes, Boss."

The chief and a petty officer helped Crispin climb down a ladder to the RHIB. A sailor at the foot of the ladder took hold of the young man's arm and helped him aboard. Crispin looked up the side of the ship. "See, Shaq, there's no need for you to be afraid anymore."

"I'm gonna kill 'em, Boss."

"He's just trying to be encouraging." Moyer caught the chief grinning. "Why don't you go next?"

"I don't mind bringing up the rear."

"You know, you do look a little green. It's gonna be worse in the dingy so let's shake a leg. You'll feel better on the fishing boat."

"No, he won't." The chief was still grinning. "No stabilizers on that craft."

"You're enjoying this, aren't you?" Shaq's voice had lost its edge.

"Who? Me?"

A voice came over a loudspeaker. "Speed it up, Chief."

"If you don't mind, Sergeant Major. Your team is putting me on the skipper's dirt list."

"Understood, Chief." Moyer turned to Rich. "In the boat, pal."

Two minutes later, a petty officer in the small wheelhouse of the boat hit the throttles, sending the rubber-hulled boat skipping over the swells and white caps. Moyer began to feel like Rich looked.

It took only a few moments for the RHIB to cross the distance from the *Michael Monsoor*. Standing at the gunwales were three Japanese men. One looked to be in his forties, the other two in their twenties. As the transport craft neared, the younger Japanese fishermen dropped a rope ladder over the side.

The petty officer at the wheel slowed and turned to Moyer and his men. "This is the dicey part. I have to get close but not smash us into the boat's hull. We're going to get bumped around some, so be careful of your footing. One person on the ladder at a time, no more. Get up to the deck as quickly as possible but be careful of your step. You really don't want to go swimming."

"You got that right," Rich said.

"Who's first?" the petty officer asked.

"That'd be me." Moyer stood and moved to the port side of the craft. "Let's do this, sailor."

"Aye, aye." He feathered the engines so the RHIB inched closer.

The cold wind whipped around Moyer and bit at his ears. He was glad it wasn't winter. He pointed at each of his men, giving them the order in which they would climb the ladder.

"Stand by." The petty officer turned the boat sideways as he neared the larger vessel. A swell lifted the craft and slammed into the fishing boat's metal hull. "Go." The man didn't yell, but he made sure he could be heard.

Moyer didn't hesitate. He scrambled to the ladder. Ocean spray stung his eyes and as he took his first step on a tread, the RHIB dropped from beneath him as swell turned into trough.

"Whoa!" Moyer tightened his already viselike grip on the ladder. The fishing boat tipped toward the trough and the ladder swung away from the hull before the trough became swell. Moyer wasted no time moving up. Before he reached the ship's rails, two pairs of hands seized him by the arms and yanked. Before he could speak, Moyer was seated on the deck, everything intact but his dignity. He pushed himself to his feet and moved to the rail. Below were his wide-eyed men. "Piece of cake."

"Yeah, bet me." Shaq shook his head.

Next up was J. J. He grinned the entire time and made it look effortless. Moyer hated youth.

The others followed, each helped over the rail by the crew. Rich was the last aboard and the moment his foot hit the deck, the RHIB roared away.

"Welcome aboard the *Komagata Maru*." The speaker was the older of the three men, Moyer saw as they approached.

"Thank you. Um, your English—"

"Thanks, I've been working on it. It's not hard. I was born and reared in Michigan."

"Oh, sorry. I assumed—"

"That's the idea. Every member of the crew is U.S. born." He held out his hand. "Commander Sam Sasaki, United States Navy. I'm the skipper of this fine vessel."

"I don't mean to be rude, Commander, but to my untrained eye, it looks a little worse for wear."

"It took a lot of taxpayer money to make it look this way."

Moyer nodded. Camouflage applied to more than uniforms. "We appreciate the ride. Is the whole crew Navy?"

"Maybe." Sasaki smiled. Moyer didn't press. "I understand you're on a tight schedule."

"Yes, sir."

"I've received word the package you're looking for is off schedule. Impact is expected sooner."

"Then we had better put the pedal to the metal."

"Sorry, no can do. We must keep up appearances."

Moyer tilted his head. "I don't understand."

"We're supposed to be a fishing boat. If I go screaming across the ocean, it might draw attention on someone's radar. We're small but noticeable. I can get you close in a few hours."

"Close?"

"I can't sail into Russian waters." The commander shrugged. "That'd put an end to the mission pretty quick, and we'd all be answering questions we don't want asked. I can explain my Japanese crew, but I can't explain armed soldiers. If you catch my drift."

"I catch it. Please do what you can, Commander. There's a lot at stake."

"So I've been told."

CHAPTER 8

J. J. LOOKED UP from the small Bible he was reading and watched Crispin slip into the booth on the opposite side of the table. The *Komagata Maru's* dining area was a cramped space next to an even smaller galley. How a crew of six could sit in such a tiny space and eat meals was beyond J. J. Until Crispin entered, J. J. had the space to himself, something for which he was grateful.

"You by yourself?" Crispin slid across the worn Naugahyde bench.

J. J. glanced around, then grinned. "I don't see anyone else."

"Yeah, I realized how stupid the question was as soon as I said it. Let me try again: Where is everyone else?"

"I'm not sure. Rich is trying to sleep off his seasickness. I think Boss is topside. Maybe the wheelhouse."

Crispin looked at J. J.'s now-closed Bible, his place held with a finger. Crispin nodded at the small black book. "Let me guess. It's too thin to be a full Bible so it must be just the New Testament."

"Right. I was reading—"

Crispin held up a hand. "I'm not done impressing you."

"That a fact? All right, carry on."

"Your finger is marking a spot near the back, so you're reading one of the epistles. The apostle Paul wrote most of the books of the New Testament, so the odds are good you're reading one of his letters." Crispin eyed the little book. "Not far enough back to be Revelation. Maybe one of Peter's letters, but I'm going to go with . . ." He put a finger to each temple as if trying to read J. J.'s. thoughts. "Wait, it's coming to me." He grimaced as if in pain. "You're reading Second Timothy . . . yes, Second Timothy, chapter two . . . verses . . . wait, wait, here it comes. Got it. Second Timothy chapter two, verses three and four."

It took a few moments before J. J. could speak. "Wait, you must have seen the page when you entered."

"Nope."

"You stood at the door and peeked over my shoulder."

Crispin shook his head. "Nah. That'd be cheating."

"Then how?"

Crispin tilted his head back and closed his eyes as if he dozed off. "'Suffer hardship with me, as a good soldier of Christ Jesus. No soldier in active service entangles himself in the affairs of everyday life, so that he may please the one who enlisted him as a soldier.'"

J. J. opened the Bible and read the passage he had just been studying. "Okay, you've amazed me; now tell me the trick."

"No trick. I've known quite a few Christians in uniform. Many of them read that passage before each mission. It gives them the sense God is watching over them."

"That doesn't explain how you can quote the verses word-for-word."

"My father made me memorize it when I was a teenager."

"Your father?"

Crispin looked away. "Yeah. He's an Episcopal priest. He did two years with the Marines, then went to college and seminary."

"Did he see any action?"

"Some. First Gulf War. I think it was what turned him religious."

"That's an interesting phrase: 'turned religious.'"

"I don't recall him being all that spiritual when I was a kid."

"Battle changes men, Crispin. Some it strengthens; others it drives mad. No frontline soldier can pass through the fire untouched. Your dad wouldn't be the first to find faith while bullets streaked overhead."

"I suppose. Is that what turned you religious?"

J. J. huffed. "There's that phrase again: 'turned religious.' No, I was a person of faith before I enlisted. So was my brother."

"The chaplain Major Scalon mentioned."

"You were paying attention."

The new team member acted stunned. "You wound me. I always pay attention." He pursed his lips. "So what's it like having a chaplain for a brother?"

J. J. shrugged. "Paul is Paul. He's a good man, a good soldier, and a great Christian. He's been a help to me and a few of the unit."

"Really? This unit?"

"Everyone knows him. He performed the funeral for one of our members and helped Jose's wife a couple of years back."

"What happened to his wife?"

"Life-threatening pregnancy. It all turned out fine, but Jose was a little shook. We were out of country at the time. Boss tried to send him home, but Jose wouldn't go. A team needs its medic and we were already one man down."

"Killed?"

"Hit by a car, but Pete survived."

"Pete? Our Pete? Junior?"

"That's him."

Crispin tapped the table. "Interesting. I need to ask him about that."

J. J. stared at the new man for a moment. "I wouldn't do it."

"Why?"

"His physical wounds have healed fine, but he's still a tad embarrassed about it."

"I see." Crispin seemed to be weighing his next question. "Mind if I ask about your limp?"

"You mean like you just did?"

Crispin's face reddened. "You might as well know: I'm not always as smooth as I appear."

J. J. guffawed. "Really?"

"Hey, keep the noise down out there." Rich's voice carried from the crew's quarters.

"Hey, Shaq. You know what's good for seasickness? Raw eggs. Want some."

Shaq groaned. "Get in here, pip-squeak, so I can pop you one."

"Maybe later."

Crispin was smiling. "You guys are pretty tight. All units like that?"

"I doubt it. We're lucky. We have the best there is and we like each other—most of the time." J. J. shifted on the bench seat. "Back to the limp. Didn't Boss fill you in?"

"He said you were wounded in battle."

"Yeah. Took a bullet in the leg. Stung a little."

"Stung? A little?"

J. J. shrugged. "Pain is relative."

"Relative, eh? You were screaming like a Girl Scout, weren't you?"

"Of course not. Okay. Maybe a little. Anyway, I was lucky. A little R & R, a few weeks of physical therapy, and more PT than I like and I'm as good as new."

"Why didn't you bail? You've done your duty. You were injured on mission. No one can doubt your courage."

"This is who I am; this is what I do."

"But how do you reconcile it all? I mean, being a Christian and a warrior."

A pain dug away at J. J.'s stomach. "I don't know how to answer that. I've killed but taken no joy in it. I'm proud about what the team has achieved over the last few years. There are people—including women and children—who are alive today because we were there for them." Images of Dr. Cenobio's family in Venezuela, Delaram in Italy, a dozen heads-of-state at a G-20 meeting, and others flashed strobelike in his mind.

J. J. looked down at his Bible. "The Old Testament shows heroes of the faith who were also warriors."

"Like King David."

J. J. nodded. "For one."

"But the New Testament is different. You don't find those kinds of people mentioned."

"True. Did you ever ask your dad that question? How did he reconcile things?"

"I don't think he did. To tell the truth, I think he became a minister because of guilt."

"That's a lousy reason."

"That's what I'm saying. Maybe it's why I haven't been to church since I left home. Seems hypocritical."

"But you've never spoken to your old man about this?"

"Not really."

"Then for all you know, you may have it backwards."

"I doubt it."

J. J. didn't hesitate. "But you don't *know* it."

"I guess you're right."

J. J. didn't like the response. He suspected Crispin was just accommodating him. "Look, I know there are some Christians who would criticize what I do. There are some who have been very supportive. I can tell you this: I take Jesus seriously."

"I believe you, but I don't think I could put a bullet in a man on Monday and sing hymns the following Sunday."

The words stung like a swarm of hornets. J. J. wrestled with this concept many times and knew he would continue to do so. In some ways, he envied those soldiers who didn't have to factor the spiritual into their work. At the same time, he felt sorry for them. Faith is what kept J. J. sane.

J. J. took in a slow breath. "If you're worried about me being able to pull the trigger when I need to, then you can stop right now. I haven't hesitated yet."

Crispin fidgeted and appeared uneasy. "Don't get me wrong, J. J. I'm not questioning your skill or dedication to meeting—"

"You had better not be, Newbie."

J. J. looked up to see the tall and wide form of Rich stepping into the galley. J. J. wasn't sure if such things were possible, but Rich's black skin seemed two shades paler.

"Oh, hey, Shaq—"

"Don't 'Hey Shaq' me, kid." Rich stepped uncomfortably close to Crispin's side of the table and leaned close to the man. Although a few feet farther away, J. J. could smell the seasick sour of the big man's breath. "Let me make this clear. The new guy doesn't question the integrity of the unit or its soldiers."

"I wasn't doing that—"

"J. J. has proven himself to many, and this man's Army many times over. He took a bullet doing his job. That makes him a hero in my book. Is that clear, pal?"

"Crystal clear, but I was just making conversation, Shaq."

"As the new guy you have the honor and the privilege of doing as you're told. Understood?"

"Yes—"

"The privilege of riding the team belongs to me and Boss. I'm here to make sure the team has one good-looking guy and to make sure guys like you follow through on orders. You haven't earned any rights yet. Until you do, I suggest you hold on to your opinions. Is there anything I've said that you don't understand, Newbie?"

"Yes—I mean no—I mean I understand."

"Good." Rich looked at J. J. and winked. J. J. suppressed a smile. Rich put a hand on J. J.'s shoulder and gave a crushing squeeze. "And by the way, Colt, you ever mention raw eggs to me again and you and me will have our own little conversation and I won't be using words. Catch my drift?"

"Understood."

"I'm going topside for some fresh air." Rich walked from the cabin with as much aplomb as a man his size could on a rocking and reeling boat. A second later J. J. heard him groan. Shaq was one sick man.

"Man, I didn't think I said anything that deserved that." Crispin's face was whiter than normal.

"You should have heard the lecture I got when I joined the team."

Crispin lifted an eyebrow. "He did the same thing to you?"

"Yup. In fact, you got off easy. My spine still melts when I think about it. He's just making sure you understand the pecking order. He rides everybody."

"What did you say to trigger that?"

"I said something derogatory about Broadway musicals. He begged to differ."

Crispin stared at the table. "Look, J. J., if I said anything to imply—"

"You didn't. I appreciate the conversation."

"Thanks."

"You told me your father is a believer, but you haven't told me what you believe."

"To be honest, I don't know what I believe." Crispin slid from his seat. "I'll let you get back to your reading."

J. J. let the man go. Alone again, he opened the Bible but couldn't force himself to focus. His mind raced with other thoughts. He had remorse over every man he killed, but he never hesitated to do his job, to pull the trigger when called upon to do so. Never.

Would that hold true in the future?

CHAPTER 9

VICE PRESIDENT ANDREW BACLIFF sat at the desk for the last time that day and probably forever. The interior of his office in the West Wing combined elegance and dignity with Bacliff's love of simplicity. Tall, gold-colored curtains covered mullioned-arched windows. A walnut desk that once belonged to Admiral Nimitz occupied an area near the windows and looked over two padded yellow sofas and several other chairs. This was his working office. He, like VPs before him, had a set of ceremonial offices in the Eisenhower Executive Office Building near the West Wing. It was where he held interviews and meetings.

He had no need to visit those offices. They would only sprinkle salt in his wounds. He loved his role in politics and his current job. Bacliff made no secret of his desire to be president. The *Washington Post* once called him an ambitious man with a heart. Power never tempted Bacliff. Power for him was a tool to be used to help others. Now he needed help.

He rose from his executive chair and paced the deep pile, blue carpet, his hands clasped behind his back. Not one given to visible displays of nerves, he was surprised to notice the clenching and unclenching of his hands, hands moist in the palm.

Around him were the trappings of power. A short walk down the hall and he could be in the Oval Office, consulting with one of the most powerful men on the planet. He could pick up the phone and summon generals and admirals into his presence. He could preside over the Senate or ring up almost any world leader, and they would feel obligated to take a call from America's second in command. A few days ago he took pride in all of this, satisfaction that he earned such luxuries and influence. That seemed a lifetime ago. Where once his mind was filled with global concerns and how best to represent his office, that of the president, and the American people, his thoughts were now riveted on his captured son.

For the briefest moment, he envied "normal" parents; mothers and fathers who might know a son or daughter went missing while overseas but knew nothing more. Bacliff not only knew his son was missing in action, he knew he was captured. The intelligence agency sent a blizzard of paper his way.

That would stop soon. The president promised to keep him in the loop, even letting him attend meetings in the Situation Room. It was a stretch of protocol, perhaps even illegal. President Huffington assured Bacliff that anyone trying to keep the VP—former VP—out would have a fistfight on their hands. Such statements were fine bravado but lacked teeth. What Huffington planned on, and what Bacliff hoped for, was time. It would take weeks for anyone to raise a big enough stink to force the president's hand.

Not that such an objection was without merit. Technically, he became a private citizen the moment he resigned his office. His office would remain vacant until both houses of Congress confirmed

Helen Brown as required by the Twenty-fifth Amendment. That would take a little time, but he had no doubt she would win approval easily. He would pull whatever strings and twist whatever arms necessary. Not that it mattered. He was already out.

The desk phone sounded. He punched the speaker button. "Yes."

"Your car is ready, Mr. Vice President."

Shirley Potts, his longtime, long-suffering secretary hadn't been told yet. "Thank you, Shirley. Please have the staff come into my office. You too."

There was a long pause. On more than one occasion, Bacliff would have raised his right hand and sworn the woman was psychic. "Yes, sir."

Time to say good-bye.

THE SECRET SERVICE DRIVER pulled the 2009 Cadillac—dubbed "Cadillac Two" because of its similarity to the president's limo and as a nod to the VP's airplane, Air Force Two—onto the grounds of the United States Naval Observatory and stopped at the front of a mansion built in 1893. The residence of the vice president looked as if it were built last year, not over a century before. The house at Number One Observatory Circle in northwestern Washington, D.C., served as home to vice presidents since the mid-1970s. It would be his home for a few more weeks, then, for security reasons, Helen Brown would move in.

Was it possible he'd lose his son, his career, and his home in the same week? Depression followed him like the cloud over Joe Btsfsplk, the well-meaning *Li'l Abner* character whose very presence caused harm to others. It was an irrational thought, but depression and fear seldom traveled the same road as rationality.

Bacliff walked through the doors of the mansion, set his briefcase down, and turned in time to see the VP limo pulling down the drive, the flags of the vice president's office flapping on their perches atop the front fenders. He had no emotion for the car, but its withdrawal into the obsidian night reminded him of all that happened.

He moved through the lobby and into the den. There he found his wife, Gertrude, seated in one corner of a sofa, a glass of scotch in one hand. Even in the dim light he could see her red lipstick smeared on the edge of the glass. Next to her was a crystal decanter half-filled with the golden liquid. He was certain it was full when he left this morning.

Gertrude looked up from the glass. She didn't smile. She didn't speak. She just stared. He removed his suit coat and threw it across the back of a chair, pulled his tie from around his neck, and sent it sailing the same direction. He stepped to her, bent, and kissed her on top of the head. Like her, he had no words. He retrieved a glass from the wet bar, poured three fingers of the whisky, and sat next to his wife.

She leaned against him. Her tears soaked through his shirt.

He finished the first glass in two gulps.

GINA MOYER SAT AT her small desk in front of the window of her small bedroom where she lived with her family. The desk was small because the room was small; the room was small because the house was small. Not tiny, but not half the size of the "McMansions" in the next neighborhood over. Her mother and father bought the home when Gina was seven. It was near schools and near Fort Jackson, South Carolina. She was fourteen now. "Fourteen going on thirty," her dad said so many times the phrase lost its humor a while back. She always gave a courtesy giggle whenever he said it.

She looked up from her American history book and gazed out the window. Gazing back was the reflection of a young lady with straight brown hair and blond highlights.

Her dad was gone—again. Most weeks he was home in the evening, having dinner with the family and "schooling" the family in digital bowling on the Wii. Truth was, he was horrible at the game, but he took it in stride. He was good at so many things that being lousy at video games didn't matter.

He often took trips to other military bases, but he told the family about those well in advance of his absence. When he just didn't come home, it meant he was in danger. Gina didn't know all her father did. He never offered details. It was only a few years ago she learned what he really did. She understood he was in the Army, but she seldom saw him in uniform. She should have suspected he did secret things when he sat her and her brother down and taught them "the story." How many times had he made her repeat it?

"My daddy, he's in business. Sometimes he travels around the country selling stuff. Office stuff." If pressed, she was just to shrug and plead ignorance.

A sound carried through the open door. Her mother was rinsing dishes and putting them in the dishwasher. It was the only sound. The television sat silent, unusual for this house, but Gina noticed a change in her mother. In the past, whenever Dad was away, her mother would watch the news, wondering if a clue to Dad's whereabouts might come over the airwaves. That stopped last year.

It hadn't been talked about, but Gina couldn't miss the fact one of her father's team came to the monthly barbeque on crutches. She also overheard talk about "Data's recovery." It would be months before Gina met the man they called Data. She learned his real name was Jerry Zinsser. He looked thin, moved slowly, and sat more than stood. She also saw him take pills, pain pills she assumed.

Mom began to change over the next few months. She seemed more nervous, spent her days cleaning and running errands, where this time a year ago she used to invest hours in reading. Gina did the mental detective work: J. J. and Jerry were wounded on mission, maybe even came close to being killed. If it could happen to them, then it could . . .

She closed her eyes, not wanting to finish the thought.

"Hey, Squirt."

Gina swiveled in her seat, a chair that matched the old desk: a desk that belonged to her grandfather then her father. It was a hand-me-down, but her father preferred to call it "family seepage."

Her tall, lanky, dark-haired brother stood in the doorway. "Hi, Rat Face."

"Rat Face? Really? Rat Face. That's just plain cruel."

"I mean it the best possible way." She grinned. "I suppose it is cruel—to the rats."

"Still think you're funny?" Rob entered and sat on the edge of Gina's bed.

"I don't think; I know."

"I don't think you know, either." He grabbed a pillow from the bed and tossed it at her. She caught it.

"That joke is as old as the hills." She tossed the pillow back at him. "I didn't hear you come in. How was your first day of work?"

"This may sound strange; it was a lot like work. I'm tired and I only worked four hours."

"Flipping burgers can be grueling."

"I wasn't flipping burgers. I'm too new. The guys who have been there longer get to do that. I cooked french fries."

"That explains the smell."

"That is the odor of a man making minimum wage. It won't be long and I'll be rubbing my new iPhone in your face." He set the pillow back at the head of the bed. "Whatcha doin'?"

"American history. I have a test tomorrow."

"My favorite class."

Gina narrowed her eyes. "You barely passed."

"But I passed and that's why it's one of my favorites. Need help?"

"Getting a D? No, I can do that by myself." She waited a moment, then added, "I'm okay, Rob."

"You sure?"

"Yeah. I mean, I'm worried and all, but I'm doing okay. It's not like it's the first time."

Rob nodded. "I wonder where he is."

Such comments from Rob still surprised her. A year ago he wouldn't have talked about their father except to criticize him. Rob changed. Some of it was age, but much of the improvement came from the time her brother was spending with Chaplain Paul Bartley. It was Bartley who reached out to Rob when their father was on mission. Being an Army brat was more difficult than people realized. Being the son of a Spec Ops team leader was worse. Yet Rob moved from wishing his father would die on mission to worrying about him when he was gone.

Of course, Rob would deny it all. He was like Dad in that way, but Gina could tell.

"He'll be all right, Gina. He always is."

"I know."

"I wish he were here. I want to tell him about my first day."

"Tell Mom."

He shrugged. "I will, but it's different. I—" Rob stood, his eyes directed out the window.

"What?" Gina turned but saw nothing.

"I thought I saw something."

"Can you be more specific?"

"A shadow."

"Um, it's nighttime, Rob. Not many shadows out there."

"Near the streetlamp, Squirt." Rob moved to the light switch and flipped it. The room went dark.

"Hey, it's hard to study in the dark."

"Hang on." He moved to the window and leaned close to the glass. "I could've sworn I saw someone in the yard."

"I don't see anything."

"Maybe it was a dog."

"Yeah, that must be it: a two-legged dog."

He lowered her blinds and then turned to the door.

"Where are you going?"

"To make sure the doors are locked."

CHAPTER 10

THE *KOMAGATA MARU* ROSE and fell with the swells, its bow plowing through six-foot seas. "I suppose we should be grateful."

Eric Moyer turned his eyes from the churning sea to the smooth Asian face of Sam Sasaki. "How's that?"

"Seas are cooperating. A little choppy, but not the twelve-footers I thought we might be riding."

"Only a Navy man would call this calm seas."

"You only have to ride out one North Pacific storm to appreciate how tiny these waves are."

"Spoken like a man who's staying on the boat."

Sasaki chuckled. "Yeah, well there is that. In some ways, I wish I were going along."

"Really? 'Cuz I can make that happen."

"No, not really. Do I look crazy? If I wanted to ride a rubber boat over cold waters in the middle of the night, I would have become a SEAL."

A crewman stepped forward and whispered in Sasaki's ear. "Very well. Make ready the CRRC." The crewman gave no acknowledgment. He slipped from the forward deck to an area behind the wheelhouse where a door waited for him.

Moyer walked through that door several times over the last few hours. It led below decks to the crew's quarters, galley, heads, and another companionway leading into the belly of the ship. Where once tons of crab were kept alive for market in the hole, it now held sophisticated tracking equipment meant to spy on communications from the nearby mainland and to keep an ear out for submarines prowling deep below the surface.

Moyer and his men were given a short and vague tour of the operations. Sasaki spoke of receivers and passive sonar without giving details. Moyer knew better than to ask. He was, however, impressed by the amount of equipment the decrepit, beleaguered-looking fishing boat held.

Moyer risked one question. "Do I want to know what happens if the ship is boarded by hostiles?"

"Then the hostiles go to the bottom with the rest of us."

Moyer's opinion of the man and his crew rose several levels. Salty spray came over the bow as the steel hull dug into a swell, bringing Moyer's attention back to the moment.

"Time to kick this pig, Sergeant Major. You may want to get your men."

Moyer nodded and followed the same path walked earlier by the crewman. He moved slowly, partly to make sure of his footing on a wet, moving deck; partly to avoid stumbling over anything he couldn't see in the dark. Commander Sasaki ordered lights out an hour before. They were making fifteen knots in pitch black. Not even a cigarette, whose glowing end could be seen at a distance, was allowed on deck.

Once through the door beneath the wheelhouse, Moyer descended a stairway in the dark. Another doorway opened to the crew's mess. In the soft glow of a single low-watt light, Moyer found his team. Four played cards. Crispin sat to the side, earbuds in his auditory canals. Every face turned his way when he crossed the threshold.

"We go in ten."

There was no hoopla, no exclamation of bravado. Experience taught his men the work they did was no game, no clip from a war movie. Each man was here as a volunteer; each willing to lay down his life for a team member and for the mission.

Crispin rose but the others remained seated. Last year they nearly lost two of the team; the year before they lost Martin "Billy" Caraway. Over time, a new tradition rose. Rich led them off. He reached in the breast pocket of his battle dress uniform and removed a photo of his wife, Robyn. Jose followed with a photo of his wife, Lucy; seven-year-old Maria; eight-year-old Matteo; ten-year-old Jose, Jr.; and the newest Medina, two-year-old Tito. He kissed the photo and set it on the table. Pete Rasor drew a photo of his pretty wife from his uniform and, like the two men before him, dropped it on the table. J. J.'s hand trembled slightly as he studied the image of Tess. He set her photo on the pile. Moyer stepped to the table, retrieved a picture he studied for a long moment, letting his eyes linger on the smiling faces of Stacy; his daughter, Gina; and his son, Rob. His eyes burned. He set the picture down, as if a quick motion would shatter it.

Shaq put a hand on the pile of photos. J. J., Jose, Pete, and Moyer stacked hands on top of his. There was a pause and Shaq looked at Crispin. "Get over here, Hawkeye."

"I didn't bring a picture."

"Doesn't matter," Shaq said. "Get a hand in here."

Crispin complied. Rich looked at Moyer. Moyer straightened his back and said, "For them, and for those like them, we do this."

The team repeated the words. "For them, and for those like them, we do this."

A second passed in silence.

Moyer withdrew his hand. "Showtime."

"I TAKE IT YOU'VE done something like this before?" Sasaki motioned at the Combat Rubber Raiding Craft setting on the deck near the stern. Lines attached to a crane formerly used to hoist crab pots were secured at key points.

"Not off a fishing vessel." Moyer and his team moved to the fifteen-foot-long, inflatable rubber boat.

"I'm sure it's exactly the same as you've done before, except different in every way."

"You are a comfort, Commander."

"I like to be encouraging. Just make sure you don't scratch anything."

"Mount up, men." Moyer stepped into the rear of the boat.

"Is this what you guys call a rubber duck?" Rich joined Moyer in the back.

"Sometimes. Rubber duck. Zodiac. Floating coffin. It's all the same." Sasaki placed a hand on one of the lines while the rest of the team took their places. "We don't want to leave any evidence of your arrival, so my man will be bringing the CRRC back. Which means you'll be on your own."

The comment was not news. Moyer and the commander went over the details several times. "Understood." Moyer checked his men. "On your order, Commander."

Sasaki stepped back and twirled a finger in the air. The small crane lifted the boat easily. Several crewmen held hand lines attached to the small craft to keep it from swinging out of control. The moving ship, which Sasaki slowed to just a couple knots, made the inflatable boat swing like a pendulum. Two minutes later, the crane operator moved the boat over the rail. Where once the hard deck was below, now there was a black ocean. Waves slapped the side of the fishing vessel.

"Yea though I am lowered into the ocean of death, I shall fear no evil—"

"Colt," Shaq said.

"Yeah?"

"Shut up."

"Roger that, Shaq."

"Okay, gentlemen, prepare to cast off lines on my say-so. We need to be quick. If we take too long we'll smash into the hull a few too many times for my liking. Clear?"

"Clear," Moyer said.

The boat hit the water at the top of a swell and then immediately dropped several feet into the trough. The crane operator wasted no time slacking the line.

"Now," the petty officer snapped. J. J. and Pete who were at the boat's bow freed the lift lines. Moyer and Rich did the same at the stern. Crispin and Jose sat in the middle, each holding the man in front of them.

"Bowlines free," J. J. said.

"Aft lines free," Rich shouted.

Before the night could swallow the last syllable, the petty officer powered the outboard motor and steered away from the *Komogata Maru*. From the ocean surface, the fishing boat seemed ten times larger than it did from the deck.

Moyer lowered his NVGs. The night vision goggles turned the dark into green daylight. He first scanned the sea for other ships, although he knew there were none. The electronic equipment aboard the *Komagata Maru* assured them of that, but Moyer wanted to see for himself. Any ship with nighttime running lights would be visible to the unaided eye but would light up like a tiny sun through the electronically enhanced goggles.

Satisfied no other ship was in the area, Moyer turned his attention forward to the dim shore of Russia and remembered the stack of photos they left behind.

CHAPTER 11

MAJOR BRUCE SCALON STOOD in the STRATCOM video conference room, what his team started calling the "bull pen." It was the same room where he and Eric Moyer's team discussed mission parameters. This time, however, it was not the gruff, stern-looking Colonel MacGregor filling the screen. Instead, Scalon and his aide Captain Tim Bryan had their gazes fixed on a dark, nearly featureless image. To the right side of the screen was a dark shape with well-defined lines; to the far left the mass of dark lightened some and a few bright splotches of light appeared.

"Coastal towns." Scalon pointed at the lights, as if commenting on a painting in a museum.

Tim nodded. "They made a wise choice. I don't see much standing between them and the shore."

"It's the things we don't see that worry me." The major put his hands behind his back and tried to look nonchalant. Inside, however, a Category 5 hurricane raged. He admired Tim, who looked as comfortable as a man in his living room watching a documentary.

"We all worry about that, sir."

"Do you think they'll succeed?" Scalon kept his eyes glued to the monitor.

"No one knows, sir. We always went in full of confidence—at least on the outside. If we had doubts, we kept them to ourselves. It's the way of our breed. Moyer and his men might belong to a different branch of the military, but at times like this, we are all brothers. I don't have a full background on the team, but they struck me as being tops in the game."

"If only it were a game."

"There were other teams they could have called, yet the brass chose these guys. I gotta believe they had good reason."

"You are worried, aren't you?" Scalon cut a glance Tim's way.

"Worried?" He paused. "I suppose so."

"Wish you were with them?"

Tim gave an almost imperceptible nod. "It's been decided that, for me, those days are over, sir. That being said, I wish I could be there when they rescue our own."

"If they rescue our men."

"That's a big 'if.' There's always something that can go wrong."

Scalon watched the image. The KH-14 satellite was in its second low orbit pass of the day, just 175 miles overhead. During daylight, the thirty-thousand-pound satellite could resolve items less than a foot across. At night, using infrared and low-light intensification technology, the bus-sized eye-in-the-sky could still see objects less than two feet across.

Between the fishing vessel *Komagata Maru* and the empty stretch of beach on the eastern Russian coast was a small object leaving a white streak in its wake. The moment the small craft stopped its forward motion, Scalon picked up the phone.

"Get SECDEF on the horn." Thirty seconds later, Scalon heard the secretary of defense's voice.

"Mr. Secretary. Major Scalon here. Team is feet dry." Scalon listened for a moment. "Yes, sir. We wish them Godspeed as well. Good night, Mr. Secretary."

Scalon hung up.

PRESIDENT HUFFINGTON NORMALLY SLEPT soundly. Seldom did the pressing problems of leading a country with 350 million residents keep him from falling fast asleep. His declining position in the opinion polls, something that happened to every president, hadn't deprived him of a single wink. Tonight, however, was different. His mind, which ran like a race car eighteen hours a day, had a stuck throttle. He stared at the ceiling, flopped around on the bed as gently as possible to keep from waking his wife, and tried to bore himself to sleep citing cases learned in law school.

Sleep refused to come.

Several times he tried to ignore the cause of his anxiety, but each time his internal argument lost ground. As president, he sent men into harm's way many times. The history books wouldn't record most of those. He also knew Spec Ops teams went into action without his knowledge. That came by plan. He simply couldn't oversee every detail and had to trust his military leaders to act with wisdom and discretion.

Moyer's team was different. Those men saved his and his wife's lives and that of other G-20 leaders. The men were not nameless warriors. He knew each one and even made it possible for one to have his wedding in the Rose Garden. To lose a soldier he didn't know tore at his gut; to lose any of these men meant the loss of a friend. It was the reason he tried to avoid friendships with those he might have to send to their deaths.

The BlackBerry phone by his bed vibrated and the screen glowed. He retrieved it and read a brief message from his secretary of defense.

FEET DRY.

There would be no sleeping tonight.

CHAPTER 12

MOYER KEPT AN EYE on Crispin as they approached shore. Insertion into hostile territory would frighten any man with half a brain. Moyer knew how the other members of his team would react. He had been in dicey situations with them in a dozen different countries. Crispin, however, was the unknown. It was one thing to excel in training; it was a completely different matter to go up against a real enemy.

Over the years of his service, Moyer saw men who were brave and steady on the military base but stumbled on feet of clay the first time a bullet whistled by their ears. He never criticized those individuals. They were probably smarter than he.

So far Crispin did everything well and without hesitation. He even removed the almost ever-present earbuds without Moyer's prompting.

The petty officer slowed the CRRC a mile out and even more when they were a hundred yards from the shore. The outboard motor was noisy and sound carried over water very well. The insertion point was selected carefully. It was a short span of sand surrounded by rugged rocks and low cliffs. In theory, no one would be around, but theory had a way of going south. One old insomniac who enjoyed a little nighttime surf fishing could blow the whole operation.

The petty officer guiding the boat operated it like an Indy racer, familiar with every nuance of the craft and of the sea. Moments ago, he steered through low surf, timing his approach to ride the incoming waves. The boat beached as if the sailor practiced the maneuver at this spot a hundred times.

Moyer gave no orders. There was no need. The thick, rigid, rubber hull slid up the sand and his men sprinted from the craft. J. J. and Pete were first and ran two yards and dropped to their bellies, weapons pointed before them, sweeping the beach. J. J. carried an M110 Semi-Automatic Sniper System; Pete an M4A1 carbine.

Jose and Crispin were on their heels, taking positions a few yards to either side of the first two men.

Moyer followed Rich from the boat. Both men stopped, turned, and pushed the Zodiac back into the water. The petty officer would have a challenge getting back through the surf without cranking the throttle enough to be heard a mile away, but Moyer was certain, based on what he already saw the man do, the sailor would make it happen. Had there been houses, industry, or towns nearby, they would have rowed the last hundred yards and another sailor would have been aboard to help row back out. That wasn't needed here.

Moyer's eyes, aided by the NVGs he wore, scanned the area. Nothing in the green, light-enhanced image.

He started for a small cliff on the south side of the beach, jogging through the thick sand. A glance to his side revealed his men doing exactly as they planned: weapons at the ready and moving from side to side and up to the high ground.

The sand gave way to broken shale and loose rock. Using the sling on his M4, Rich shouldered his weapon, put his back to the cliff face, and cupped his hands. Moyer estimated the top of the drop-off at nine feet, an easy scale.

Moyer pointed at J. J. who stepped forward, placed a foot in Rich's hand, and stood as if he were standing in a stirrup. Pete and Jose kept their weapons pointed at the top of the cliff. Crispin and Moyer kept an eye on the beach around them.

Slowly, J. J. peered over the cliff's edge. "Now."

Rich lifted and J. J. pulled himself over the edge. Moyer couldn't see what J. J. was doing, but he knew anyway. His weapons expert would be flat on his stomach, surveilling the area.

"Clear."

The announcement came over the earpiece Moyer and the others wore. He motioned to Crispin who followed J. J.'s example. Jose went next, then Pete. Moyer was next. Rich, whose strength still amazed Moyer even after so many missions, put a little extra into the lift. For a moment, he was sure his friend was going to throw him up the cliff.

Moyer and Jose leaned over the cliff. Rich took several steps back to get a running start. He planted a boot in the side of the cliff and reached for the upper edge. Moyer and Jose each grabbed an arm and helped the big man up and over the side.

Jose triggered his tactical throat microphone. "You ever heard of Jenny Craig, big guy?"

"You want your kids to grow up without a father, Doc?"

"Hey, I'm just sayin', *amigo*. You're just a few pounds away from looking good."

"Boss, permission to squash Doc like a bug."

"Denied. For now." Moyer was on his feet and moving to an asphalt road a short distance away. The macadam had so many holes it reminded him of a bombed-out runway.

As planned, the team split into two teams of three. One squad on each side of the road. Rich led Jose and Crispin on the eastern side of the road; Moyer took point on the western edge. Also per plan, Rich's group stayed fifty yards to the rear giving one team the opportunity to come to the aid of the other should the need arise.

Moyer set off in double time, his eyes ever forward looking for headlights or movement that would indicate they were no longer alone.

He picked up the pace, keeping in mind it did no good to wear his men out before they were thirty minutes into a mission.

TWO KILOMETERS LATER, THEY departed from the road without seeing another human. Moyer could only imagine what someone driving down the road might think if they caught sight of six heavily armed, helmeted men jogging along the path.

The area around them was bare with areas of low shrubs. Hills still clinging to what remained of their snow blankets loomed to the west.

Moyer slowed his men as a weatherworn building came into view. It looked like a two-story barn without the accompanying farmland. Its wood siding was stained from years of resisting rain, snow, wind, and months of freezing temperatures. It was the kind of building a landscape painter would enjoy replicating on canvas. To Moyer, it represented the next step in the mission.

A small grove of Siberian larch stood a few yards from the road. Moyer and his team took cover behind the trees. It was still several hours before sunrise, a realization that made his mind run home. There was almost a fifteen-hour difference between here and his South Carolina home. What was his family doing with their afternoon? Moyer refocused his thoughts. He had business.

Moyer raised a small pair of M25 stabilized binoculars to his eyes and studied the building and the few small shacks around it. No indications of life; no activity. "Place looks abandoned."

"Look at this place," Rich said. "Would you hang around? Cold, desolate, no fast-food joints."

"It's a good thing we're trained to endure such hardships." Jose kept his voice low.

"Desolate is what we want right now." Moyer lowered the binoculars. "That's our building. We go in quiet but loaded. Shaq, you take Junior and cross the road. Approach the structure from the rear. I'll take Hawkeye and we'll come in from the north side. That should keep us from view of anyone who might be watching from the other buildings."

"You sure you don't want me to take the new guy?"

"Thanks, but I don't want him showing you up. Hawkeye, leave your toys." Moyer turned to J. J. "Colt, you and your M110 take a sniper position forward and keep an eye out for problems. Doc, you be his extra eyes."

"Roger that, Boss." J. J. worked his way to the front of the small stand of trees and removed the lens cover of the AN/PVS-174 night sight. The Army Navy/Portable Visual Search device turns night into day. Moyer watched as Jose took a position a few feet to J. J.'s right.

"Let's do this fast and sweet, Shaq."

"Will do, Boss. Will do." Rich turned to Pete. "Let's hit it, Junior."

"On your six, Shaq."

The two sprinted across the narrow road and a dozen yards farther on. Each man moved quickly but with caution. Moyer gave them two minutes before following his assistant team leader. He wished for more cover but nothing was available. It was one reason they worked at night.

The industrial building grew in Moyer's NVGs but still no motion. What little intel they had for the region gave no indication hostiles waited for them, but there was—somewhere—an Air Force Spec Ops team that might beg to differ.

Rich and Pete made it to the back of the building without incident; Moyer and Crispin arrived at the side of the building moments later.

"I got a door here." Rich's voice came over Moyer's earpiece.

"Understood. Colt?"

"All clear, Boss."

The wall by Moyer had a series of six double-hung windows, each covered in grime. He saw no lights. Still, he raised a pair of fingers to his eyes, then pointed at the windows. Crispin nodded, then glanced in the window nearest him and immediately pulled his head back. With a shake of his head he indicated he saw nothing. Moyer did the same with the window close to him: nothing but blackness.

Moyer lowered his head and scrambled past the window, not taking the chance someone with a gun might be sitting in the dark. Moyer checked half the windows; Crispin eyed the remaining three. The best Moyer could tell, nothing but darkness filled the building.

Reaching the corner with Crispin in tow, Moyer joined Rich and Pete. A sharp, upraised hand by Rich stopped Moyer in midstep. Rich gave a hand signal directing Moyer to look in the rear window near where Rich stood.

Moyer approached and glanced through the glass: A small, red glow floated four feet off the floor. Laser sight? Ghost?

Rich brought two fingers to his lips, then pulled them away. *Cigarette. Good catch, Shaq.*

Two feet north of the window was a door covered with peeling red paint. Moyer took a position to one side, Crispin immediately behind him. Rich took the other side, Pete on his six.

Moyer eased a gloved hand onto the knob and turned it with painful slowness. It rotated. Unlocked. Moyer's eyes drilled into Rich's.

Rich nodded and turned on his tactical light, a small flashlight attached to the underside of his M4. The others did the same.

Moyer pushed the door open and crossed the threshold, his light slicing the black, his weapon pressed into his shoulder. Other beams swept the area looking for any threat.

The floating red glow was near the middle of the wide, empty room. Moyer drew down on it and the dim shape behind. The others followed suit until all four beams were fixed on a man seated in a wood chair, a cigarette in his lips.

"Gentlemen. I've been expecting you." The voice was calm and the accent thick. He leaned to the side and extended his arm.

"Don't move." Rich took a step closer, close enough that the barrel of his M4 was only inches from the man's head.

"Slow down, cowboy." The man continued to extend his arm. Moyer heard a click, and a dim light pushed back the darkness. Seated in the chair was a bald man with a half crown of hair running from ear to ear. He was round in the middle and slump shouldered. He wore glasses with thick lenses and a wire frame. His clothing was that of a working man: dirty jeans, heavy flannel shirt, and work boots. He looked like he'd be more comfortable with a platter of nachos and a six-pack.

The lamp sat on a battered folding table and shared the space with a pot of tea, an unidentifiable half-eaten sandwich, and a nearly empty bottle of vodka.

Moyer signaled Pete and Crispin to finish securing the building. Moments later they returned. "Clear," Pete said. "But you won't believe what we found."

Moyer kept his focus on the bald man. "State your name."

"You know my name. I'm why you're here."

"State you name," Moyer repeated. Rich put the barrel of his weapon to the man's temple, putting the exclamation point to the order.

"Lev."

"Lev what?"

"Lev Nikitin. Now, can you call off your dog?"

"He's our man." Moyer waved Rich off.

Lev grinned. If Rich put any fear in the man, it didn't show. Lev had the look of a man who had seen a lot, maybe too much.

"I don't have much to offer. I'm afraid I finished the tea. The vodka . . . well, you are on duty, are you not?"

Moyer frowned. "Yeah, just like you."

"Ah, I see. You think I'm drunk. Well, I'm Russian. Drunk is a long way off."

"Are you sure this is our guy?" Rich's disdain was clear.

"What? You don't like my looks?" Lev stood. "You think I should wear a tie and suit coat? How many agents do you think are willing to work in this area? Vodka is a staple of Russian diet.

It got my father and mother through the Cold War years and my grandparents through Stalin."

"I'm just saying a little personal pride—"

"Fine. If you don't want me, I'll go to what passes for my home. You can find your satellite and lost men by yourself." He started for the door when Moyer stopped him by placing a hand on the man's chest.

"The wordplay is over, Lev. I've been ordered to meet with you and meet is what we're going to do. I have no orders for what happens to you after that. You do understand what I'm saying, don't you?"

Lev grinned. His breath smelled of cigarettes. "I don't intimidate easily, Mr. Sergeant, sir. You don't grow up in Siberia like I did without making friends with fear. Now do you want my help or not?"

"Yes." Moyer had a growing desire to plant a fist in the man's face.

"Then come with me."

Lev led them in the direction Pete and Crispin were a short time before. At the end of the building was a large, white panel truck with blue and orange letters painted on the side: FedEx.

"You're kidding me." Rich looked stunned. "You have FedEx here?"

Lev shook his head. "FedEx is everywhere. We might be remote, but we are not backwards." The Russian opened the back doors of the truck. Inside were white cardboard boxes here and there. "Unlike most delivery trucks, this one has rear seating."

"What's in the boxes?" J. J. asked.

"This and that. Food, water, a few other things."

Moyer cocked his head. "Other things?"

Lev seemed proud. "In one of the boxes is something you might need: a way of carrying radioactive material. You didn't think you could throw it in your backpacks, did you?"

"I've been wondering about that," Rich said.

"How did you get all this?" Moyer stepped into the cargo area.

"Overnight delivery, of course."

"You got a sense of humor, I'll give you that." Rich slapped the man on the back.

"You see, everyone loves Lev."

"We ain't buddies yet, pal."

Lev shrugged. "It's a start." He stepped into the back of the vehicle, opened a small box near the driver's area, and removed something that reminded Moyer of a large iPhone. "Your people will send information to this device."

"We have satellite phones." Moyer studied the device.

"Do they have displays? Do you know how a submarine gets its information?"

"Well, there are several ways—"

"Data is sent from satellites in compressed digital packets. They are called 'burst transmissions.' A submarine comes close enough to the surface to extend its communication mast, then receives a burst of information. It takes only a few seconds so the submarine can submerge to deeper, safer waters. What you hold is a version of that."

He took the device from Moyer and caressed it. "It's an amazing piece of work. Did you know I studied to be an electrical engineer? Of course not, how could you." He handed it back. "With this device you can do more than talk as you do on a satellite phone. There are electronic ears in this area. Satellite phones are easy to track, even if they encrypt their transmissions. In fact, encrypted messages tend to raise suspicions."

Moyer faced Pete. "Think you can handle this?"

"Yes, Boss. If it runs on electrons, then I can handle it."

"Boss," Lev said. "How . . . quaint." He paused, belched, then scratched his belly. "We should be going."

"We?" Moyer raised an eyebrow.

"I'm your driver."

"You're kidding." Rich took a step back. "I hate to tell you this 007, but you're drunk."

"See, I'll fit right in."

"Bad idea," Moyer said.

"Really? Which of your team speaks Russian?" Lev crossed his arms.

Moyer had a bad feeling. The agent had a point. Given the time, the brass might have sent a Russian-speaking soldier with them, but the clock was working against them. In a matter of hours, Angel-12 would plummet to earth, and there were the captive men to consider.

"Mount up, men."

"Boss, you can't be serious." Rich looked stunned. "I can't remember the number of times I've jumped out of airplanes, some at high altitude. I did so without a second thought, but this has disaster written all over it."

"I said, mount up." Moyer keyed his throat mike. "Colt, status report."

"All clear, Boss. I saw a rabbit. Does that count?"

"You and Doc haul yourselves in, double time, and bring Crispin's gear."

"Roger that."

Moyer turned to Lev and smiled. The Russian grinned back. In a blink, Moyer seized the man by the front of his flannel shirt and rammed him into one of the fixed seats mounted to the truck bed.

"At the moment, I am a man with mixed emotions. You've done us some favors, not the least of which is this truck, but so far you seem to be taking this lightly; too lightly for my tastes." Lev's eyes widened. "I haven't had much sleep, I've been traveling for I don't know how many hours, so I'm a little on edge. Are you following me?"

"Yes, I follow." A slight tremble ran through the man.

"If you do anything that endangers my men, hinders my mission, or puts those captured men at greater risk, I will bust you up so bad, buzzards will puke when they see you. Is there anything you don't understand?"

"I assure you that my intention—"

With one arm, Moyer lifted the man from the seat and slammed him back down hard enough to force air from his lungs. "I asked you a question."

"Yes, I understand. I understand completely."

"Good, you have five minutes to sober up." Moyer released him and then jumped from the back of the panel truck.

"If you ask me, Boss, you just made him sober."

CHAPTER 13

Columbia, South Carolina

STUDY GROUP WAS GOING well and Gina was pleased with herself for the gathering. She and three other girls from her junior high school met twice a week to study and cram for tests. Gina didn't need the help, but she enjoyed the warm sense of accomplishment that came from helping others. Well, she didn't need help with academic classes. Science, social studies, English, Spanish, and history came easy to her. It was speech class that gave her nightmares. The class reinforced what she long suspected: She was a high-order introvert. Among family and friends, she was a wit, quick with a jab, a soft sarcasm, or a suggestion for an outing. Standing in front of a class and talking was a different matter.

Tomorrow she would have to do the emotionally painful act of giving a three-minute speech. Three minutes! Why did it have to be so long? Her stomach already hurt.

Gina repositioned herself on the floor, crossing her legs. The girls gathered in Pauline Wysocki's house three blocks south of

Gina's home. Pauline was the first to practice her speech: "How to Properly Brush Your Teeth." Gina suggested something a little more serious might be in order.

"Dental hygiene is important, girl." Pauline's straight black hair bounced when she spoke. Petite and several inches shorter than anyone else in the group, Pauline was powered by boundless energy. Everything she did, she did at accelerated speed. Gina guessed the girl would have to write a six-minute speech to reach the three-minute minimum. "I mean, have you seen Vinny's teeth?"

"Eeeeew." Sharon sat on the floor, her back against Pauline's sofa.

"You just like the subject because your dad is an Army dentist." Beth was stretched out on the sofa. Tall and lanky, she covered the entire length of the piece of furniture.

"And what's wrong with that?" Pauline crossed her arms.

"Nothing wrong with it. I'm just sayin'." Beth studied her nails, the notes for her speech resting on her flat belly. Life kick-started her growing years, leaving her a half-a-foot taller than any girl in her class. To her credit, she took the teasing in stride. Her unflappable nature was one of the things Gina admired about her. That, and she was the smartest girl in the school and Gina's constant competition for the higher grades.

Sharon sighed loudly and for effect. "Come on, guys, let's get on with this. I gotta be home by nine, or my parents will ground me again." She pushed her blond bangs from her eyes. Sharon was the darling of the boys. Her short hair with the streak of pink in it, bright blue eyes, and thousand-watt smile drew the attention of every seventh, eighth, and ninth grader with a Y chromosome.

"Okay, you go first, Pauline." Gina lifted a stopwatch she borrowed from her brother. "I'll time you."

"Why me?"

"It's your house," Beth said.

"What's that got to do with anything?"

"It doesn't." Beth pulled her long legs in, turned on the sofa, and sat facing Pauline. "We're all going to give our speeches, so what does it matter who goes first? Get it over with, girl. There's a program I want to watch on television."

"But—"

"Just do it." The other girls spoke in unison. The unplanned chorus drew giggles from them all.

"Okay, okay." Pauline stepped to the middle of the living room, straightened her back, and raised her notes. "High blood pressure, diabetes, and heart disease. Very few people know these diseases can come from poor dental health . . ."

THE STUDY SESSION LASTED another ninety minutes, lengthened by Pauline's mother's insistence they reward themselves with chocolate chip cookies and milk. Gina didn't want any so she ate only three of the largest cookies.

She told her mother she'd be home by eleven and her watch told her it was five minutes past that. It would take less than ten minutes to walk the three blocks north to her house, not late enough to call home. Mom was always tolerant of Gina's study nights.

The May air was still warm; South Carolina warmed early and stayed hot far too long for her tastes. At this hour, however, things had cooled to a comfortable level although the humidity refused to leave.

Had Rob made it home from McDonald's? He said he might have to work late, so maybe not. She spent more time lately thinking

of her brother. Maybe it was because of the change she watched
in him over the last two years; maybe, at the age of eighteen, he
became the protector of the family when her father went away on
mission. Maybe.

The neighborhood looked sleepy. Only half the houses had
lights burning; from a few the sound of a television rode the gentle
breeze. In the distance a night bird sang. Weariness settled on her.
After a day of school, an afternoon of study, and an evening of
study group, Gina was ready for her bed.

The headlights of a car approaching from behind washed the
road with illumination. Gina turned and saw a red 1970s Cadillac
approaching. She had seen the car before. An elderly couple owned
the vehicle, apparently unable or unwilling to buy something made
in this century.

She turned her attention to the sidewalk extending before her.
Just two blocks to go. Another pair of lights came toward her: a
new Volkswagen Beetle. She eyed it with admiration. A red Beetle
was on her wish list. All she needed was to grow a little older and
find a way to finance the car. Like the Cadillac, she had seen the
car before.

She paused at the curb, ready to cross the last street and walk
the last block. Gina shifted her speech book to her other arm and
started across.

A car engine started.

Tires rumbled on asphalt.

Gina turned to see who was pulling from the curb at this hour.
Instead, two large men appeared. Before she could think, before she
could react, one of the men pulled a hood over her head. It smelled
of chemicals. A hand clamped over her mouth.

She screamed anyway but couldn't manage any sound with
volume.

Dizzy.

Her legs gave out. Her last memory was of being lifted and carried. A few moments later she felt motion, forward movement. A vehicle?

Gina tried to focus but nothing happened. Shouldn't she be afraid? Yes she should, but she couldn't keep her eyes open. The smell turned her stomach. Thoughts bounced randomly in her head: no order . . . no reason . . . no emotion. The chemical smell deprived her of reason. Her last conscious thought struck her as odd.

She hoped her mother wouldn't be angry about her not coming home. Stupid thought.

Then she couldn't think at all.

Khabarovsk region of eastern Russia, near Enken

THE FEDEX VAN MOTORED over the rough, potholed surface of the road Moyer and his men followed a short time before. Irritation and weariness mixed with adrenaline, leaving Moyer on edge. There was something else; something he couldn't put a finger on.

Lev told them what to expect. After Moyer's little conversation with the man, Lev became very cooperative. Moyer didn't know how long it would last. Lev didn't seem like a man who would stay intimidated. Moyer just hoped it lasted through the trip.

The team sat on seats specially installed for this purpose. They were small, they were uncomfortable, but they did the job.

Rich sat across from him. They made eye contact and the big man tilted his head.

"Something on your mind, Shaq?"

Rich nodded. "Yup."

"Spill it."

He leaned forward and Moyer did the same. Moyer could feel Rich's breath on his ear. "You okay?"

"Solid. Why?"

"You seem a little out of sorts, even for you."

Moyer leaned back. "I'm gonna forget that last comment."

Rich rested elbows on his knees. "All I'm sayin', Boss, is that you seem edgy."

His second in command had to speak up to be heard over the roar of the engine and the rattle of the truck's metal sides. Moyer glanced at the other members of the team. Not one made eye contact.

"What's your point?" Rich leaned forward again but Moyer waved him off. "Just say it, Shaq."

"Okay, I will. You were a little rough on our man up there." He motioned to Lev with his thumb.

"*I* was rough. You put your gun to his head."

"True, but that's me. Someone has to play the bad soldier and I do that well. You're supposed to be the good soldier."

Moyer frowned. "This isn't good cop, bad cop, Shaq. The man needed some sobering."

"Agreed, but that's what I'm here for."

"So you're ticked because I didn't let you put sense into the man?"

"No. I'm just asking if you're okay."

"I'm fine."

"Okay, if you say so, Boss. Just checkin' because it's my job."

"You've checked and I've answered."

"Understood, Boss. You're doing just peachy. Got it. I read you."

"You don't sound convinced."

"Is that a requirement?"

"Let it go, Shaq."

Rich leaned back. "Already have."

"Good." Moyer stretched forward to look through the delivery driver's passage that joined the cargo area with the cab. He could see nothing through the windshield.

"Coming up on the paved road . . . Boss."

Lev was getting snippy again.

Moyer ignored him and leaned back. Why was he so ill at ease? Rich was right, but Moyer didn't want to indicate that now. He'd make good with his friend later. He turned to the other men. Pete and Crispin were chatting quietly about the communications device. "You boys making any headway with that?"

"Yes, Boss," Pete said. "Hawkeye heard rumors about it back in the States."

"Rumors? It didn't come with a digital instruction manual?"

"Not that we can find."

"What rumors did you hear, Hawkeye?"

"Electronic transmission is my gig, unmanned and the like. Of course, you already know that. There's been talk about these babies. Lev was telling the truth when he said it's designed to send and receive encrypted messages in bursts. The sender records what he wants to say, loads up whatever files he wants, then before you can say 'boom goes the dynamite,' the transmission is sent and downloaded. What you don't get is real-time dialog, that's the bad news. The good news is, the transmission is so short it can't be traced. The other good news is that files can be sent: maps, schematics, whatever you want. In that sense, it's like sending e-mail with attachments."

"So you can make it work?"

"No doubt, Boss. It's very intuitive." Pete looked at Rich. "I bet even Shaq can operate it."

Rich didn't miss a beat. "Good, that means we don't need a nerdy communications guy."

"This is why I stick with guns," J. J. said. "Teams always need a shooter."

"And a medic," Jose added.

"That's true, Doc." He gave Jose a fist bump. "Saved my life and my leg."

"Wait until you get the bill, Colt."

"Write it off as professional courtesy."

Moyer removed his helmet and ran a hand through his hair.

For some reason, he kept thinking of Gina.

CHAPTER 14

LI PENG, SHANG WEI—a captain in NATO military classification—in the People's Liberation Army of China, wasn't certain whether to be thankful or not. His team was tasked with recovering a falling satellite that was supposed to crash within fifty miles of their location in Heilongjiang just south of the Russian Jewish Autonomous region. The bad news was the scientists who did the math were wrong and Peng was just learning of it. The good news was that glory and military honor could still be his. His recovery team was to continue their mission.

More bad news. The latest calculations put landfall in Russia. To make a success of this mission, all he had to do was find a way to sneak his unit into another country, one which had already seen conflict along its 2,738-mile shared border.

He had confidence in his team, even greater confidence in himself, but his job had become exponentially more difficult. The Russians would certainly send a recovery team, as might one of the military splinter groups known to be in the area. Perhaps most challenging of all, the Americans would do their best to retrieve or destroy the device. He would if he were in their place. That couldn't be allowed. He hoped his superiors would not give up the cause because of the unexpected change. Given the chance he would honor them with success.

On the plus side, he was in one of the most remote, least-populated areas in the country. Peng stood on the banks of the Amur River, one of the largest waterways in Asia. It flowed 1,755 miles from Mongolia and along the border between his country and Russia. He stood on Chinese soil and looked into what was once the Soviet Union, a fellow Communist country. Now it was something they called a federal semi-presidential republic, whatever that meant. From here, with a little wind at his back, he might be able to hit the country with a stone.

He glanced southwest. Three of his men stood on the same bank as he, fishing poles in hand, pretending to fish the Chinese side of the Amur. Pretending was too strong a word. His soldiers, dressed like Chinese businessmen on vacation, pulled in several fish they kept in pails farther up shore.

Peng held a fishing pole, but his line had yet to hit water. His mind was on a place a few hundred miles north. When he asked how the satellite could fall so far from course, he was told it was not part of his mission to know. He accepted that. Perhaps a small error in space converted to a much larger error on earth. Of course, what did he know? He was military, Chinese Special Forces, Hong Kong Special Ops Company, Macau Quick Reaction Platoon, otherwise known as the "Five-Minute Response Unit." They had been on this mission more than five minutes.

Wei Dong called from the camp of tents fifty meters from the river's bank. He said nothing, just shouted to get Peng's attention. Peng set the fishing pole on his shoulder and walked back to camp.

He doubted they were being observed. The Russian economy was so bad they thinned their border protection until it was little more than a joke. Still, he had earned his rank by hard work, diligence, and more than a little paranoia.

He entered camp and stepped into a tent. Wei Dong, a Si Ji Shi Guan—sergeant first class—held a satellite phone to Peng, then stepped to the side of the tent, showing deference and a readiness to help in any fashion his team leader demanded.

"Peng." The team leader pushed a camping chair aside, choosing to stand as he spoke. He listened for several moments and then said, *"Ting dong le."* In truth, he didn't understand as much as he would like.

Peng set the satellite phone on a card table. "Get the others. We're leaving."

"May I ask where we are going, Captain?"

"North, Sergeant. We are going north, but not directly."

Thirty minutes later, the team had loaded a BAW Zhanqi SUV and started for Fuyuan about twenty minutes in a straight flight, but they weren't flying. They were winding their way over uncertain roads.

Fuyuan was small but still several times larger than the scores of other villages in the area. This was remote China, far from the megacities holding millions of citizens. Here Peng was far from belching industrial stacks, gridlocked traffic, and wealth. Here, there was mostly poverty and subsistence living. Here the people were as tough as the unmerciful winters. Peng knew, he grew up not far from here.

The People's Liberation Army was his way out. Military service was compulsory but seldom enforced because of the large number of volunteers. Peng was one such volunteer. At the age of eighteen he enlisted, becoming one of three million people making up the world's largest military service. He showed skill, interest, and enthusiasm and was soon selected for officer training.

He had been part of the Macau Quick Reaction Platoon for four years and team leader for the last two. His work took him into several Baltic states, former members of the USSR, Africa, and the Middle East. He relished every mission and each ended with success, placing him in good standing with his superiors. Rumor had it a successful conclusion to the satellite recovery would deliver a promotion and better quarters. Peng was ambitious and Army life suited him. He had no plans for life away from the military.

Runoff from residual snow made the roads muddy and slippery. Wei Dong worked the steering wheel as if the thing were trying to escape the cab. One of the men in the back made a lewd joke about Dong's ability to handle things. Peng let the laughter continue. His mind was elsewhere. They passed several villages, none of which could harbor more than a few hundred people—people who worked farms under the guidance of their collective.

There were three hundred million farmers in the country, toiling in difficult conditions to raise rice, sorghum, wheat, potatoes, and scores of other crops. At one time, the government owned all farms, but in the late seventies, before Peng was born, they began to release property and control back to the farmers. One such farm served as Peng's home for the first eighteen years of his life. He was certain his familiarity with the area was one reason his team received the mission. Still, being back made him uneasy.

The SUV was large but five men made it feel cramped. Peng would be glad to be out of the vehicle. Dong found a stretch of hardpack road that soon gave way to pavement. The smoother ride was welcome.

In the distance, lights from Fuyuan still burned, even though the sun had been up for over an hour. Winter was gone, but at this latitude the sun still hung a little lower than it did in late summer.

"Stay to the south of the city." Peng pointed out the windscreen. "There is our ride."

Dong leaned over the steering wheel. "The helicopter?"

"What else do you see in the sky?" Hsu Li was Peng's second in command. A young lieutenant and the only other officer on the team.

"Nothing we can ride on, sir."

Peng watched the slow-moving aircraft as it banked over the small city, making a full circle. Even in a moving car and still five kilometers away, Peng could hear the thumping of the helicopter's rotors.

As they drew closer to the selected landing area—an empty field ten kilometers southeast of the city—life inflicted another irony on Peng: the aircraft was an Mi-17V7. Russian made.

CHAPTER 15

Columbia, South Carolina

STACY MOYER WOKE WITH a start. Had she heard something? She straightened on the couch, cocked her head, and strained to hear whatever awakened her. The only thing she heard was the soft droning of a late-night talk show host yammering on the large flat screen mounted to the wall opposite the sofa.

She waited for the noise to reappear but heard nothing out of the ordinary. *I'm snoring again.* Over the last few months, for reasons she couldn't explain, she started snoring. Eric assured her it wasn't loud or disruptive, but what did he know. He spent many of his nights sleeping in the company of men in a tent, on a plane, or in some concealed location. If he lay down in a safe place, he could sleep through earthquakes, tornadoes, and tank movements. On mission, he once told her, he could be awakened from a sound sleep by a fly rubbing its legs together. That was her husband: soldier, father, teller of tall tales.

Stacy rubbed the back of her neck. She hated it when she fell asleep on the couch. A stiff neck always followed. Her back didn't feel much better. To make matters worse, she had been drooling.

"How embarrassing. Good thing no one is around to see me in all my glory."

On the cushion next to her rested a sketch pad, a thick book titled *Functions of Interior Spaces*, a box of colored pencils, and four issues of *Architectural Digest*. The sight of them made her smile.

Earlier in the year, Stacy initiated the adventure of remaking herself. Why shouldn't she? Rob had just turned eighteen, had a job, and would graduate high school in a few weeks. Eric needed minimal care, fresh meat for his barbeque when he was home, beer in the fridge, and his beloved big-screen television. Gina, although just in the second of her teenage years, was always more mature than her chronological age. Although there were moments when she acted like the junior high girl she was, she never presented a problem. If there were a magazine called *Perfect Child*, Gina would be on the cover every month.

Feeling freer than she had in many years, Stacy enrolled in the local junior college and began classes in interior design. The topic had always interested her and her professors said she showed a flair for the art. Perhaps. Even if she didn't, she enjoyed attending the classes, trying something new, and making friends. The family was supportive. In fact, Gina pushed her to step out and "get her design on." Stacy smiled at the recollection—

Gina?

Stacy looked at her watch. Just after midnight. *Wow. I must have really been out. I didn't hear her come in.* Retrieving her sketch pad, she studied the drawing she had been working on before dozing off. It was due soon and drafting was Stacy's weakest skill. She picked up the pencil and set the point to the coarse paper.

She stopped. Something nibbled the back of her brain. Setting the pencil and pad down, Stacy rose, stretched her aching back, and walked to Gina's bedroom.

The door was closed. Nothing new. Gina always kept her bedroom closed. She glanced at the threshold, looking for light seeping beneath the bottom of the door. Gina often stayed up at night to study or watch a video on her computer. Tonight she appeared to have gone straight to bed. *Good for her.*

Stacy started to turn away but stopped before she took her third step. She returned to the door, took hold of the knob, and gave it a gentle turn. The tongue of the lock retracted into the door. Slowly, trying to avoid any squeaks, she pushed the door open and looked through the narrow opening.

Gina's bed sat in the middle of the room, the headboard pushed to the wall. The pale glow of Gina's computer monitor gave the space an otherworldly look. Stacy saw the three stuffed animals Gina always kept on the bed. Every morning, her daughter would make her bed and place the toys in a particular order. Hoseface the Elephant rested on the left; Bandit, a one-foot-tall Panda bear occupied the center of the mattress; and Donnie the Donkey rested on the right side.

The toys were in their usual places, mute witnesses to the fact Gina was not in bed.

Stacy opened the door to the stops and stepped in. She must be seeing things wrong. She stepped closer to the bed.

Empty.

Stacy's heart seized like a fist and she raised a hand to her chest. Instinct drove her to flip on the light. The room was empty.

Easy, girl. Panic doesn't help. A few steps later, Stacy stood in the hall bathroom. Also empty. The heart that refused to beat began to pound against her breastbone.

"You picked the wrong day to become a rebellious teenager, young lady." She hoped that was all that was going on.

In the minutes that followed, Stacy checked the other rooms of the house. She was alone. Very, very alone. Returning to the living room, Stacy snatched her cell phone from its resting place on the coffee table and checked for messages. None. She dialed Gina's cell number. It rang five times, then went to voice mail.

"It's after midnight, young lady, and I told you to be home by eleven. You had better have a good explanation." Stacy ended the call.

Her heart recruited help from her stomach, both determined to tear her up from the inside.

The sound of a car door closing pressed through the walls. Stacy crossed her arms and waited for the front door to open. Both barrels of her emotional shotgun were loaded.

The door opened.

Rob entered, closing and locking the door behind him.

"Oh, it's you."

"I missed you too, Mom. Sheesh. Should I leave?"

"No, no. I'm sorry. I heard the car door close and thought it might be Gina."

"First, Gina doesn't drive and doesn't have a car. Second, she said she was going to her study group at Pauline's. Third, no one has ever mistaken me for Gina."

"You know what I mean. I thought maybe Pauline's mother or father had driven her home."

"I take it the Golden Child is late."

"Don't be contrary, Rob. I'm upset."

"Yeah, I can see that." He slipped off his McDonald's shirt and started for his room. "Have you called the Wysocki's yet?"

"No, it's after midnight."

"You don't have to tell me. I didn't think this day would ever end. Closing isn't as much fun as it sounds."

"I mean, it's too late to call over there."

Rob stopped. "Not if Gina's there it isn't. You want me to do it?"

"No. If I wake her parents I'll just apologize."

"Good thinking. You know Gina; she's probably studying the night away with her geek friends. I'm gonna change. I smell like a hamburger."

Stacy took a deep breath and let it out in a long exhalation. Retrieving the number from the contact list in her cell phone, she placed the call. She had only spoken to Pauline's parents a few times and felt bad about the late night—no, she corrected herself—early morning call.

"Hello." A sleepy female voice answered.

"Mrs. Wysocki, this is Stacy Moyer. I'm sorry to call so late. I hope I didn't wake you."

"After midnight. Why would I be asleep?"

The sarcasm was clear. "Again, I apologize. I wonder if I might speak to my daughter. She's not answering her cell phone."

"Gina." The woman's tone turned serious. "Gina's not here. All the girls left about eleven. I remember Gina saying she had to hurry, she was running late."

"Are you sure?"

"Of course I'm sure . . . Wait a minute. I'll double-check. I suppose she could have come back for some reason."

Stacy heard a slight grunt and assumed the woman was crawling from bed. A few moments later: "I've checked everywhere. I even went out on the porch. My daughter is in bed."

"Alone?"

"I beg your pardon?"

"Sorry. That did sound bad. What I mean is, Gina didn't fall asleep or something."

"No. She's not here." Her voice softened. "Maybe she went to another friend's house."

"That's not like her. I'm getting scared."

"Do you want me to come over?"

Stacy hadn't expected that. "No, thank you."

"Please keep me informed. Let me know if I can do anything. We'll be praying."

"Thank you." Stacy hung up and doubled over. Something was wrong, very wrong.

"So anyway, closing up a burger joint is more work than I thought. You know me, I'm allergic to work—" Rob stopped. "Mom? What's wrong?"

"Gina left Pauline's house over an hour ago."

"But it's only a three block walk—" He spun and walked back into his room and reemerged a few moments later, car keys in hand. "Get your shoes on. We're going Gina hunting."

Rob was starting to sound like his father and that gave Stacy a moment of comfort.

STACY LET ROB DRIVE. She didn't trust her nerves. First they reversed the path Gina would have taken home but saw nothing. Rob then drove the side streets covering routes Gina probably wouldn't have taken but might have if she was feeling adventurous—a quality she never displayed before. Again nothing.

They drove half-a-dozen ever-widening circles with Pauline's house at the center. During that time, Stacy called the police and received the usual, "She has to be gone for forty-eight hours to be declared missing." They did promise to dispatch a patrol car to search the area and would issue a BOLO. Rob had to explain that meant "be on the lookout."

Twenty minutes into the search Rob said, "This is nuts." He turned the car around.

"What are you doing?"

"Going back to Pauline's. You're going to drive."

"Why?" Tears burned her eyes.

"I feel like we're missing something. I'm going to walk from Pauline's to home. I want you to follow."

Rob wasn't asking; he was telling her this was the way it was going to be. He stopped in the middle of the street, removed a flashlight from the glove compartment, and exited. Stacy moved to the driver's seat and watched as her son started at the Wysocki porch, lowered his gaze, and began to walk slowly toward home. She could see his head moving from side to side as he scanned the area in front of him and shone the light beneath every car parked along the curb or left on a driveway.

One block gave way to the next as Stacy crept along the street, forcing herself to not only focus on Rob, but on where she was directing the car. At times Rob would disappear behind some curbside vehicle, then reappear a moment later. They came to a pickup truck and Rob peered into the cab and then the truck bed. The thought of him finding her daughter hurt or worse, lying in the back of a 1980s Chevy pickup, came as a waking nightmare. Her hands shook as they gripped the steering wheel.

Rob started across an intersection, then paused in the middle of the street. He looked down one street, then the next. Stacy didn't need a conversation to know he was wondering if Gina might have tried a different way home. Possible, but not likely. Gina loved her habits. She rose at the same time every day. When her friends longed to sleep in until the crack of noon, Gina would rise at six on school days and seven on weekends. The ritual never changed.

Just like her father.

Stacy wished with all her might Eric were here. He'd know what to do. He would have found her by now. And if someone . . . She couldn't complete the thought, but God help the person who would harm his little daughter.

Rob stopped suddenly. Stacy pulled forward until she could see him through a gap between parked cars.

He picked up something.

Her heart stuttered. Stacy slammed the car's transmission into park and exited, leaving the vehicle idling in the middle of the street, the driver's door open, the overhead lamp shining in the dimness of the late hour.

"What?" She approached, her stomach so tight and twisted she couldn't stand erect. Rob held a book. "What is it?"

He turned. "I think this is hers." He held up the tome. It was thick with a worn cover and dulled corners, the abuse from a student who had it before Gina. "I've seen it on Gina's desk."

Stacy took it from her son and studied the cover: *Basic Speech Communications*. Stacy had also seen the book in Gina's room. She wanted to deny it, to consider it a coincidence, to assume the book belonged to someone else's little girl.

She sucked in a lungful of air and opened the front cover. Pasted to the inside cover was a white card with WARDLAW JUNIOR HIGH SCHOOL printed in black ink at the top. The card bore the names of students who had been assigned the book in previous sessions.

"Oh, God. Oh, dear God. Please no." A glint in the light of a streetlamp caught her attention. A small cell phone lay in the gutter—Gina's cell phone.

She started for it, but Rob placed a hand on her shoulder. "No. Let me." He stepped close to the device. Stacy followed just two feet behind. Even in the dim light she could tell the phone was dropped and the scratches in the case suggested it was kicked or thrown to the side.

Stacy stepped around Rob and started to reach for the phone.

"No." He pulled her back. "Don't touch it. Let the police do that."

"But—"

"Mom, leave it alone." His tone was firm but kind. "Give me the book. I want to put it where I found it."

Reluctant to release the textbook, Stacy pulled the book to her breast. Rob eased it from her embrace. It seemed like she had just released her daughter. Her hands shook, then her arms. Gooseflesh covered her skin. Her legs wobbled. She was hot. Emotional pressure built in her like a runaway boiler.

"Gina! GINA." Her screams rolled down the street. "Where are you, baby? It's Mommy. Where are you?"

A pair of hands seized her by the shoulders and pulled her close. "Stop it, Mom. That's not helping."

"But—"

"You know what Dad would say. 'Keep the main thing the main thing. Keep focused on the mission.' We have to keep it together or we will be of no help to Gina. Do you understand me?"

It was as if she were listening to Eric. "Yes. Yes, I think so."

"Okay, I'm calling the cops."

"They already said she hasn't been missing long enough."

"They don't know about the book and cell phone."

Rob keyed his cell phone, put it on speaker, and waited. Then, "I want to report an abduction."

"You saw an abduction?" A woman's voice, tired and disinterested.

"My sister hasn't come home and we've found one of her textbooks and her cell phone in the street."

"Are you sure she's not at a friend's house?"

"Positive."

Stacy could hear the tension in Rob's voice.

"How old is your sister?"

Rob sighed. "Fourteen. Can you send someone out?" He gave the address.

"How long has she been missing?"

"She was supposed to be home almost two hours ago."

"Sir, two hours is not very long."

"As I said, we found her textbook and cell phone in the street. Are you going to send someone?"

"We prefer that a person be missing longer than a couple of hours."

"I want you to send someone right away." His words had a sword's edge to them.

"Sir, I don't need the attitude."

"Lady, I don't care what you need. It's not your sister who's missing."

"In most cases the person usually shows up on her own."

"And what about the other cases?"

"Sir, I'm just trying to do my job—"

"And I'm trying to make sure my sister is all right. Now are you sending someone or not?"

"Our patrol cars are very busy with crimes—"

"Kidnapping is a crime. Send someone."

"Sir—"

Rob's knuckles whitened as he gripped the phone. "Okay, lady, I'll make a deal with you." He looked at his watch. "It's 12:32. In ten minutes I begin breaking windshields, setting off car alarms, and putting bricks through bedroom windows of every house on the block. Will that get your attention?"

"Sir—"

"You have a little over nine minutes before the first brick goes into someone's living room." Rob hung up.

CHAPTER 16

THREE SQUAD CARS PULLED onto the street and turned toward Rob and his mother. *It's about time.* Rob crossed his arms and tried to disguise his fear. He was harsh with the dispatcher; no doubt that information was conveyed to the street cops.

"Thank you for coming."

Rob could hear the terror in his mother's voice. Although he felt the same, he used every brain cell and nerve ending to act like he was in control. He had never been so out of control in his life.

"It's my daughter—"

"Who made the call?" A city officer, who stood four inches taller than Rob and weighed a good fifty muscular pounds heavier, approached. The officers in the other patrol cars emerged and stepped forward until they formed a semicircle around the two.

Rob took one step in front of his mother. She stepped to the side and spoke. "I made the first call." Her voice trembled. "Something has happened to my daughter—"

"I made the call." The firmness of his voice surprised Rob. Copzilla took another step closer and dug his thumbs beneath his Sam Browne belt. Rob glanced at the other officers who kept their places but made no attempt to conceal their grins.

"You threatened our dispatcher?"

A fourth police car appeared and pulled to the curb. A stocky man with gray hair slipped from the driver's seat. Rob noticed three stripes on the man's sleeve.

A metal name tag over the breast pocket of the big man read: D. SAMPLER. "No, officer, I threatened to break windows. I didn't threaten the dispatcher."

"But you threatened to commit a crime?"

"A small crime compared to ignoring the desperate pleas of one of the people you're sworn to protect."

"What? You think you're smart?" Another step. Two more and Gigantor would be standing in Rob's pocket.

"This isn't about me, officer; it's about my sister . . ."

"You know threatening a dispatcher is pretty much like threatening a cop."

Stacy pushed forward. "Officer. I'm sorry you're angry, but my daughter is missing—"

"Ma'am, I'm going to ask that you shut your mouth and let me take care of this."

Rob glanced at the other officers. Their grins were gone.

"Hey, Don, lighten up," one of the officers said.

"You telling me how to do my job?" Sampler turned on the officer.

"No, but I am." The police sergeant pushed past his other men and approached Officer Sampler.

"Hey, Sarge, I was just trying to get to the bottom of the situation."

"So I see. You can go back on patrol."

"But Sarge, I was just doing my job."

"And doing it badly. Do you really want another complaint in your jacket? Pretty soon they're going to need a file cabinet just to hold all the complaint forms filed against you."

"Look, Sarge, I know you're a short timer and all, but—"

"Watch it." The field sergeant raised a finger. The two mute officers took a step back. Apparently they knew something. Another glance at Sampler showed a crack in his armor. "I may only have two weeks left on this job, but it only takes me two minutes to ruin your career. Would you like to test me on that?"

"No, Sarge, but I don't know what the big deal is."

"That's because you don't have a daughter. Beat it. You're embarrassing me and the uniform."

Sampler retreated to his patrol car, slamming the door so hard Rob expected the light bar to fall from the vehicle's roof. The engine roared to life and Sampler drove away.

The sergeant turned to the other men. "Am I going to have a problem with you too?"

They shook their heads and one said, "No, sir, we're with you."

The sergeant turned to Rob and Stacy. "I'm Sergeant Tony Crivello. I apologize for Officer Simple . . . I mean, Sampler. Please don't judge us by him. We have a good department with good people."

"My daughter is missing."

Rob put his arm around his mother. "Her name is Gina; she's fourteen and she's not the kind to be late without calling." He pointed to the cell phone. "That's hers. We haven't touched it." He motioned to the book. "That's hers too. We did pick it up."

"I see. Do you have a picture of her?"

"I do," Stacy said. "In my purse. It's in the car."

"Go ahead and get it, ma'am." Crivello studied Rob; Rob let him. "You the guy who gave our dispatcher trouble?"

He stiffened his spine, ready for whatever onslaught the officer would unleash. "Yeah, that's me. I didn't know any other way to get you guys out here."

Crivello smiled. "It was a good one. I was in dispatch when you called. I was listening in. How old are you?"

"Just turned eighteen."

"I figured it was something like that. When this is all over, I may have a little talk with you, but for now, let's focus on your sister. What do you think happened?"

"I think someone took her." Rob stuffed his emotions to appear strong for his mother, but cracks were developing. A tear ran free. "I'm sorry. I've never been through anything like this."

"Never apologize for love, boy."

Stacy reappeared and handed a photo to Crivello. He turned to one of the officers. "Get this out. Tell 'em we have an abduction. I want every man not dealing with a violent crime combing the streets. Got that?"

"Got it, Sarge." The man moved to his car.

Crivello pointed at the other officer. "I want you to canvass every house that can see this spot. Wake 'em up and if they have any complaints, give them my name."

Crivello returned his attention to Stacy and Rob. "Okay, we've got the ball rolling. Now tell me everything. Start from the beginning."

THE MI-17V7 HELICOPTER MADE the two-hundred-mile trip in short order. Peng watched the sun begin its daily crawl up the sky's dome. Golden light fell on farm fields and industrial buildings spread throughout the many small towns. A new day had begun, as it had for countless years. What would the sun see today? He hoped it would be witness to his team's success.

He looked at a dark sky turning blue and thought about the large satellite due to plunge through the atmosphere. When he first heard his assignment, he wondered if there would be anything worth salvaging after such a high-speed plunge. Peng kept the question to himself. It was enough for him his superiors believed so. What he thought didn't matter. He was a highly trained machine of flesh and blood. It was his job to do as he was told without question.

The Mi-17 slowed, drawing Peng's attention from the heavens above to the earth below. The pilot led them next to a long, wide strip of concrete. The Jiamusi Airport sat just south of National Road and was a minor destination for several airlines from the larger cities to the southwest. It also served a dual role with the military.

The moment the craft's wheels touched the tarmac and its two BK2500 engines began to power down, Peng popped his safety belts and stood. His men followed his example. The aircraft could hold thirty-six passengers or twenty-four fully equipped troops. At the moment it held only five soldiers and three crewmen. The flight mechanic opened the side door and cool air, propelled by the still-beating rotors, pushed into the cabin. Peng started forward but the flight mechanic, a thin but hard-looking man, stopped him.

"Forgive me, sir, but I have been asked to give you a message. You are to proceed without hesitation to the aircraft on the taxiway."

"Which aircraft?" Peng had to shout to be heard.

"There's only one, sir. It is waiting for you."

"Then what?"

The flight mechanic shrugged. "I'm sorry, sir, but that is all I know."

Peng nodded, patted the man on the shoulder, and exited the craft, his head low to keep the rotor blast from his face. He carried a large bag over his shoulder as did each of his men.

A dozen steps later, the pressure from the spinning blades lessened and he stood erect, letting his eyes trace his surroundings: a large building loomed on the other side of the taxiway, its doors shut; its windows blacked out. At the distant end of the runway waited a China Express MD-90 jet. A covered airstairs mounted to a truck bridged the distance from runway to doorway. A man in a white shirt and dark pants, typical of commercial pilots worldwide, stood at the base of the stairs.

Peng marched his direction. He didn't bother checking on his men. He knew them well enough to know they would follow a few feet behind.

The morning air brightened as the sun continued its climb. Light glinted off the unpainted areas of the cargo plane. Often used as a passenger plane, several of China's air-cargo companies used them for package delivery around the world. Blue and green paint ran the length of the plane's skin meeting at the tail and sweeping up the rear fin, forming a stylized dragon's head.

"*Nǐ hǎo*," the pilot said as Peng approached, bowed, and extended his hand. Peng acknowledged the greeting. "Please." The air captain motioned up the stairs. Peng jogged up the metal steps.

The air inside was warmer than he expected and the cabin different in configuration. What Peng thought he'd see was an open space filled with boxes of cargo or fuselage-shaped metal cargo containers. Instead there were six rows of seats, three rows to a side. Behind the last row of seats, running from the midpoint of the cabin and along the centerline of the craft were three large objects, each covered with a white tarpaulin.

"Unexpected." Hsu Li set his bag in one of the seats.

Li Peng's second captured his first impression. Then it came to him. "I know what this is." Peng moved deeper into the plane, making room for the others.

"Then you know more than me, Captain."

"I believe we will know in a moment if I am right."

The pilot entered the space last, pulled a microphone from a mount by the open door, and said something. Seconds later, the motorized airstair backed away from the opening. The captain closed the door hatch and locked it down.

"Welcome aboard, gentlemen." The pilot's smile seemed genuine. "Do you know where you are?"

"*Qīpiàn*," Peng said.

"Yes, Captain, you are right. You are aboard the *Deception*."

CHAPTER 17

SCOTT MASTERS FELT FEVERISH. He couldn't see the growing perspiration on his forehead but he could feel it. He could also feel the wet spot his body created between his shoulder blades and the small of his back—puddles of sweat slowly oozed into the dirty mattress. The smell of urine intensified.

He groaned. He tried not to. Signs of pain encouraged his captors and he wanted to withhold anything that might be useful to them, no matter how small.

Still, the moans, the groans came more frequently. His guts were baking in his body, his skin aflame. The fever made thinking difficult. He tried to focus on the problem, running escape scenarios through his mind, but he couldn't come up with a viable first step: getting out of the restraints binding him to the bed frame.

Behind him the IV pump continued to beep, reminding him lifesaving antibiotics were just three feet away. Bound and infected, his weakening thoughts of cooperating percolated to the top of his mind. Each time, he stuffed them into a mental vault.

In his training, he was taught the mind could rationalize almost anything—even murder. When captured, when tortured, the first thing the brain wants to do is give in. Humans—all humans—have a threshold of tolerable pain. Masters had not reached his. Yet.

An hour ago, a thickly built man with three days' growth of beard entered the room, a tool kit in one hand, a box in the other. He set the kit down, left, and returned with a ladder. He didn't speak, didn't look at Masters for more than a moment. It was as if Masters faded to invisible over the last few hours.

He watched the workman. His clothing said he was a soldier, but the material of the uniform look faded and inconsistent with modern Russian field uniforms. The camo pattern looked bleached and the fur collar indicated it was a winter uniform from the days of the Soviet Union.

The man showed himself to be a lousy craftsman. Using a hammer and a large Phillips-head screwdriver, the worker created a half-inch hole in the wall, three feet from the door. He then hung the box on brackets put in place with screws. A wire hung from the box and the worker fished it through the rough hole he created a few minutes before.

It took twenty minutes to do the job. Five minutes after that, the man disappeared with the tool kit and ladder.

Despite the growing pain in his neck, Masters studied the box. A security camera? No. A speaker. An old-fashioned speaker in a plywood box with fabric covering the hole in the face.

He would have preferred the security camera. He could only think of one reason to go through so much trouble. He prayed he was wrong.

He wasn't.

A voice drifted over the speaker. "Sit him down." Egonov's voice.

"What . . . what are you doing?" Another familiar voice. The unit's communications man, Chaddick, was the newest member of the team.

Egonov's voice: "You have had many opportunities to cooperate. This is your last opportunity. Why have you and the others invaded my territory? Why are you here?"

"My name is Staff Sergeant Dave Chaddick—"

The sound of a brutal slap followed by a howl of pain drifted from the speaker. "My patience is gone, Staff Sergeant."

"My nime isth Divvid Cheddick."

Something was wrong with Chaddick's speech. A broken jaw? Masters's heart deflated like a balloon. Chaddick was a good man, the joker of the group. Masters never saw him down, never heard a complaint. He was a family man with a pregnant wife and two young children. Masters had been around enough to know that even if they walked out of this place safe, Chaddick would never be the same.

"Take off his boots." Egonov's voice betrayed no emotion. Masters had no idea how many other men were in the room with Egonov, but he could hear boots shuffling.

"What are you doing?" Terror filled the man's voice.

"I gave you opportunity," Egonov said.

Masters heard the squeak of a door. It was close. All the action was taking place in a room just a few feet away.

"Just his feet."

He heard fluid splashing.

"No. Don't."

"What you must understand, Staff Sergeant, is that I can get my information from one of the others."

Masters caught a sniff of something familiar, something pungent.

"No. For the love of God. Please don't."

"I do not believe in God. I certainly do not believe in the love of God." There was a pause.

"Oh, God!"

"Light it."

Masters continued to smell gasoline. Then he smelled burning flesh.

The screaming minced his soul.

J. J. PRAYED. HE often prayed. Not just before or during missions, but he prayed on his day off; in country, out of country; in uniform or out; alone or with his wife. Prayer was second nature for him. Some soldiers became believers in foxholes or the urban streets of distant cities; some found faith only after bullets streaked overhead or a land mine exploded nearby. Not J. J. He attended church since he was a child. It was a family thing. His twin brother was an ardent believer and now served the Army as a chaplain. It hadn't been his first choice, but after washing out of Ranger training, Paul Bartley decided he needed something more. It was then he found his real calling. He finished college and attended seminary, returning to duty as an officer.

There were many things to pray for. J. J. prayed for Tess. How was she handling his absence? They married the previous year. Being a soldier's wife was not for the easily faint. Many marriages hit the rocks with the long, unexpected absences. Often the for-better-or-for-worse vows went by the wayside when a soldier, hardened, embittered by conflict and war, returned changed, withdrawn, even reclusive.

J. J. depended on his faith to keep him honest, brave, and unchanged. He saw enough abrasive horrors to grind any man's brain to powder. It was one of the things he prayed about as the FedEx truck moved along a pothole-laced road. His team leader seemed edgy, out of sorts. The assistant team leader not long ago put the muzzle of his weapon to Lev's head.

Were they losing their grips? It had happened to other teams. Although rare, history recorded a team of soldiers doing the unthinkable. It happened in Iraq, Vietnam, and other foreign fields.

J. J. shook off the idea. It was stupid. Boss and Shaq were solid-gold soldiers with intellects and wills forged in the furnace of life-threatening danger. J. J. would trust either man with his life—not just *his* life, but Tess's too. They proved their willingness to die for others.

So why the edginess? They were short on sleep and were called into action on short notice. They were undertaking a mission unprecedented in Army history. There was no time for specialized training. In many ways, they were out of their element. But then again, it would be for any Spec Ops team. Satellite recovery was different than anything they'd ever done.

J. J. looked at the small Bible in his hand.

"I know that look." Moyer had only one eye open.

"What look is that?"

The team leader straightened and fixed his gaze on J. J. It made him feel uncomfortable. "The one that says you have something on your mind."

"Sorry, Boss. It's the only face I have."

Rich chortled. "That is one piece of miserable luck, Colt."

"I get by."

"So, you got anything in that book for us, Colt?" Moyer closed his eyes again. He looked weary. Not just physically, but emotionally.

"There's always something good in here, Boss."

"Let's hear it."

It was the first time Moyer had made such a request.

"Okay. This is a New Testament, but I've been thinking about something David wrote in the Psalms." J. J. stared at the floor, his mind drawing forward a passage he had been memorizing. "It's from Psalm 18 and goes like this:

> As for God, His way is blameless;
> The word of the LORD is tried;
> He is a shield to all who take refuge in Him.
> For who is God, but the LORD?
> And who is a rock, except our God,
> The God who girds me with strength
> And makes my way blameless?
> He makes my feet like hinds' feet,
> And sets me upon my high places.
> He trains my hands for battle,
> So that my arms can bend a bow of bronze.
> You have also given me the shield of Your salvation,
> And Your right hand upholds me;
> And Your gentleness makes me great.
> You enlarge my steps under me,
> And my feet have not slipped.

The group was quiet for a moment, a stillness broken by Lev. "Amen."

"Nice words," Pete said.

"So why is that on your mind, Colt?" Moyer studied his hands as if he had spilt something on them.

"I just like to remind myself we don't do what we do alone. King David was a warrior. He didn't complain about war, but he did depend on God's guidance. We're not exempt from trouble, just empowered in it. There's an old saying: 'God doesn't lead us to a desert; He joins us in the desert.'"

"I hope you're right, Colt," Moyer said. "I hope you're right."

CHAPTER 18

THE MD-90 AIRLINER DUBBED *Qīpiàn*—"Deception"—took to the air at a steep angle, its aft-mounted International Aero V2500 engines humming through the hull and filling Peng's ears. It wasn't the sound of the engines that occupied his mind; it was what waited under the tarpaulin shrouds behind the seating area.

Shortly before liftoff, Peng learned he made a faulty assumption: The man in the white shirt and dark pants was not the pilot. He was Shang Xiao Jiang Tao. Colonel Jiang's smile disappeared shortly after the door to the aircraft was secured. He had hard almond eyes and a reputation to match. Although Peng had never met the man, never served under his direct command, he knew of the colonel's exploits. In the PLA, he was a hero, an example to all soldiers.

The disguise should not have surprised Peng. After all, he and his team were dressed like vacationing fishermen. The items in their duffle bags would give them away immediately, but no one would get close enough to peek in the canvas bags.

Once the cargo craft reached altitude and leveled off, its nose pointed toward the east, Jiang rose from his seat and faced Peng and his men.

"We have only a short time and there is much I need to tell you." He looked at Peng through those dark eyes. Did the man ever blink? "Know this, Captain, the mission is still yours. I am here to give you information we do not want transmitted over open lines, even encrypted lines. Understood?"

"Yes, Colonel." Peng kept eye contact. He was being judged and he wanted his superior to know he did not intimidate easily.

"You have seen what is under the tarpaulins. Are you familiar with them, Captain?"

"I have only seen them, Colonel. I have not trained with them, nor have my men."

"I will brief you. You will have, as they say in the West, on-the-job training. I will teach you what you need to know; the rest you will learn on the way down."

"On the way down" sounded ominous and theatrical. Peng had met men like Jiang before: They thrived on danger and enjoyed seeing fear in the eyes of others. Peng wouldn't give him the pleasure. "Yes, sir."

Jiang looked at his watch. "Let us not waste these precious moments. We have forty minutes before our left engine goes out and we lose hydraulics."

"I'm sorry, sir. I don't understand."

Jiang smiled and the sight of it chilled Peng.

STACY MOYER COULDN'T SIT. Sitting was the same as doing nothing and she had to do something, anything. She fought the urge to unload the dishwasher. The urge was natural and unnatural. Her mind wanted to focus on the mundane, the unimportant, the routine, as if pretending nothing bad has happened would mean nothing bad had happened. She couldn't bring herself to do it. Instead, she paced. A female police detective sat on her sofa, fresh out of questions to ask. Stacy was weary of hearing, "We will do everything we can."

What difference did that make? Every second that passed meant finding Gina grew more difficult. A car traveling at sixty miles per hour put a mile under its wheels every minute: five minutes equaled five miles; ten minutes meant ten miles. It had been three hours. If someone took Gina and put her in a car, then they could be one hundred and eighty miles away, and with every mile, the search area grew exponentially.

"Mom, we need to talk."

"I don't want to talk; I want to find Gina." Stacy put an edge to the words.

"So do I, Mom."

"But we're not doing anything. The police aren't doing anything—"

Rob approached and took her in his arms. She tried to push him away. She didn't want to be comforted. Everything was wrong; every word irritating; every motion infuriating. She loved Rob down to the marrow of her bones, but his touch seemed toxic.

She tried to push him away again, but he'd have none of it. His arms wrapped around her like a straitjacket. She could feel the muscles in his thin arms tighten into a gentle squeeze. Again she tried to pull away but Rob held on.

Unreasoning resistance shattered like chalk in a vise. She shuddered. She convulsed. She sobbed, laying her head against her son's shoulder. In the last few hours, she had watched him go from often self-absorbed teenager to a man.

She let him hold her as tears and emotions poured from her. Water filled her eyes, mucus filled her nose, despair filled her heart.

"I made a call." Rob spoke softly, just a few decibels above a whisper.

"A call?" Her voice sounded raspy and muted against his shoulder.

"Yeah. I called Chaplain Bartley."

"He can't help. I don't need a sermon. I don't want a sermon."

"Mom, stop it. You know he's not coming over to preach."

"He's coming over? Tonight? Now?"

"Yeah. I got him out of bed. That's what he gets for giving me his cell number."

"You shouldn't have done that, Rob." Calmer now, she eased away from her son. "There's nothing he can do at this hour."

"He can be here. He's good at listening. He listened to me when I needed it, when I was being such a pain."

"But—"

"Mom, listen to me. You need to think. This may have something to do with Dad."

"Dad?" Detective Angie Wells, a middle-aged redhead, stood from the sofa. "I thought you said your father is out of town."

"We didn't, Detective." Rob offered nothing more.

Angie eyed them. "Could he have taken her?"

"No." Stacy drew a hand across her cheeks. "Not possible."

"You know if he did and you're protecting him—"

"We're not protecting him." Rob's tone revealed his impatience. "You don't understand."

"Then you'd better explain it to me."

"I can't."

A knock came at the door.

"That can't be Chaplain Bartley. I just called a few minutes ago." Rob moved across the living room and peered through the door's peephole. "It's Sergeant Crivello." Rob opened the door.

"I don't have any information," Crivello said quickly. "I'm sorry, but no word yet." He entered the house and gave a nod to Detective Wells. Rob closed the door behind him. "I've contacted Highway Patrol. The APB will alert all the other law enforcement agencies in the area. I've also made a run by the local hospitals."

"What about the canvassing?" Detective Wells said.

"We woke up a lot of people, but no one heard or saw anything." Crivello shook his head. "I'm sorry, but we're coming up zeros. I take it she hasn't called home."

"No." Stacy had to force the word out.

"Nothing on this end, Sergeant." Wells turned to Rob and Stacy. "They were just about to tell me about Gina's dad."

"He's not out of town?" Crivello sounded suspicious.

"We told you he was." Stacy bit her lip. "Sorry. I'm not at my best."

"That's understandable." Crivello look puzzled. "What's this about your husband, ma'am?"

Wells answered for her. "They say they can't talk about it."

Crivello's brow furrowed. "Why can't you . . . ?" The man looked around the living room as if secrets were written on the walls. His eyes fell to the coffee table. A stack of magazines rested on the surface.

Stacy followed his gaze to two interior design magazines, a
periodical for gun lovers, and a news magazine.

"Is your husband in the military, ma'am?"

"He's a businessman," Rob said.

Crivello's smile was sympathetic. "You've been saying that for a
lot of years haven't you, young man?"

Rob didn't answer.

"Look, we're not here to blow anyone's cover. All the detective
and I want is to find your daughter."

Stacy looked into Rob's eyes and saw agreement. "Yes, my
husband is military. How did you know?"

"Spent a few years in the Army. That's how I landed in South
Carolina. I'm originally from central California. That and seeing
a gun magazine and a conservative news magazine gave credence
to my suspicion. That and having Fort Jackson so close. I'm going
to make another guess. He's part of the Spec Ops group out of
Jackson. Not many people know about that."

"I know I don't." Wells seemed put out.

"You're not supposed to know about it, Detective. It's a bit of
a secret."

"But you know."

Crivello nodded. "Only because I had a couple of buddies who
did something for the group. I still don't know what they did.
They don't tell and I don't ask." He turned back to Stacy. "He's on
mission now?"

"Yes."

"Do you have any reason to believe your daughter's disappearance
might be related?"

"I don't see how. We never know when or where he's going.
Sometimes all we get is a phone call. Gina certainly doesn't know
any more than we do."

"What's your husband's name?"

"Eric. Sergeant Major Eric Moyer." Stacy swallowed hard. It hadn't occurred to her that Eric's mission and her daughter's disappearance might be connected.

Crivello looked at Wells and waited.

"What?"

"I don't want to interfere with your investigation, but you might want to ask who the sergeant major's commanding officer is."

"Because . . ."

"Because he needs to know about the girl's disappearance; because he may have a way of informing Mr. Moyer; and because he may know something useful."

Detective Wells seemed embarrassed.

"Colonel MacGregor," Stacy said.

"Does he have a first name?" Wells pulled a smartphone from the pocket of her pantsuit.

Stacy shrugged. "I don't know. Eric just calls him Colonel Mac or Mac. I've never heard a first name."

"I don't suppose you have a number?"

"No, sorry."

Rob said, "Chaplain Bartley might have it. He should be here soon."

"Then we'll wait on him." Wells sat on the sofa again.

Could there be a connection between Eric's mission and Gina's disappearance? The thought terrified her. If it were true, then Gina was in the hands of some very dangerous people.

THE PHONE BY FORMER Sergeant First Class Jerry "Data" Zinsser, now special agent for USACIC—United States Army Criminal Investigation Command—rang, launching Zinsser a foot above the bed.

He let it ring twice more before answering, mostly to allow himself a moment to slow his heart. He snapped up the receiver and glanced at the clock: a few minutes after two in the morning.

He put the hand piece to his ear. "Someone had better be dead."

"I hope not."

There was no humor in the comeback. It took a moment for him to recognize the voice. "Paul?"

"You weren't asleep, were you?"

"At two in the morning? Of course not. I was doing push-ups and reading *War and Peace*. Is your brother all right?"

"As far as I know." Tension permeated Chaplain Paul Bartley's voice. "Look. Bad news. Eric Moyer's daughter is missing and the police think she's been abducted."

Zinsser sat up, now wide awake. "What?"

"Rob Moyer called. Gina didn't come home. They found one of her textbooks and her cell phone in the street. I'm headed over there now. Is there anything you can do?"

"I'm on my way."

Five minutes later, Special Agent Jerry Zinsser was in a pair of tan pants, a dress shirt, and blue Windbreaker with the emblem of an eagle perched over a gold shield. CID was printed over the front left breast. In a holster on his hip was a 9mm, M11, Sig Sauer P228 sidearm.

Zinsser had been to several of Eric Moyer's famous backyard beer and barbecue gatherings so he needed no directions.

On the way a flood of memories, most unwanted, crashed like storm waves on his mind. Zinsser was awarded the Distinguished Service Cross for valor displayed in the Somali backwater town of Kismayo. He saved lives that day but almost lost his mind in the process. Flashbacks plagued him to such an extent he nearly killed the leader of his new team: Eric Moyer. His post-traumatic stress disorder almost cost more lives than he saved.

Moyer could have dropped him from the mission—Moyer *should* have dropped him and pressed charges for more violations of the Code Military of Justice than could be imagined. Moyer didn't. He saw something in Zinsser he didn't see in himself.

Still his actions cost him. He could no longer work foreign missions, but because of his bravery and the fact he helped save the president's life, Zinsser was given a new start as a special agent with Army CID.

Memories swirled in his head and every one brought him a new, cutting pain. It was like standing in a blizzard of razor blades. He tried not to think of his failings. Chaplain Paul Bartley and others helped him focus on the good he did, not what his disorder caused him to do.

One thing was certain: He owed Eric Moyer big time. If Moyer's family needed help, then he would do anything and give anything to be there for them.

Zinsser pressed the accelerator to the floor and made hash of the South Carolina vehicle codes.

PAUL BARTLEY PULLED TO a stoplight and dialed his phone. He had another call to make.

The phone rang and a weary man answered. "Fort Jackson, Corporal White speaking, may I help you?"

"Corporal, this is Chaplain Paul Bartley. I need to speak to Colonel MacGregor."

"But, sir, it's just after two in the morning. The colonel will have me skinned."

"I didn't call for the time, Corporal. This is an emergency. You can either give me his home number or patch me through; I don't care which as long as it happens in the next few seconds."

"Yes, sir."

Bartley waited a few moments, then a gruff voice poured from the phone. "It's never a good thing when a minister calls at 2 a.m. What's wrong?"

"It's Gina, Eric Moyer's daughter."

"Oh no."

Bartley explained as he drove.

CHAPTER 19

"WHAT'S HE SINGING?" JOSE leaned forward and rubbed the back of his neck. The trip was getting to everyone.

It had only been a few hours, but much of it was uphill on bad, twisting roads. Every bone in Moyer's body hurt from the constant jarring and cramped confines.

"You don't recognize that, Doc?" Crispin had a self-satisfied grin plastered on his face.

"Two problems, Newbie: First, he's singing in Russian; second, he's a lousy singer."

"I heard that." Lev turned to look at the men in the back, then jerked the wheel when he realized they were headed off the road.

Rich reached for his 9mm. "Let me just wound him; a nick, maybe crease his scalp."

Moyer pretended to give it some thought. "Maybe later. If you're good."

"Thanks, Dad."

"I ask again: What is he singing?"

Crispin's grin widened. "I still can't believe you don't recognize it. It's a classic. Even young guys like me know about it."

Jose turned to face Crispin, took hold of the wires that ran to the earbuds planted in Hawkeye's ears, and yanked. He leaned close. "Okay, smart guy. School us."

"Paul McCartney's 'The Long and Winding Road.' Get it? A long and winding road. Kinda clever."

J. J. asked, "How can you hear what Lev is singing with those things crammed in your ears?"

"I am a man of many talents."

"We'll see about that," Rich said.

Moyer leaned to the opening between the truck's cab and cargo. "How much longer?"

"Soon, Boss. Soon."

For some reason, hearing Lev call him by his nick irritated Moyer. Everything was irritating Moyer.

"Yeow!" Pete jumped, almost dropping the new communication device.

"What?" Moyer snapped his head around.

"Sorry, Boss. Thing just came to life. I think we're getting a message."

Crispin leaned close to Pete. "Amazing. We're not getting a message, Boss—we just got a message, in like, a second. Ya gotta love this."

Pete studied the display. "Hawkeye is right." He handed the device with its glowing screen to Moyer, who took it. High tech was not his thing, but he knew his way around a computer. How hard could this be?

Moyer touched the screen and it brightened. "There are six squares and an onscreen keyboard."

"It wants you to enter a security code." Crispin stretched his neck to see.

"Ya think?"

"Is that a problem, Boss?" Rich studied Moyer, more interested in the man than in the device.

"No one gave me a security code."

"Oh."

The group sat mute, the silence filled by the bounding, twisting, rattling truck body.

"How many numbers?" J. J. looked thoughtful.

"Six. Why? You got an idea?"

J. J. scratched the side of his face. "What's the only code we all know?"

Moyer studied his weapons specialist. "The Concrete Palace."

"It's worth a shot," Rich said.

The Concrete Palace at Fort Jackson was the heart of one of the Army's new Special Operations, still unknown to many even in the Army. Many operations were run from the location and the building was, therefore, a highly secured facility. No matter how many times Moyer entered the building, he had to enter a code, have a thumbprint read, be cleared by a security officer inside a locked foyer, and enter another code to enter the inner workings of the windowless building.

Moyer entered his six-digit code. The screen changed and a small box appeared in the bottom, right-hand corner of the screen.

"Biometric reader," Pete said.

"I figured that." Moyer placed his thumb on the square. The screen blanked, then a message—an aerial image—appeared. Moyer could see a small red dot near the center of the image. He tapped it, and the device zoomed in. "It's us. A satellite photo of the FedEx truck on the road."

"Real-time satellite surveillance." Pete seemed impressed. "Not new, but sending it to us in moments is."

"Hello," Moyer said. "What have we here?" A pulsing blue light appeared in the upper-right corner. A light blue line ran from the dot to the west.

"Tap the blue dot."

Crispin stood to improve his viewing angle. The man clearly loved his tech. Moyer shot him a gaze that could freeze a flame.

"Um, sorry, Boss."

Moyer placed a finger on the blue dot. A series of numbers appeared: coordinates. The name of a town appeared in white letters. It reminded Moyer of Google Maps. "Hey, Lev, do you know where Nov Arman is?"

Lev turned and the truck again veered to the right. Lev snapped the wheel back just in time, jarring everyone aboard.

"You don't have to make eye contact to talk, Lev. Keep your eyes on the road."

"Yes, I know Nov Arman. It is not far from the river Arman, hence the name."

"That's our new destination: a few klicks north of Nov Arman. Over the river."

"There is very little there. Just a few farms."

"That's good. The fewer the better."

Lev thought for a moment. "I know of a bridge south of the river. It is not the best bridge, but it should hold us."

"Should?" Rich said. "Should? What do you mean 'it should hold us'?"

"As I have said, the village is small, maybe a few hundred people. Such places don't get fancy bridges. Don't worry; we will be safe—probably." He smiled.

"I can't figure if he's yanking our chain or if he just enjoys making us nervous."

Moyer ignored Rich. "How long, Lev?"

"Maybe another hour or two. Much of the trip is uphill, but there is a road of sorts that leads to the town."

"Make the most of it. We have less than two hours."

"Understood." He paused. "I have been driving for some time now. I could use a break and maybe some refreshment."

"If I see a flask of booze anywhere near your mouth, I'll place it somewhere where you can't reach. Got it?"

"Yes . . . Boss."

THE MD-90'S INTERCOM SYSTEM carried a voice from the cockpit calling Jiang Tao forward. The cockpit door remained open and Peng watched the colonel slip on a pair of headphones. A moment later, he removed a smartphone from his pocket and studied it. He said something to the pilot, then returned to the cargo area with a smile. As he did, the aircraft, now over the Sea of Japan, banked sharply to the right.

"Our scientists have more accurately determined where the satellite will fall. They have an exact trajectory. It is farther north than we first estimated, but not so much as to change our mission."

"Time?"

"Two hours. We will be in position in ninety minutes. You and your men will be ready in one hour."

"Understood, Colonel. One hour."

Fifty minutes later, Peng led his men as they removed the tarps from the cargo strapped to the deck. Beneath each beige cover rested a vehicle, the kind used to travel terrain with no roads. Except these vehicles differed from what ran through the back country of the world: These were not designed for pleasure or thrills. They were made for the Chinese military.

When Jiang revealed the plan, Peng knew the man had lost his mind. He kept the opinion to himself as did his men, but he could feel their tension.

They had a right to be tense. They were just told they would be driving these things out the rear exit of the MD-90. Each buggy was fitted with a propeller encased in a fiberglass surround. The propulsion unit was mounted to the back of the frame. A small gas engine powered the fan and then could be switched to power the wheels. The buggy could reach speeds of eighty kilometers an hour, and the reusable parachute could become airborne again with just fifty meters of flat ground. They would win no races, but it could help his men move over the uneven terrain faster than marching. Each vehicle could seat two and had a small storage area for backpacks and mission-needed equipment.

"But what about noise, Colonel?" Peng had seen powered hang gliders and smaller powered parachutes but deemed them unfit for stealthy insertion. A gas-powered motor was hard to keep quiet and an electrical motor required an unwieldy battery.

"You will be landing in a remote area. Very few people around to hear you."

Out loud he said, "Yes, sir." He didn't dare speak what he said in his mind.

Jeng took a little over an hour briefing the men. It was time for *Qīpiàn* to live up to its name: Deception.

The deception began as the MD-90 crossed into Russian airspace. Jiang and Peng listened to the radio exchange through auxiliary headsets. In one way it was an honor for Peng to be included. Technically, he did not need to know these details, but Jiang insisted because, "Someday you will be in a position like mine." Peng thanked him.

A thickly accented voice came over the headset. "Unidentified aircraft bearing 315, you are entering Russian airspace, please identify yourself." The conversation was conducted in English.

"Pushing 121.5 now," the pilot said.

Jiang nodded his approval. He leaned in Peng's direction. "The pilot just set the transponder to 121.5. It will show up on Russian radar as an emergency in progress."

"Mayday, mayday, mayday. This is China Express two-four-nine bound originally for Tokyo declaring an emergency."

"Tokyo? You are far from Tokyo, two-four-nine."

"Understood, Control. We are experiencing engine trouble in our port engine and have lost most of our airfoil hydraulics."

"Do you have control of the aircraft?"

"No, Control. Not fully. We are steering with engine thrust but can't hold altitude. Dropping to twenty thousand feet."

"So you are declaring an emergency."

"Moron," the pilot mumbled, then activated his radio. "Affirmative, Control. We are declaring an emergency."

"How many souls on board?"

"We are a cargo craft ATC. Just the two-man crew."

"Understood, two-four-nine. Please hold your altitude."

The pilot swore in Chinese. "Control, we cannot hold altitude— now at fifteen thousand feet."

"Two-four-nine, can you make Khabarovsk?"

"Stand by, Control." Then, "Khabarovsk may be too far. Request permission to try Yakutsk."

"That's still pretty far."

"We're open to ideas, Control."

"Stand by, two-four-nine."

Jiang turned to Peng. "It's time. We'll be at ten thousand feet soon."

Peng removed the headset and walked to the back. He could feel the consistent bank of the aircraft and its ever-slowing speed. He inhaled deeply, raised a hand and extended his index finger, and made a circling motion. Without a word, each man entered one of the three powered parachutes, one in the "driver's" seat, the other to his side. Peng would operate his alone. Some of the team's gear was stowed in the seat next to his.

Jiang stepped to a panel at the rear of the aircraft. In the commercial application of this aircraft, this area would be used for restrooms and the rear flight attendant area. The MD-90 was designed with a rear exit. For this mission, the steps of the airstairs had been covered with a ramp. Peng had jumped from many planes and learned to enjoy it. This time, however, he was jumping while strapped to a small vehicle. Parachute jumps were done with larger pieces of equipment and even snowmobiles, but this was different.

Jiang donned another headset and waited. A few minutes later, he removed the headgear, opened the panel, and pressed a large red button.

The rear exit opened slowly, creating more drag. The aircraft bounced and shifted. The craft's speed slowed noticeably. Jiang moved to Peng's car and pulled the quick-release buckles, pulling away the straps used to secure the contraptions.

Peng waited, looking out the opening into a pale gray shroud of nothing. He thought of his parents and the wife he had yet to find.

Jiang reappeared and pointed at Peng, who started the engine that drove the rear propulsion fan. Jiang watched the others do the same. The colonel looked pleased, looked proud.

Jiang bowed deeply and held the position.

Then he stepped to the side, making a grand motion to the void.

Peng pressed the accelerator to the floor and drove into the nothing.

CHAPTER 20

THE THIN MAN IN the white doctor's smock, who Scott Masters saw when he first opened his eyes in the rundown room of the aged, uncared-for building, entered and moved to the bedside. The man eyed the restraints keeping Masters strapped to the bed. He was afraid.

Masters licked his lips and swallowed, hoping to free his voice enough to speak with conviction. "Hey, Igor."

"My name is not Igor." Whiny voice. No conviction.

"No? Then what does your master call you?"

The words struck a nerve. "He's not my master. We are comrades."

"Ah. Silly me. I have a question, Comrade Igor. Egonov called you a doctor. Are you really a doctor?"

"Does it matter?" He leaned over Masters and examined his facial wounds. Igor shook his head. He then moved down to the bullet wound in Masters's side and removed the dressing. A foul odor rose from the wound. The doctor put it back.

"You talked like a doctor when you were describing my wounds."

"Yes, I'm a doctor. I studied in Moscow."

"It takes a lot of work to become a doctor."

The man nodded and shone a light in Masters's eyes. "Pupils still equal and responsive. The sclera is slightly swollen and discolored."

"So, when you were spending all those hours studying to become a physician, is this what you imagined? Is torture part of the curriculum in Moscow Medical or wherever you went?"

"You are a very sick man. I suggest cooperation. It is the only way to save your life."

Masters ignored the comment. "Why medicine, Igor? There are easier degrees to get."

"I told you, my name is not Igor."

Masters forced a grin. It made the side of his head ache. "Will you tell me your real name?"

"No."

"Then Igor it is. Answer the question, Igor. Why medicine?"

"My father was a physician. He groomed me for the profession."

"So you live your life for him. I can understand that. My dad wanted me to sell paint. You know, in a paint store." It was a lie, but it made him think of the man in whom he could find no fault. To Masters, he was more than a father; he was a hero. *How I've let him down.*

Igor shook his head. "He's dead."

Masters forced the image of his famous father from his mind. "How long?"

"How long what?"

Masters frowned. "Don't play games, Igor. You're too smart for that. How long has your father been dead?"

"Five years."

"And yet you're still living out his dream for you. No wonder Egonov has you in his pocket."

Igor stiffened. "I am in no man's pocket."

"Yeah, right. You are a free man, free to do whatever you like. Is that it?"

"Exactly."

Masters laughed. "Sorry, Igor, I know a lapdog when I see one."

"Careful, Captain Masters. I am the man who can save your life."

"And yet, *Doctor Igor*, you do what no reputable doctor would do: torture people."

"I have tortured no one."

"You're torturing me. You tortured my man."

"I had nothing to do with that."

Masters shifted in the bed. "Are you familiar with the concept of tacit consent, Doctor?"

Igor turned away.

"Maybe not. Tacit consent means that if you don't stop an evil, then you, by your inaction, agree with the evil."

"So."

"So, Doctor, if you did nothing to stop what they did to my man, then you agreed with what they did."

"It's not my place—"

"YOU'RE A DOCTOR!" Masters was surprised by the volume of his own voice. "Of course it is your place."

"You don't understand."

"Yes, I do. You're afraid, terrified of Egonov and whatever thugs he surrounds himself with. You are a coward."

"And you, sir, are a man with deep infections that will soon attack the vital organs."

"I'm prepared to die."

Igor tipped his head. "We'll see." He started for the door.

"Doc?"

He stopped. "Yes?"

"How is Sergeant Chaddick?"

"He's alive for now. Burns are difficult to treat and require medications and tools we do not have here." He paused and seemed embarrassed. "Just so you know, he told Egonov what he wanted to know. The sergeant slipped into unconsciousness shortly after. That is probably a good thing."

The doctor turned to the door, placed his hand on the knob, then stopped. "I'm going to ask that you be allowed to have the antibiotics."

"Do me a favor, Doc: Give them to Chaddick. He needs them more than I do."

"Perhaps, but your man is going to die from his injures."

Masters turned his gaze away, choosing to look at the ceiling instead of the man by the door. "I've got a feeling I won't be far behind him."

"I will see if Egonov will allow it."

Masters heard the doorknob turn and the door squeak on its hinges.

"Before you go, Doctor, one more question."

"What is it?"

"If your father were alive today, would he be proud of you?"

Igor said nothing.

Masters heard the door shut.

COLONEL MAC DIDN'T WANT this meeting. Most Spec Ops happened without reading the president in. He needed the deniability and no president could keep track of the details of every mission. That's why there were generals, admirals, and—in his case—colonels. This, however, was no ordinary mission. The vice president's son was involved and that fact alone kicked it up the pucker chart.

Mac left Fort Jackson at o-dark-thirty. In the few hours he had between Chaplain Bartley's call and the time he boarded the Army's VC-20 Gulf Stream IV, he called his assistant Master Sergeant Alan Kinkaid, dragging him out of the sack. They met in the Concrete Palace, in Mac's Spartan office.

For seventy minutes, they discussed the pros and cons of the decision before them, then at five that morning, Mac called General Ian "the Borg" Bourg, head of Special Operations. General Bourg was scheduled to fly to Europe and wouldn't be able to attend the meeting. "It's all on you, Mac. Don't screw up."

The president's personal secretary ushered Mac and Kinkaid into the Oval Office, the president, former Vice President Andrew Bacliff, and Chief of Staff—soon to be VP—Helen Brown were already waiting, coffee cups on the table between the facing sofas. In full uniform, Admiral Gary Gaughan, Chairman of the Joint Chiefs, sat in one of the wingback chairs in the seating area. President Ted Huffington sat in a matching chair.

As the president and Admiral Gaughan stood, Mac and Kinkaid stood at attention. "As you were, gentlemen." The president shook their hands. "You already know everyone in the room . . . or have you met Gary?" He motioned to Admiral Gaughan.

"I've not had the pleasure, sir." Mac shook the chairman's hand.

"I've heard a great deal about you and your men, Colonel. General Bourg brags on your team all the time."

"Thank you, sir."

"Have a seat, gentlemen." The president motioned to the empty sofa. "Coffee?"

"Always, sir."

The president poured two cups from a silver pot, then set it back on the table. "Good flight?"

"Yes, sir," Mac said. It was the idle talk men engaged in before getting down to business.

The president let the men have a sip, then, "Okay Mac, let's have it. Bullet points, if you don't mind."

Mac set his cup down. "At about 2300 last night, Eric Moyer's daughter went missing. Abduction is suspected. The local cops are on the case. An Army chaplain is present with the family. I've also received word a representative from Army CID is present. There has been no contact from the kidnappers."

"CID is already in place?" the admiral said.

Mac hesitated. "As I understand it, one special agent is there. Jerry Zinsser—"

"Sergeant Zinsser? The man on your team?"

"Formally on the team. You're aware of his unique situation, sir."

"I'm the one who made CID break the rules to bring him on board."

"I don't know the details," Admiral Gaughan said.

"Jerry Zinsser is an Army hero. He's been awarded the Distinguished Service Cross for valor in Somalia. Unfortunately, he suffers from post-traumatic stress disorder. He received treatment and is back on the level, but he's not field eligible anymore."

"So he's doing police work now?" The admiral narrowed his gaze.

"Yes, sir. I hear he's doing a great job."

"But he's not leading the investigation, right?"

"CID is not officially on the case yet. He's there because it's Eric Moyer's family that's involved."

"Still—"

"The man saved my life, Gary. Let it go." The president thought for a moment. "Okay, let's talk about the gorilla in the room. You think this has to do with the mission? Someone trying to get to Moyer through his daughter?"

Helen Brown spoke up. "I think we have to assume that's the case."

Andrew Bacliff groaned and brought his hands to his face.

"You okay, Andy?" Concern covered the president's face.

"Let me see if I have this right." Bacliff lowered his hands. "Moyer is risking his life, partly to save my son, if my son can be saved, and it may cost him his daughter?"

"We can't assume that, sir. It might not be related to the mission at all. It could be a simple abduction for—"

"We get the idea, Brownie." The president's gaze bored into Mac. "What do you suggest, Colonel?"

"We are in the bind that every commanding officer dreads. Moyer has a right to know. His family needs him, but he's on the other side of the world, deep in the mountains and valleys of Magadan region of Russia."

"Can you make contact with him?" President Huffington reached for his coffee cup.

"Yes, sir. Contact is no problem. We can use satellite phones or a new device we're using in the field. It delivers messages in short bursts."

"Like submarine flash messages," the admiral said.

"Exactly, sir. We've been following them in real time by satellite, so contact is the easy part."

"Then what's the hard part?" Helen Brown asked.

"The most difficult part is whether or not we should tell him. Knowing might change his focus. It sure would change mine. If we do tell him, then how do we extract him? It's not like he can take a bus out of the region. We're not supposed to be there."

"That's an understatement," Huffington said. "What are our options?"

Mac didn't hesitate. "Option one: We recall the whole team."

"That's not much of an option," Brown said. "There's too much at stake."

"Yes, ma'am. I'm just giving a range of options. I'm not saying that's the way to go."

"Carry on, Mac." Mac sensed impatience in his commander in chief.

"Option two: We keep the info to ourselves, telling him when the team is on the way home. Option three: we tell him the truth and let him carry on with his mission."

"Which he will do?" Bacliff whispered.

"I've known Moyer for a very long time. He'll finish his mission. I'd stake my career on it."

The admiral pressed his fingertips together. "That's what you'd be doing, Colonel."

"Tell him," Bacliff said. "We ask the man to risk his life time and time again. We owe him honesty."

"With all due respect," Brown said, "I think that's a bad idea. He and his team can do a better job if they don't know."

President Huffington stared at Mac. Mac returned the honor. "He's your man, Colonel, what should we do?"

"Tell him."

"You don't want to think about that?"

"I've been thinking about it since two this morning, sir."

The president rose and paced his office. No one interrupted him. A full minute later he said, "Do it."

"Yes, sir."

"Now, what can we do to help find Moyer's daughter?"

MAJOR SCALON WATCHED THE large monitor in the satellite control center. Radar verified their calculations. Angel-12 was headed home. The Army insertion team was less than three miles from the expected impact area.

"Godspeed, gentlemen. It's all up to you now."

VITALY EGONOV SWITCHED OFF the satellite phone on his desk and leaned back in a 1950s desk chair. It creaked. The young soldier's information was correct, and his man in Moscow confirmed it. He smiled. The heavens were about to give him a gift, something he could use in negotiating with the reigning government or could sell to the highest bidder. Although negotiation was several items down his wants list. Mostly he wanted to overthrow it and return things to their proper standing, just as they were in the great days of Khrushchev and Brezhnev; back when the Russian Federation was *Soyuz Sovetskikh Sotsialisticheskikh Respublik*. Things were tough back then, but the current global economy made the current system worse.

A third of the government was influenced by criminal elements and corrupt businesses. To Egonov, the country didn't need a new direction; it needed to return to an old one.

He sprang from the seat and marched to the door. They had more than one hundred kilometers to cover in short order. It was time to leave.

In the hall, the same large man he sent to install a speaker in Captain Masters's room strolled by, cigarette in hand.

"Nikolay, gather the men and vehicles. We're going on a mission."

"How many men?" His voice sounded as if he spent his mornings gargling sand.

"A small team. Make it six. All armed. Well armed. Also, I want a team to prepare a truck, a flatbed."

"We will be transporting something, sir?"

"Yes, my friend, we will. Now go, do as I say."

Egonov's heart picked up a few beats. If all went well, they would have the satellite without opposition. If things went really well, they might be able to kill a few people along the way.

CHAPTER 21

EVERYTHING ABOUT GINA'S BEDROOM reminded Stacy of her daughter. The wee hours of the morning became the walking hours. Sounds of cars on the street in front of their house seeped through the wall and window; noises made by people going about the same business they went about the day before: work, shopping, taking children to school. Yesterday, she took no notice of the sounds; today they were laden with irony: the tragic happened and the world remained unchanged.

Gina was gone and the world kept spinning. Business would open, transactions would occur, airlines would take wing as if nothing so soul crushing as an abduction had happened.

In the living room sat three girls, the friends with whom Gina studied the night before. Each received word, most likely from Pauline's mother. The police interviewed the family. The girls—Pauline, Beth, and Sharon—refused to go to school. Unlike the rest of the neighborhood, they could not pretend nothing had happened.

At first, Stacy didn't want them in the house, not because she blamed them, but because she didn't want to be distracted with guests. Still, when the tears in their eyes and terror on their faces appeared, she couldn't close the door. For the last few hours the trio sat in stunned silence, staring at the floor, or the walls, or out the window as if Gina might stroll up the walk any moment.

Stacy pulled a tissue from a box by Gina's bed and blew her nose. It was one of the few things she was able to do: cry and blow her nose.

Pink tissue paper. Gina always wanted pink tissue paper. "Blue is for boys," she often said. She was five when she first said that, but she kept the preference as she grew.

Rob once said, "Insisting on pink tissue means you're psychotic."

Gina had replied, "I think you mean neurotic. There's a difference, you know."

On most days, Stacy was certain Gina was the smartest person in the house.

Stacy closed her eyes and inhaled deeply. The room smelled of Gina; the air was charged with the essence of Gina; and if she listened carefully, she could hear her daughter humming.

The tears came again. Stacy, seated on Gina's bed, pulled a pillow to her chest and buried her face. More Gina. The smell of her shampoo.

Tears turned to deep, body-racking sobs.

She felt a presence and looked up. Chaplain Bartley entered the room. He pulled Gina's desk chair within reach of Stacy and sat. He said nothing. Tears streaked his face.

"You don't have to stay, Chaplain."

"I know, but I'm staying out of a sense of self-preservation and to uphold an old family tradition."

"I don't understand." She continued to hug the pillow.

"My brother is on your husband's team. You know that. What you may not know is how much he admires your husband and your family. A few weeks ago, he told me he hopes to have a family like yours. If I'm not here for you, J. J. will make sure I get a weeklong butt kicking."

"Our family isn't perfect."

"No family is, Stacy. Perfection isn't the goal. Love is."

She took another tissue and dabbed at her eyes. "What's the family tradition?"

"No one gets to cry alone."

The words made her cry more. The weeping faded. "Chaplain, why would God do this to us? Is He punishing us for not going to church?"

He shook his head. "I don't think God is that small or vindictive. I've been a Christian for a long time and I've seen good come to bad people and bad to good people. The rain falls on the just and the unjust. No, I don't think God is doing this to you."

"But He allowed it."

Bartley folded his hands. "That's some thick theology, but in a nutshell, you're right. He did allow it."

"Why?"

"I don't know. I believe God is all powerful and all knowing, which means things do not happen without His knowledge. I also know He loves us and wants the best for us."

"How do you reconcile the two?"

Bartley shrugged. "I don't. Oh, I used to try to explain the whole thing away. I tried to defend God's honor, but I came to realize He didn't need my help. Bad things happen. They always have. Disease, poverty, greed, violence, and war. I became a soldier to help stop some of that; I became a chaplain to help those affected by such things."

"I still don't know how a loving God could let my little girl be snatched from the street."

"I know you don't. I don't either, but my not knowing the why doesn't overpower my belief in the Who."

"I'm sorry, Chaplain. I guess I'm not at my best." She looked past Bartley at the photos Gina kept on her desk. One was of the family taken in an in-mall photo business; the other was of Gina with her friends at a school function. Her gaze traveled back to the family photo and fixed on Eric.

Never before had she needed her husband more and he was somewhere in the world cleaning up other people's messes. He should be here. It wasn't a rational thought; it was emotion. Still, it was no less real. She was mad at Eric. Mad at the world. Mad at herself. She was especially angry with God.

"Tell Him."

Stacy looked at the man sitting in her daughter's chair. "Tell who, what?"

"If you're angry with God, then tell Him."

"Right now, Chaplain, I'm not sure I believe in God."

"I understand and I think He does too."

She didn't know how to respond and was too tired to try. "Do you know where he is?"

"God? Sorry, you mean Eric."

"Yes."

"No. Unless I'm deployed with a unit, I never know. It's not necessary for me to know, and as I'm sure Eric has mentioned, the fewer people who know what's going on, the better."

"Doesn't seem to be working this time, does it?" The words were prickly. If they bothered Bartley, he didn't let on.

"No, it doesn't. If Gina was abducted and the kidnapping is related to your husband's mission, then there's a serious problem in security."

"Will they tell him?"

Bartley's face went blank. "I don't know, Stacy. It's one of those things mission leaders debate and never resolve. I've seen it go both ways. Since I have no idea where the team is or what its mission is, I can't hazard a guess. I do know this: You remember the problem Lucy Medina had with her pregnancy a couple of years ago? You were a big help to her."

"I remember. She almost lost the baby and her own life."

"Colonel Mac made sure Jose knew of the problem and offered to extract him from the mission. That doesn't mean he'll do the same this time. Every mission is different and—"

"And Eric is team leader." She sighed. There was so much she didn't know. "I hate not knowing."

"I understand. Worry is the hardest work any of us will ever do." Bartley stood. "I'm going to give you some privacy. Just know that I'm here if you need me."

"Thank you, Chaplain."

He walked from the room and it seemed he took all her hope with him.

JERRY ZINSSER WALKED THE area around the Moyer home. It was the tenth time he did so. Each time he covered a slightly different path. Rob Moyer had been by his side the whole time.

"You've been up all night, son. Don't you think you oughta head back and rest a bit?"

"No."

"It's no disgrace—"

"Forget it."

Zinsser studied Rob for a moment. He looked beat, worn by fear and impotence. He guessed the teenager matured fifteen years in the last few hours. His hair was disheveled, his eyes red, and the peach fuzz that passed for a beard was turning into a vague shadow on his face.

"Okay, pal. It's your call."

"Would you go home and rest if it were your sister?"

The corner of Zinsser mouth lifted. "Of course I would."

"You're lying to me, aren't you?"

"Yup. Lying through my teeth. Just trying to do what's best for you."

"What's best for me is to find my sister and kill the guys who took her."

"Ease up on the killing talk, Rob. Killing a man isn't nearly as satisfying as you might think. I speak from experience."

"Hey, Zinsser."

He turned to see Chief Warrant Officer Terry Wallace. The man was a walking, talking example of "nondescript": average height, average build, and—to Zinsser—average intelligence. He wore an identical blue blazer to the one Zinsser wore. He had been on Wallace's bad side since he first showed up on Wallace's doorstep, fresh from apprentice agent training. Wallace dismissed Zinsser's Army record, much of which was redacted, leaving out missions that would never be discussed except by those who were there. Not knowing why Zinsser earned a free pass through the acceptance process remained a big, pointy burr under his heavy saddle.

"Uh-oh," Zinsser whispered.

"Trouble?" Rob looked worried.

"Not for you. Trouble with a capital *T* for me."

"Why? Who is—?"

Zinsser raised a hand. "Now might be a good time for you to head back to the ranch."

"I told you, I'm sticking with you."

Zinsser sighed. "Okay, just keep your mouth shut. Got it?"

"I can do that."

"I hope so."

"Zinsser, you and me need to talk."

"Sure thing, Chief, but aren't we already talking?"

The man's hazel eyes seemed to darken. Once again, Zinsser successfully ticked off his boss. "You know what I mean. Why are you here?"

"Working, Chief."

"Last I looked, I made case assignments."

Zinsser smiled sweetly but not sincerely. "That was true last I looked too."

"I didn't assign you to this case. It didn't come through channels. If the police hadn't called to complain about your presence, I wouldn't even know about it."

"I'm sure they meant well."

"I want an explanation and I want it now. No sugarcoating, no cute talk."

"Gina Moyer was apparently abducted last night."

"Who is Gina Moyer and why is it any of your business?"

"She's my sister."

Wallace glared at Rob. So did Zinsser. "Who's the kid?"

"Rob Moyer. Rob, this is my immediate superior, Chief Warrant Officer Terry Wallace, Army CID. He heads the office out of Fort Jackson."

"Pleased to meet you, sir."

Rob held out his hand, but Wallace looked at it like the boy just sneezed in it. He ignored the offer of a handshake. "I need to talk to Special Agent Zinsser."

The rebuff offended Rob. "Go ahead."

"I want to talk to him alone."

"Then get a room."

"You little snot, who do you think you are?" Wallace made a confrontational turn to Rob.

Zinsser put a hand on his boss's chest. "Easy, Chief. I can explain."

"Remove that hand, Zinsser, or I'll take it off and feed it to you."

Ice water flowed through Zinsser's veins. The hand remained. Zinsser looked deep into Wallace's eyes. A second later, Wallace took a step back.

"Rob Moyer is Stacy Moyer's son. His sister is the one who's missing. Since his father, Sergeant Major Eric Moyer, is on a Spec Ops mission, I felt the abduction fell under CID jurisdiction. Kidnapping is a felony."

Wallace frowned and faced Rob. "Your dad's overseas?"

"I don't know where he is. We never know. He just leaves when he's told to."

Wallace nodded. He was a pain in the department's collective rear end, but he always showed respect to the family of soldiers on foreign fields, although it seemed to give him indigestion.

"Why didn't you call me as soon as you heard, and by the way, how did you hear?"

"Chaplain Bartley called me at about two this morning."

"And why would he call you?"

"I served with Moyer."

Wallace raised an eyebrow. "You know the girl? You know the family?"

"I've knocked back a few beers at their house and eaten some pretty good barbeque."

Wallace worked his lips, as if doing so would send ideas to his brain. "That means you're not a disinterested investigator."

"Listen, Chief, I know there's a bit of a strain between us, which puzzles me—me being so lovable and all—but this case matters to me."

"I should remove you."

"You can if you wish, but I'm not going anywhere."

Wallace crossed his arms as if Zinsser had just given him a way out. "Then I can drum you from CID."

"If you must."

"You'd ruin your career over this?"

"I'd give my life over this. I owe Moyer a lot. More than you know."

"What? Did he save your life or something?"

"Something like that."

Wallace clenched his jaw and worked his lips even more. He raised a threatening finger but stopped when his cell phone sounded. He fetched it from his pocket and answered without taking his eyes from Zinsser. "What?"

He blanched.

Zinsser smiled.

"Yes, General. I'm on the scene now." A pause. "Yes, ma'am, I'm with Agent Zinsser right now." A longer pause. "I'm sorry, ma'am. Who called you?"

Wallace blanched some more. Another shade lighter and people would confuse him with an albino. Zinsser exchanged glances with Rob. "Wait for it," Zinsser whispered.

"Yes, General. Of course. I'll do exactly that. No, ma'am, there will be no problem. I will put every resource I have on it. Yes, ma'am. Thank you, General."

Wallace clicked off the phone. Zinsser thought of twenty piercing quips but kept them to himself.

"Brigadier General Irene Gore? *The* Irene Gore? Head of USACIC?" It took work for Zinsser to keep the corners of his mouth even.

"You know it was. It appears POTUS has made a personal appeal. So did the chairman of the Joint Chiefs."

"The president and the chairman of the Joint Chiefs of Staff. Seems like overkill to me. Whatever could they want?"

"You know what they want, Zinsser. I don't know who you've been sleeping with to get such favorable attention, but they want you on this case—no matter what."

"You should have told them you were going to drum me out of CID."

"Stuff it, Agent Zinsser. Fill me in."

"Will do."

COLONEL MAC SAT IN the aft-most seat of the CV-20 Gulfstream IV with a legal pad in front of him. On the floor around his seat were a dozen wadded pieces of paper. Mac was as good with a computer as most people but some things required pen and paper.

For the thirteenth time, Mac began writing the message he did not want to see. It comprised only a few lines:

Gina missing from home. Suspect foul play. CID and police on job. Chap there. Zinsser too. Can't extract. Continue with mission. Will keep you posted.

"Sergeant!"

Alan Kinkaid strode down the aisle of the aircraft. "Yes, sir?"

Mac handed the paper to the aide. "Send it. Make it happen quick."

"On it, sir."

Mac looked out the window, seeing only the tops of clouds and thought about the man he admired, the man he would call friend if rank and responsibility didn't prohibit it.

It didn't happen often, but every once in a while, Mac wished he had become a plumber.

LEV STOPPED THE VAN on a narrow cow path near the top of one of the highest hills south and across the river from Nov Arman. They were operating in daylight now, so the first bit of duty required reconnaissance to make sure they were alone. In the distance, Moyer could see a tiny village nestled in the foothills and a full klick from the Arman River, a lazy moving body of water that, based on the terrain, once ran deep. Now it seemed anemic.

Moyer studied his surroundings: no military vehicles, just small shacks that passed for houses, horses, goats, cows, and the tilled fields of subsistence farmers—people who cared nothing for the outside world, international intrigue, or politics. He imagined their big concerns revolved around weather, farm animals, and meager crops. These were a people for whom fifty was elderly.

"Boss."

Moyer didn't bother lowering his binoculars. "Whatcha got, Junior?"

"Connie has come to life again."

The military had a long history of naming inanimate objects. For some reason "Connie the Communicator" had been chosen for the new digital device.

"Read it."

"Can't, Boss, it's Eyes Only."

"What? The thing is already encrypted six ways from Sunday."

"Can't explain it, Boss, but I have a guess."

"Which is?"

"It's personal."

Moyer secured his binoculars, rolled to his side, and reached for the device. "Personal? For me?"

"It's all I got, Boss."

Moyer pushed himself into a sitting position, crossed his legs, and set the communicator on his lap. He went through the security protocols.

A message appeared.

He read it, then covered his face. A moment later he slumped to the cold, damp ground.

"Boss?"

Moyer heard Pete but couldn't respond.

"Boss, you okay?"

He still couldn't move; couldn't think; couldn't speak. Bile rose in his throat. Tears flooded his eyes. A tsunami of fear tore though him.

"Boss, what's wrong?"

Moyer managed to shake his head.

Pete keyed his throat mike. "Shaq, Junior, Boss needs you on the double. On the double, Shaq. Boss, talk to me."

Pete picked up Connie. A second later he heard a long chain of curses.

PETE'S VOICE RATTLED IN Rich's brain. *Shaq, Junior, Boss needs you on the double. On the double, Shaq. Boss, talk to me.*

Rich was a big man. Linebacker big, but that didn't mean he was slow. He was moving before Pete could finish the sentence. He and J. J. had been scouting the high ground: a peak fifty feet higher than where they stopped on the back of the hillside. The run was down hill and Rich ran recklessly. Pete's message would have gone to each member of the team. The sound of J. J.'s bootfalls followed Rich.

It took less than two minutes to cross the distance, but it felt like two days to Rich. He found Moyer lying on his back, Pete kneeling next to him. Instinctively, Rich raised a hand, bringing J. J. to a stop, and raised his M4, scanning the area. He had heard no shot, no cry of pain, no echo of gunfire, but he was trained time and time again not to assume anything. From the corner of his eye, he watched J. J. do the same.

Jose and Crispin were jogging up the path. Crispin was in the lead, but Jose caught him by his pack and yanked the inexperienced soldier back. Jose raised his weapon. Crispin got the idea.

Slowly they advanced.

Pete caught sight of them and waved them over, something he wouldn't do if hostiles were involved. Three steps later, Shaq was at full speed again. He reached Moyer and Pete, and dropped to his knees. "Report."

Pete handed Connie to Shaq, who read the message. He said nothing. Instead, he handed the device to J. J., then sat down by his friend.

He put a hand on Moyer's arm. It was the only communication he could muster.

Lev stepped from the back of the FedEx truck, saw the scene, and approached. Rich watched him read their expressions. To the man's credit, he kept his mouth closed.

CHAPTER 22

PENG WAS A GRATEFUL man. When he pressed the small metal accelerator on the buggy and drove down the rear ramp and into empty air, he was certain his life would end fifteen thousand feet below. How long would it take to fall that far? Did it matter?

The cold air stung his face and cut through his field uniform as if the fabric were silk. The impact of the freezing air took his breath away. He forced himself to breathe even though every breath stabbed his lungs.

Thankfully the small cart, which Peng assumed would nose over the moment the rear wheels left the ramp, dropped wheels down, something the parachute needed in order to open correctly.

Parachuting equipment was not new. He saw trucks and Humvees dropped from large cargo planes. What he was in was light enough to make a parachute drop less complicated than dropping several tons of engine and steel siding from a moving aircraft. Equipment drops usually didn't include people strapped into the seats.

A few seconds after "departing" the altered MD-90, above the whistle of rushing air, Peng heard the flapping of the parafoil above his head. He turned his gaze up to a dark, rectangular-shaped parachute. It filled with air and his descent slowed. Twisting in his seat, he watched the other members of his team descending under successful parachute deployment.

"Not dead yet," Peng said to the open air. With the turn of a switch on the small metal dashboard, Peng transferred the power of the engine from the rear wheels to the propeller behind him. His forward motion increased. He used the throttle to increase the propeller's speed and control handles to either side of him to adjust the pitch and attack of the parachute. It took a little practice, but Peng soon had the hang of it.

The fog in his goggles caused by the sudden change in temperature cleared. While it never obscured his vision, it did give the world a milky-white appearance for the first few moments.

Once he had control of the craft, he began a slow circle to allow himself a quick look at the plane he left seconds before. It continued a gradual downward angle. Black smoke began to pour from the left engine. Jiang prepared him for this. For the ruse to work, the *Qīpiàn* needed to look in as much distress as possible. It looked real enough to Peng.

Below Peng was a patchwork of mountains, valleys, and uncountable tributaries. There were no cities, no towns, but he could see one village, nothing more than shacks and sheds, a short distance away. Patches of farmland covered every reasonably flat area. If it wasn't a mountain or a river, it was a furrowed field.

Per plan, Peng increased the rate of his descent. His orders were to get to the ground as fast as possible. Jiang thought through every aspect of the plan and its timing. During the briefing the colonel made clear his belief the ever-paranoid Russians would try to turn the craft around. Decades ago, China and the Soviet Union were good neighbors, but tensions and border clashes divorced the parties. Diplomats spoke in civil tones but trust was impossible. The year before, Russian spies were caught recruiting military contractors as agents. Peng was shocked; his own country engaged in the same activity. All large countries did. For China it was easier; it was one of the few major countries with a healthy economy. It had problems for a short time, but rebounded faster than anyone thought possible. Russia still struggled. Many of its people lost work and lived in poverty. Money made such people easy to recruit.

Exhilaration replaced Peng's apprehension and for a few moments he allowed himself to enjoy the adventure of flying over such beautiful albeit rugged terrain. He caught himself smiling.

The joy passed as he focused on the chosen landing site: a bit of ground identified as suitable by a Chinese spy satellite and a group of technicians specializing in photo interpretation.

Peng did another wide circle over the chosen landing area, gauging the wind and ground. He would have only one chance at this. The longer they stayed in the air, the greater chance someone would see them. As it was, the farmers he could see working the fields would take notice of them. Jiang assured the team the people in this area had little contact with larger populations. It was one reason they stayed mired in the nineteenth-century way of life.

Patches of snow remained on the higher mountains and in the shaded areas of some valleys. The field where Peng and his team would set down looked free of residual ice. It also looked free of large rocks that might upend him or one of his team. It was remarkably free of such things. Peng assumed it was a field left to fallow.

Peng adjusted his glide path and let off the throttle. Moments later his wheels hit the damp surface and the parafoil collapsed behind him. He switched the drive train to his wheels, and drove to the edge of the field making room for his team.

He popped his restraints and scrambled from the buggy and turned to face the incoming buggy controlled by Hsu Li. Zhao Wen was in the seat next to him, holding the side rails as if trying to keep the contraption in the air. They touched down without incident. Two minutes later, Gao Zhi and Wei Dong came to a successful landing and stop.

Peng returned to his buggy and gathered the parafoil, carefully folding it and placing it in the storage bin just above the fiberglass-shrouded propulsion fan. Two of his men took defensive positions while he and the remaining two members secured their vehicles.

Ten minutes after touchdown, Peng and his unit were marching to an area a few kilometers north and into one of the wider valleys.

RICH READ THE MESSAGE on Connie again and handed it back to Pete. "Acknowledge the message as received and understood, Junior. Then I want you, Colt, and Hawkeye to surveillance positions. I don't want someone sneaking up on us."

"Roger that, Shaq."

They hesitated, then J. J. asked the question: "Is there anything we can do? Is the mission still a go?"

"Colt, it's a go until Boss says it isn't. Now give us some space." The three soldiers hustled off.

Rich looked at his fallen team leader, felled not by a bullet or IED, but by something more devastating than an improvised explosive device: fear for a loved one.

Sentences and phrases battled for attention in Rich's mind. What was needed? A word of comfort? A "chin up ol' boy"? Should he get in his friend's face and remind him how much was at stake?

He didn't know what to do, so Rich sat on the ground next to his friend and kept his silence.

THERE WAS A SMALL space between the arm Moyer used to cover his eyes and his face. Through one eye he could see a cerulean sky. A flock of ducks flying in V-formation ambled through the sky, headed for one of the many lakes and ponds dotting the area. A bird of prey, probably some kind of eagle, circled overhead. Maybe it was the first of a series of vultures. Moyer didn't know. Moyer didn't care.

A voice played in his head; a soft, youthful female voice.

"Look, Daddy, I made a family picture." Gina at five. "And, and, and you're in the middle and everything."

"We'll just see what you've done." Moyer picked her up and set her on his lap. "Did you draw this with your new crayons?"

"Yes, Daddy; the ones you brung me."

He studied the photo. "I like it. I see the blue sky, and the green grass and . . . wait a minute. I thought you said this was a picture of the family."

"It is. I made everyone look like a bear. See there's Mommy Bear, and Robbie Bear, and me, Baby Bear."

"Who's that?" Moyer pointed at the crudely drawn image in the middle.

"It's you, Daddy. I told you dat you was in the middle."

"But I don't look like a bear. Everyone looks like a bear but me."

"That's because you're a porky-pine."

"A porcupine? You made your daddy into a porcupine?"

"Yeah. See you have an itty-bitty nose and lots of stickery hairs."

"Quills, baby, porcupines have quills."

"Okay, grills."

"Not grills . . . never mind. Why did you make your handsome, kind, bringer-of-crayons daddy into a porcupine?"

"Because when you don't shave your face feels like a porcupine." She giggled.

Ah, the giggle, the sweet music. No matter how angry he became, Gina could disarm him with a giggle.

Moyer's stomach burned and roiled.

Gina at twelve. The dinner table. "Gina, we need to talk. Three boys have called for you since four this afternoon."

"Four boys. You missed one."

"Four? What's going on with you, young lady?"

"Just growing up, I guess. I didn't ask them to call."

Moyer raised an eyebrow. "Then how did they get our phone number?"

"Oh that, well, I may have given it to them."

"May have."

"I'd say there's a good chance I did give them the number."

He exchanged glances with Stacy, who was losing her battle not to smile. "I don't like boys calling the house."

"Why? They're not calling for you."

Gina smiled and Moyer's heart melted. "Did you tell these boys I carry guns for a living? Great big, terrifying guns?"

"Now, Daddy, you know that would only discourage them."

"That's the point."

She grinned again. "Go easy on them, Daddy, or I'll make life miserable for you."

Moyer set his knife and fork down. "Oh, and how do you plan to do that?"

"I'll grow up beautiful then—marry a sailor."

Gina at fourteen, two months ago. On the front porch swing.

"Dad, when will you stop going away?"

"It's my job, sweetheart."

"But it's a job you choose, right?"

Moyer looked away, choosing to focus on the neighbor's dog trotting free down the street. "What I do is important. There aren't many men who can do it."

She sighed and a tear escaped her eye.

"What's wrong, honey?"

"What if you don't come back?"

"I always come back."

"Does everyone who goes out on a mission come back?"

Moyer studied a bee hovering around a rose. "No."

"Then how can you say you'll always come back?"

At first he did not answer, then, "Because you need me. I will always be here for you."

MOYER WASN'T THERE FOR her. He was lying on his back in wet grass in a forgotten, empty part of eastern Siberia. He should be home. He should have been there to protect his daughter, to hold his wife, to guide his son. But no. One more mission. One more sudden trip to a place no one has heard of to do work no one will know about.

"Daddy! Daddy help!"

The words were real. They didn't enter his mind through his ears. It was his imagination that uttered the words; it was his imagination that painted vivid pictures of Gina being held in some dank place, being harmed—

He wouldn't allow the thought; wouldn't give it a place to grow roots in his gray matter.

Moyer moaned and shut his eyes. In the course of his service, he had been shot at, barely escaped capture by swimming to a submarine, fought off Afghan rebels who outnumbered the team ten to one, endured a situation-close bombing in which explosives were dropped a few feet over his head, made high-altitude jumps, disarmed bombs, lost men . . . The list was too long to recite. Of all the wounds and injuries he received, this hurt the most; of all the terrifying situations he faced none undid him as the message he just read.

"Oh, God, oh God, oh God." Moyer opened his eyes to the sky above, hoping God would answer. Instead, he saw the eagle and the powered parachute—

He blinked. "What the—?"

"Eric . . . Look man, I don't know what to say."

Rich was staring at the ground, fiddling with a long blade of grass.

"Shaq?"

"They'll find her, man. We gotta believe that."

"Shaq, look up."

"Looking up is good, Boss. I mean—What?"

Moyer pointed to the sky. "Check me. Is that what I think it is?"

Rich craned his neck. "Well, I'll be . . ." He reached for his binoculars and trained them skyward. "It's a powered parachute of some kind. It looks like a small dune buggy hanging from the silk."

J. J.'s voice came over the earpiece. "Shaq, Colt. We've spotted some airborne craft. They're landing on the other side of the river, one, maybe two klicks from the village."

Rich keyed his mike. "We see 'em, Colt. Any idea who they belong to?"

Moyer reached for his binoculars and, still on his back, pointed them at the small craft. With the unaided eye, Moyer could see three parafoils. Through the high-magnification tactical binoculars, Moyer could see what looked like two men in a dune buggy.

J. J.'s voice came over the earpiece again. "I can't be sure, Shaq, but I have a good idea."

"You gonna share it or make me guess?"

"I'm eyeballing one chute now. Two men aboard . . . aboard whatever that thing is. One is packing what looks like a QBZ-95. If I'm right, then those guys are a long ways from home."

"So are we, Colt. Bottom line it for me."

"A QBZ-95 is an assault rifle. A Chinese assault rifle."

CHAPTER 23

MAJOR SCALON SHIFTED HIS eyes from one corner of the large display screen in the communications room at Offutt Air Force Base to the image of the nation's highest-ranking civilian. The large screen was electronically divided to allow Scalon and Captain Tim Bryan to see the other members of the teleconference. Facing them were the larger-than-life images of Colonel MacGregor and Admiral Gary Gaughan.

"Telemetry shows atmospheric insertion in three, two, one." Scalon did his best to look and sound interested but unemotional. It was a hard thing to do. Angel-12 was his baby and it was about to plunge to earth in a fiery display, be gutted by Moyer's team, then destroyed. Life wasn't fair. Of course, he was safe and warm in STRATCOM. Moyer and his men had a much rougher go of things.

"How long before they can see it?" Huffington asked. The audio system made it sound as if he were in the room.

"Three minutes, sir. People in the UK, the Baltic states, and much of Asia will be able to see it but only for a moment. They'll call it a meteor."

"And it's on track to hit the bull's-eye?" Admiral Gaughan said.

"It should be close."

"Close. What do you mean close, Major?"

Tim answered. "Begging the admiral's pardon, but no one can predict with great accuracy where an object from space will fall. We have data from several hundred space junk reentries so the coordinates we gave, we gave with high confidence."

"I detect a 'but' coming." Gaughan leaned closer to the camera.

"But, factors such as object tumble and the physical shape can change things. We have good photos of the damage done by the Chinese attack satellite and have factored that portion in, but chaos theory—"

"Chaos theory, Captain?" The president looked suspicious.

"Yes, sir, it's the old story about a butterfly in Africa beating its wings and through a long chain of events, causing it to rain in New Jersey."

"Meaning?" the admiral said.

Scalon took over. "Meaning, Admiral, we've accounted for everything we can, but we can't account for everything. Still, I believe Angel-12 will land right where we say it will."

The phone on the table behind which the two Air Force officers stood beeped. Scalon snatched up the receiver. "Scalon." He listened. "Feed it in." Scalon turned to the tech sergeant operating the controls of the video conference. "Recon is sending us taped images. Put it on the screen, Sergeant."

"Yes, sir."

The bottom right quadrant of the screen lit up. A time code on the video revealed the image was less than five minutes old.

"What do you have?"

"One moment, Mr. President." Scalon quickly added, "If you don't mind, sir."

Scalon watched the blurry images of five men and a truck on the side of a large hill not far from a sinuous river. Something much too large to be a bird swept by. The satellite operator, perhaps alerted by the quick movement, pulled back on the zoom. Three powered parafoils came into view.

"Mr. President, our men have company."

"I GOT SMOKE," HAWKEYE said. "Looks like a jetliner of some kind trailing black smoke."

Moyer pushed off the ground and stood. "You hear that?"

Rich turned his head to the side. "I hear a distant roar. Sounds like . . . like . . . jets."

Moyer snapped his head around. Two dark objects were approaching from the northwest. He raised his glasses. "PAK FA T-50. Russian stealth."

"Not good." Rich raised his glasses, then keyed his mike. "Incoming aircraft. Take cover. Repeat, take cover." He put a hand on Moyer's shoulder. "We need to beat feet, Boss."

"I don't think they're here for us. They banked south. Isn't that where Hawkeye saw the airliner?"

"Roger that. I still think we should spread out and hit the ground."

Moyer removed the binoculars from his eyes and moved up the hill to an area of low-lying brush. He and Rich crawled beneath the cover. Moyer crawled forward to the edge of the foliage and took a visual bead on the jets. Rich inched to his side.

"Still got 'em?"

"Yeah, they're definitely chasing the airliner."

"You don't suppose the big plane and the Chinese guys are connected."

Moyer looked at Rich. "You mean that they somehow drove their toys out of the plane?"

"We've done stranger things."

Moyer had to agree. "So our Chinese friends haven't given up on our satellite."

"They did go through a lot of trouble and expense to knock it out of the sky and try to steal it. Who can blame them?"

"I can."

"Boss, Colt. Incoming target off our left, ten o'clock high."

Rich shook his head. "Man, for a backwoods area, there sure is a lot going on."

Moyer searched the area J. J. indicated. A white streak crossed the sky on a descending angle. He tried to follow the streak with his binoculars, but it was difficult to track. He did get enough of a view to know he was watching Angel-12 become a Fallen Angel.

It hit in the distance, sending a tremor through the ground. Moyer guessed the impact area to be a half-dozen klicks away. "Junior. Get on the horn and let the folks at home know we have earth-fall, then stand by. They should be able to give us an exact fix."

"Got it, Boss."

"Boss, Hawkeye. The airliner is continuing south. The T-50s have taken escort positions. The airliner continues to descend, but its rate of fall has decreased. All three aircraft are moving away from us. They're almost out of sight."

"I'm starting to like that kid, Boss."

Moyer rolled to his side and stared at his friend.

"What? I shouldn't like the new guy?"

"Shaq, I may be compromised. My brain is mush; my emotions are boiling over. You may have to take command."

Rich moved his head back and forth. "No way. You have always led this team. I know I questioned your decisions a few times, but you were always right."

"Shaq, I'm not kidding. If need be, you push me out of the way. The mission is too important. Don't let me screw things up. Don't let me slow things down."

"No matter how bad things get, you can go on instinct better than anyone can with every brain cell firing at once."

Tears rose in Moyer's eyes; something that had never happened on mission. "Shaq, I'm giving you an order."

Rich looked angry and heartbroken at the same time. "Yes, Boss."

Moyer nodded and wiped a tear from his face. In the last few minutes, he saw a disabled craft, Russian fighter jets, a Chinese Spec Ops team, and all he could think about was his daughter. Every action required additional focus. His emotions swung like a pendulum. One other thought percolated in his mind: *I am no longer fit to serve.*

CHAPTER 24

GINA'S HEAD HURT. HER eyes hurt. Her stiff neck throbbed. The space between her shoulder blades cramped. Her vision was blurred and a gray mist seemed to fill the space in front of her.

More pains: her fanny, her feet, her hips. She closed her eyes, then opened them again. It was dim.

What time was it?

Where was she?

Thoughts, questions, confusion swam in her head. She felt ill. For a moment she was certain her stomach would empty.

She leaned forward. No, she couldn't lean forward. Something held her in place; something wrapped around her chest. Another restraint over her bare thighs kept her from rising.

Her mind began to clear and with it, her vision. She shook her head as if trying to fling the fog from her brain. The action made her head ache and she tried to bring a hand to her temples. Her arm wouldn't move. More restraints.

Bare thighs? The thought returned, this time with a truckload of emotion. She looked down. Lit by a small incandescent bulb—a bulb similar in size to a refrigerator bulb dangling from wires overhead—Gina's legs came into focus. They were bare. Hadn't she been wearing jeans? Yes. She was sure of it. She put the pants on before walking to Pauline's house. Surveying herself, she learned her thighs were not the only thing bare. Her blouse was gone. Gina sat in a dark, closet-sized room wearing nothing but her underwear.

Had she been . . . ? She couldn't complete the question. The thought was too horrible, too frightening. Tears rose. Her limbs began to shake. The nausea she'd been fighting climbed in her throat.

I'm alive. Focus on that. I'm alive, I'm alive, I'm alive. She inhaled deeply. Then again. And again. Her stomach settled; the tears trickled but the flood did not come.

I'm alive. That's a good thing. I hope.

She didn't feel beaten, couldn't detect any sensation she had been molested. It might be a false comfort, but she would take it.

As her thinking grew sharper, her fear grew. Who would do this to her? Why would they do it?

Panic is everyone's enemy. She heard her father say that several times. He learned that in the Army. "I had a drill sergeant who made us recite that fifty times a day. 'Panic is everyone's enemy. Panic will get you killed. Worse, it will get the men in your unit killed. If you panic, you die.'" Her dad smiled. "That may be the greatest bit of wisdom the Army ever taught me. Calm thinking beats out screaming like a Girl Scout every time."

I will not panic. I will not panic. I will think. I will be calm.

She repeated those words until she beat the fear back. What else did her father teach her? Why hadn't she listened more?

His voice became almost audible again. "Don't deny fear; use it. The man who denies fear is a fool; the man who uses fear is its master." He was talking to Rob then. It was two or three years ago. At the time it was funny. He sounded like a teacher in a kung fu movie.

Okay, I'm afraid. I admit it. But I am fear's master. It sounded good, but the thing she most wanted to do was cry and scream for help. She wanted her father, needed her mother. Still, she remained calm despite the storm of terror lashing her insides.

Gina did what she was good at: compartmentalization. In her mind, there was a room for school, one for family, one for friends, and one for herself. Neat. Tidy. She overheard her mother bragging to a friend: "The only thing more organized than Gina's room is Gina's brain."

Use that. Think. Think. Think.

She drove back the persistent urge to panic by cataloging her situation. She was in a chair. An old-looking dining room chair with arms. Oak. Nylon ties bound her wrists to the arms, not so tightly as to cut off circulation. That meant something: They were worried about hurting her.

She could feel the same kind of nylon ties at her ankles. A canvas belt bound her thighs and a similar one was across her chest, just above the bottom of her ribs, again not so tight as to restrict her breathing. They wanted her alive.

There wasn't much to see in the room. Directly across from her was a metal door with a wired-in glass window in it, similar to what they had in some rooms at school and in hospitals. A dingy, white pull-down shade attached to the other side of the door kept her from seeing through the glass.

A vague light reflected off the glass in the door. It was the shape of a rectangle set on its short end. A window. There was a window behind her, but the glass wasn't clear. She tried to turn and face it but couldn't. The chair wouldn't move. She didn't know how, but the chair was anchored to the floor. She suspected brackets of some kind.

The floor was concrete; the ceiling, plaster. While examining the ceiling she noticed something. A small, black cylinder was mounted above the door, where ceiling met wall. She blinked several times, then strained her eyes trying to focus her attention. A lens. A camera. A video camera. Next to it was a small white speaker.

She was being watched.

Next her gaze traveled along the baseboard and lower part of the wall. Two things struck her. First, everything looked new; second, there were no electrical outlets. The room had been designed for her. What did a captive need with outlets?

She paused in her thinking and fear filled the void. No matter how much she tried to act like an adult, to follow the firm, even attitude exhibited by her father, she couldn't. She wasn't her father, hadn't been Army trained. She was fourteen, just starting her teen years. Some days she was more little girl than young woman.

Although Gina willed herself not to, she began to cry, and crying turned to weeping and weeping to sobbing. She could only whisper one word:

"Mommy."

DESPITE THE COOL AIR outside, it was stuffy in the FedEx truck. The men returned to their seats. Lev listened from the driver's seat. He kept wiping at his mouth, a clear sign he was jonesing for a drink. Moyer couldn't bring himself to feel sorry for the man.

"Okay, ladies, listen up." Moyer's eyes felt full of sand, his ribs had turned to concrete, and the skin around his chest constricted like a straitjacket. "I'm only going to say this once. I doubt I could say it twice." He dropped his gaze, waiting for the words to line up in formation. "You know about Gina . . . the situation with Gina. Naturally, I'm having trouble thinking about anything else. But we still have a mission. Other lives depend on us. We have brave men to rescue."

He leaned back on the small, anchored chair. "Shaq is under orders to take over the mission if I falter, if for any reason I become more detriment than help. If that moment comes, you will obey him as you obey me. There will be no argument; there will be no discussion; there will be no hesitancy. Is that understood?"

"Boss—"

"I asked a question. Do you understand?"

"Yes, Boss." They spoke in unison.

"Good. Now let's get down to it. We have to assume the Chinese air circus that just landed is after the same thing we are. It can't be anything else. We also know a group of Russian dissidents have taken the surviving original Spec Ops team captive. We have to assume they've tortured the men and that one of them cracked. If so, then we may be facing a bunch of armed Russians too. There isn't anything I like about this mission."

Moyer continued. "If we get in trouble, then we are on our own. We're too deep in country. We can't call in air support, can't call for artillery, and can't call for an extraction team. It's been a tough trip getting here; it's about to get a whole lot worse. Are we clear on that?"

Another chorus. "Clear, Boss."

"Junior, get me a map on Connie."

"On it, Boss." A moment later Pete handed the device to Moyer.

"Lev, I see several small towns along the road beyond Nov Arman. Are you familiar with them?"

"No, but they are probably farm settlements like this one."

"Would our truck stand out?"

"People would notice it, but I know deliveries are made this way. I checked that out before I arranged for the truck."

"Really, FedEx delivers all the way out here." J. J. sounded skeptical.

"Yes, young man, they do. So does UPS. Not often, but at least once every couple of weeks."

"All right then." Moyer made eye contact with his men. "Are we good to go?"

"Hooah!"

"Lev, kick it in gear. The Chinese are making ground on us."

"Through the backwoods. We'll use the roads."

"Fine by me. We have a package to pick up."

GINA WAS UNCERTAIN HOW long she had been crying, but the tears ceased coming, even though the scorching fear still raged and the black despair still blanketed her. Her body ached from the physical exertion of sobbing. She could feel mucus hanging from her upper lip.

Desperate, she pulled against the nylon straps binding her wrists to the chair. The sharp edges dug into her skin. Blood began to ooze.

Despite the pain, she tried again, hoping that if the strap wouldn't give, the arm of the dining room chair would. Then she noticed the threaded rod that ran from the chair's arm to the solid oak seat. She pushed her right arm out as much as she could and saw the round, smooth top of the long bolt. It had been countersunk deep enough in the arm that Gina's arm didn't rest directly on it. They thought of everything. That realization frightened her all the more. Intelligent, calculating bad guys were more dangerous than simpleminded hoods. At least they were in the movies.

Panic welled up in her. She pulled at the bindings, shook her arms and legs, moved in any way she could on the impossible hope something would give way.

"You will only hurt yourself."

She froze. A voice. From overhead. She looked up. A small, round, perforated metal cover painted the same color as the ceiling was situated just a short distance from the dangling incandescent bulb.

The voice infuriated her. She pulled at the straps again trying to free herself. More blood.

"If you want to feel pain, I can arrange it."

"Who are you?" The question erupted as a scream.

The soiled shade on the other side of the window snapped up. Even through the door Gina could hear it smack the top of the door.

She gasped.

Through the glass she could see a figure. His face was covered by a black knit mask. Not even his eyes could be seen. It was like looking at a three-dimensional shadow, solid, thick, animated.

The man—she assumed it was a man because of the voice she heard a few moments before and because of the observer's size.

"Let me go."

He opened the door and stepped inside as casual as a man entering his own home. "No."

"Why are you doing this?"

"Because I can."

The voice was deep and smooth, FM radio smooth.

"I want to go home." Gina jerked at the restraints, which dug deeper into her flesh.

"Of course you do. That's the idea."

The observer moved closer, walking around Gina, circling her. The motion made her think of a shark. He stopped behind her. She turned her head but he remained out of view.

"What are you doing?"

"Look up, Gina. Look into the camera."

"How do you know my name?"

"I know everything about you, Gina. You'd be surprised what I know about you, and your brother, Rob, and your pretty, pretty mother. I know a great deal about your father as well."

"This is a mistake. You have the wrong person."

He chuckled. "They all say that. No mistake, young lady. Too bad your father is so far away taking care of others when he should be home taking care of you."

"My father is just on a business trip. That's all."

"Really. I think you're old enough now to know what your father does for a living. I'm sure he's told you."

"He's a businessman. I told you that."

"Yes, you did, and you're right, if your father's business is killing people. That's what he does, you know. He goes places he's not wanted and when he leaves, people are dead."

"That's not true." Tears returned.

"Look at the camera, sweetheart. I want everyone to see how pretty you are. Your father is Sergeant Major Eric Moyer, United States Army, leader of a Spec Ops team."

The man ran a gloved hand down Gina's hair, then caressed her jawline. He kissed the top of her head.

"Stop the mission."

It took a moment before she realized he was speaking to the camera.

Then the gloved hand took hold of her jaw and another hand gripped the back of her head. She erupted in sobs and waited for the sharp twist that would snap her neck.

CHAPTER 25

CHIEF WARRANT OFFICER TERRY Wallace clicked off his cell phone, glanced at Jerry Zinsser, and turned to Rob Moyer. "You guys have a computer?"

"We all have computers. Well, Mom and Dad share a computer."

"I need something with fast download."

"My room." Rob rose from the sofa where he had been sitting with his mother. "The whole neighborhood has fiber optics, but my computer is a gamer. It's the fastest one in the house."

"Why do you need a computer?" Stacy inched forward on the sofa.

"I just got word someone sent a video to our office. My people are putting it up on the server so we can see it from here."

"What kind of video?" Stacy rose.

"I don't know yet, but you should let Agent Zinsser and me take a look first."

"Not if it concerns Gina, I won't."

"Ma'am, please. Let us do our jobs."

"I'm her mother; I have a job too."

Zinsser stepped close. "Let us have first look, Stacy. Okay?"

Stacy said nothing.

Rob led Zinsser and Wallace into his room. The place was a shambles, and Zinsser couldn't help comparing it to Gina's neat-everything-in-its-place bedroom. On the bed lay a dirty shirt from the burger joint where Rob worked, four pairs of sport shoes lay near the bed, two pairs of jeans hung on the back of a chair by his small desk, just three feet from the closet. On the wall were posters of grunge rock bands whose careers ended before Rob was born. An electric bass guitar sat on a stand in the corner, dust indicating that it hadn't been used in some time. On the desk, next to a keyboard so used the letters were worn from the keys, sat several college catalogs.

Good for you, buddy.

"How long will it take to boot up?" Wallace seemed oblivious to the untidiness, but then he had a teenage son living at home. For all Zinsser knew, this might appear good and clean to what he faced each day. Zinsser could make no judgment. While he cleaned up his act, he was still working on his apartment.

"I leave it on all the time." Rob pulled the jeans from the chair and tossed them on his unmade bed. Zinsser slipped into the seat before Rob could turn around and tapped a key, waking the computer from its digital sleep.

"It wants a password."

"Oh, yeah." Rob hesitated. "Beatles. Capital *B*."

Zinsser typed: *B-e-e-t-l-e-s.*

"No, the band, not the bug."

"Really? You like the Beatles?" Zinsser tried again.

"Hate 'em. That's why I use it as a password. No one who knows me would ever think of that."

"Okay, kid, let Agent Zinsser and me take it from here."

"No."

"Look, kid, I don't want to argue—"

"Good, neither do I. So it's settled, I'm staying."

"We don't know what's on that video, Rob." Zinsser turned in his seat. He admired the boy's courage.

"You will after you play it." He motioned to the computer.

Zinsser accessed the CID's private server and found the video file. He clicked on it. A moment later the player on Rob's computer loaded and the video began to play.

They watched Gina struggle; they watched her weep; they watched her cry for her mother. They watched her turn brave and challenge the man who entered the room. Then they watched him put his hands into position to snap her neck.

"Oh God, oh God, my baby. No."

Zinsser keyed the pause button and turned to the door. Stacy stood there; Chaplain Bartley had to hold her up.

"I told you—"

"Let it go, Boss." Zinsser spoke softly but firmly. "If it was your kid, you'd be in here too."

"You know what's about to happen don't you, Zinsser?"

"I know what it looks like, but I got a feeling he's playing with us." Zinsser hit play and watched as the captor lifted Gina's head slightly, forced her chin to the left, then sharply pulled his arm to the right.

"NO!" Stacy's scream shook the windows.

"Hang on." Zinsser raised a hand. "She's okay. He didn't do it."

"She's alive?"

"Yes."

The captor looked into the camera. "End Moyer's mission now, or next time won't be pretend."

The video ended.

Zinsser heard a retching sound. Rob had just vomited on the floor; the stench of it filled the air. Zinsser ignored it and returned his gaze to the flat-screen monitor. "I'm coming for you, Gina. Hang in there, baby." His eyes shifted to the man in black. "I'll find you. I don't care if I have to look in every dark corner of hell, I will hunt you down, and then you will learn what real pain is."

SPECIAL AGENT WALLACE MARCHED to the bedroom door and helped Bartley escort Stacy back to the sofa. He could feel her tremble in his arms and it made him furious. Once Stacy was seated, he pointed at the chaplain. "You, come with me." He turned to Gina's three friends. "Keep an eye on her."

"I should stay with—"

Wallace shot out a hand and seized Bartley's uniform shirt and pulled him out the front door. The part of his brain not awash in anger told him he just assaulted an officer. This would be hard to explain, but at the moment Wallace didn't care. He shoved Bartley off the porch, slammed the door behind him, and took hold of Bartley's arm—another bit of assault and battery. When they reached the middle of the yard, Wallace spun him.

"I didn't want Moyer's wife to see the video. I've seen stupid in my day, Chaplain, but you take the prize. How could you bring her into the room? For all we knew she might have had to watch the murder of her own daughter."

"Agent Wallace—"

"I should arrest you for interfering with an investigation. You may have scarred her for life."

"I was in the latrine when you guys went into the room. I didn't know what was going on."

Wallace could feel heat emanating from his face. "You should of checked with me."

"And where were you when I came out? You were in Rob's bedroom using his computer. What did you want me to do? Call you on the cell phone?"

For a chaplain, Bartley had a good set of lungs. "You were wrong to do that."

"What? Hit the head?"

"No, let her see the video."

"I know God made us all a little different, but why He filled your head with concrete I'll never know. I didn't *let* her do anything. She was gone when I came back to the living room. The girls said she went down the hall. I went to check on her. I got there at the last moment. What would you have done? Dragged her away by the hair?"

Wallace raised a finger and stabbed at Bartley. "I would have . . . You should have . . ." He sighed.

"Got nothing?"

"Not a thing." Wallace looked down. "Sorry. I have a daughter and that, well, it just got to me. Sorry about roughing you up."

"I don't consider that rough, but apology taken."

A woman in a dark business pantsuit approached. "Are you guys done spraying the area with testosterone?" She was five-five, with blond hair pulled back into a ponytail. Suspicious blue eyes peered at the two.

"Who are you?" Wallace snapped.

She produced a badge case. "Special Agent Brianne Lazzaro, FBI."

"We have jurisdiction," Wallace said.

"You CID guys amaze me. Every time we show up to render aid, you guys go paranoid. I'm not here to take your case away from you."

Wallace eyed her. "Then why are you here?"

"When the POTUS calls the director of the FBI in Washington who calls the assistant director for my region who calls the director of my office who tells me to get my fanny over here, then I cart my fanny over here. So, are we going to have a problem?"

"Probably not." Wallace's anger subsided.

"Good. I was given the basics. What can the FBI do to make the CID look good?"

"Come with me. There's something I want you to see."

"Such as?"

"A video. Maybe your white-coat guys can give it a good look."

Brianne nodded. "You have the original here?"

They reached the porch. "No. It was sent to my office electronically. Your people can retrieve it off the server. Hang on."

Wallace stopped and looked back at Bartley. "Hey, Chap. We good?"

"When all this is over, you can buy me some lunch. Then we'll be good." Bartley smiled.

Wallace could only muster a nod.

SCOTT MASTERS WAS SURE the dirty sheet beneath him would catch fire any moment, ignited by the fever boiling through his body. Every joint hurt. His head ached and he couldn't shake the idea that ants were crawling in the crevices of his brain. He began to wish for death.

The door to his room opened and the doctor entered. He closed the door behind him. In his hand he carried a small but deep metal tray. He set the tray at the side of Masters's bed.

"Sorry, Igor. I'm still alive."

"My name is not Igor. We've been through this." He spoke softly as if exchanging secrets. "Being alive is good."

"Is it? Doesn't seem so good from where I sit—lay—lie. Sorry, my grammar seems to have escaped me."

"It's the fever."

"How do you know I have a fever? I don't think you've done as much as a casual exam, other than to describe my wounds to Egonov."

"I can see it from here." He stepped close and touched Masters's uninjured cheek, then his forehead. "I was right."

"Doctoring at a distance. You'd be a hit in the States. What can I do for you, Doc? A drink. A light lunch. Oh, wait, I can't get up. I'm strapped down. What was I thinking? Come to think of it, don't have anything to drink or eat. I guess you're on your own."

The doctor looked sad and his already thin frame seemed smaller than the last time Masters saw him. He also looked like a man who doubled in age in just a few hours.

"You know, most doctors ask how their patients are feeling."

"Useless small talk. I know how you feel." He walked to the ever-beeping IV pump and pulled it close to the bed.

"So what's it going to be this time? A little more torture? Have some dirt or manure to rub in my wounds to speed up the arrival of gangrene?"

The thin man removed a sealed needle from the tray and peeled away the protective plastic. He attached it to the flexible line that ran from the fluid-filled bag to the business end of the IV line. He

stepped to the side of the bed and examined Masters's restrained
arm. Holding the IV line between the fingers of one hand, the man
removed a small packet from the tray, opened it, and removed a
cotton ball. Master could smell the pungent alcohol.

"What are you doing?"

"Just lie still."

The sharp prick set off an electric pain that ran up Masters's
arm. The doctor taped the IV needle in place. "I told you to give
the antibiotics to my man."

"Won't do him any good."

Masters didn't like the sound of that. "Why?"

"He died an hour ago."

He looked away.

The doctor continued. "I did what I could for him, but this is
not the most sanitary place. The burns on his feet sent him into
shock. I couldn't bring him out of it. He needed better care than
I could give."

"What he needed was not to be tortured by guys like you."

"I've already told you, I wasn't there."

"But you knew about it, didn't you?"

"Egonov doesn't inform me of very much. Just what he wants
me to know."

"Where is he?"

"Who? Your man, or Egonov?"

"Both." Anger swelled in Masters.

"Your man—Sergeant Chaddick—is still in the room. We will
bury him as soon as possible."

"Room. You mean cell, don't you?"

"I suppose so. Egonov was able to confirm what Chaddick
revealed to him. He has followers in every area of the government.
He has gone to look for the satellite."

The news sucked the air from Masters. "Why are you doing this?"

"Because if you do not receive the antibiotics, you will die, and I have seen enough death today."

"Why tell me about Egonov, Igor?"

"Because telling you doesn't change anything. Egonov is already gone."

"If he knows you've helped me, won't he kill you?"

"I'm not that lucky. Now hold still. The torture is about to begin." He removed a large plastic bottle of medical alcohol, opened it, and poured some on a gauze pad. "Turn your head to the side." He leaned over Masters's damaged face. "This might hurt."

There was pain, but nothing hurt more than learning he just lost another man. By his count, there was only one other man on his team still alive.

He had a feeling that wouldn't be true much longer.

For thirty minutes, the doctor cleaned Masters's wounds, irrigating them with water then with antibiotics applied directly to infected tissue. It hurt. A lot. Masters took it without complaint, although a large part of him thought it was just an effort to keep him alive long enough so they could kill him later.

The doctor packed up the soiled and bloody gauze pads and walked to the door, placing a hand on the knob. He paused and turned.

"No, Captain Masters, my father would not be proud of me." He seemed to drift away. "In fact, he would be furious."

Masters stared the man in the eyes. "You know what my father used to tell me? He used to say, 'Doing the same thing over and over again and expecting a different outcome is the definition of insanity.'"

"Meaning?"

"Meaning, results will only be different if you change what you're doing."

"If only it were that easy."

"He never said anything about it being easy."

"Do you and your father still speak?"

Masters moved his head from side to side on the pillow. "He's dead. Died two years ago." It was a lie, but the last thing he needed was for this group to know about his real father.

Igor nodded then left the room, leaving Masters to his own thoughts and to wrestle with the knowledge that his team had been whittled down to just two.

CHAPTER 26

"YOU KEEP REPLAYING THAT video. What are you looking for?" Rob entered his room again. Zinsser sat in the chair in front of the computer, FBI agent Brianne Lazzaro and CID agent Terry Wallace sat in chairs taken from the dining room. They were shoulder to shoulder with Zinsser.

"Clues, Rob. There are always clues."

"You've found clues?" Rob stepped closer.

"We've found information, but nothing very helpful. At least not yet." Zinsser advanced the video a frame at a time.

"What kind of information?" Zinsser could hear the anxiety in the young man's voice. Talking might ease some of the pent-up frustration, give him a sense of participation.

"First, how's your mother?"

"Not good. I've never seen her this way. She's always been so strong."

"I think she's showing remarkable strength," Brianne said. "When it's your kid in trouble, things change."

"What have you found?" Rob stood behind Zinsser and leaned on the seat.

"Ease up on the chair, pal."

"Oh, sorry."

Zinsser turned and smiled. "No problem." He addressed the monitor again. "Okay, the FBI is breaking out all their video kung fu tricks and will have more information for us ASAP. Right now, we have only our eyes but we've noted a couple of things." Zinsser paused. "Are you sure you want to look at this thing again? I mean, it's your sister."

"I want to do something to help. Sitting around is making me crazy. I'm gonna start punching walls if I can't be involved."

"Do you know how much you sound like your father?"

"There was a time when that would have been an insult. I wish he were here now."

"He's where he's supposed to be." Zinsser pointed at the monitor. It was time to teach, if for no other reason than to distract Rob for a few minutes. "Okay, Rob, there are two ways to look at things: first is the big picture; second are the details. Big picture: We're looking at a room designed to hold Gina. It's not a regular bedroom in a house or apartment."

"How do you know that?"

"No electrical outlets for one," Brianne said. "There's only one. It's on the wall, just behind Gina. We can only see about half of it. She and the chair block the rest from view, but it's there."

"That means the back wall is part of the real structure." Zinsser ran the video stream forward a bit. "Cash is about to enter."

"Cash? You know who this guy is?"

"No, Rob. He's dressed in black—Johnny Cash—the man in black. Always wore black."

"If you say so."

"Anyway, the kidnapper is about to enter. Now your eye is going to want to follow him. I think that's planned, but for now just watch the wall to Gina's right." Zinsser started the video stream again.

"It moved."

"Exactly. The wall isn't permanent; it wasn't fastened down well. Okay, no electrical outlets, phone jacks, cable jacks, and a wall that wiggles when Cash walks in. They've staged the area."

"How does that help us?"

"It means this was planned but had to be put together quickly."

"Couldn't they just be sloppy?"

Zinsser agreed. "They could but they thought about the other details. My gut tells me they had to work fast, which fits with your dad's mission. It came up quick, as they usually do."

"It also gives a bit of a lead," Brianne said. "I have agents going to hardware stores and home-improvement outlets asking questions. It will probably lead to a dead end but sometimes we get lucky. There will be thousands of purchases, but we know that we're looking for someone who bought wood studs and drywall. By estimating the length of the three walls, we can guess at how many studs were purchased. At the very least we have a range. The room is maybe eight feet by eight feet. Studs are normally spaced every sixteen inches, but let's assume they spaced them one to two feet apart, then we need someone who bought twelve to twenty-four studs. Something in that range."

"Also," Wallace said, "we think the wall height is eight feet. Drywall panels are four feet by eight feet. That equates to about six sheets of drywall, assuming they didn't drywall the other side, and why would they if they were in a hurry. It's not exact, but it will reduce the invoices we have to go through."

"Look at the window, Rob, what do you see?"

"Just a window."

"It's not just a window. Do you have a window like that in your house?"

He looked closer. Zinsser gave him a moment. "No."

"It's called a double-hung window. The window doesn't move left and right, the bottom section moves up and down. We can't see out the window because they have it blocked off, but we can see enough of the window itself and it looks like an old double-hung, so . . ."

"So it's an older building."

"Right."

Rob sighed. "It's hopeless."

Zinsser turned in his seat. "Never give up hope, Rob. I don't know how this will turn out, but right now we need to take every bit of information we can get. Crimes have been solved with less."

"I know, I just . . . I don't know what to think."

"That's why we're here, son." Wallace sounded kinder than Zinsser had ever heard him. "Let us do the thinking."

"Got anything else?" Rob's despair dripped from every word.

Zinsser said, "A few things. The kidnapper is a male. Using the height of the window as a guide, we think he's six foot two, maybe six-three. Strong build, broad shoulders, confident bearing. Maybe military trained. When he was pretending to . . ."

"Snap Gina's neck," Rob prompted.

"Yeah, that. He used the same motion we learn in Spec Ops. And that's another thing. He used the phrase "Spec Ops." That doesn't prove he's ex-military or paramilitary, but it makes me think he's tied to the service one way or another."

Brianne said, "He sounds American but there is a hint of an accent. FBI linguists will go over it. We can't make out an accent that might apply to an ethnic group or a terrorist country. My guess is we're dealing with a white male."

"The question is: How many of them are there?" Zinsser leaned back. "These things aren't usually done alone, especially when they have a political agenda."

"Now that's interesting, isn't it?" Brianne said. "How do they know about Moyer's mission?" She turned to Wallace. "Do you know where Moyer is?"

"Not a clue."

"What about you, Zinsser? You in the know?"

"Nope. I'm not part of the team anymore. They wouldn't tell me if they wanted to. I don't know where they are or what they're doing."

"Then how does this guy know?"

Zinsser rubbed his eyes. The question conjured an answer he didn't want to give. "Spec Ops has a mole, or at the very least, an insider in the Pentagon."

Wallace groaned. "That, Agent Zinsser, is a terrifying thought." He rubbed his chin for a few moments. "You had better call Colonel MacGregor."

"I think I should make it a personal visit. I also think you'd better come with me."

"Why?"

"Because Colonel Mac is going to go ballistic and I may need someone to hide behind."

"Thanks."

"I try to spread the love." Zinsser pushed back. "Let's do this. Agent Lazzaro, will you bring Stacy up to speed?"

"Yeah. I need to check on the tech guys. Make sure they have the trace set up in case Cash calls."

"Come on, Boss, let's go get our heads handed to us."

ANDREW BACLIFF HAD A decision to make and he was having trouble making it. He sat in his office in the West Wing. So much had happened in the last few days his resignation seemed a month ago. Truth was, the formal letter still sat on President Huffington's desk, unannounced in the White House, still unknown on Capitol Hill. Functionally, however, Bacliff was out and soon Brownie would occupy the space.

Staff had already packed many of the personal items but kept the action and the boxes out of sight. If one reporter saw the bare walls or the sturdy cardboard boxes being moved from the office, the world would know about it by the end of the news cycle. The amount of attention such news would generate would spread around the world and might even make it to his son's captors, who might make a connection Bacliff needed kept secret.

As yet, there had been no communication from the Russian splinter group holding his son. That didn't mean much. The timing was in their control, not his. If they, through torture or other means, learned that Captain Scott Masters was son to Vice President Andrew Bacliff, it was game over for his boy.

He pulled the phone close and mulled over his decision. When he first revealed to his wife the news about their son's situation, she wept, became angry, threw things, and beat his chest with her fists, blaming him for encouraging their "baby" to go into the service. It took almost an hour for the fury and fear to dissipate enough that she could talk rationally. When she could, she'd wrung a promise from him: "You keep me in the loop, do you hear? I don't care if national security is at stake. I have a right to know what's going on with Scott. No secrets. You share everything you know with me."

He agreed. He was too shell-shocked to do otherwise.

Bacliff fingered the phone and looked at the bare walls. The furniture remained and would until Brownie officially moved in. Keeping his promise meant calling and telling Gertrude about Eric Moyer's daughter. He could tell her the mission is still a go and nothing was going to change, but she wouldn't hear that part. Her mind would translate the information into something darker and more hopeless.

Lying. He considered the option. After all, he had already kept something from her. Angel-12 was so highly classified that standing law made it illegal for him to discuss it even with his wife. That was good news. He had no idea how to tell Gertrude the rescue of their son was second on the mission list, not first.

He picked up the receiver and called home. He could imagine the phone ringing in the mansion on the grounds of the Naval Observatory. Gertrude answered on the second ring.

"Yes."

"Hi, sweetheart. I'm still at the office, but I wanted you to know that the overseas business is starting."

"How long before we know the outcome?"

"It will be some time. I can't give an exact time. Too many variables. Do you want me to come home or monitor things here?"

"I need you, Andrew, but I also need you there. You'll let me know how things turn out?" Her voice cracked.

The line was secure, but over the years, they developed the habit of speaking in generalities. "Of course. I'll be able to keep an eye on things."

"I understand."

She did. As the VP's wife, she was invited to the White House many times for social events, but she was also given a private tour, seeing things about which tourists could only guess. As VP he was, to use the media cliché, just a heartbeat away from the Oval Office. That meant he had to be dialed in on all security protocols and sit in on intelligence briefings. It also meant being aware of how things in the Situation Room operated. It was the one room in the White House that most impressed Gertrude.

The pause was as heavy as a saturated wool blanket.

"Have you spoken to my favorite daughter-in-law?" Bacliff asked.

"Yes. Twice today. She's . . . she's having trouble with it all."

"We all are. Is there anything I can do for her?"

"No, just keep telling us the truth. We'll make it one step at a time."

The truth. The very thing he was keeping from her.

"Is there something else?"

Bacliff hesitated a moment, rolling the prickly decision around in his head. "No."

"Andrew?"

"I'm just a little distracted, Gertrude. There's nothing else." Politics taught him how to lie and to lie well.

"Okay, if you say so." She didn't sound convinced, but she had been a public servant's wife too long to start questioning him over the phone.

"You know I love you." He struggled to take a breath. Fear and sadness bound his lungs. The next time they spoke, he might have to deliver the worst news any parent could hear.

"I know, Andrew. And I love you."

Bacliff hung up, pushed the phone away, crossed his arms, and lowered his head like a kindergartener told to rest at his desk.

Except Bacliff found no rest.

VITALY EGONOV RAISED A small, green, handheld radio to his mouth, keyed it, and said, "Ostanovit." The convoy of three Tiger military vehicles—Russia's answer to the Humvee—and a flatbed truck slowed to a stop on a dirt road that normally saw only tractors and old trucks pulling animal carriers. Egonov's mottled green-and-beige Tiger slid a foot in the loose dirt, its wide tires kicking up dust and pebbles.

"What is it, *Podpolkovnik*?"

"A message from our friend in the Kremlin." What Egonov received was the military version of a text message. The satellite phone's display came to life, alerting Egonov of an incoming message. All it contained was an Internet address, coded. Egonov pulled a laptop from the space between his driver, Senior Sergeant Anton Terasov, and him.

It took only moments before Egonov had tethered the satellite phone to the laptop. A few moments later he was looking at a satellite-generated map. He turned to Terasov. "The satellite is down." He turned the computer so his right-hand man could see it. "The coordinates put it a few kilometers north of Nov Arman."

"We should avoid the town." Terasov pointed to the map. "This road will take us a few kilometers east of the satellite. We will be off the road after that."

"Time estimate?"

"Less than two hours."

"Make it much less than two hours."

Terasov put the Tiger in gear and pressed the accelerator to the floor. The heavy suspension took most of the abuse, but speeding on a dirt road meant a rough ride no matter what vehicle they were riding in. Egonov was willing to risk his kidneys.

MOYER DIDN'T KNOW RUSSIAN but he recognized swearing when he heard it. The vehicle shuddered to a stop.

"What? What's wrong?" Moyer righted himself after inertia pressed him into the small divider between the cargo area and the truck's cab.

"Vehicles." Lev kept his eyes forward either because his eyes were fixed on something or he didn't want to be seen looking behind him.

"Details, man. Give us details."

"I counted three Tigers and a flatbed truck."

"Tigers?" Rich said.

"Like your Humvees. Four-wheel drive, diesel engine."

"Military?"

"Russian military uses them, but these may belong to the group you're looking for. They call themselves Future Dawn. Those who know them have less poetic names."

"What direction were they traveling?"

"North. We can assume they're going our way."

"Great," Rich said, "sounds like a party. I hope they brought a fruit plate."

Moyer's mind began to grind ideas.

Lev turned in his seat. "What do you want me to do?"

"Did they see you?"

"Us, Mr. Moyer. Did they see us? I'm not in this truck alone."

"Okay, Lev, did they see us?"

"I don't think so. They're downhill from us. I saw a glint off their windscreen and hit the brakes."

"Good job."

"I'm glad you liked it. Can I have a drink?"

"No booze for you, Lev. I need you sharp."

Lev lowered his head. "I keep telling you: Vodka makes me sharper."

"I doubt it," Jose said.

"Everyone give me a sec." Moyer closed his eyes and let the ideas run rampant. "How fast were they going, Lev?"

"Faster than is safe."

"The Chinese already have a lead on us," Rich said. "Now we've got hostile Russians headed to the same place."

"I know, I know. I need another sec." Moyer eyed Rich. "I'm still here, Shaq."

"I believe you."

"That's what your mouth says, but your face says something else."

"My face has always had a mind of its own."

Moyer looked down, then smiled. "This could be good. Very good."

When he looked up again, he saw six men, Lev included, staring at him.

"What?"

CHAPTER 27

COLONEL MAC AND ALAN Kinkaid sat at one side of the long conference room table; Jerry Zinsser and Terry Wallace sat across from them. Mac selected one of the meeting rooms in the main administrative building. At first, Zinsser assumed they would be meeting in the Concrete Palace, but the idea faded when he was reminded he was no longer Spec Ops, and even if an exception could be made for him, it couldn't for Terry Wallace, CID or not. Technically speaking, despite the local CID director's influence and experience, he shouldn't even know about the Spec Ops control center.

Zinsser only served under Colonel Mac for one mission. He met with Colonel Mac several times before being assigned to Moyer's team last year and before making a hash of his career. Zinsser's first impression of Mac was a positive one. The man was built like a brick, had a quick mind, was a no-nonsense leader, and had eyes that could bore through a steel plate. He had never seen Mac angry and never wanted to. Zinsser knew the type. He could intimidate a rabid pit bull with just the tone of his voice.

"Fill me in, Jerry." Mac leaned back and folded his arms. Kinkaid took notes on a notebook computer.

"You received the web link I sent you?"

"Yes. Received and viewed."

Sometimes Mac acted like he had to pay real money for each word he spoke.

"Someone knows about Moyer's mission."

"Maybe."

"Sir, with all due respect, the kidnapper called Moyer by name and mentioned the mission."

"Correction, Agent Zinsser. The kidnapper mentioned *a* mission."

Wallace leaned on the table, putting weight on his elbows. "Colonel. I know you have secrets to keep. I've been around the Army for a long time, but we are facing a different kind of case here. A young girl's life is at stake."

"I know that. People higher up the food chain know it as well."

"I can't speak to that," Wallace said. "My only concern is the girl."

It was a slight motion but Zinsser saw Colonel Mac's jaw tighten. Not good. "I'm aware of the problem."

Wallace drummed his fingers. "Sir, what mission is Moyer and his team on?"

"That's classified."

"It may be pertinent to our investigation." Wallace scooted closer to the table. Zinsser wanted to leave.

"The mission is classified above your level."

Wallace ran a hand over his face. "Colonel, I didn't expect you'd show up with blueprints, but I have to ask the nature and goal of the mission. It is an integral part of our investigation."

"There is nothing I can tell you."

Wallace stood and leaned over the table. "Colonel, I try never to go over an officer's head—"

"Sit down, Agent Wallace."

"Perhaps you don't understand. I—"

"I said, sit down."

Wallace did, but his face grew three shades of red.

Mac straightened in his chair. "Agent Wallace, have you ever met the president?"

"I know he's pulled strings on this investigation, but no, I haven't met him."

"Well, if you want to go over my head, he will be the guy to talk to. On most missions that's not the case. It is the case for this mission. If you catch my drift."

"I don't catch your drift."

Mac's attention shifted from Wallace to Zinsser. He sighed. "The colonel is saying the president is involved. That implies the level of secrecy is way above our pay grades and probably deals directly with national security. We're not going to get anywhere here."

Wallace sprung to his feet. "I don't believe this. It's your own man. Don't you care about that? You are willing to let some homegrown terrorist torment a fourteen-year-old girl. What kind of man does that?"

"A man who knows how to follow orders."

"So you're not going to tell me anything?"

"At this moment, my men are entering harm's way. I don't need a desk jockey to bust my chops about this."

"I'm trying to save a life."

Mac was on his feet. "So am I, Agent."

"Really? Because I don't see it."

Mac looked at Zinsser. Zinsser wished he hadn't. "You need to put a leash on your lapdog, Data."

"It's not Data anymore, Colonel, and Agent Wallace is not my lapdog. I work for him. Besides, he's right. And just for the record, I have met the president."

"You know better than that. My hands are tied."

"I know, Colonel, but you're tying our hands. If we don't act quickly, we will be attending the funeral for Eric's daughter. I've faced a lot of frightening things in my life. Standing at Gina Moyer's graveside scares me to death."

"Gentlemen, I can't help you. I wish I could . . ." Mac grew silent, then glanced at Kinkaid. "You want a cup of coffee, Master Sergeant."

"No thanks, I'm fine." He looked into Mac's eyes. "Come to think of it, I do want coffee. Do I want a donut too?"

Mac nodded. "Yeah, you do. Take Agent Wallace with you."

"I'm not going anywhere. I'm leading this investigation. I will not be dismissed."

Zinsser frowned. "You want coffee, Boss. It will do you good. Trust me on this."

Wallace shoved his seat back so hard it fell over. Kinkaid was already at the door, holding it open for the fuming CID director.

The moment the door closed, Mac sat again and folded his hands on the table. Zinsser sat in silence, giving his former commander time to think. He was asking the man to, if not break security protocols, at least bend them beyond recognition. It was a career ender.

"Colonel—"

"Shut up, Jerry. You've put me in an impossible situation."

"Only because I'm in the same spot."

Mac gazed at the table. Silence filled the space. Zinsser could hear the man breathing.

"Colonel, let's try a different spin on this. You have multiple issues here, one we haven't touched on, mostly because my boss has a mouth problem."

Colonel huffed. "He is a piece of work. His CID protection allows him to talk rough to an officer, but even a gentleman like me has his limits." He chuckled, something that seemed to come from need more than humor. "Okay, let's hear your spin before I end my career."

"Here are the factors. One, you have a team in the field on a covert mission; one apparently of high order. Two, you also have the daughter of a team leader whose life is in danger. I'm guessing Eric knows about this."

"You'd be right. I owe him that much and more."

"Okay, if we can rescue his daughter, it will help him in the field."

"I'm listening."

"The third problem, the one we haven't mentioned is this: There's a mole in the system, someone who knows about the mission and who is in on it. How can that be? I don't know, but I do know that not only Moyer's mission, whatever it is, must succeed, his daughter needs to be saved, and the mole needs to be eradicated. True?"

"True."

"By helping us, Colonel, you are enhancing the success of Moyer's mission and plugging a hole in military security."

"You should have been an attorney."

"Nah, they don't let you carry weapons on duty."

"Okay. I'm going to give you the skinny. You talk to no one, not even your boss. Guide him the best you can, but I don't want him in the know about the details."

"Understood, sir."

"A few days ago, a Chinese satellite we believed to be long dead came back to life and targeted one of our birds . . ."

Fifteen minutes later, Zinsser stood at the door but facing Colonel Mac. "I don't know what to do with all this, Colonel, but thank you. It might prove useful."

"Find the girl, Data. Find her and the men who took her. I don't care what you do to them, just give her back to Moyer. His country owes him."

"Yes, sir. I will do my best." He paused. "Ready?"

"Yeah. I'll see you at the Oscars."

Zinsser smiled, then cleared his throat. He raised a finger and pointed at his one-time commander. "You are a disappointment, Colonel. It shames me to think I served under you."

Mac matched his volume. "You best evacuate this room before I have you tossed in the stockade."

"Go ahead, call for help."

"I don't need help to deal with you!"

Zinsser snapped the door open and slammed it behind him. In the hall, were Wallace and Kinkaid, both wide-eyed.

"Let's go, Boss. This place is starting to turn my stomach."

CHAPTER 28

PENG DIDN'T KNOW WHETHER to be thankful for the lack of deep forest or apprehensive. Five Chinese men in mottled blue-white-green-gray camouflage military field dress scooting along animal paths and open fields in half-sized off-road vehicles made of metal tubes couldn't be more noticeable. The only thing working to their benefit was the lack of population. This area of east Siberia was mountainous with little ground flat enough for good farming. Not to mention the harsh winters that would cause any sane family to leave for a place easier to scrape out a miserable living. Those who stayed, he surmised, were those who had no choice or were unwilling to give away their land. There were many similar areas in China.

The land was marked with hundreds of tributaries starting to swell in the mid-spring melt off. Most still had sandy, stony shores that the buggies handled easily. The animal paths were created by centuries of migrating moose, deer, wolf, and other creatures that called the larch forests, lower grassland, and barren slopes home.

The fact the sun made good progress toward its zenith made driving easier, but it also made it easier to be seen from ground, air, and satellite. He pushed the worries from his mind. Worry wouldn't change anything. All he could do was carry out his mission with as much care and speed as possible. With luck, he would return home a hero. If unlucky, he wouldn't return at all.

A small mirror on the driver's side of the vehicle allowed him to catch a glimpse of the team behind him. The two buggies followed at a distance. Grouping was unwise. If something happened to him—such as driving off a cliff—his team would see it and avoid committing the same mistake.

Peng's buggy came equipped with an onboard compass and GPS unit. He glanced at the latter. *Just a few more minutes.*

The motor in the rear, which operated the propulsion fan in flight and the transmission on the ground, seemed too loud. Low vis was preferred, but being low visibility in this situation was impossible. Even when in the expanses of larch forest, they could still be heard. After all, there were three motors chugging away. In the open, they could be seen and heard. A poor way to carry out a mission. Peng had no idea why the fallen satellite was so important, but it was significant enough for his government to break treaties, international law, and risk the best Spec Ops team in the People's Liberation Army.

He moved along another animal path, down the steep side of a hill, in and out a coppice of larch trees, and into a small spread of open grassland. Ahead was another hill. He accelerated to gain momentum to help him up the slope. The engine could drive the buggy close to one hundred kilometers an hour on open, solid ground, but on this terrain he had not been able to make half that. By necessity, the engine had to be small. Nonetheless, its power impressed Peng.

As he climbed the hill he steered around trees and brush, something that required slowing, and slowing meant the engine had to work harder to push him up the hill. It did its job. Peng crested the hill and braked to a stop.

Snow clung in the shadowed areas created by rock outcroppings. Trees lined the slopes of hills to the east and west, hills creating a valley down through which a shallow stream meandered. No houses. No shacks. No sign of humanity anywhere.

He switched off the engine and exited, his QBZ-95 carbine in hand. He dropped to a knee as the rest of his team arrived, each stopping a short distance from their team leader, again avoiding grouping their assets. The men poured from the vehicles, taking positions along the ridge and seeking what cover they could.

With the engines stilled, Peng strained to listen for any sound that might indicate they were not alone. He heard only wind and birds.

Peng turned his attention to the gulch floor. A broken streak, like a dotted line, of churned and broken earth ran just north of the stream, ending in a small, comet-shaped crater a hundred or so meters from the base of the hill where he and his men had taken position. Peng didn't need to be a scientist to know what happened: The satellite came in at a shallow angle and skipped along the ground, losing momentum with each bounce until it came to rest in the soft, wet ground at the base of the hill. Along the path he could see bits of metal, part of a solar array, a chunk of what looked like it might have been an antenna at one time, and other items Peng couldn't even guess about. It was the large, battered piece of junk in the crater that kept Peng's attention. The heart of his mission was just meters away.

"Gao, reading?" Peng looked to his left where Gao Zhi lay on the damp earth. The man slipped off his backpack and produced a small, handheld Geiger counter.

"Background radiation only."

Peng looked to his right. "Wei, report our status."

"Yes, Captain." Wei Dong sent a coded text, impossible to trace. "Situation reported. Acknowledgment received."

"Understood." Peng studied the shallow valley. He listened again but still heard only birds. It was time to get this done and leave the area. "Wei, Gao, Zhao, I want a three-point perimeter."

Zhao, the ranking member of the three, answered for them. "Yes, Captain."

"Hsu, you're with me."

"Yes, sir."

Peng pushed to his feet and moved slowly down the slope, his men on either side of him. A glance to Gao showed he was taking constant readings on the Geiger counter.

When they reached the satellite, Peng was finally convinced they were the only ones in the area. He relaxed.

PRESIDENT HUFFINGTON WAS UNFLAPPABLE, most of the time, but sitting in the Situation Room watching the real-time satellite feed of a military team other than his own reach Angel-12 first undid him. He pushed his chair back, paced, and used language his wife would spend weeks scolding him for. At the moment, that was the least of his concerns. The Chinese beat them.

"I don't believe it. They beat us."

"It's not over yet, Mr. President," Admiral Gaughan said. He sat two chairs down from the head of the table where the president had been sitting a moment before. To the left of the president's spot was Helen Brown. Across the table from her, his head resting in his hands, sat Bacliff.

Huffington rubbed the back of his neck. "How did we get behind? Despite their statements to the contrary, we know the Chinese have been planning this for some time, but we have the better technology."

"It's not how advanced out technology is, Mr. President," Brown said. "The Chinese don't need superior technology—and let's not lie to ourselves, they have great tech—they just need adequate technology. Tracking satellite motion doesn't require the latest tech, just good-enough tech."

Huffington stared at the screen. He had been watching the Chinese team inch their way closer to the downed bird. He pulled out all the stops. The president turned to Brown. "Brownie, I want the Chinese ambassador in the Oval Office as soon as possible. Tell him, I'll be calling his premier in one hour."

"Yes, sir." Brown excused herself and stepped from the room.

Huffington turned to Gaughan. "Where are our men now?"

"They're still a ways out. They're following a convoy of trucks."

"The ones we assume are from the Russian splinter group?"

"Yes, sir. They're staying well back."

"How could they let themselves fall into third position?"

Gaughan cleared his throat. "Well sir, the Russians were already in the area. We assume they got some of their information from moles in the legitimate government of the Russian Federation. That's how these things usually work. And the Chinese . . . well, they were just sneakier and more brazen than we were."

"Maybe they could teach us something. Have you confirmed they exited from a wayward, crippled cargo jet?"

"Confidence is in the 95-percent range. When the pilot of the MD-90 squawked his transponder to the emergency frequency, we picked it up and tracked the plane with radar in Sapporo, Japan. We also had a few intel assets near the Sea of Okhotsk that followed the radio traffic between the Chinese pilot, the Russian escort planes, and Chinese traffic control. Bottom line: The aircraft made it back to Chinese airspace but at very low altitude. It then switched off its transponder. We think it used a false signal. We don't believe it crashed."

"So the whole thing was a ruse?"

"Yes, sir, and a good one."

"But your earlier report said the aircraft was an MD-90 used by a Chinese cargo company. Hardly the kind of thing troops would parachute from, especially using those things Moyer described."

"Yes, sir, the powered parachute. We can only guess, but the MD-90 has a rear emergency exit. It's possible they used that to make their jump."

Huffington looked at the video feed. "Let's get Colonel Mac on the feed. I know he's watching this at Fort Jackson."

"Yes, sir."

A moment later the video image of Colonel MacGregor appeared on one of the screens to the side of the large main screen.

"Mr. President."

"Can you explain your men, Colonel?"

"Sir?"

"I'm starting to feel like the fourth runner-up in a three-man race. Why is the team behind the Russians?"

"I don't have specifics, sir, but I can assure you they're doing everything they can."

"You know what my fear is, don't you?"

Mac grimaced. "My guess is you would have several fears."

"I do, and right now they all center on one thing: Is the team behind because of Moyer? Has news of his daughter hampered his ability to lead the mission?"

Even over the video link, Huffington could see Mac's expression sour. "Sir, such news would knock anyone off their pins. Moyer is reporting in just as he should, and I'm sure he's doing the best possible work given the circumstances."

"So what do we do about the Chinese?"

"Sir, on my first mission I learned one thing that has guided my leadership through the years. A soldier is at his best if he concentrates on what is in front of him. If that changes, the mission changes. We don't know the condition of Angel-12. It might take hours for the Chinese to strip out the electronics and optics. Our men will be on scene long before that."

"Then what? A gun battle?"

"Maybe, sir. That will be Moyer's call. The Chinese getting there first changes things. What they do will determine what we do."

"So we do what?"

"Wait, sir. There is nothing else that can be done, at least not in the field."

"I can think of several things." Huffington returned to his chair. "I don't like any of them."

"Such as."

Huffington hesitated. "That will be all for now, Colonel."

The video link to Colonel Mac was closed.

"Admiral."

"Sir?"

"Is the *Monsoor* still in the area?"

"It is." The admiral stiffened. "They're waiting to help with extraction."

"Move them as close to Russian waters as possible and have them stand by for my orders."

"What orders, sir?"

"If I have to, I will put a Tomahawk cruise missile on the site."

Bacliff's head snapped up. "That might endanger our team and it would put an end to the rescue operation."

"I know, old friend, and I'm sorry, but I can't let that technology fall into the hands of the Chinese or Russians. I'll destroy it and everything around it if I have to."

Bacliff pinched the bridge of his nose. "Don't you mean destroy everyone around it?"

"Yes, I mean that too."

"Sir, firing a cruise missile into Russian territory will be impossible to explain and may create problems taking a decade to undo."

"I'm aware of the ramifications. It's the last thing I want to do."

"You will let our men know first, won't you?" Gaughan asked.

"If possible, yes."

"If possible?"

"You heard me, Admiral. Now make the order and pray we don't have to use it."

Huffington stared at the monitor and watched the Chinese team as they reached Angel-12. "You know," he said to no one in particular, "I sometimes wonder what I ever saw in this job that made me want it."

No one spoke. That was fine with the president.

CHAPTER 29

GINA SPENT THE LAST few hours staring at her bare legs. She had cried all she could, but the emotional roller-coaster ride continued. Fear gave way to despair, which moved over anger which, in turn, surrendered depression. All positive emotions like happiness and peace seemed like distant sensations experienced in a dream.

She tried to occupy her mind with escape. The cut flesh beneath the nylon ties was her own doing and now the skin burned and itched. She studied the ties. She had seen the kind before. Her father used them in the garage to strap things together. Once he used them to bind the many cables behind the television, satellite receiver, and sound system into neat bundles. He also used them to keep an extra hose wound in place and hung on a wall. When he took the hose down months later to use it for some work he was doing in the backyard, he didn't release them; he cut them with wire cutters. That's what she needed: a free hand and wire cutters.

The door to her cell opened and another black-clad figure entered the room. Like the first, this person wore black pants, a black top like a sweatshirt, black gloves, and a full over-the-head mask. Even the sport shoes the person wore were black.

But this was not the same person. The suit could not disguise the shorter height, the rounder hips, and the breasts.

She carried a tray with a plate on which sat a sandwich and potato chips. There was also a clear plastic bottle of clear fluid. Gina assumed water.

The woman set the tray on Gina's lap, reached to a back pocket of her pants, and removed—wire cutters. A snip later and Gina's right hand was free.

"Do you see the video camera over the door?"

"Of course I do."

"Good. There is someone watching you at all times."

"Must be pretty boring, since I can't do anything."

She shrugged and looked at Gina's wrists. "That little tantrum did you more harm than good. I'm going to leave your hand free so you can eat. I'll be back with some medication for those cuts. Don't be stupid and try anything you'll regret. Remember—"

"Someone is watching me all the time."

"Smart girl. Do you have to go to the bathroom?"

"Yes. You going to videotape that too?"

"You do have a mouth on you. Get your attitude from your father?"

"What do you know about my father?"

"I know he's gone when you need him most. Eat the sandwich. I'll be back. Try and be a good girl while I'm away."

The woman left and Gina picked up the sandwich. Baloney. She hated lunch meat but took a bite. She hadn't eaten since dinner the night before. She had no idea what time it was, but her stomach told her she missed breakfast and maybe lunch as well. The sandwich tasted good. It had mayo, something else she despised but not enough to refuse to eat. The potato chips were salty and greasy but the best part of the meal. There was nothing special about the water other than it was lukewarm.

She consumed the meal in just a few minutes. The sustenance settled her stomach a little. The woman in black returned with a first-aid kit, a towel, and a sports bottle of water.

"You made short work of that."

Gina didn't respond. Instead, she examined the tray, looking for anything she could use to help free herself. She hoped for a plastic knife but found nothing useful. These weren't the kind of people who made mistakes.

"Let me see your arm."

Gina didn't move.

"I'm not going to hurt you."

"Really? Silly me, being kidnapped and tied to a chair must have made me a little paranoid."

"Just let me see your wrists."

Finally Gina held out her free arm. "Happy?"

"The cuts aren't deep but I bet they sting. I'm going to rinse the wounds, dry them, and put on an ointment that will keep them from hurting so much."

"I didn't say they hurt."

The woman's shoulders dipped. "You are a tough little girl. I was the same way at your age. We have something in common."

"Except I don't kidnap and terrorize teenagers."

The woman moved Gina's arm so it extended to the side and raised the water bottle, squirting a stream in the wounds. The cold water stung and dripped from her arm to the floor. Her captor dabbed the area dry, then spread the ointment over the wounds, covering it with a self-adhesive gauze patch to hold the medicine in place.

She freed Gina's other arm and repeated the steps. "Better?"

"I guess. How about my clothes? That would make me feel better."

"We'll see. First, I'm going to take you to a bathroom. To do that, I'll have to blindfold you, and of course, I'll have to release the rest of the restraints. You will cooperate with me. Do you hear? I'm a nice person at heart, but somewhere along the line I lost my conscience, so if you give me any trouble, I'll put your head through a wall. If you try to run, it'll be your head through a wall. If you scream—"

"My head, your wall. I get it."

The woman produced an opaque band of cloth and wrapped it around Gina's eyes. Moments later the nylon ties around her ankles were clipped away and the band over her thighs and the one around her waist slipped away.

A strong hand pulled her to her feet and led her slowly from the room.

"YOU'VE BEEN AWFULLY QUIET since we left the colonel." Wallace insisted on driving the CID-issued sedan, which was fine with Zinsser: He had a lot to think about.

"Yeah, lots on my mind."

"He booted his aide and me out because he wanted to talk to you privately. He was protecting us. Am I right?"

"No, he was protecting Sergeant Kinkaid. He hates you."

"Well, the feeling is mutual."

"What you need to know, Boss, is this: This may hit the fan and if it does, you're going to cover Colonel Mac's six."

"I am? Are we forgetting who's in charge here?"

"I haven't forgotten a thing, but this case is different. In most cases, I'm an outsider coming to the crime scene. Here, well, I know these people and I owe them a lot. I know I'm being a little footloose with rules and regs. I've always been that way. I need you to bear with me on this."

"You've been a pain in my butt for a long time, Zinsser. Why should I?"

"Because you can't resist my baby blues."

"I'm gonna need more than that, bub. Your baby blues do nothing for me."

"This isn't a typical murder, AWOL, drug trafficking, or embezzlement from military funds. This is real war, Boss. What we do may impact the lives of a lot of people."

"I know what real war is, Zinsser. I've done a couple of tours in Iraq and one in Afghanistan."

"Then you know what I'm talking about. Look, you can fire me when all this is over if you want. I'll go make lattes in some coffee shop, but for now, give me some leeway."

"You're asking me to trust you."

"Yes, I am."

"Well, why didn't you just say so? Understand this, when it hits the fan, I want you standing in front of me."

"Count on it, Boss. Count on it."

TESS WAS PACING HER apartment. She was supposed to be working on a short course for a seminar at the Army War College in Carlisle, Pennsylvania. Since marrying J. J., she reduced her hours so she could live near Fort Jackson with him. Not willing to let her go, the War College talked her into teaching a few days each month in seminar form. She was happy to do it. Study and teaching were her life. It was her way of contributing to her country. She still taught symposiums on suicide bombers, especially the rise in female bombers, but she also had intel expertise. More than once she worked with one of the alphabet soup intelligence agencies.

Colonel Mac used her skills on a few occasions, especially when the team was in Italy and other countries last year chasing down a group of female suicide bombers. Now her husband was in Russia without an invitation. Her last meeting with Mac gave her chills and robbed her of any appetite.

She was in a unique position. No other team member could reveal to his family what J. J. could reveal to her. Her expertise and previous involvement with a mission gave her inner-circle access. Unlike the other wives, Tess knew the dangers her man had faced; not in general but in detail. While wanting to feel privileged by her special standing, being married to one of the men in the field caused her more concern; knowledge brought sharper, serrated fear.

Tess put on a pot of tea. Its shrill whistle demanded attention. She walked from the small apartment living room to the smaller kitchen and took hold of the pot's handle. Her hand was shaking. Instead of water pouring from the spout in an even stream, it jiggled and sloshed. Still, she managed not to spill. A few moments later, the cran-apple flavored herb tea had steeped, and Tess carried it to the dining room table. She sat and opened a Bible—J. J.'s favorite Bible.

She had no reading plan, no particular passage in mind. She just needed to read words providing some comfort, some confidence, some reminder God was still on His throne.

She opened the text to the middle of the book and found the Old Testament book of Psalms, a collection of song lyrics written by many godly people, but mostly by King David. J. J. loved David's psalms. She remembered asking him why.

"Because he was a poetic warrior, a leader, a soldier, a ruler. Not perfect by any means, but in good and bad he clung to God and never apologized for it. At times he had to flee to save his life; at other times he had to wade into battle. In some ways, we are alike."

"You and King David?" She chuckled, then stopped. He was being serious.

"I know he was a far greater man than I'll ever be, but the same mouth that gave orders to enter battle was the same mouth that sang praises to God."

J. J. was always honest with Tess. They had, on many occasions, discussed the tension between his faith and his duty. It was the kind of conversation that could only be shared among intimates, but it was also the kind of topic in which she could offer no advice. Ironic. She advised intelligence agencies and military leaders, but she couldn't guide her own husband through the winding, oftentimes uphill path of the soul.

J. J. was a kind man, a man honest with himself and therefore with Tess. "I've killed men, Tess, but only because I've had to." He spoke of the narco-terrorist in Mexico who held innocents captive and how, as team sniper, he had to down several men, shooting them while they stood near the window of a warehouse used to store drugs and the firefight that came after that—a firefight that left him wounded and bleeding nearly to death. He survived by God's will and the quick work of his team. He spoke of killing innocent shepherds that he and the team believed were part of a terrorist camp in Afghanistan. There were other stories, and J. J. told each one with a measure of pride doused in regret.

Once he said: "Do you know what my greatest fear is, Tess?"

She didn't, but said she did.

"My biggest fear is losing my sense of regret. On mission, I can't think about my feelings, can't second-guess an order, can't doubt a mission. When I pull the trigger, I need to do it because there is no other choice, but if I forget that I'm taking human life, then I stop being human. I'm afraid of losing my spiritual conscience."

Tess knew military lifers and saw what a stripped conscience could do to a person. She also knew enough heroes to know that being a soldier doesn't require the surrender of one's mind. J. J. would never become a flesh-and-blood machine.

Tess flipped through the pages of J. J.'s NIV Bible and found a passage marked with yellow highlighter, Psalm 144:1–2:

> Praise be to the LORD my Rock,
> who trains my hands for war,
> my fingers for battle.
> He is my loving God and my fortress,
> my stronghold and my deliverer,
> my shield, in whom I take refuge,
> who subdues peoples under me.

Tess raised her trembling hand, interlaced her fingers, closed her eyes, and prayed for J. J., the team, and Moyer's family.

The phone rang, startling Tess so much she nearly knocked her teacup over. She glanced at the clock. She had been praying for half an hour; it seemed like moments.

It rang again, its sound foreboding.

Tess set her hand on the cell phone and raised it. It took another second for her to tap the talk key. "Yes."

"Tess? It's Colonel MacGregor. I need you."

"My husband—"

"No change in status. I'll see you soon." He hung up. Mac was never one for pleasantries.

Two minutes later, Tess was out the door.

CHAPTER 30

"YOU'RE THINKING AGAIN, COLT."

J. J. looked up from his uncomfortable seat near the FedEx truck's rear door. "How can you tell, Shaq?"

"There's smoke coming out your ears."

"Sorry, I forgot to oil my mental gears."

"So what's got you so preoccupied?"

Now everyone in the back of the van was looking at him. He was certain if Lev could pull it off, he'd turn around in the driver's seat and stare too.

"What? A man can't think?"

Moyer spoke, breaking thirty minutes of silence. J. J. had seen the man in every kind of situation. He saw Moyer when he was deep into his beer, when he was leading the team in physical training, when he faced off with high-ranking officers, and when he was in the heat of battle. But nowhere, at anytime, had he seen the mask of neutrality the team leader had been wearing since he received word about his abducted daughter.

"You're the thinker of the group," Moyer said in a flat tone. "When you think, we all get nervous."

"Hey!" Pete said. "I think. So does Doc. Shaq, well never mind."

"You know you're within arm's length, don't you, Junior?" Icicles hung from Rich's words.

"Can it, guys." Moyer didn't bother to open his eyes. "We still good, Lev?"

"No. There's a vodka shortage in the cab."

"When this is all over and if we're not moldering in some field, I'll buy you a vat of the stuff so you can drown yourself in it. I ask again, are we still good?"

"Yes, Mr. Boss. The Russians are still well ahead of us. They can't see us, but I can see the dust they're kicking up."

"Good." Moyer opened his eyes and directed them at J. J., who not only saw this but somehow felt it. "Okay, Colt. Spill it. You got a sermon to share or something?"

J. J. laughed. "Preaching isn't part of my skill set, Boss. The last thing you need to hear is me preaching."

"Uh-huh. So what's on your mind?"

"Just batting ideas around."

"You're avoiding the question."

"Yeah, Colt," Shaq added, "you're avoiding the question."

J. J. grew nervous. "I was thinking about your situation, Boss. You and your family."

"What about it, Colt?" The words were hard.

J. J. smiled. "I've been thinking about a phrase I heard in a song. It's been haunting me."

"What phrase? What song?"

"The song's been covered by several people, but I keep hearing Rufus Wainwright. The song is 'Hallelujah.'"

"Leonard Cohen wrote it in 1984." Crispin removed the earbuds. "Colt's right, at least a half-dozen people have recorded it. It was in one of the *Shrek* movies. That made it famous."

All eyes shifted to Crispin.

"Hey, I know a little bit about music."

"Carry on, Colt," Moyer said.

"The song uses biblical stories. To be honest, it's sort of a mishmash of things that raises more questions than it answers. Sometimes the singers change the lyrics. For example, Cohen uses the phrase 'the holy dove.' Wainwright and others use 'the holy dark.' That's the phrase I've been thinking about. 'Holy dark'."

"Does this go anywhere? What does that have to do with my . . . situation?"

"Okay, here's where it gets preachy. People—by which I mean guys like me—always associate holiness with light. Nothing wrong with that. Saying 'the holy light' just sounds right and fits with what the Bible teaches, but the reverse—although it doesn't sound right—is true."

"Holy dark," Moyer muttered.

"Yes, Boss. What I've been thinking about is that God might be in the dark as much as in the light. My brother once preached a sermon about Solomon building the temple in Jerusalem. When he finished Solomon said, 'The Lord said that He would dwell in thick darkness'—a holy dark."

"Deep stuff for such a shallow mind." Rich delivered the words with a grin.

"All I'm saying is that God is in the darkness with you. There is a holy dark."

"Thanks, Colt. I know you mean well, but I'm just not feeling it. I can only feel one thing right now: fear for my daughter."

"Understood, Boss. I'm just sayin'."

"I hear ya, Colt. Maybe it will mean something to me someday."

Lev's voice wafted to the back. "If the church service is over, I should tell you we're coming up to the coordinates you gave me. What do you want me to do now?"

Moyer moved from his seat in the back and leaned into the cab. "Leave the road. Drive as far as you can. We need to conceal the truck."

"I can see a stand of old trees fifty meters up the slope."

"Do it. We'll go the rest of the way on foot."

"Won't that slow you down?"

Moyer put a hand on the Russian's shoulder. "We like to be fashionably late."

Lev slowed and turned up a grassy slope, accelerating to gain traction. "You know, I'm leaving tracks they can follow."

"They don't know we're here and I've got a feeling they're going to have other things on their minds."

"If you say so, Boss man."

"I say so."

Moyer turned to the team. "Okay, let's see if Colt is right about God being in the dark."

"But it's still light outside," Crispin said.

"It's a euphemism, Hawkeye," Pete said.

"Oh."

ROB HEARD THE SOFT voice of Special Agent Brianne Lazzaro. "You're not doing yourself any good by watching that tape over and over again."

"I'm not trying to do anything good for me; I'm trying to do some good for my sister."

Brianne sat in one of the dining room chairs brought in earlier when Zinsser and Wallace were going over the video. "We have specialists working on it, Rob."

"So what? Another pair of eyes won't hurt anything."

"I'm worried about you. That's all."

He snapped at her. "Maybe things would work better if you worried about my sister."

She put a hand on his arm. "I'm not the enemy here. You know that. CID and the FBI are doing everything that can be done. Your mother needs you to be strong and to be present, not hiding out here."

He turned to face her. She was gorgeous on a dozen different levels, although older than him by fifteen years. He could lose himself in her eyes—any other time but now. The only thing he could think about was Gina, the times he teased her too severely; the times he made fun of her friends; the times he upset her world by bringing discord into the house.

The muscles constricted in his chest, and for a moment his heart seemed ready to burst like a balloon, leaving ripped tissue fluttering in the center of his chest. Fearing a nervous breakdown, he turned back to the computer. His eyes pointed at the screen but he saw nothing. Nothing. Nothing. Nothing.

"You all right, kid?" Brianne's hard FBI special agent tone turned nurturing.

"Yeah. I guess. I just keep thinking we're missing some clue in this video."

"You can't see what's not there."

"Something has to be here. No one is perfect. There must be a goof, a mistake somewhere that leaves a clue."

"Rob, let the professionals do this."

"I'm not stopping them."

Brianne opened her mouth to speak again when her BlackBerry went off. She answered, rose, and left the room.

Rob was glad she was gone. She didn't understand. Couldn't understand. To her, this was just another kidnapping, another task to be completed on her to-do list. He would do whatever he could. Minutes mattered.

Minutes mattered . . . mattered. Rob covered his face with his hand to hide the tears he could no longer hold back.

ZINSSER STEPPED FROM THE car the moment Wallace pulled to the curb. Wallace insisted they return to the office where they would have more assets available to them. It made sense, but Zinsser wanted to check on Rob and Stacy. Wallace acquiesced, clearly weary of arguing. As Zinsser slipped from the passenger seat, Agent Lazzaro stepped from the house, as if she knew what minute they'd be arriving. She had her phone to her ear. She nodded several times as if the caller could see her.

He started to walk past her when she took his arm in an unexpectedly strong grasp.

"Got it. Good work." She put the phone away.

"Do you mind?" Zinsser glanced at his arm.

"Oh, sorry." She let go. "Good news. The video forensic team has made a discovery."

"What discovery?" Wallace joined them.

"They've identified the kind of camera used to make the video."

"That was quick," Wallace said. "Faster than we could have done it."

Brianne shrugged. "Like I said, the president calls the FBI director and motivation sweeps through every corner of the bureau. How did you get such a powerful friend, Agent Zinsser?"

"We like the same kind of pancake syrup." He waited for a laugh but when he didn't get one, he continued. "Long story, one which I can't tell you even if we had the time. What'd your team find?"

"Some video cameras, especially the higher-priced ones, come with a metafile, watermark creator. You know, invisible markers placed in the digital fabric of the video. These can be read with the right kind of software. It just so happens we have that software. The video was made with a Sentratronics XG200 security camera. It comes with a digital recorder that works like a store security camera catching only a few frames every few seconds, or it can be used at regular recording speeds—which our black hats did."

"Okay, but that helps us how . . . They sell these in home-improvement stores?"

"You're getting it, Zinsser. And here's the bonus: These things are at the upper range of the cameras sold in such stores, meaning—"

Wallace jumped in. "Meaning they sell fewer of those than lesser-priced security systems."

Zinsser smiled. "That lowers the number of candidates. There might be hundreds of people who buy two-by-fours, drywall, and white paint. We search for someone who bought those items, maybe some tools, but also the security system."

Brianne nodded repeatedly. "It narrows things quite a bit."

"It's time to pull out the stops." Wallace reached for his cell phone. "Can you get more agents hitting these stores? We're smaller than the FBI, but I'll pull everyone out of the office and get them on it." Wallace looked at Zinsser. "What about the cops? Did you offend them so much they'll refuse a little interagency cooperation?"

"Um, you may want to call them. Detective Angie Wells wants to control everything, but I believe she's a committed cop. Police sergeant Crivello is a stand-up guy. I'd work through one of them."

Wallace turned and started making phone calls.

"How're Rob and Stacy doing?"

Brianne saddened. "Not good. Rob is trying to man up and take charge of things, but he's way out of his depth."

"He's barely eighteen."

"I'm not being critical; I'm giving a report. Stacy has yet to sleep. She looks like she's been run over by a very long train. Gina's friends have gone home. I pushed them out the door so Stacy could rest. She kept fixing drinks and food for them."

"Understandable. The chaplain?"

"Bartley is still here. He said another chaplain will be over tonight. He's called the wives of some of Moyer's men. A couple are coming over with dinner for the family. Maybe they can get them to eat."

PRESIDENT HUFFINGTON HAD ENTERTAINED Ambassador Hui Xu on several occasions. One of the hallmarks of his administration was tightening the bond between China and the United States. Huffington was about to blow that out of the water.

Huffington stewed as he sat in his high-backed leather chair behind the presidential desk. Hui was late and there could only be two reasons: One, he was conferring with his home office, or two, he was making known his displeasure about being summoned on short notice. Either way, the man succeeded in making Huffington angrier than he already was.

The phone on his desk beeped. He punched a button and heard the gentle voice of his personal secretary. "Ambassador Hui is here, sir."

"Show him in."

Helen Brown entered a moment before Hui, took one look at the president, and sighed. "This isn't going to be pretty, is it?"

"Not by a long shot."

The door to the Oval Office opened and Hui, a thin, aristocratic-looking man entered, a disingenuous smile glued to his face. Brownie moved to him, bowed slightly, and held out her hand. Hui took her hand and held it for ten seconds. He then bowed to her.

"It is always my highest pleasure to see you, Ms. Brown. I hope you are well."

"I am, Ambassador Hui."

They turned to face Huffington. What was supposed to happen, what had happened in the past, what Huffington originally planned was this: The president would stand, step to his guest, bow, take the man's hand in a gentle but protracted handshake, praise him for coming on such short notice, and ask about his health. He would refer to the man by his title and family name. Never his given name—which in China always appeared second—and use his title frequently.

That was what was meant to happen, but Huffington decided he had enough of small talk and social customs.

"You're late, Xu."

Two insults in three words. A new record for the president.

The color drained from the ambassador's face, replaced by a red tinge. "Yes, Mr. President. I had urgent business that delayed me."

Here is where Huffington was to offer Hui a seat. He didn't.

"Remind me, Mr. Ambassador. Whose country are you in?"

The man paused and pressed his lips together. "Why, I live in your wonderful country."

"Do you like it, Hui?"

"Very much, Mr. President." The man had to press the words through clenched teeth.

"I see. Well, since you are so busy as to keep the president of your host nation waiting, a president with some pressing business of his own, I'll get down to business."

"I can sense some tension, Mr. President. Perhaps we should sit and discuss what it is that is bothering you."

"You will not sit in my office until I'm satisfied with the next series of events." Huffington stood and motioned Brown to open the doors of the custom entertainment center where a large flat-screen television sat.

"I don't understand the source of your anger, Mr. President. Perhaps I should come back at another time." He turned.

"If you walk out that door, you will need to go to your embassy and pack, because I will have you, your family, and your staff escorted out of the country." Huffington rounded his desk and stepped close to the ambassador, invading his personal space. "I'm going to talk. You're going to listen."

"I'm not used to being treated so rudely."

"You'll live, even if your career doesn't." The president took a breath, the kind a man takes when he's about to let loose a tirade. "Not long ago one of your satellites targeted, impacted, and knocked one of our satellites from the sky."

"Sir, I have already apologized for the inadvertent—"

"There was nothing inadvertent about it! We have done a trajectory analysis and know for a fact you targeted that one satellite with hopes of bringing it down in eastern China. But we moved it at the last moment. Not much, but enough to change its path of entry. It landed in eastern Siberia. This you know because using a very clever ploy, you dropped five men into the area. They're at the crash site right now."

"Sir, I know nothing about this."

"I think you do, Ambassador. I know for a fact you do. Do you know how I spent my time while waiting for you to show up? I spent it talking to President Urie Solovyov. Have you met him? Nice guy. A real progressive. I asked a favor." He turned to Brown. "Hit it, Brownie."

She touched the play button on the DVR just below the television. The screen brightened and ran a thirty-second video of a cruise missile leaving a Navy destroyer, then cutting away to it striking a bunker. Brown turned the screen off.

"That, Ambassador, is an older version of one of our TLAMs— that's Tomahawk Land Attack Missiles. Forgive me for not giving details, but the one I have in mind is newer and, shall we say, more effective. I can put one of those within ten feet of any target I like. Right now that target is my fallen satellite. Of course your men are there."

"You would fire on the Russian Federation? I think not."

"Think what you will, but I already have permission from the Russian government. Once Solovyov heard it was Chinese military that invaded their land under a ruse, well, he was begging me to pull the trigger."

"I shouldn't have to remind you that you have a team within their borders. We have our sources too, Mr. President."

"I'm sure you do, Mr. Ambassador."

Hui frowned. "It causes me pain to be so rude as to bring up the enormous debt the American people owe my country—"

"I'm aware of the debt created by previous administrations, but be careful about throwing that in my face. We've made our payments as scheduled. Your name means 'wise,' Mr. Ambassador. It would be unwise to challenge me on this. Do not think because we are indebted to you that we are owned by you."

"Mr. President—"

"We're done, Mr. Ambassador. Your tardiness has caused me to be late for an important meeting. I want your men clear of the satellite in the next hour, or you will be picking up their pieces for months to come."

"I will speak to my government."

"Thank you, Mr. Ambassador. You now have fifty-nine minutes."

Ambassador Hui Xu walked from the room.

"Ouch. I knew you were going to blindside him, but I didn't expect you to beat him with a verbal bat."

"I'm a little irritable tonight."

"You normally have me in the room when you talk to heads of state. How hard did you have to work President Solovyov?"

"Are you kidding? I didn't talk to him. The runt hates me. He'd never give permission for a cruise missile skimming his eastern mountains."

"You amaze me."

"You should see my poker game."

"I think I just did."

CHAPTER 31

PENG STOOD NEXT TO the still-smoldering wreckage of the American satellite and tried to wrap his mind around the thought that the object, not that long ago, was circling tens of thousands of miles overhead. It was an interesting truth, one he might have dwelt on were it not for other concerns on his mind. Gao, his master sergeant, passed the Geiger counter to Peng and took one of the three points of the triangular perimeter his team established. The three lowest-ranking men lay on their bellies, scanning the forest line a short distance off for any movement. Hsu, the only other officer on the team, stood with Peng at the satellite.

Peng passed the handheld device over the crumbled, burned, bent, metal corpse. "No radiation beyond background. The fuel cell must be intact."

"A good thing for us. I plan on having more children—normal children."

Peng seldom joked but couldn't resist. "Think of the advantage of having a boy who glows in the dark. Easy to find."

"Yes, sir."

"You're agreeing just to be polite."

The lieutenant smiled. "Yes, sir."

Peng glanced around the area one more time, then confident they were alone in the wilderness, called for the tools.

Hsu dropped his pack and fished out a kit of battery-powered microtools. They were lucky, one of the items they were tasked to find was within easy reach, the result of a lucky bounce. Peng focused on a scarred and scorched plastic window. He ran a gloved hand over the surface and brushed away mud, grass, twigs, and leaves. He cupped his hands, blocking the glare, and peered into the space behind. A large lens was mounted in what looked like a universal bracket that allowed the lens to move in two dimensions. He was told the lens system was probably a compound system of several lenses, a charged-couple device that converted images gathered from space into digital format for enhancement and transmission.

The technology was well beyond him, but he knew enough to know he was looking at the latest advancements. He was also looking at billions of dollars of research and development. A little back engineering and his government could make great strides in a very short time.

Peng was also to photograph everything. Carrying off in-flight propulsion units would be useful but impractical. Thruster design had not changed dramatically over the last few years—or so he was told. In truth, his government excelled in that area. However, optics were highly specialized.

The team was also to retrieve the "brains" of the satellite, the computer that monitored position, analyzed image integrity, and communicated with ground control.

He was also ordered to remove anything that looked interesting and if he couldn't remove it, to photograph it in detail. Peng had no idea what his superiors might consider interesting.

Hsu removed a small, battery-powered set of sheet metal shears, set the sharp jaws into a gap formed by buckled metal, and pulled the trigger. The noise set him on edge, the sound of it echoing down the narrow valley.

Peng hoped there was no one else to hear.

MOYER, OUT OF IMPATIENCE born by too much time in the back of a delivery van, took point, jogging at a slower rate than his mind begged. Six men—he left Lev to hide and protect the FedEx vehicle—tramping through a thin forest at full run would be heard at distance. Moyer didn't want to be heard.

The slower pace gave him another problem. It gave him time to think. Normally a good thing, thinking had become problematic: 98 percent of his thinking was about Gina. Even now as he ducked beneath low branches, her image flashed on his brain like a strobe light. His stomach twisted into a tighter knot; something he didn't think possible. The urge to fall to his knees and weep alternated with the pressing desire to scream at the top of his lungs and shoot anything that moved.

Although no scholar, Moyer did enjoy a good read. His wife gave him Edmund Morris's *Theodore Rex*, the story of Theodore Roosevelt and his rise to the presidency. Teddy Roosevelt was a military man's president, tested in battle and not afraid to unleash soldiers into battle.

One part of the book touched him. He hadn't known Teddy lost his mother and wife on the same day, in the same house. A young New York legislator at the time, the future president raced home by train and buggy in time to hold each as they died.

The sudden deaths so grieved him he lost himself. He wrote in his journal, "Today the life has gone out of my life." He took his newborn child—Roosevelt's wife died in childbirth—and presented her to his sister. He then took care of the funerals, left home, went hunting in the wilderness, and killed everything that moved. The list of animals he felled numbered in the hundreds. When Moyer read the account, he assumed Teddy overreacted. Now he understood. Killing something sounded good.

Pushing aside unwanted thoughts, he forced himself into soldier mode; something he seldom had to do while on mission. It lasted thirty seconds. As he trudged up the slope he thought of Stacy. She must be beside herself. How could he not be there for her? What good were a husband's strong arms when they were so many miles away?

Then there was Rob. More teenager than man. Never tested by hardship; never forced to face danger; never called upon to step up. He missed his son.

A sound, mechanical but distant, pushed through the noise of his footfalls and heavy breath. He snapped one hand up in a clenched fist. His team stopped midstep. Moyer raised a cupped hand to his ear, signaling he heard something. The sound of birds filled the air, then the noise reached them again. Moyer, a lover of tools, recognized it immediately. Someone was using a power tool on metal. The fact he could recognize it told him they were close to the satellite, and as he expected, the Chinese were already there.

Moyer moved to the crest of the hill and took cover behind a fallen tree. Shrubs grew around the moldering trunk. Before dropping behind the tree, he extended his left arm to the side, calling for an abreast configuration. His men spread to the side forming a line, each separated by three or more yards, depending on the cover they could find.

Moyer raised his binoculars and studied the situation. The battered remains of Angel-12 lay partially buried in the soft dirt of the valley. Surrounding the satellite stood five Chinese soldiers in full gear. Two worked on the satellite; three formed a perimeter.

"I make five armed hostiles," Moyer whispered, the throat mike picking up every word.

"Roger that, Boss. I make the same." It was Rich's job to confirm the situation. "I count four QBZ-95 automatics and a QBU-88 good-guy killer."

"Boss?"

"Go, Colt."

"The QBU-88 is an anti-personnel, anti-material sniper rifle. Suggest we target him first. I don't want to eat any rounds, but I sure don't want to eat one that treats my body armor like tissue paper."

"Colt, you're on him but don't fire unless I tell you. That goes for everyone." He sighted the area. "Shaq, you take the guy with the tool; Junior, I want you sighted on his partner. Doc, you take the perimeter man on the east. I got the other one. I repeat, no shooting until I give the go."

Moyer scanned the forested area to the northeast. That's where they'd approach. He saw nothing. He listened but heard only the action of the power tool on sheet metal. The tool was laboring. Apparently the beast was made of sterner stuff than the Chinese anticipated.

"Hawkeye?"

"Go, Boss."

"Time to do your magic. Break out a nano."

"Roger that, Boss. Got just the thing."

Moyer looked to his left. The newest team member was pulling gear from his rucksack. Crispin was part of the team for this very reason: He was an expert in nano UAVs. The tiny, remote-control aircraft were growing in use for recon work. Unmanned Aerial Vehicles ranged from full-sized aircraft to small planes like the Wasp III micro air vehicle used by the Air Force Spec Ops. Its wingspan was just a little over two feet. Still, that was too large for this situation and difficult to carry in backpacks.

The Defense Advanced Research Projects Agency—DARPA— had been developing these small aircraft for years. MAVs, sometimes called nanos, were so small that at a distance they could be mistaken for birds or insects. Crispin's toys were a little larger, but not by much.

Moyer pushed back from the log and crawled to Crispin's location. When he reached the young soldier's hidey-hole, he found him busily setting up what looked like a toy.

"I'm assuming a hovering recon would be best, as opposed to a quick flyover. I've got both." He opened a padded box and removed a white plastic plane with rear wings and a rear propeller. It looked like a great toy, except it was far more expensive. From nose to tail it was just a few inches long. Crispin opened another box and removed a four-inch-long helicopter. "I recommend the *Voyager*. We don't have much wind and it has good gust control."

"Will they hear it?"

"Not likely. I can keep it high enough that they shouldn't see it or hear it."

"Just the same. I want to keep it out of view of the Chinese."

Crispin looked at him. "I thought you wanted a bird's-eye view of what they were doing."

Moyer shook his head. "I already know what they're doing."

"Ah, you're thinking the Russians."

"You got it. Now earn your nick, Hawkeye. Send your toy around the tree to that area over there." Moyer pointed northeast. "If I've guessed correctly, our new friends are going to come through

there. They need an area with few trees to get that truck in. If they're
not there, then you can do a flyby over the Chinese, but make sure
it comes from across the valley. If they see little Binky, I want them
to think it came from the direction opposite us. Got it?"

"Got it, Boss." Crispin pulled a device from his bag. It reminded
Moyer of a game controller, except it had a screen. "I can have
Voyager up in two minutes."

"Take three minutes if you need it."

"Gee, thanks, Boss."

Moyer returned to watching the Chinese. The tall man was
switching batteries in the tool.

"What now, Boss?" Rich's voice came over Moyer's earpiece.

"We wait, Shaq. We wait for the others."

"But we can pop these guys now, then set up for the
Russians."

"We wait, Shaq. That's it."

"If you say so, Boss."

"I say so."

Two minutes, thirty seconds later, Moyer heard a buzzing to his
left. The micro helicopter rose from a flat bit of ground directly in
front of Crispin. Deftly he guided it through the trees to the edge
of the clearing, then along the edge of the forest. Moyer soon lost
sight of it and switched attention to the display screen Crispin was
using to fly the diminutive craft.

"How's it going?"

Crispin grinned. "Sa-weet, Boss. Man, I love this stuff."

"Let's see if you like what comes next." The grim tone in his
voice surprised Moyer. Of course, he had a right to be grim. For
Crispin, this might be a high-tech camping trip, but in a minute his
mettle would be tested.

The monitor showed, in black-and-white, the valley floor scrolling by. A rabbit sprinted from one bush to another. The first pass revealed nothing.

"Can you take it higher? Above the trees?"

"Sure can, Boss. Just so I don't go too far out there and lose my signal."

The view in the monitor changed from valley floor to treetops. Moyer watched with the kind of interest reserved for the best action movies. These scenes, however, were not pretend. Something evil moved through the woods and Moyer wanted to know where it was.

"Target." Crispin kept his voice low.

Moyer saw it too. "Make another pass, but keep it high. Don't get too close."

Crispin followed the orders without a word. Moyer counted close to eight men, each armed with AK-47s. Their dress varied. At best they were a ragtag squad, but Moyer had no doubt they knew how to use the weapons in their hands.

"Listen up. Eight hostiles on foot; military grade automatic weapons and sidearms; approaching tree line a half klick to our right."

He paused and Rich used the opportunity to ask a question. "Target priority?"

"Hold your fire. Do not engage unless they engage us."

"Understood, Boss. We take out the survivors."

"Negative, Shaq. We do nothing."

"What about the satellite, Boss?" That was Pete.

"I want the Russians to have it."

"Excuse me, Boss."

"You heard me, Shaq. We do nothing. We let the Russians take the Angel."

There was a long pause, then Rich said, "Boss, a word."

"You know where I am."

CHAPTER 32

J. J. FOLLOWED ORDERS. He always followed orders, including those he didn't understand. He was told to site down on a particular Chinese Spec Ops member but to hold fire. Fine with him. But he was uncertain what to do with the idea of watching a Russian military splinter group sneak up on a Chinese covert unit. In one sense, they had done the same thing. Okay, fine. But release the satellite to the Russians without squeezing off so much as a shot just seemed wrong on a dozen points. Hadn't they been tasked with retrieving the radioactive fuel, then blowing the thing up?

He tried to ignore it, but the thought crawled around in his brain. Had Boss lost it? The stress of his daughter's abduction may have unhinged him. Had J. J. received word while on mission that someone harmed Tess, he had no idea how he would respond. He was pretty sure he'd lose his mind.

The missions he conducted under Moyer's leadership were rough, painful, and deadly, but no fault could ever be laid on the leadership.

J. J. prayed for his team leader.

TESS PRAYED FOR J. J.

She had just spent fifteen minutes with Colonel Mac in the Concrete Palace conference room. At first, she was admitted into the Special Operations Command Center situation room, where Mac sat with Sergeant Alan Kinkaid. Mac greeted her, but Tess barely heard it. On a large, wall-mounted monitor was an overhead view of men in a field. She counted five, one short of J. J.'s team.

As if a mind reader, Mac looked at her then at the monitor. "That's not them. The team is fine."

"Who is that?"

"Chinese Spec Ops. They got to the satellite before we did."

"Oh no. Where is . . . ?"

"I tell you what, Tess, let's step into the conference room for a few minutes. This won't be long and you'll have fewer distractions."

"Yeah. That's probably wise."

Mac opened the door for her and as she crossed the threshold she heard Mac say, "Sergeant, I want to know if the situation changes."

"Yes, sir. Understood."

Mac led Tess into the conference room where they sat at the far end of the long table. The Concrete Palace had many rooms, but she had only seen the briefing room and Colonel Mac's office. J. J. told her there was a basement where they kept equipment. She didn't ask what he meant by "equipment" and he didn't volunteer an explanation.

"No time for pleasantries, Tess. Jerry Zinsser was here. He's investigating Gina Moyer's abduction."

"How's that progressing?"

"Slow. They're doing everything they can. CID and the FBI are covering the case as well as the local cops. They believe they're dealing with professionals and that's the problem. The abductors know at least something about the team's mission and about Eric Moyer. The question is, how? Zinsser thinks we have a mole. How do we find them?"

"Why ask me, Colonel? CID has trained investigators for these things."

"Yes, they do and they're on the case, but I need someone who thinks outside the box. Besides, it may not be an Army problem. It could be someone on the civilian side, someone in one of the intel groups, a politician in the know. I'm a soldier, Tess, not an investigator. You and Zinsser are mavericks in your thinking."

"Still, Mac, I'm not an investigator."

"Sure you are. You're a scholarly investigator. I don't need you to lift fingerprints. I need you to answer one question: Who benefits if we bring the team back? The Chinese? The Russians? The splinter group? A politician? I'm open for ideas. That's what I want: ideas."

"Where do I get information?"

"I'll brief you with what I know. After that, Zinsser will be your contact, but the way he's working, you'll have trouble catching up to him." Mac stood. Tess followed his example. "If anyone gives you grief, let me know. The president has our backs. Not many people give him grief."

"No, sir, I guess not." She debated whether to say the next sentence that came to her mind. "There's a price, sir."

"Oh, brother. There's always a price."

"How's the team doing?"

Mac clenched his fists and placed them knuckles down on the table. "Okay, come on." Mac marched from the conference room and into the situation room. Tess had to walk briskly just to keep

up. He stopped at the door and passed his smartcard badge over
the security lock situated near the right jamb. Tess heard a click
as the automatic lock surrendered its position and Mac walked in,
holding the door for Tess.

"Any change, Sergeant?"

"Yes, sir. Just a moment ago Junior just sent a flash message
that the Russian splinter group is approaching. We've located their
vehicles a short distance away. Best guess is the Russians will engage
the Chinese once they reach the open area. They have the advantage
of surprise and better cover. Chinese don't have a chance."

Mac shook his head. "I can't figure out why the team didn't
take out the Chinese, grab the fuel, and blow the thing to kingdom
come. They had enough time. They could have done the deed
and been back in the cover and headed to their vehicle, but Moyer
hesitated."

"Why did he hesitate?" Tess marveled at the image. She was
seeing live action on the ground in eastern Russia. She glanced
at her watch. It was early evening now. That meant midmorning
tomorrow there.

"That's my point. I don't know. That's the first part of their
mission. Now they have to engage the Russians which number
. . ." He looked to Kinkaid.

"Junior's message said eight men armed with automatic
weapons."

Kinkaid spoke as if discussing an ongoing baseball game.
His words turned her stomach. Then an idea hit her. "What's the
second part of the mission?"

"You already know that, Tess."

"I do know that, but I'll bet you a pizza that's your answer."

"I don't follow."

"It's simple, Mac. Their mission is to destroy the satellite and do what?"

"Rescue whatever Air Force Spec Ops men remain alive."

"Where are those captives?"

"We don't know exactly."

Tess studied the image on the screen. She couldn't see the team and assumed they were undercover nearby. "How then can the team rescue the men—?"

"Sons a—"

"Watch it. There's a lady present. Me."

Mac looked at her. "See, I told you you think outside the box." He rubbed his chin. "Sergeant, let's get POTUS on the line."

AMBASSADOR HUI XU POURED another glass of warmed *shaojiu*. His third and he had yet to have dinner. Normally a wine man, he took to distilled spirits when anxious and he was anxious. Earlier, the self-righteous president of the United States insulted him repeatedly, then made demands; demands he didn't intend to honor.

He had called his government, not because Huffington told him to, but because any meeting with a head of state had to be reported. He did his duty and reported the conversation and threat. His superior listened patiently, then hung up without a word. Hui knocked back the drink.

Had his career, maybe even his life, just ended?

JERRY ZINSSER'S MIND RACED despite his weariness. During Ranger training he learned to get by on little to no sleep. In some ways, he felt sharper; in others he felt dull and insipid.

He and Brianne were doing their part in tracking down home-improvement stores. The hidden digital manufacturing watermark on the video enabled them—rather, enabled the FBI video gurus—to track the maker and the model. Brianne had her team make calls, so they had a list of stores that carried that brand of security camera. The problem was, they had no idea how far the abductors took Gina. Were they even in the same state? The FBI and the far-more-limited CID offices in three states were doing the same thing as he and Brianne: going from store to store, rousting whatever manager was there, and asking questions about purchases.

This was the fifth Home Warehouse they visited. They were in a community forty miles north of Columbia. Zinsser found a parking spot near the front door.

"Lucky driver," Brianne said. "If I were driving, we wouldn't find a spot within two blocks. I'm unlucky that way."

"If that's the only bad luck you have, then you may be the luckiest person on the planet."

"I have a confession to make."

"Let me guess. You're a Russian spy."

"Nah, couldn't master the language. No, my confession is this: While I was gone, I did a little research on you."

"Uh-oh. Do I owe back taxes or something?"

She studied him for a minute. "Are you always this glib?"

"Yep. It's a coping mechanism."

"I learned you're a hero. Won an award."

"I don't talk about it." He opened the car door.

"Seems you should be proud of it."

"Seems that way, but most people I know who carry medals are proud of their service but prefer to forget what they had to do to earn it. It may not be true for everyone but it's true for me."

"Message received." Brianne opened her door and exited.

Home Warehouse was a Home Depot–Lowe's style home-improvement store, a do-it-yourself supermarket with tall metal shelves and workers in yellow work aprons. Zinsser walked to the help desk. A large, sweaty man in a T-shirt and dirty jeans was chewing out some college-aged employee. She looked on the verge of tears.

Zinsser stepped close to the man and looked at the lone employee. "Excuse me. I'm sorry to interrupt—"

"Beat it." The man stunk of beer and cigarettes.

Zinsser moved an inch closer. "This is official business."

"Do I look like I care? I was here first and I'm not done straightening this girl out. So you and your chickie can just wait your turn."

Zinsser removed his badge and ID holder and opened it, pushing it close to the man's face. "Sir, I'm with CID—"

"What's that? Some kinda rent-a-cop thing? I'm not impressed."

Brianne elbowed between the two and flashed her badge. "Maybe you'll like these letters better."

"FBI. You? I don't believe it." A lecherous grin spread across his face. "Of course, if you wanna come over to my place you can try and convince me." He set a beefy hand on her shoulder. "I like to play cops and robbers." He winked.

The man outweighed Brianne by 150 pounds and looked to have some muscle hiding beneath the fat. Zinsser leaned an inch forward, ready to school the man in the proper way to treat a lady, when Brianne became a blur. Zinsser had time to blink once before he realized the man was on the floor, his offending arm twisted behind his back at an angle that made Zinsser's shoulder hurt in sympathy. Even more painful was the knee Brianne had pressed into the man's neck, pinning his head to the tile floor. Zinsser couldn't help smiling.

"Whatcha think, Agent Zinsser? Drunk and disorderly?"

"Nah, he'd be out on bail in no time."

"How about ugly and stinky? Think we can make that stick?"

"No doubt, but I'd go with assault on a federal officer. That's a felony. Wait, I know. He's interfering with our investigation. That makes him suspect in my eyes. What say we hold him for seventy-two hours?"

"I like it." Brianne pulled a set of black handcuffs from the holder on her belt, hidden beneath her coat. She wiggled them in front of the man's face.

Three men pressed through the crowd. A name tag on the man's work apron helped Zinsser recognize him as the store manager. He guessed the other two were store security.

"What's going on here? I'm calling the cops."

Zinsser raised his badge. "We are the cops. I'm with Army CID and she's FBI."

"Oh. What do you want me to do?"

"Just sit tight for a moment. We need to talk to you." He squatted next to Brianne. "It's your call, but we have to think about time."

She nodded then spoke to a man whose arm, thanks to her, would ache for the next week. "So what's it gonna be, friend? You gonna give me any more trouble, or would you like to spend a couple of days behind bars?"

"No more trouble, Agent."

"Hey, you found your manners. If I let you go, are you gonna walk out the door and not look back?"

"Yes, ma'am. Out the door. No lookin' back."

"That's a good citizen."

She stood. The man lay still for a moment, then rolled to his back and sat. He rubbed his shoulder, then struggled to his feet. He glared at Brianne then Zinsser but kept his jaws locked. Without a word, he walked away.

Brianne looked at Zinsser, then did a double take. "What are you grinning at?"

"That was so hot. May I kiss you full on the mouth?"

"Professionalism, Agent Zinsser. Professionalism."

"Pity." The action had taken his mind off the urgent business. It came back with tsunami force. He addressed the manager and formally identified himself and Brianne. He asked the other men if they were store security. They said they were.

"I need to talk to you."

"Whatever you need." He paused and looked at the young lady behind the customer service counter. She looked close to fainting. "You better take your break." The employee was gone two seconds later.

The manager—the name tag read "Ben Elliot"—led them to the back of the store, past the employee break room where the customer service clerk sat dabbing a tissue at her eyes, and into an office made crowded by two large desks and cardboard boxes. For a store that made millions selling decorating supplies, the office was as dull and bare as a cave.

"That was really something out there." He pulled out a couple of folding chairs and offered them seats. Elliot looked like a man who had worked construction sites most of his life. What propelled the man to leave the field for an indoor job? "He's been a problem before. Hopefully you scared him away for good."

"Glad to be of service," Brianne said. "Now we need your help. We're investigating an abduction and we believe one or more of the people involved may have been in a home-improvement store like yours."

"Do you know how many home-improvement stores there are?"

"As a matter of fact, Mr. Elliot, we do." Zinsser crossed his legs. "We have people canvassing every one of them."

"Okay, let me put it this way: Do you know how many people come through this place every day?"

"I'm sure it's a lot," Zinsser said. "Maybe you could let us ask the questions."

"Oh, sure. Sorry. I've never been interviewed by federal agents before. You know, I once considered becoming a cop—"

"Mr. Elliot."

The man stopped and scratched his thick goatee. "Sorry again."

"You track purchases by computer. Is that correct?" Zinsser kept his tone even, pressing down his impatience.

"Of course. It's how we track inventory. By comparing what has gone by the registers and what's on the shelves, we can also estimate how much shoplifting goes on."

Zinsser pressed on. "My understanding from talking to other stores in your chain is that you can access your database locally."

"Yes."

"I need you to do a Boolean search for a set of items associated with a single purchase. At least we hope it was a single purchase."

"I have no idea what you just said."

Zinsser simplified. "Sorry. I spend a lot of time with computers. A Boolean search is a technique for using several search terms to narrow results. For example, if you go on the Internet and search for 'home improvement stores in South Carolina,' then your first results will include all those terms."

"Okay, I got it. I didn't know the term. This Boolean guy is some kind of Internet ninja?"

"Nineteenth-century English mathematician. You can look him up later. Can you access the database from the computer on your desk?"

"Yes." Elliot tapped a key and the computer came out of sleep mode. "Okay, the senior manager is the one who usually handles this."

"Look." Zinsser stood and rounded the desk. "Let me have a crack at it."

"Don't you need a search warrant or something?"

Zinsser stuffed a few more emotions.

Brianne leaned toward the desk. "Mr. Elliot, you have a right to ask for a search warrant; you have a right to call your superiors; you have a right to remain silent—wait, sorry. Force of habit. We are not trying to find out if you're stealing from your company. We're trying to find a teenage girl who's been abducted."

The man lowered his head. "I have a six-year-old daughter at home."

"Imagine if someone took her." Zinsser hated playing on emotions, but it was that or yanking Elliot from the chair and breaking the law by conducting the search without a warrant.

"I can't imagine that, but I don't want to lose my job."

Zinsser leaned close. "If you lose your job over this, I will come back and have a chat with your boss. If we find what we're looking for, you will be a hero."

"I don't care about being a hero, but I do care about the girl. Have at it, but if I lose my job, I'm moving in with you."

"Deal."

"Call up the database and then give me some room." Elliot did. From memory he typed in the name of the security camera system and the estimated materials necessary to create the small room. A few moments later, a result appeared. "Bingo."

"You got a hit?" Brianne shot to her feet.

"Two days ago, six in the morning. We're off on the number of studs and drywall but we're close, and they bought the camera." Zinsser turned to Elliot. "I need two things, hero: one, the receipt for the purchase; two, I need to see your recordings. Please tell me you have the recordings."

Elliot grinned. "You bet we do."

"Mr. Elliot, I could kiss you full on the mouth."

Zinsser looked at her. "Hey!"

CHAPTER 33

MOYER WAS LOOKING THROUGH his binoculars. He should have been seeing the clearing, the Chinese unit, the forest line, Crispin's nano spy helicopter, or the approaching Russians. Instead he was seeing Gina curled up on the love seat reading a novel. He swept the image from his mind and tried to focus. His brain refused to process the real world, choosing instead to substitute a different event from last month.

Moyer was sitting in his easy chair reading *Popular Mechanics.* Stacy was cooking grilled-cheese sandwiches; Rob was reclined on the sofa, playing a handheld video game.

Gina walked into the room and paused. Moyer lifted his eyes. "Uh-oh."

"Daaaady." Her grin had a touch of mischief in it. She walked over and sat on his lap.

"Every time you say *daddy* that way, my wallet starts hurting."

"I love you, Daddy."

"You're toast," Rob said.

"The answer is no."

"But, Daddy, I haven't asked for anything." She laid her head on his shoulder. She smelled like apple-laced shampoo, and a mind-numbing, free-will paralyzing aura emanated from her.

"I'm on to your tricks. I'm not that easily manipulated."

Stacy's laugh wafted in from the kitchen. "You're a goner. How long, Rob?"

"He's acting pretty tough. I give thirty seconds."

"Everyone's a comedian."

Gina nuzzled his neck. "Daaadyyyy. I'm going to the movies with my friends. Pauline's mother is driving, but I don't have any money."

"You have plenty of money. You save your allowance like no other kid I've ever seen, especially your brother."

"Leave me out of this."

"But, Daddy, that's to help with college. I'm trying to do my part. Movies are expensive these days."

"You got that right."

"I don't need much. Please, Daaadyyy."

"How much?"

Stacy laughed again. "And Rome falls."

"Just a little, maybe forty dollars."

"Forty dollars?" Moyer shook his head. "Movies haven't gone up that much."

"But there's popcorn and I might find something in the mall."

"I don't know, sweetheart. We're trying to cut back."

Gina raised her head so Moyer could see her lower lip shoot out. She sighed. "I understand. I suppose I could get by with thirty."

"Get by?"

"It'll be tough."

"Oh, please, Daddy."

"Okay, but you'll have to move. I can't reach my wallet with you pinning me to the chair."

"You're the best, Daddy."

Rob turned from his video game. "While you have your wallet out—"

"Shut up and get a job," Moyer said it with a smile.

"Hurricane Gina takes down another city," Rob said.

Gina moved and Moyer retrieved a pair of twenties.

"Oh, Daddy, you're the best. I love you . . .

. . . I love you . . . I love . . ."

THE MEMORY SHREDDED HIS heart as if someone had taken his KA-BAR tactical knife and had at it. Moyer lowered his head and buried his face in his arm. Every fiber of his being, every cell in his brain was fighting back the tears, once started, he knew would never end.

He never felt sorry for himself. Two years ago he thought he had colon cancer, news he kept to himself on a mission to Venezuela. J. J. had enough suspicions to question him on it. Ever loyal, J. J. offered advice, comfort, and kept the secret to himself. Now Moyer was awash in self-pity and self-hatred. Every minute the emotions grew more powerful; the sense of helplessness unbearable. He bore up anyway. He had no choice.

"Boss?"

The mission was critical for reasons not yet fully revealed to him. He long suspected there was more to the satellite than what was being said.

"Boss?"

Then there were the Air Force men still being held. He had to think of them. They might be dead, but there was only one way to find out. The fact the Russian group was advancing through the forest at this moment indicated one of them talked. That meant torture. They might be Air Force but they were Spec Ops, brave men, and Moyer did not leave brave men behind.

A hand touched him. A big hand. It shook his shoulder. "Boss!"

Moyer looked up into the worried, black face of his closest friend. "Yeah?"

"You are scaring me, man, and I don't scare easy."

"I've scared you before. In fact, I scare you on every mission."

Rich's eyebrows shot up. "True that." He paused. "I gotta ask. They're your orders: You with us?"

"I'm with you."

"You good to go?"

"Those are the first words I uttered." He took deep breath. "I'm good to go, Shaq. It's time to kick this op into gear."

Moyer activated his throat mike. "Hawkeye, bring your toy home."

"Roger that, Boss."

"Colt, Hawkeye. You're with me. We move in sixty."

Shaq asked, "What's the plan, Boss?"

"I'm splitting the team. You, Junior, and Doc are going to observe from here." He looked Rich in the eyes hard. "This isn't going to make sense at first and I can't explain it all because I'm doing this on the fly, but you are to see to it the Russians win the skirmish. They shouldn't need any help since they outnumber the Chinese almost two-to-one and have surprise on their side. I doubt they make it to cover."

"You want us to help the Ruskies?"

"Only if you have to."

"I don't get it."

"I'm giving them the satellite."

ZINSSER AND BRIANNE FOLLOWED Elliot across the store to a narrow stairway leading to the second floor. The upper story was a narrow projection stretching only a third of the building's width and held a few offices, but most of the floor space was taken up by the security office. Large, tinted windows overlooked the sales floor, enabling security personnel an eagle's-nest view of events. It was one reason they arrived at the scene of Brianne's confrontation with stinky man. There was also a bank of monitors displaying video feeds from within and outside the store.

"How far back do your video records go?" Brianne asked.

Elliot seemed proud of the system. "It's all digital these days; no more tapes to store. Since we can compress the video files, we store several months of video footage. Unless something has happened, there's no need to keep it beyond that."

"Outstanding. Let's take a look at the records from two days ago around six in the morning."

"Inside or out?"

"Both." Zinsser hovered over one of the plainclothes security officers. "Let's start with inside."

Elliot told the guard what he wanted and the fiftyish man with a shiny bald head complied. "The files show the person or persons checked out by the lumber section, which fits with the list of materials you gave."

Brianne's cell phone chirped. She stepped away as she took the call. She returned a few moments later. "Interesting."

"That was about the number on the receipt?"

"Yes. It reads like a MasterCard but it's a blind account."

Elliot looked confused. "What's a blind account?"

Zinsser and Brianne exchanged glances. "Without going into too much detail, it's a bank account set up in the name of a business. The business is a sham as is its masthead of executives. The account, however, is real. The credit card company does an automatic withdrawal each month so it's always paid on time. Enough money is kept in the account to keep the bank happy. Money flows into the account from another artificial business. There are several more layers. You have to be a CPA to unravel it all."

"Sounds like something a spy organization would do," Elliot said.

"Yes, it does," Brianne said.

"Got the video." The bald security guard worked a keyboard, advancing the video frame by frame. "Okay, we should be coming up to the time of the purchase."

Zinsser leaned in close. He wanted to see everything he could on first pass. Brianne moved to his side, close enough for their shoulders to touch.

Two men pushed a large cart, the kind used to hold lumber, drywall, or any other bulky, heavy items. They stopped at the register. The man closest to the register had bleached blond hair, was tall, and had broad shoulders.

"This guy could be the one in our video." Zinsser pointed at the screen. He watched as the checkout clerk rang up the purchase. The second man, shorter but built like a tank, carried a large box. "Could that be a security camera system?"

Elliot leaned in. "Stop the video." He squinted. "Yeah, that's what that is."

"So Guy 2 is definitely with Guy 1." Zinsser pulled at his lower lip. "Hit play."

The security man did.

"Who's that?" Brianne asked, indicating a black-haired woman standing close to Guy 2. "Is she with them?"

"Body language says yes. No one stands that close to a stranger." Zinsser crossed his arms. "That's three players."

"None of them have looked up," Brianne said. "It's like they're avoiding the cameras."

"I'm surprised they're not wearing hats."

She shook her head. "They're overconfident. I'll bet you this isn't their first time."

"Maybe not, but I'm going to make sure it's their last."

"*We* are going to make sure it's their last."

Zinsser faced Elliot. "This is the loading area?"

"Yes. It's where customers can drive their trucks to the door and load things up. We have confrontations there all the time. Someone gets ticked off at someone else for hogging the space or parking a trailer so no one can share the space. We have a fistfight at least once a month."

"Let's see it."

"On it." The security man called up another file. The image of a covered area open on three sides appeared. A dark, full-sized Toyota pickup waited by the door. The windows were tinted. Zinsser judged it to be a late model, maybe less than five years old. They watched as the trio loaded the back of the vehicle.

"She's definitely with them," Brianne said.

"I can get the license number," the guard said.

"Go ahead," Zinsser said, "but it won't do any good. I'm sure the plates are stolen. So is the truck."

"I'm on it." Brianne was on the cell phone before Zinsser could respond. A few moments later, she returned. "I had my office run the plates. They belong to a 1995 Ford Mustang."

"I'll bet a check of reported stolen vehicles will turn up a Toyota Tacoma double cab."

"They're checking." Brianne returned the phone to her pocket. She touched Elliot's arm drawing the man's attention from the monitor. "Do you have a good broadband connection here?"

"Sure."

"Good, I imagine these files are large. Okay, we're going to send these files to the FBI. I'll fill in the e-mail address. I want to do that now. They'll be able to enhance the video, then our video forensic guys and gals will tear into it."

"Facial recognition?" Zinsser marveled at the resources available to the FBI. CID had to do with smaller facilities, distant labs, and sometimes independent contractors.

"You betcha. When they're done, we'll know how many eyelashes each of the perps have."

"I'd be happier with an address. That's our next problem."

After sending the video files, Zinsser and Brianne shook the hands of Elliot and the security guard.

"You may have saved a girl's life, Mr. Elliot. You're okay in my book."

"Thank you, Agent Zinsser. Let me know if there's any way I can help."

"There's one thing you can do. Give that young lady who took the verbal beating the rest of the day off."

Elliot grinned. "Will do, Agent. Will do."

MOYER RAN ON POINT, J. J. and Crispin behind. Time was more important than stealth. He knew where the Russians and Chinese were. He doubted they could hear him plowing through the thin forest. Running with full gear was difficult at best; running through a wooded area and downhill was tough. It required focus, the one thing Moyer lacked . . .

Gina's eighth birthday party . . . pink dress . . . ten sugar-fueled girls.

Gina in the backseat of his car with two friends, all talking at the same time, no one listening, driving Moyer nuts.

Gina getting an award at school.

Gina in junior high drama doing her best with the few lines of the *Crucible* she had.

Gina pelting him with marshmallows during a family camping trip.

Gina saying, "Ew, ew, ew, ew," when he taught her how to bait a fishing hook.

Gina at thirteen starting to look like her mother.

Gina . . . Gina . . . Gina . . .

His vision blurred and he took a small branch in the face. He touched the stinging flesh and saw blood on his glove.

"You okay, Boss?"

"Peachy, Colt. Just peachy."

He started jogging again. Fifty steps later the sound of automatic fire rolled along the hills and valleys. The three dropped to the ground.

More shots.

"It's started." Moyer's thoughts ran back to the field where the Chinese were trying to pop open the satellite. It had only taken minutes for the confrontation to start. "Let's move."

Moyer was on his feet again and charging down the hill toward, not the FedEx van, but to the area where Crispin's nano-copter found the Russian vehicles.

They had work to do.

CHAPTER 34

PENG'S FIRST INDICATION OF trouble was the red splatter that hit the satellite and dotted his face. The noise of power shears masked the shot. Peng looked up from his work in time to see what used to be Hsu Li's face, now a mass of red meat.

He released the tool and dropped to the moist ground.

Pop-pop-pop.

Peng pulled his weapon close, fingered off the safety, and tried to assess the situation. To his left he could see Zhao Wen facedown in the grass; to his right Gao Zhi lay in an awkward position, his arms and legs bent in unnatural angles. Even at distance, Peng could see the man had breathed his last. Especially sad. Gao had two children.

The shooting stopped and Peng had an idea why. If he were hunkered behind a boulder or some other natural defense, there would be bullets flying everywhere. Whoever was shooting was avoiding putting holes in the satellite. It was, perhaps, the only reason Peng was still alive.

Three men down. That left him and Wei Dong, and he couldn't see Dong. Peng crawled along the body of the satellite and peered around the cover. He still couldn't see his man. He activated his radio. "Dong, can you hear me?" Nothing. "Wei Dong, do you read?" Nothing.

He failed. He failed in his mission; he failed his men; he failed his country. He wanted to see where the fire came from, to see who took the lives of his men by ambush, but to lift his head meant certain death. Four men died before Peng knew there was a problem. His enemies were professionals.

What would he do in their place? He knew. He would advance several men for the final kill. One would approach straight on, others from the side. Peng guessed he had five minutes to live, if that.

He pushed the lever that turned his QBZ-95 to full automatic.

He bolted to his feet.

He screamed.

He pulled the trigger.

Bullets spit from the end of the carbine at nearly one hundred rounds per minute, but with only thirty rounds in the clip, the weapon fell silent a few moments later. He was up long enough to see that his first estimate was right. Three armed men were approaching, spaced four or five meters apart. He hit each one. He didn't hear screaming, so he assumed he killed them. He saw something in the tree line that chilled his blood: a glimpse of several other men.

Peng's life was over. But the knowledge didn't bother him. He had long suspected he would die in battle. He just didn't expect it to be today.

His failure ate at him as he slammed a new clip into the weapon. If he failed, maybe he could make his attackers fail as well, steal their glory, make the death of their men meaningless.

THE M110 FELT AWKWARD and large in Rich's hand. This was J. J.'s weapon. Although Rich trained with it, fired a similar weapon many times, he preferred his more familiar M4. Moyer insisted on the switch. He needed J. J. for something else and the remaining half of the team needed a long-range shooter.

The Russians fired from just inside the tree line. Rich counted nine shots felling four men. Not bad considering the situation, but in the end, it was a massacre. Only one man remained. He just made a valiant attempt to even the odds and had some success, but Rich knew what the Chinese soldier didn't: three dead Russians meant five still alive.

Rich watched the action through the high-powered scope on the sniper rifle. "Doc, situation."

"Russians still in the trees. I see some motion to the sides. They may be trying to flank him."

"I concur, Shaq." Pete spoke in a whisper.

"Stay on them. I've got— What's he doing? Junior, check me on this."

From the corner of his eye he saw Pete move his binoculars to the area around the satellite. "Grenade. If Colt were here he could tell the kind."

"Grenade. He can't throw that far enough to do any good."

"Shaq, I don't think he's planning on throwing it."

Rich was puzzled. "What else would he—?" He swore under his breath, pulled the butt of the rifle tight into his shoulder socket, and sighted on the man, setting the illuminated, red crosshairs on the man's head.

He watched the man hold the grenade in one hand and reach for its top with the other. Rich balanced the weapon on its collapsing bipod. The sound and flash suppressor on the end of the barrel added four inches to the M110's length.

Rich compensated.

PENG KNEW HE HAD very little time. The satellite was his goal, now it was his shield, but the attackers wouldn't wait forever. He had to do the deed and do it now. The grenade was heavy in his hand.

The idea was simple. Arm the handheld bomb and drop it in the opening Peng cut in the satellite's skin, destroying the optics and electronics. If he lived through that, he'd repeat that act with the white phosphorus grenade attached to the side of his pack. Explosion and heat should destroy the inside of the big device—at least the important part of it.

He took a deep breath, fingered the arming mechanism, recalled exactly where the hole was he created—

—black.

SOMETIMES I HATE MY JOB.

Shaq took another deep breath and kept his sights trained on the Chinese soldier. There was no doubt the man was dead.

"Nice shot, Shaq." Pete nudged Rich's shoulder.

"Whatever."

"I only meant—"

"Let it go."

A moment of silence.

"What now, Shaq?" Jose kept his voice low.

"We follow Boss's orders."

"About Boss, Shaq—"

"Don't go there, Doc. If you're going to tell me he's acting a tad weird, I already know. If you're going to tell me that it's your job to judge his fitness, I already know. So just can it."

"Got it."

Shaq let his gaze drift back to the battlefield. Soon the Russians would make their move and find one more dead Chinese soldier. The M110 and the AK-47 fired a similar size round. They would assume they got lucky.

"We're outta here."

Rich was up and moving down the hill headed for the FedEx truck, his mind trying to sort out events and his friend.

MOYER SLOWED AND PREPPED his M4 for action. He motioned for J. J. and Crispin to spread out. He moved from tree to tree, eyes scanning from side to side, ears straining for the sound of boots on the ground or an unexpected engine. His senses sharpened but he felt slow, as if weights were tied to him. It wasn't a physical weariness, although he was short stocked on sleep and food. This weariness came from the expenditure of emotional energy; something he was unfamiliar with.

More popping, the sound of gunfire but distant. If the Russians were there, then they weren't here. Moyer harbored concerns a man or several men were left behind to guard the vehicles, being this deep in a wide expanse of nothing didn't require such caution, but Moyer wasn't going to risk the lives of his men or the success of the mission by being careless now.

He took a knee and again scanned, listened, and this time he sniffed. Soldiers were notorious smokers and he had worked with enough foreign forces to know the habit was universal. He sniffed again but only the smells of a damp forest reached his nostrils.

Moyer motioned for his men to huddle up. He laid out his plan. "You got five minutes. Got it. Five and only five. Don't make me come out and get you. Clear?"

The reply came in unison. "Clear."

Then a one-word command. "Go."

THE PRESIDENT ATE DINNER in the Situation Room. He canceled several appointments to track the activities on the ground. One more day of that and the press would notice.

He kept dinner simple: a couple of ham sandwiches and a glass of iced tea. When had Moyer and his team last eaten?

He carried the plate with one sandwich still untouched and the glass of tea half-consumed. Huffington blamed Ambassador Hui for his loss of appetite. That and what he just witnessed in the real-time display. The Chinese unit was down and not by Moyer's team.

It wasn't the loss of life that concerned him. Huffington was still ready to send a cruise missile over the sovereign territory of a government with a nuclear arsenal, a country with strained relationships with everyone and near chaos within its borders. There were times when Huffington wondered who really stood at the wheel of that country.

Hui did not do what he was asked to do. All right, *ordered* to do. Perhaps Huffington could have handled things better, but he was trying to work the psychology of the situation. Hui had to believe his country's Spec Ops team was about to become part of the distant landscape. Apparently that didn't matter, at least not to Hui. He made the call but did little to convince his superiors the president wasn't kidding. They called his bluff, and if Colonel Mac hadn't called with a reason why Moyer wasn't pursuing the prize, Huffington would have given the order.

Now he had to wait. Now he had to trust. Despite his bluster, he was still thankful it was Moyer's team on the ground.

CHAPTER 35

"SO CLOSE, YET SO far." Brianne pulled from the parking lot. "How do we find her?"

For the first time, Zinsser was seeing a crack in Brianne's ironclad armor.

"We should assume she's fairly close. We're forty or fifty miles from the Moyer's neighborhood. The abductors stayed close because they had to get the holding cell built, snag Gina, and make the video."

"You don't know that."

"You're right, I don't, but I think I'm on target. They could have traveled across state lines, but why bother? Surely they know doing that would bring in the FBI."

"If they're smart, then they'd know the FBI investigates crimes against children, which includes abductions. State lines have nothing to do with it. They'd also know the moment they attempted to interfere with a military mission, we could investigate under our counterterrorism arm. In theory, we are limited in the crimes we investigate, but just between you, me, and the fence post, we investigate whatever we want."

"Okay, maybe they stayed within a hundred miles for other reasons. I still think timing has something to do with it."

Brianne leaned her head back against the headrest. She looked weary. "What I can't figure out is how they know about Moyer's mission. They have inside info."

"There's definitely a mole somewhere. Leaking sensitive information isn't new. Private First Class Bradley Manning sent classified documents to WikiLeaks in 2010 by the boatload. Retired Chief Warrant Officer John Walker Jr., did spy work for the Soviet Union from the late 1960s to 1985. The list goes on. The government and the military are huge organizations. The U.S. military is the second largest armed forces in the world, second only to China. With 1.5 million active-duty military, there's bound to be a few bad apples and twisted minds. There are nearly 2 million civilians working for the government. That brings the number to well over 3 million people."

"But only a handful has access to secret material."

"I'll give you that, but I bet the number is larger than you might guess. The whole Private Manning and WikiLeaks thing was stunning because Manning was close to the bottom of military rank yet easily stole information." Zinsser stopped at a red light and looked at Brianne. "Play the numbers. Let's say there is one person in ten thousand willing to betray his or her country. Between military and government employees that leaves something like three hundred people."

"Ever the optimist, aren't you? By the way, the light is green."

Zinsser frowned. "You wanna drive?"

"Yep."

"Too bad." He pulled through the intersection. "You get my point. I have no idea how many people can or would spy on their own government or sell information, but history shows there are plenty who will."

"That part of the story is someone else's problem for now. Gina is our pressing concern." A second later she asked, "What would you do? If you were the black hats, I mean."

"I've been thinking about that. If we were dealing with your typical gravel-for-brains crook, things would be easier, but everything we've seen tells us these guys are several rungs up the intelligence ladder. If I was running the operation, I'd ditch the Tacoma as soon as I unloaded it." He paused. "I'd also choose a spot where I could carry a fourteen-year-old girl into a building without being seen. That's not something you can do in an apartment building or a hotel."

"Agreed. What about security cameras? Would you worry about those?"

"Absolutely. We saw how cautious they were in the home-improvement store. They did their best to keep their faces turned away."

"Which is impossible to do in a store with fifty cameras."

"Right. They have no reason to believe we'd be tracking down that kind of lead." Zinsser pulled to the side of the road. His brain had just hit the afterburners. "Okay, we know it's an older building because of the old-style, wood-frame, double-hung window. We know they built the holding room to conceal the rest of the building's interior. They even covered the glass in the window."

Brianne was nodding. "And we assume they would do this in a building where no one would notice someone carting building material around and banging nails."

"And the place has to be away from prying eyes and security cameras."

"An abandoned building."

"An *old* abandoned building, away from security cameras or traffic lights."

Brianne snatched her cell the way a gunslinger snatches his six-shooter from its holster. She punched a single button. "Operator, this is Special Agent Brianne Lazzaro." She followed that with her badge number. "I need the number for the central police station for Fairfield, South Carolina." She paused. "Yes, I know I could call information, but I called you. What part of 'FBI' and 'emergency' don't you understand?" Another second. "Thanks." She dialed another number and waited. Zinsser admired her straightforward approach to everything. She put it on speaker.

"Fairfield Police. Sergeant Presley speaking." He sounded bored.

Again, Brianne identified herself by name and badge number. "I'm in your city with Special Agent Jerry Zinsser of Army CID. We believe a young girl has been abducted and may be in your city."

"How can I help?"

"I'm going to tell you what we're looking for. I don't have time to answer questions, just give me your best answer."

"I'm ready. Shoot."

Brianne rattled off the criteria she and Zinsser had just discussed. There was no response. "You still with me, Sergeant?"

"Yes, ma'am. I'm thinking. Hold on." More silence. "You got GPS in your car?"

"Yes."

"There are several small industrial buildings in the old part of town. Built in the fifties. Some real estate developer bought them a few weeks ago. Plans to tear them down this summer. If I recall my patrol days correctly, there are four two-story structures on the three thousand block of Regency, cross street Polk."

"Got it." Zinsser punched in the information. "Polk and Regency."

"You want me to send patrol cars?"

Zinsser nodded. "Yes, but keep them well back. If they see marked cars, they might bug out. Worse, they might harm the girl."

"Understood. I'll be there in an unmarked car."

"No need," Brianne said. "We can take it from here."

"You're in my jurisdiction, Agent. I'm not going to lose my job because I have to tell the chief I sat on my butt while this was going on."

"You plainclothes?"

"I will be. Blue jeans, blue pullover shirt. Padres cap."

"Padres?" Zinsser looked at Brianne's phone. He couldn't believe what he was hearing. "Really?"

"I started off as a cop in San Diego, before my wife moved us to small-town life. I just don't want you to shoot me."

"Padres? I may shoot you anyway."

"Funny guy."

Brianne hung up and Zinsser pulled from the curb.

MOYER SUCKED COLD AIR in rapid inhalations. Perspiration ran down his face, soaking his knit mask. He was so focused on getting back to the FedEx truck on time, he almost missed it. Lev did a fine job concealing it behind brush and trees. Moyer backpedaled and ran up the slope where Lev had backed the vehicle. Crispin and J. J. were just steps behind. He could hear their heavy breathing. They had a right to be sucking air, the trip back was eight kilometers of uneven ground, branches, and roots trying to slap a face or grab a foot.

Moyer paused as he laid his hand on the handle of the back door. J. J. and Crispin walked the last few steps, Crispin bending as if he were about to deposit the contents of his stomach on the bedding of leaves.

He looked up and raised a hand with a thumb up. He couldn't speak, but he could still let it be known that he wasn't about to die. Moyer wanted to smile but he seemed to have lost the ability.

With a sharp motion, Moyer flung the door open, then stumbled back. Looking back at him were three muzzles. "Easy, boys, it's just me."

Rich frowned. "This is why we have radios, Boss."

"So . . . I . . . see. Sorry, Shaq. I'm a tad winded."

Rich, Pete, and Jose lowered their weapons and Moyer stepped into the back of the van. The rest of his team followed. Moyer removed his helmet and his black balaclava. J. J. and Crispin did the same.

"Man, I'm getting old." Moyer closed his eyes and focused on slowing his heartbeat. "Report, Shaq."

"Just as predicted, the Russians massacred the Chinese and now have access to the very thing we were supposed to keep them from."

Moyer ignored the jab. "They got all the Chinese?"

"All but one."

Moyer opened his eyes and looked into the stony face of his second in command. "The last man?"

"I had to bag him. He was about to toss a grenade into the satellite." Rich turned to J. J. "Here's your weapon back, Colt. I want my M4."

"Come to papa, baby."

They exchanged weapons.

Jose looked puzzled. "So what? Part of our mission is to blow the thing up."

"Radioactive fuel, Doc," Crispin said.

"Does that matter out here? Chernobyl did much worse. There can't be that much radioactive fuel."

"Leaving a part of a foreign nation's forest glowing in the dark and sprouting six-foot-tall rabbits would be frowned upon." J. J. removed the suppressor from the M110.

"Then why not just take out the Russians after they picked off the Chinese? From our position, we could have taken them out easily, especially if we waited until they brought in the truck to load up the blasted thing."

"We need them," Moyer said.

"We need them?" Jose raised an eyebrow.

"Yup, Doc. We need them."

Crispin pulled his nano recon controller from his pack. "Boss, the signal is weaker than I like. I think it's the metal sides of our truck. I need to run an outside antenna. Is there a hole somewhere that I can use to run a wire?"

Rich stood, removed his Benchmade Infidel tactical knife, and drove it through the metal skin of the truck above Crispin's head with a single, violent thrust. He did it again, forming an *X*. He used the blade to push the metal back, creating an inch-and-a-half hole. "There ya go, Hawkeye. Need anything else?"

Crispin, who had been covering his head with his hands looked at the opening. "Okay, it's official now; you are the scariest man I've ever met."

"I do what I can." Rich sat again.

"I'll be right back." Crispin grabbed his pack and exited. Seconds later, a wire came through the opening. Crispin entered the truck again and attached the wire to the controller he used to guide *Voyager*. "That's better. The signal is still weak, but it will get stronger as they approach."

Moyer turned to Lev who was following the conversation from the driver's seat. "How much has to be done to free the truck from the camo?"

"Nothing, Boss. I just press on the accelerator and we're gone to go."

"Good to go, Lev, not gone to go."

"Whatever. It will scratch the paint some, but who cares?"

Moyer turned in his seat and started to speak.

"They're moving, Boss." Crispin smiled. "I have an image. Not bad for improvisation."

"You wired the Russian convoy?" Jose said.

"Just one car." Crispin looked sad. "*Voyager* will never be the same. She was my favorite."

Rich stared at the new guy. "Admit it, you were one of those guys who made a girl robot so you would have someone to take to the prom."

Crispin looked wistful. "Her name was Rosie. You know, like from the *Jetsons*."

"Stow it, guys. Here's what we're doing next."

CHAPTER 36

TESS WAS GIVEN A conference room, a computer, and Master Sergeant Alan Kinkaid. The last addition surprised her. Kinkaid was Colonel Mac's right-hand man, and she never imagined he would cut the man loose to work on anything but the mission in Russia. Although she didn't know the details, she knew several other missions were underway in other countries. Assigning Kinkaid to her was proof Mac was spooked.

Kinkaid was an organizational genius, quiet, reserved, the kind of man who let his work speak for him. First time she met him, he was in full uniform and she took notice of the Ranger tab on his shoulder, chevron and rockers rank insignia on his sleeve, and a chest full of ribbon-metals including those indicating service in Afghanistan and Iraq.

"Where to begin?" Tess was thinking out loud.

"If I may make a recommendation, Dr. Rand." Kinkaid sat at the laptop he set up in the conference room. He sat so straight she wondered if someone had fused his vertebrae. She didn't know a man could sit at attention.

"I'm open to suggestions, Sergeant."

"I have a brother who works in air-traffic control for the Army. He once said a man could often tell where an aircraft was headed by the path it already traveled."

"Is that your way of saying, 'start at the beginning'?"

"In one way, yes ma'am, but I meant something more. I suggest first asking who knows of the mission in general and Sergeant Major Moyer in specific."

"Okay. Sounds good." She paused. "Can you get a stack of index cards? I want to go old school on this."

"I can." He left the room and returned in less than a moment. "I assumed a marker might be in order."

"So you read minds as well as run this operation."

"Colonel MacGregor runs the operation, ma'am."

"Yeah, sure he does." She paced beside the long side of the table. "Okay, let's brainstorm. I'm going to toss out names. You write one per card no matter how ridiculous the suggestion. I'm not making accusations at this point; I'm just throwing spaghetti at the wall and seeing what sticks."

"Yes, ma'am. Spaghetti at the wall. That's just how we say it in the Army." He smiled, something she never saw before.

"I married an Army man. I know how it's said in the Army."

"Yes, ma'am, but not from Colt. He's squeaky clean. He's a man of faith."

"He's talked to you about his faith?"

Kinkaid shook his head. "No, ma'am. Our time together has been limited. We've never talked outside this building, but I know a Christian when I see one."

She studied him. "Because you're one yourself."

"Yes, ma'am."

"Would it be inappropriate to ask about Colonel Mac?"

"It's safe to say the Colonel and Jesus have yet to meet."

"He knows of your conviction?"

"Yes, ma'am. I make no secret of it."

"I'm glad you told me, Sergeant. Maybe God will give us a few ideas. I need them."

"I'm ready for the names, ma'am."

"Okay, let's start with the ridiculous. President Huffington, Vice President Bacliff, Chief of Staff Helen Brown—"

"Why do you consider these ridiculous?"

"The president conspiring to end a military mission? All he had to do was order the end of the mission."

"But he would also have to explain himself."

Where was Kinkaid going? "Your point?"

"Don't cross off names too soon."

"Okay. In that case, let's add the COS for the vice president, the assistant COS, the secretary of defense, the members of the Joint Chiefs of Staff." She paused to give Kinkaid a chance to write. He passed the cards to her with a box of pushpins he brought in with the index cards.

Tess turned to the wall covered with a padded fabric meant to be stuck with pins. She put them in pecking order with the president at the top. At the bottom of the stack she found three unexpected cards: Colonel MacGregor, Master Sergeant Alan Kinkaid, and Dr. Tess Rand-Bartley.

"You put yourself on the list."

"Yes. I have detailed information of the mission. I know more than you and put your name down as well."

"Fair enough. What about intel agencies? Several have been involved, but all I can do is list the head of the division that deals with Special Ops. Who he talks to is kept secret. So that's a blind corner for us. Would they know which team is sent out?"

"One man would," Kincaid said. "He was responsible for getting a local operative involved."

"Do you know who that man is?"

"Yes." He wrote something on a card and sent it across the table.

"Mr. X. At least his name is easy to spell."

"You work with intel. You know how they are."

"We'll just go with Mr. X for now. We can deal with him if things point his way." She studied the list. "The thing that sticks in my throat is the fact Gina's abductors mention Moyer by name. This group would know that, but who else would? Who briefed them?"

"There is a string of contacts. The team was headed back to Fort Jackson when the mission came up. We intercepted them midflight and redirected them to Offutt in Nebraska. STRATCOM is located there. They were briefed by Major Bruce Scalon." He wrote the name down.

"Anyone else?"

"A Captain Tim Bryan assists the major. My understanding is he was responsible for picking up the team."

"Did the team interact much with other people at STRATCOM?"

"I don't have firsthand knowledge, but I'm certain there were those who saw them come and go. Most likely there was another driver."

"Can we get his or her name?"

"Yes, ma'am."

"Walk me through the rest of the team's prep and travels."

Twenty minutes later, Tess was more lost than ever.

GINA WAS ALLOWED TO use the bathroom several times and each time she looked for a means of escape; each time she realized the impossibility of it. She never saw a face, just several people in black outfits and black masks. She was never able to get a count, but based on the few people she did see in an open room just past the bathroom and the number of different voices she heard, she guessed there were as many as six people. They had more than black outfits in common: Everyone wore a gun on their hip and she caught sight of a shotgun.

Once strapped back in the chair, Gina began to make peace with death. Her dad's face appeared in her mind, then her mother's. Rob's was there too. Snippets of family trips, time spent with friends, and the unending teasing that was the hallmark of the Moyer family floated on the currents of her mind.

She was going to miss them. Everyone. Even her rat-faced brother.

"I'm sorry, Dad. I'm so sorry, Mom . . ."

ZINSSER PULLED ONTO REGENCY Avenue keeping the car just above the speed limit like any local would do. He was antsy and he didn't know why. Over the years of training and forged by missions he wished he could forget, he came to trust his gut. All good soldiers did, especially those in leadership. Sometimes the brain saw things but kept them hidden in the subconscious.

His skin crawled; his brain shivered. Every sense sharpened so much and so quickly, it gave him a moment of confusion.

"You okay?"

"Something's wrong."

Brianne looked around as the car moved along the street. "What? I don't see anything."

"I don't see anything either. I feel it."

"Great, a psychic agent."

Zinsser didn't respond. He was too preoccupied with what set his senses off. "Bingo."

"We're playing bingo?" Brianne swiveled her head, still looking for whatever couldn't be seen.

"Down the street. Three blocks. Right side. Lousy park job."

"The truck? The truck!"

Zinsser's keen eyes had spotted the shape of a large pickup—a Toyota Tacoma double cab. "Roger that, Agent Lazzaro. A great big truck."

"That's the place?" She reached for her phone.

Zinsser stopped her with a touch. "Not now; not here. They wouldn't park the truck this close to base of operations, but I'll bet my boss's annual pay they're within a few miles of here." They approached the parked vehicle. "Don't stare at the truck but snag the plate number."

Brianne did. "Same as in the security video."

Zinsser's eyes narrowed and his head dipped one inch.

"I ask again: You okay? Because you look really, really—"

"Focused."

"Not the word I was going to use, but, okay, focused. The last time I saw that look was during *Shark Week*."

Zinsser looked at the GPS display. "I'm going down Dixon Street and over to Emerald. It runs parallel to this road. Our only outside clue is the size and shape of a window, and the fact it's covered."

Moving slow, Zinsser guided the car a mile down the road, east over a side street and up Dixon. As he neared the aged business section, he saw several blocks of old office buildings, the area looked deserted. A rusted Buick sat at the curb in front of one of the buildings, a structure representing a past generation, a building forgotten by the twenty-first century. He turned down the street, looking at the windows on his side of the road while Brianne did the same on hers.

Nothing.

Zinsser rounded the block and started the same process. Several homeless men wandered the street, no doubt using one or more of the buildings as a free flophouse. The street smelled like urine.

On the third block, Brianne said, "Got it." She said it like she'd found a lost pair of sunglasses. When Zinsser looked at her, she was gazing out the windshield. The woman deserved an Oscar.

"Where?"

"Two buildings back. My side. Second floor. One window with the glass covered. The covering is the same color as the one in the video."

"Understood." Zinsser drove on until he reached the end of the street. Three blocks down, in a residential area, a local police car waited. Behind it was an unmarked vehicle of the same make and model. *Not very creative.* Zinsser parked across the street and exited. He heard Brianne do the same.

"You Agent Lazzaro?" The fiftyish man in blue jeans, a polo shirt, and a Padre hat looked at Brianne as if Zinsser weren't there.

"Yes." Brianne showed her ID. "I take it you're the sergeant I spoke to on the phone."

"Lee Presley. This is Officer Andy Arnold. He's the shift lead. Any luck?"

"We think so," Zinsser said.

Presley gave Zinsser the once-over. "You must be the CID guy who doesn't know diddly about baseball."

"If you say so." Zinsser stripped off his CID blazer and suggested Brianne do the same. "Can you get a few more men here?"

"I have some on the way. They'll be here in five minutes."

"Good. This is a CID operation, but I'm going to need your help. I can't get a team out here in less than an hour without using helicopters and those things are a little noisy."

"We need a warrant to enter a building," Officer Arnold said.

Presley closed his eyes for a moment, then opened them slowly. "Not if we believe a life is in peril." He faced Zinsser. "Is that what you're telling me? This girl's life is in danger?"

"I believe it is. I believe immediate action is needed."

Presley's gaze met Brianne's. "Agent?"

"I believe the same."

"Well, I can't allow that in my town. Who's calling the shots?"

Brianne nodded to Zinsser. "CID was first on scene. Besides, if we're going to do what I think he's going to suggest, then I want all the blame to fall on him. I still have a promising career."

"Not if you keep hanging out with me." Zinsser looked up the street. "Got a clipboard, Sergeant?"

"No, but I've got some office folders. I was taking a little paperwork home. Man-hour allocations and all that."

"Don't you have a chief of police?"

"Yes." Presley shrugged. "It's because of him I'm taking work home."

"Get the folders, Sergeant, and let's see if we can't turn a bad day into a good one."

"What are the odds of turning a bad day into a really bad day?"

"Don't ask."

"Great."

"YOU'VE BEEN STARING AT those cards for some time now, Dr. Rand."

"I don't have enough information. I'm used to doing detailed investigation, asking questions, formulating hypotheses, and starting over again until I've refined the result."

"That's a great process in the academic world."

Tess tipped her head. "Are you saying I'm not living in the real world, Sergeant?"

"No, ma'am. I'm suggesting you're not thinking in the real world. I assume you read a lot."

"More than most. What's that got to do with anything?"

"Recently I read a book by Malcolm Gladwell called *Blink*. It's a good read."

"You read Malcolm Gladwell?"

"Doesn't everyone?" Kincaid pushed his chair back, walked around to Tess's side, and looked at the cards pinned to the wall. "Gladwell gives many examples of people who come to the right conclusion in the blink of an eye. It's called, 'thin slicing.' I'll loan you the book, but for now all you need to know is to trust your instincts."

"Trust my instincts. I think this is a little too important to just trust my instincts."

"Forgive me, ma'am; it is precisely because it is so important that you do." He folded his arms and hunched his shoulders in a way that reminded her of a kindly professor she had while an undergraduate.

"I don't follow."

"There are some things that cannot be taught in leadership school." He rubbed his eyes, the first sign of weariness she had

seen. She had forgotten he had been up and moving as long as
Colonel Mac had. "I'm good at what I do, ma'am. If I'm not being
too self-aggrandizing, I'm pretty good at organization and mission
planning. However, in the field I learned very quickly that I'm not
a leader of men. On base, sure. Under fire, I'm cool and thoughtful,
but that's not enough. Mission leaders—men like Eric Moyer—are
people who know what to do even when they don't know why.
They size up a situation in a moment and make a decision without
long analysis. Later, when asked why they did what they did, they
can't tell you." He motioned to the cards. "Pick."

"Sergeant—"

"Pick."

"Fine. Anyone ever tell you you're one pushy man?"

"Colonel MacGregor has been known to mention it—every
day."

Tess stepped to the card-littered wall and studied it. She
grabbed two cards and handed them to Kinkaid.

"Really? Are you sure?"

"I thought the whole point was to let the subconscious do its
part."

"I would never have picked these two."

"I'm not saying they're the ones. I just have a feeling about
them. Can we do backgrounds on them?"

"Right away. In the meantime, we need to think this through.
I'm not going to Colonel Mac and say, 'We have a good feeling
about this.'"

"What? This was your idea."

"Not the way I plan to tell the story."

CHAPTER 37

ZINSSER DECIDED ON A team of three. He asked Brianne to sit this one out. She told him what he could do with the suggestion. He, Brianne, Presley, and Arnold huddled.

"I'll be first in. We move quickly. There will be no hesitancy. Understood? A half-second delay and one of us gets killed. When we go in, we go in committed. Can you do that?"

That got three yeses. Moments before Zinsser tried to talk them into letting him go into the building alone. That idea was killed before he put the period on the sentence.

He looked at Brianne, Presley, and Arnold and feared for them. He should wait for a team. He should wait until the building was surrounded and the "talkers" tried to convince the perps to walk out with their hands up. That's what he should do, but he knew there would be a firefight and Gina could be caught in the middle. So, never hindered by procedural rules, Zinsser made his decision. To his surprise, Brianne agreed as did Presley.

"We do this the military way. I don't know what your training included, but let me give a word or two of advice. First, this is not a drill. If you do not shoot bad guys, bad guys will kill you where you stand. We have reason to believe these guys are professionals." Zinsser poked a finger in the middle of Presley's chest. "You probably already know this, but make your first shot a body mass shot. Aim for the center of the body. If they're wearing their armor, the force of the shot will cause enough pain for you to take a head shot. Make sense?"

They agreed.

"If you can't do this, tell me now. This is no movie. There will be real blood. If we do this right, it will be their blood."

Zinsser took a few moments to describe the room Gina was in. As he did, Brianne's phone chimed. She answered and stepped away. A moment later she returned.

"Ever heard of Green Zone?"

Zinsser groaned. "Don't tell me. Facial recognition came back."

"My team got enough markers off the Home Warehouse security video to identify two of the three suspects—both the men. Both have military backgrounds and were dishonorably discharged for thefts they committed in Iraq. Somehow they ended up with Green Zone."

"Green Zone?" Presley said. "I think I've heard of them."

Zinsser rubbed his face. "You may have. They're one of many private contractors who provide civilian soldiers in war zones for a hefty fee. Some of the groups are filled with brave, experienced, loyal men. A couple are filled with military rejects." He looked down the street.

"Your expression tells me this is bad." Presley looked worried.

"The plan remains the same but the degree of difficulty has gone up. They're former military and probably some of Green Zone's elite." He thought for a moment. "I should go in alone."

Brianne rolled her eyes. "Yeah? Well, it's not going to happen. Besides, it's not about you; it's about the girl. We go in together or we wait for backup."

Zinsser used his cell phone to call his boss.

"It's about time you called, Agent Zinsser."

Zinsser filled him in on most of the story, leaving out his plan to enter the building. "Agent Lazzaro's people have used the video to identify two of the three suspects. They're part of Green Zone."

Wallace sent a stream of curses over the cellular system. "Give me the names."

"Brianne is texting you the info. We need to let Colonel MacGregor know. He still has to help run down the mole."

"Did she tell you about the other video?"

Zinsser didn't like what he was hearing. "No. What other video?"

Brianne looked up, puzzled.

"We just sent it to her crew in the FBI. Same message but . . ."

"But what?"

Wallace's voice dropped a dozen decibels. "They were holding a gun to the girl's head."

"That tears it." Every muscle in his body tensed.

"Zinsser, what are you planning?"

"Thanks for passing that on, Boss."

"You found the hideout, didn't you? You know where the perps are."

"Gotta go, Boss."

"You will do nothing until I get there. What's your exact location? Zinsser? Zinsser!"

Zinsser closed his phone. "Cell phones off."

"That didn't sound good." Brianne quieted her phone. "I could hear him like he was standing next to me."

"You must have heard wrong. He said to go on it."

"Sure he did." Brianne took a folder from Presley and started down the walk.

"I think she likes you, Agent."

"I can see why you never made detective."

MOYER WATCHED CRISPIN. The young soldier hadn't moved his eyes from the small screen on the controller despite the bumps and twists Lev was putting the truck through. Crispin's focus remained welded to the device in his hands. Every few minutes he would say, "Good. Still good."

Moyer, like the others, took his turn peeking at the small monitor.

"Exactly what was it you put on the vehicle?" Pete eyed the device like a lion looking at his next meal.

"I used the MAV. Wired it into the grill of the lead car."

"How did you know which car would be the lead?"

"We didn't. The cars were in a line and the flatbed was at the rear. Boss guessed the first car in would be the first car out, so I wired it to the grill. Anyplace else and the thing would be noticed."

"It looks like a little jet except it has a propeller," J. J. said. "I can't believe something that small can fly."

"Bees fly and they're a lot smaller." Moyer assumed Crispin had dealt with such objections before. "Small is good for recon. Harder to see; impossible to target."

"And it has a tiny camera sending a live video back to you." Pete leaned forward to steal another look.

"Yes. Granted it's not a great picture, but it's detailed enough. Ironic in a way."

"How's that?" Shaq asked.

"The most important thing on that satellite is its secret and advanced optics and here we are following something a thousand times smaller and with a much cheaper camera."

Moyer addressed Lev. "Not too fast. We don't have to be on their tails. We can use the MAV's radio as a beacon if we lose them. I don't want them to know we're here."

"Fine with me." Lev kept his eyes on the road. "I do not want them to know we're here either."

"They're slowing."

Everyone looked to Crispin.

"Distance?" Moyer asked.

"Best I can tell we're still two klicks behind . . . fork in the road . . . turning left. Road narrows. Potholes. The image is pitching and yawing like crazy. Rough ride."

Moyer moved to the back of the van, struggling to keep his feet beneath him, using the sides of the van and the shoulders of his men to steady himself. He hovered over Crispin. A large white block appeared in the monitor. "Is that a building?" The image settled.

"Slowing more, Boss. This may be it."

Seconds passed with agonizing slowness. Only the sound of the motor and the twisting of the frame and body of the truck on the rough road hung in the air. Moyer's heart picked up its pace.

"Stopped. Boss, they've stopped."

Moyer drew in the image on the screen. The forward motion ceased and he could see people moving in front of the camera. They walked around the vehicle. Moyer assumed the others were tending to the satellite loaded on the back of the truck. Time was crucial.

"Pick it up, Lev. Get us a klick away."

"Understood."

Moyer looked at his men and they stared at him. "Brave men need our help. You guys ready to lend a hand?"

"Hooah!"

"We bring them home. Dead or alive, we bring them home. Am I right?"

"Hooah!"

Moyer paused. "Look, gentlemen, I know I've been off my game; I know I'm missing a stride because of my . . . my daughter. Know this. I serve with the best. You are the best. I don't know what's ahead, but I know we are going to leave a mark." He paused and inhaled deeply. "If any one of you gets dead, I will kick your butts. Understood?"

"Yes, Boss."

"This may be rough. The enemy is well armed and well trained. We have the advantage of surprise. That and I think we're pretty ticked off."

"Heard that," Shaq said.

"They have what belongs to us. It's time to wipe the smiles from their faces." Moyer moved to his spot in the van. "Lock and load, gentlemen. Lock and load."

ZINSSER, HOLDING A MANILA file folder, walked down the middle of the street. To his left walked Brianne; to his right Sergeant Presley. Both held similar folders. Zinsser stopped every few steps, pointed at one of the abandoned buildings, and made notes on the outside of the folder. Occasionally, Brianne would do the same.

They took no defensive positions, did not stay in the remaining shadows and growing gloom of early evening. They walked like people who belonged there, like people simply doing their job.

They neared the building Brianne identified. A quick look told Zinsser she was right about the window. The color of the covering was right, the size and shape of the window matched, the presence of the Tacoma seen in the video surveillance parked a couple of miles away convinced him they were in the right place.

Zinsser used the time to study the buildings closer. They were laid out in a style long out of fashion, with one access to the lower floor stores and an enclosed stairway with access from the street and leading to a second-floor office.

As they reached the target building, the front door from the stairway opened and a man exited, closing the door behind him. He was big, thick, and looked like he lived in the gym. He also wore a black shirt and black pants. He looked at Zinsser. "What you guys doing?"

Zinsser smiled. "Oh, I didn't know any of the buildings were occupied—well, by anyone other than the homeless."

"I asked you a question."

"Yes, that you did. I'm sorry, but we're with the county and we have to survey the streets in the area. You see, some people have filed a complaint against the new owners who want to tear everything down to make way for new construction." Zinsser approached the man as he spoke. "Some people think the buildings are historic landmarks." Closer. "Maybe you're one of the people who filed a complaint."

"I don't know anything about that."

"Well, I'm confused." Zinsser scratched his head. "My associates and I were told the buildings were empty. Are you doing construction in there? Because if you are, I have to ask if you have a permit."

Closer. Zinsser was now on the sidewalk, just three feet from the man in black.

"No construction."

"Then why are you here?"

"That's none of your business." He reached for the knob on the door and turned it. The door opened a few inches.

"I'm sorry. I didn't mean to be rude. I'm one of the CPA types. Like to have all my numbers in order, if you know what I mean. Look, let me give you one of my cards."

Zinsser started for his back pocket as the man faced him, his hand still on the doorknob. Zinsser's hand never reached his back pocket. His right fist impacted the man's throat. As he raised his hand to reach for his crushed larynx, Zinsser brought the same hand back then up into the man's nose.

Before the man in black could drop, Zinsser had him by the front of the shirt, and, without losing hold of the file, he held the handgun he concealed beneath it, threw him over his hip and head first into the concrete. Zinsser heard a bone snap. He didn't bother checking.

Brianne and Presley took positions to either side of the door; both dropped the folders they had been using to conceal their weapons.

Zinsser looked into their eyes and was happy to see determination rather than fear. He took a deep breath, then, "Fast, calm, no turning back. Got it?"

"Give the word," Brianne said. "We're behind you."

Zinsser held up three fingers and silently counted down. When he retracted the last finger, he flung the door open and stepped into the dim stairway.

He heard voices.

Too many voices.

Zinsser started up the stairs, his P228 pointed up and to the corner where the stairs wrapped around a wall, making a ninety-degree turn. Brianne was two steps down, her Glock 27 out and pointed down and away from Zinsser's back. Presley followed with his Beretta 9mm pointed down.

It was a lousy situation: three people in a confined space, each with a weapon that made big holes in people. He was comfortable with Brianne's training but didn't know what to think about Presley.

Nearing the landing at the corner, Zinsser paused and listened. He identified three distinct voices, all male. What about the female he saw on the surveillance video?

A creak.

A step.

Someone was coming down the stairs.

"I'll check." He spoke loudly. "He probably decided to have a smoke—"

Zinsser stepped on the midpoint landing and rounded the corner.

Another man in black.

Two taps. One round hit the man in the sternum, the other punched through his right cheekbone. Zinsser ignored the splatter and charged up the last few stairs. He had to catch the others flatfooted.

The stairs ended in a wide, open area. The floor was asphalt tile, the kind popular four or five decades ago. Two men sat at a folding table playing cards. Man Two on the video was dealing.

Zinsser ended his game with two rounds to the chest. He pointed the business end of the pistol at the second man who lay facedown on the table, a pool of blood oozing from his head. Brianne had made one shot. It was all that was needed.

Zinsser's ears were ringing; the loud report of the guns in a confined area were doing damage.

The three stood ready, waiting for someone else to appear. The cavernous space gave them a clear view of most of the floor, but several rooms—offices and a pair of bathrooms—lined the back wall of the space. There was one other room: one freshly made with no drywall on the exterior of the stud wall.

Gina.

Handgun ever before him, Zinsser moved, slow step after slow step, closer to what he had come to think of as a cell. He had a decision to make. There was at least one other actor: the woman. Two bathrooms, three additional doors to what he assumed were offices. His biggest concern was if someone was with Gina, ready to kill if backed in a corner.

Zinsser motioned for Brianne and Presley to check the side rooms. He moved to the cell. Behind him he heard a door open.

"Clear."

Good. That's one.

Zinsser reached the cell, stopping short of the door with its wire-laced window. A shadow from inside played across the textured glass, a shadow that could only be made by someone standing.

Zinsser laid a hand on the doorknob.

His heart chugged like a locomotive. He couldn't remember the last time he took a breath. His hands were slick with sweat. *Let her be alive. Let me do this right.*

He flung the door open.

CHAPTER 38

THE APPROACH TO THE buildings was fast at first, but as they closed the last one hundred yards . . . Anyone seeing the approach of six men in camo, body armor, packs, sidearms, helmets, and more would know exactly what was going on. That's why Moyer was moving slowly.

He split the team. Rich, J. J., and Doc approached from the north; Moyer, Pete, and Crispin came from the south.

Before they left, Moyer ordered Pete to report their situation. Moyer spread his men out, knowing Rich would be doing the same.

"It looks like a hospital," Crispin said.

Peter corrected him. "It looks like it used to be a hospital."

"Well, riddle me this: Why is there a hospital way out here?" Crispin slipped off his pack.

"We're not that far from Nov Arman." Moyer raised his binoculars. "There used to be a government mining operation a couple of decades ago—Soviet Union days. The mine ran out or became too expensive to run. We don't know."

"Makes a good hideout," Pete said. "It's like the Hole-in-the-Wall Gang hiding out in the wilds of Wyoming."

"You ready, Hawkeye?"

"I will be in one. What have you got?"

Moyer scanned the buildings from his hiding spot behind a pair of trees. "I see a main building with two smaller buildings in the back. Those look abandoned. Padlocks on the doors. Broken windows."

"Boss, Shaq." The earbud buzzed in Moyer's ear. "We have a good view."

They were in position. "Roger that. I believe the back two buildings are unoccupied. Do you concur?"

Thirty seconds passed. "Concur. No activity on this side. Everyone seems to be inside. Chow time, maybe."

"Stand by."

"Hawkeye. Put *Voyager* up and make a wide pass."

"Working on it, Boss." Crispin worked quickly but carefully. The little helicopter came to life and rose under Crispin's control.

Moyer moved to Crispin's side. The little craft worked perfectly, giving Moyer a moment of confidence. Crispin guided *Voyager* high and kept it a good distance from the buildings, trying to be invisible and quiet.

Moyer broadcast what he was seeing to Rich and his team. "High-set windows on the south side. Maybe patient ward. Bigger windows on the east side. Assume offices. Big windows on the north. Should be visible to you. Assume cafeteria. More small, high-set windows on the west. Maybe a second ward. Wait one."

Moyer leaned closer to Crispin. "Back up."

Crispin turned the craft around. "Shaq, Boss. Back door open."

"Understood."

"Colt, Doc, you take sniper position. The rest of us move on my signal." Once more he scanned the area. Only God knew what was about to happen. He hoped J. J. was right: that God was in the holy dark. Images of his family flooded his mind and he forced them back despite the urge to dwell on their faces and voices.

Moyer pulled his balaclava mask over his face, then switched off his M4's safety. "Colt, Boss. You ready?"

"Just waiting for the go."

Crispin brought *Voyager* back and put it by his pack. He grinned at Pete.

"What's got you so happy?"

"While I was busy stuffing the MAV into the grill of the car, Colt was busy stuffing something else."

Peter turned his head slightly. "Such as?"

Moyer answered for the new guy. "Come on, Junior, what do you think Colt would be doing?"

Pete's eyes widened. "He didn't."

"Oh yeah, man," Crispin said. "He did."

"Shaq, Boss, start your move."

"Roger that."

Crispin stood. "Boss, before we left the *Michael Monsoor* we said we do this for family. We do this for Gina."

Pete triggered his mike. "For Gina."

J. J.: "For Gina."

Rich: "For Gina."

Jose: "You bet."

Moyer blinked back tears, then activated his radio. "Thanks, guys." Inhale. "Colt, go."

Three seconds later one of the Humvee-looking Tigers burst into flames and flew several feet in the air before landing on its side. A half second later, car two did the same, landing as a burning hulk. It was joined by the third vehicle bursting into a ball of fire.

"C4 is a wonderful thing." Moyer began his run to the back of the building where he saw the open door.

THE M110 SNIPER RIFLE was an extension of J. J.'s body. The collapsible stock was extended and fit perfectly in the socket of his right arm. He waited until the first four men ran from the front of the hospital, AK-47s in hand, before he stroked the trigger. He chose the last man out as the first to die. The others had a greater distance to run back to the building.

He dropped a second man when he heard Jose's M4 come to life. A burst of bullets cut down the third. J. J. inched his rifle to the side and put a round high in the man's chest. He staggered back, then twisted to the ground.

THERE WAS AN ENDURING thought in the Army. Train a man hard and long and when the chips are down, he follows his training more than his instincts. Moyer was in full operation mode. His vision narrowed, his senses became supersensitive, and adrenaline coursed through his veins, fueling every muscle.

Moyer pushed through the back door, kicking bags of garbage and scraps of food. He discovered the reason the back door was open. Someone was getting ready to take out the trash. In Moyer's mind, that was his goal too.

Moyer cut into the first room he encountered: the kitchen. He heard Rich move past to the next room. The kitchen was clear and Moyer emerged into the hall that separated the kitchen from a staff dining area.

Pete was now in the lead as they moved single file down the hall. The hall formed a *T* with another hall. The interior was confusing and ill planned, perhaps changed over the years. Those were questions for others to ask and answer.

The *rata-tat-tat* of automatic fire drew Moyer's attention. It came from his right. Rich moved the same direction, a few steps ahead. He motioned for Crispin and Pete to search the other rooms. The hall led to the front of the building and opened into a small lobby.

Rich lowered into a crouch, then to a knee, and pointed the barrel into the lobby. Four men were firing out windows in the direction of J. J. and Jose.

One of the men fell backward, blood running from his throat. J. J. was on his game. Moyer raised his weapon. One of the men who turned to see his fallen partner caught a glimpse of Rich. He turned and raised his AK-47. He was dead a moment later. Both Moyer and Rich fired. Four bodies lay on the tile floor.

"Lobby clear." The message was meant for J. J. more than anyone. He needed to know that he could save his ammo.

Moyer heard a scream and then a loud bang. Rich fell and rolled to his side, unconscious, the skin along his right temple and over his eye a mess of blood and tissue. Moyer had never seen Rich unconscious. Then Moyer noticed more blood on the floor—his.

The room began to spin. A motion to his right caught his attention: the sole of a boot hit him in the face.

Pain ran down his neck. Driven by instinct, Moyer tried to raise his M4. Through pain-fogged vision, he saw a stout man with a hate-filled sneer on his face and a Russian sidearm in his hand.

"You picked the wrong camp to invade." The heavy accent made it difficult for Moyer to understand. He did, however, know what it meant when an angry man raised a gun and pointed it in another man's face.

Moyer managed two words: "Bite me." Darkness poured into his eyes.

Two sounds drifted into Moyer's brain: "Egonov!" and a very loud bang.

CHAPTER 39

ZINSSER CRAMMED EVERY EMOTION into a dark, secret place near the corner of his soul. It was what he did when the situation needed more machine than man. Zinsser became that machine.

He swung the door open, the P228 at arm's length, and saw what he feared. The good news: Gina was still alive, still restrained in the oak chair they saw in the threat-video. In the second it took to glance at her, he saw no additional injuries. Seeing her strapped to the chair in nothing but her underwear made something snap inside Zinsser. The bad news: Another man stood behind Gina holding a large-caliber handgun—the kind only insecure men carried—to Gina's head, pushing her head almost to her left shoulder.

"Hold it right there," the man said. He was six foot four if he was an inch and looked to be 250 pounds of muscle. "One bad move on your part and you'll be scooping the girl's brains off the walls."

Zinsser looked deep in the man's eyes and saw a coward. "Lower your weapon and you live."

"No dice. I move this gun an inch and my life isn't worth a dime."

"It's not worth that now."

"Okay, funny man, here's how this is going to work. Your crew is going to withdraw. Young Ms. Moyer here is going to be my ticket out of here. Here's what I want—"

Zinsser put a bullet in the man's forehead. He collapsed like a house of cards.

Gina screamed. Screamed. Continued screaming. Blood and tissue covered her.

"Gina, it's okay. It's me, Jerry. You know me. I've been to your house a few times. It's over now—"

Bang. Bang-bang.

Pop-pop-pop-pop.

The sound came from the other side of the wall. Zinsser snapped his head that direction. He jetted from the room, rounded the corner, and saw three things: Sergeant Presley sitting on the floor holding his left shoulder, crimson oozing between his fingers; a dead woman bleeding from at least four holes in her chest; and Brianne pointing her Glock at the unmoving form. The gun wiggled in her trembling hand.

Zinsser stepped to her and laid his hand on her weapon, pushing it down. "It's over."

"How's that for a body mass shot?" Her voice trembled more than her hand.

"You done good, Agent Lazzaro."

"Saved my life." Presley struggled to his feet.

"Stay down, Sergeant."

He shook his head. "It's just a flesh wound." He tried to stand but collapsed again. "I think I'll just sit here."

Kneeling by the officer, Zinsser did a quick review of the wound. "In and out. Doesn't look like it hit any arteries. I see some bone frags. You'll live but won't be throwing any fastballs anytime soon."

"Got the jump on me. She came out of the head, gun blazing. I got off a shot but missed. She already popped me. Agent Lazzaro had just cleared one of the offices and, well, did that." He nodded at the corpse.

Footsteps pounded up the stairs. Zinsser turned to aim. Five uniformed police officers poured into the room. The entire operation took less than two minutes, although it seemed a lot longer to Zinsser.

"Call an ambulance," Zinsser ordered.

Andy Arnold made the call.

"How's Gina?" Brianne asked.

"Shook." Zinsser stood. "At least she's stopped screaming—" Two holes in the wall separating the open work area from Gina's holding space—two large bullet holes.

Zinsser made it to Gina's door in a sprint, flung it open, and plunged into the room.

Gina leaned forward against her restraints, unmoving.

"No. No! NO!" He lowered his weapon and drew a large folding knife from his pocket, popping the blade open in one move. "Help me! Help me!"

Zinsser the machine melted into a slag-covered pool in the heat of what he was seeing. The bottled emotions broke free. He cut the nylon ties and the straps that held Gina to the chair, tossed the blade aside, and eased the girl to the floor. There was a hole in her left arm and one in the side of her chest.

She wasn't breathing.

"Oh, God no. Please, God. Please."

Brianne knelt beside Gina's body, leaned over her head, and placed an ear over Gina's nose. Brianne shook her head. She tilted Gina's head back, pulled her jaw down, laid her lips over Gina's, and exhaled, sending air into her lungs. Blood and air bubbled from the wound in her chest. "Pneumothorax. Put your hand on the wound."

"What?"

"Your hand. Put it over the wound. Air is getting in the chest cavity and collapsing her lung."

Zinsser forced himself back into battle mode: emotionless, acute thinking, senses sharp as scalpels.

Brianne blew more air into Gina's lungs, repeating the process three times, then put two fingers to one of the girl's carotid arteries. "No pulse. Move."

Zinsser slipped further to the side but kept his hand over the wound, blood tinting his fingers. Brianne raised a fist and brought it down on Gina's sternum, executing a precordial thump. Again, she checked for a pulse. "Nothing."

She moved to the other side of Gina, laced her fingers together, placed her hands over the center of Gina's chest, and pushed, counting, "One, two, three . . ."

THE UNIVERSE WAS BLACK, ebony, Stygian. Yet Moyer did not feel blind. He was standing. He knew that much. He could feel ground or floor or something beneath his feet. He looked up. No stars. He looked from side to side, but there was nothing but more dark.

He should be filled with terror. Why wasn't he? Something real but intangible surrounded him, like he was floating in a pool of ink.

He touched his arm and it felt real. He felt no clothing but he didn't feel nude. Whatever he wore was right for this place.

"Daddy?"

Moyer turned. Behind him, bathed in a light with no apparent source, stood Gina, pretty and perfect. "Gina!" He closed the distance between them in rapid steps and took her in his arms, lifting her from the ground and swinging her in a big circle. "Baby. My girl." He set her down and stroked her hair.

"I love you, Daddy. I miss you."

Tears ran down Moyer's face like rivers. "I love you. I love you so much. I haven't said it enough in your life. I love you, adore you. I'm proud of you. You are my life."

She clung to him for a moment, then stroked his cheek, wiping away tears. "Everything is going to be fine, Daddy. Everything is going to be fine."

Slowly, Gina, bathed in ethereal light, began to move back and up.

"Where are you going? No. Stay. Stay with me. I need you, baby."

"It's going to be all right, Daddy. It really is."

Gina ascended skyward and became the only star in the ebony cloak.

"Gina!"

He was alone in the dark again—but not alone. Something was moving in the black, occupying it, filling it. Something good and comforting. Moyer heard J. J.'s voice: *"Boss, all I'm saying is that God is in the darkness with you. There is a holy dark."*

CAPTAIN MASTERS HEARD GUNFIRE and it gave him a moment of hope. He had been on enough missions and heard enough gunfire in his day to recognize the distinct sound of American-made M4s. He pulled at his restraints.

The door to his room exploded open and two men burst in. Two men in black camo and matching masks marched in, automatic weapons searching for any target. Seeing the room had only one occupant and he was strapped to a bed, the men lowered their M4s. One man approached Masters, the other turned to the door, his weapon at the ready for anyone who might have followed them.

Masters watched the soldier study the situation. The man's eyes brightened. "You call for a taxi?"

"That would be me. I'm late for the theater. Man, have I got someone for you to meet."

He shouldered his weapon and began removing the restraints. "They call me Junior. You are?"

"Captain Scott Masters."

"You able to move?"

"Yes. I'm a little weak, but I'm sure I can walk."

"Wounds?"

"Face and side. Side hurts the most."

"Okay, I'm going to release you, but I want you to stay here until—"

"You can forget that noise, soldier. Give me a status report. Did you find my men?"

"Yes, sir." Junior's voice faltered. "I'm afraid you're the last one alive."

"No, I was told—"

"We found two bodies. One has been dead for hours. The other
. . . I think someone shot him when we came in. I'm surprised to
find you alive."

The door opened and all eyes turned to a thin man in a doctor's
smock.

"No," Masters snapped. "Hold your fire."

"Identify yourself," the other soldier demanded.

The man looked at Masters and shrugged. "He calls me Igor."

"He's the doctor," Masters said. "He hooked me up with
antibiotics—finally."

"May I?" Igor nodded to Masters. "The IV?"

Junior said, "Go ahead, but don't mess with us. I still have
plenty of bullets."

Igor moved to Masters and removed the IV needle. Masters sat
up. The room twisted and spun. "Where's Egonov?"

"Who's Egonov?"

"He's the lead clown." Masters stood and wobbled, then found
his footing. Every part of him hurt. Despite the antibiotics, his fever
still raged. He needed to spend more time in bed with high-caliber
drugs, but that would have to wait. "Give me your sidearm, soldier."

"No can do, Captain. You're in no condition."

"I'm guessing I outrank you. Don't be insubordinate. I know
what I'm doing. I've been doing it longer than you. Now hand it
over or I'll knock you down and take it."

"You know there's no chance you could do that in your
condition."

"Yeah, but threats are all I have at the moment."

"Hawkeye, give the captain your sidearm."

"What? Why mine?"

"I may need mine to save my life."

"Oh, I see how it is. Nice. Real nice."

The handgun felt good in Masters's hand. "Have you cleared the facility?"

"This side. Stay here until we come back for you. We still have several rooms to check."

"Understood."

The two exited. One minute later, Masters started for the door.

"Where are you going?" Igor asked.

"My mission isn't over yet."

Captain Scott Masters put one wobbly step after another and walked out the door. With each step he grew more certain. With Igor by his side, Masters, bent at the waist from his wounds, moved down the hall.

The hall ended near the lobby/waiting area. Two soldiers dressed like those who were in his room were about to engage a group of armed men near the windows of the extended lobby.

One of the Russians fell; another turned with weapon raised; and the soldiers opened fire, gunning down the remaining men. He recognized one of the newly dead men as the bearded man who installed the speaker in his room. *Good riddance.*

A blur to his right caught his attention. A man emerged from the back of the building, a GSh-18 weapon in his hand. He pulled the trigger just as the larger of the two soldiers turned. The bullet hit the right side of his head just below the helmet rim. Another shot struck the other rescuer in the arm or chest. Masters couldn't tell.

The shooter advanced and drove the heel of his boot in the man with the head wound, then kicked the other in the face. Masters watched as the man raised his weapon.

"Egonov!"

Egonov turned and Masters pulled the trigger. The round hit his torturer in the shoulder. Masters had been attempting a head shot. He pulled the trigger again, hitting the man's right hip. Masters fired again and again.

Egonov fell, his head bouncing off the floor.

Masters fired again until he put the same number of bullets in the man as the number of dead men in his team.

Masters, now overextended, dropped to the floor, his fall broken by Igor.

The two soldiers who were in his room burst from the hall. Masters watched them assess the situation. One keyed the radio.

"Doc, Junior. Men down. Repeat, men down. We need you. Now!"

CHAPTER 40

MOYER'S EYES POPPED OPEN. He was floating. No, not floating, but he was moving. He heard voices. Different voices; one odd sounding.

". . . 'kay, Boss. You're going to be okay."

"Shaq?"

"Hey, you're awake. Enjoy your nap?" Doc's voice. Jose's voice.

The ceiling was moving. No, he was moving. That made more sense.

"Shaq?"

"Colt's with him. He came to. Won't let me work on him until you're all patched up and ready to go dancing."

"I hate dancing."

"Good, because I've seen you dance."

Moyer couldn't tell what was real and what was a dream. Had he just seen Gina? Where was he? Russia. That's right, Russia.

"Report."

"We got it taken care of, Boss."

"I told you to report, Doc."

"Okay, but try to relax."

"Ree-port!"

"Yes, Boss. Facility is secure. You've been shot and assaulted. We're moving you to the surgery for a little touch-up."

"Surgery?"

"The bullet deflected off the butt of your M4. That saved your life. But it fragmented and nicked your jugular and a piece went through your shoulder and under your arm. There's a doctor here. We're gonna stabilize you."

"Shaq."

"He'll live. A bullet grazed his head but left him with a skull fracture and . . ."

"And what?"

"His eye has been damaged."

"Take care of him first."

"No can do, Boss. Triage dictates I take you first."

"Shaq first."

"You two are a pair. He said the same thing about you. The difference is, he can still kick my butt; something you can't do in your situation."

"Rescue?"

"One man, the team leader. We found two bodies. One had been tortured. You don't want to know about that right now."

"Junior?"

"Here, Boss. Just helping cart your lazy rear end."

"Send report."

"Will do, Boss."

"First finish job. Kill the satellite."

"We're on it, Boss."

The ceiling changed as they pushed through a pair of swinging steel doors.

A strange voice; heavy Russian accent. "You have field med kit?"

Jose answered. "Yes."

"We have very little here. I may need what you have."

"It's yours."

SIRENS FILLED THE AIR and pushed their way through the old building. Zinsser could see splashes of red and blue on the covered glass.

Perspiration dripped from Brianne's face and off her nose, dropping onto her hands and Gina's bare skin. She maintained the count, but the words came out as whispers.

"Switch with me," Zinsser said.

"I got it."

"Switch with me."

"One, two, three . . . okay."

A young officer entered. "Paramedics are here." He looked things over. "Let me do that."

Before Brianne could answer, the small city cop knelt by Brianne and elbowed her out of the way and started the compressions. "How's Presley?"

"He's okay," the officer said. "He's worried about what's going on in here."

"He's a good man," Zinsser said.

"He's a pain." The officer said it with a smile.

Brianne placed fingers on Gina's neck. The officer was doing a good job; there was a pulse with every compression. Then she felt something else. "Hold it."

The officer stopped pushing Gina's sternum into her heart.

"Check me. I think I've got a pulse."

Zinsser used his free hand to touch Gina's neck. A pulse. A strong pulse. "Yes!"

Gina moaned, then opened her eyes. She seemed confused, then her gaze settled on Zinsser. "I know you."

A good sign. "Yes, you do. You had us scared."

"I had myself scared."

Zinsser kissed her on the forehead. "There, now you can't say you've never been kissed."

A weak smile settled on Gina's face. "Who says that's my first kiss?"

Zinsser laughed.

Then he wept.

J. J. AND PETE detached the fuel cell from the wires connecting it to the satellite's electrical system. The nuclear payload was small and used only to provide electricity to the transmitter and electronically controlled elements. Angel-12 also contained small tanks of rocket fuel for positioning, orbit, and attitude control. The liquid fuel frightened J. J. more than the radioactive material.

Judging by the nonstop monologue coming from him, Crispin was nervous. J. J. stopped listening after the third time he heard, "RTG stands for radioisotope thermoelectric generator and they're used in all kinds of spacecraft."

It took twenty minutes for J. J. to crack open Angel-12 and remove a long cylinder, which he placed in the transportation package from the FedEx truck. J. J. radioed Lev and told him to bring the truck into the compound.

After inserting the RTG into its new home, Pete moved it from the flatbed and carried it back to the FedEx van. J. J. took thirty minutes to place small packages of C4 plastic explosive in strategic spots. What the explosive didn't do, the rocket fuel would finish. J. J. didn't want to be anywhere close when he pushed the detonator.

As he placed the fourth block of C4, he saw something: twenty-five small rockets. On closer examination he found a mechanism that would open a door and extend the cylinder holding the three-foot-long missiles. The rockets were too small to carry much of an explosive payload, but they were large enough to take out another satellite, an ICBM, or maybe even high-flying aircraft.

J. J. couldn't be sure. He was a weapons and explosive expert, but space-based "Star Wars" like offensive weapons were beyond him. It did, however, explain some of the urgency surrounding the mission. This was not the kind of technology one shared with other countries.

He placed the last explosive package, jumped from the truck, and walked to Rich who watched from the front of the hospital. "Good to go, Shaq."

Medical gauze covered half of Rich's face. "Good."

"How's Boss?"

"Good, but still out of it. He lost a lot of blood."

"Yeah, I know what that's like. Kinda messes with the brain."

"I'm not on my game either." He looked up as Pete returned from the FedEx truck. "Colt . . . listen. Doc has given me some serious pain meds. My brain feels like it's running in second gear. Boss, can't make the calls. That means, you're team leader."

"No, you're team leader—"

"Shut up, Colt. The man in charge has to make decisions in a snap. I don't think I could tie my shoes without help. From this moment on, you're the man."

"Shaq—"

"I may be in pain and slow, but I can still rip your face off."

"I'm the man."

"That's better."

Jose stepped outside.

Pete spoke. "Hey, Doc, Colt's the man now."

"As long as it's not me."

"How's Boss, Doc? Can he be moved?"

Jose nodded. "It will be tough on him. On the big man here too."

"I can take it."

"We can't stay here," J. J. said. "For all we know, more bad guys are on the way. I don't think we just took out the whole splinter movement."

"Agreed," Pete said.

"Get Boss and Shaq prepped for the trip. We've got a lot of miles to go."

"Boss needs a faster trip. So does Shaq. We're hours from the extraction point."

"All we have is the FedEx," J. J. said. "We blew everything else up. And the flatbed will be useless once I hit the button. Most likely, the building will take a big beating. Get 'em ready, Doc."

PRESIDENT HUFFINGTON SIGNALED FOR the video conference to end. The image of Colonel Mac disappeared. He took a moment to sort through everything he heard, then rose. He put a hand on Bacliff's shoulder. Tears of relief steamed along his cheeks. "Go home, Andrew, go home to your wife. You have a lot to be thankful for."

"They're not home yet."

"I know. But they will be soon." He faced Helen. "I'm going to the Oval. I have a call to make. I want you there."

Minutes later, Huffington held the phone to his ear.

"President Huffington, I hope you are well."

"I'm well, President Solovyov. How is your wife?"

"She spends my money on parties and Western decadence."

"I know what you mean." Huffington considered his next words. "Urie, I need to tell you a story, then ask a favor, then give you a gift. The story will make you angry, the favor is more than I have a right to ask, and the gift, I hope, will make it all right."

"You have me intrigued."

"It began a few days ago when a Chinese satellite we believed dead came back to life . . ."

GINA OPENED HER EYES and once again experienced fear-causing disorientation. Her heart quickened, breathing came with great pain. She tried to sit up, but she was too weak.

"It's all right, sweetheart." The voice, familiar and longed for.

"Mom?" She turned her head and saw her mother, eyes red and puffy, no makeup, hair in disarray. Standing next to her was Chaplain Bartley. He was smiling. "You look horrible."

"Thanks," Bartley said.

"I meant my mom."

"Thanks." She took Gina's hand.

Nothing ever felt so good.

"Hey, Squirt." Rob stood at the foot of the bed.

"Hi, Rat-Face."

"She's going to be okay," Rob said.

"I'm really sore."

Her mother smiled. "It could be from the gunshot wound, or the CPR, or the surgery."

"I'm confused."

"She's the same ol' Gina." Rob's smile widened.

PETE HEARD THEM FIRST. The *whup-whup-whup* of a helicopter. "I hope those are the right birds."

"Take positions, just in case. Let's make sure Boss and Shaq are away from the windows and doors. Get Hawkeye and Doc to help you, then I want a man at each cardinal point of the building. And see if you can't get Captain Masters to stop trying to take over the mission."

"I think he has a few pent-up emotions."

"He needs to keep them in the pen."

Pete disappeared into the building. J. J. scanned the sky and found a single distant dot approaching. He retrieved his binoculars and aimed them at the dot. An Mi-26. It was a monster built, if J. J.'s memory was on target, in the mid-1980s.

It came in loud and low, making no attempt to hide its approach. J. J. took that as a good sign, although the pessimist inside reminded him the helo could carry up to eighty troops. For a moment he envisioned a steady stream of armed men pouring from the craft like water from a hose. He was part of the best Spec Ops team working, but he didn't like those numbers.

The craft found a clear corner of the compound and settled on its wheels. Only one man exited the craft. He wore a Russian Army uniform but carried no weapons. He walked with confidence and purpose. J. J. stepped out to meet him.

"I am *Srarshiy Serzhanf* Demidov, Army of the Russian Federation. I have been told to speak with a man named 'Colt.'"

"That would be me."

Demidov took a step back and saluted. "My orders are to convey you to your next destination." He looked at the giant satellite, opened his mouth as if to ask a question, then closed it, keeping his silence.

"You are a welcome sight."

"We also have medical supplies including plasma and blood."

"I could kiss you," J. J. said. The man looked stunned. "It's an American expression. I'll settle for a handshake."

It took twenty minutes to get the team and the wounded into the large helicopter. Igor the doctor—whose name it turned out was really Igor—connected Moyer, Masters, and Rich to IVs.

J. J. moved to the pilot's area. "I have one last thing to do and I can do it from the air. Take us up and out about a kilometer." The pilot nodded.

The Mi-26 lifted to five hundred feet and moved back the distance J. J. requested. He removed the remote detonator. "You want the honors, Boss?"

Moyer waved him off.

"In three, two, one." J. J. activated the detonator. The shock wave made the aircraft bounce and shift from its location. A column of fire and smoke crawled up the air. Shrapnel peppered the front of the former hospital, a hospital that held only the corpses of Russian dissidents, terrorists. The helicopter was filled with three wounded men, two corpses of Masters's team, J. J.'s team, and Dr. Igor. The latter would not be leaving the helicopter with the others. People in Moscow had questions for him, and J. J. had no doubt the man became a bargaining chip with the Russians.

Pete looked at Connie. They received another message. J. J. had never seen a bigger smile. Pete moved to the side of the helicopter where Eric Moyer lay strapped to a litter. He motioned to J. J.

"Boss. You awake?"

"Yeah, just a little loopy from the . . . um . . . um . . ."

"Pain meds," Jose suggested.

Pete lifted his head. "Listen up, team. They found Gina. She's alive and Stacy is with her."

The cheer shook the sides of the helicopter. They took turns congratulating Moyer. The moment the cheering ended, Sergeant Major Eric Moyer broke into tears.

EPILOGUE

Three months later

STEAKS WERE SIZZLING ON the barbecue in Eric Moyer's backyard. There were drinks, baked potatoes, and Moyer's closest friends. J. J., Tess, and Chaplain Bartley sat in lounge chairs, soaking in the sun. Jose, his wife, and what seemed like fifty-two kids were nearby. Pete, Crispin, Colonel Mac, and Sergeant Kinkaid stood on the lawn telling jokes. Rich and his wife sat in the shade. Even with the new eye patch covering his friend's eye, Rich looked good.

"May I have everyone's attention, please?" Moyer stood in the center of the backyard, the smell of barbecue filling the air. "The steaks are almost ready and I don't let anything interfere with such important things."

There was light laughter.

"Then get to it, Boss," Pete said. "I'm hungry."

"Okay, I'll make this quick. First, having almost everyone in one place allows me to say thank you to all of you for what you did, especially for Gina. Data, you and Agent Lazzaro did a great job. My family will never be able to repay you."

"I'm still calculating the bill."

Moyer turned to Agent Terry Wallace. "I'd like to thank you for helping to save my daughter's life."

"If you want to thank me, Moyer, then take Zinsser back on your team."

"Ain't gonna happen." Moyer pulled his daughter close. "Gina and I have matching bullet wounds. How many fathers can say that?"

"How many want to?" Gina said.

"Okay, to the announcements. First, Captain Masters—who as the world knows now is the son of the former vice president— is recovering nicely from his wounds and plastic surgery."

Some of those present applauded.

"The big news, however, is this: The Army accepted my request for retirement."

No applause, just stunned silence.

"I know, I know, but I've put a lot of years in this business, lost team members, and nearly lost my daughter. My identity has been compromised."

"What are you going to do, Boss?" Pete looked stunned. "I don't think you're ready for the easy chair."

Moyer grinned. "Well, I landed me a sweet job with a private security firm. I'll be a consultant. Good money. And not only that, Rich is going with me. The Army has given him a medical discharge—losing his eye and all."

"Anybody wanna see?"

Several women and Crispin said, "Eww."

"Hey, Robyn says it makes me look sexy."

"This leads me to the next announcement. Stand up, J. J."

"Why? Last time I did that I got volunteered for something."

"Stand up, Colt. The steaks are waiting."

"Okay, but I'm only doing it for the steaks."

"Everyone, I'd like to introduce you to the new team leader: J. J. 'Colt' Bartley."

"What?"

Applause.

"You earned it several times over." Moyer lifted his drink. "To Boss."

A chorus of "To Boss" rang out.

MOYER PUT TWO FOLDING tables together to make room for the inner circle, those in the know about the mission.

"Since your official retirement is a couple of weeks off, I feel safe in bringing you up to speed." Colonel Mac looked at those around the table: Zinsser, Brianne, his team, Kinkaid, Tess, and Agent Wallace.

"I appreciate that, Colonel," Moyer said.

"Of course, there are a few things I can't share, especially about Angel-12." Mac made eye contact with J. J. "Some of this you already know, but I asked Tess to help uncover the mole, the one who tipped off the Chinese and hired Green Zone to abduct Gina. Tell us how you did that, Tess."

Tess shrugged. "The real credit goes to Sergeant Kinkaid. He pushed me to act on my first thoughts, on instinct. He thinks everyone knows more than he thinks he knows. He wouldn't let up."

"I do what I can."

"Yeah. Anyway, I felt it could only be two people. Normally I wouldn't say something like that. I'm an academician, I like facts laid out in order."

"We didn't have time for that," Kinkaid said.

"I know. Anyway I chose—on what I first believed was a whim—Major Scalon and Captain Tim Bryan of STRATCOM. As I thought about it later, it occurred to me they knew more about Angel-12 than anyone else; they knew who was on the insertion team because they briefed them; and they knew what everyone involved was doing, because they were monitoring the situation from Nebraska."

"Okay, Scalon is a desk pilot but Tim Bryan is a decorated Spec Ops man." Rich scratched at his freshly healed facial wound.

"That's why I dismissed them at first, but my gut said one of them had to be the one."

"I love my baby's gut." J. J. gave her a squeeze.

"Still, Kinkaid gets the credit."

"Nonsense," Kinkaid said. "When you chose those two, I figured you had lost your mind."

"Oh, thanks."

"He was alone, Tess. He brought me the names and rejected the whole notion," Mac said. "Had the suggestion come from anyone else, I wouldn't have given it a second thought. But I did, and I called the president. He had the FBI do a background check. Captain Bryan had recently come into some money, much of which he put in an offshore account. A little deeper look and we found a connection to Green Zone. We checked their bank accounts—don't ask—and they received a big hunk of cash from Bryan's offshore account."

"Wait," J. J. said. "The Chinese paid Captain Bryan for information on Angel-12, then paid Green Zone through him?"

"Yes." Mac leaned on the table. "Army CID in Nebraska collared him. He's been interviewed by several organizations including intel groups. He's confessed to everything. It seems he holds a grudge because he has received no recognition for the missions he did. He thinks he should have received more credit for being wounded in action. In his mind, the Air Force just stuck him in a desk job in Nebraska."

"So he sold out," Moyer said.

"Yes."

"I think I know the answer to this," Moyer began, "but how did the president arrange for the Russian military to extract us and deliver us to the *Michael Monsoor*?"

"He told me he just laid out the truth, asked for help, and turned over the location of Egonov's group and one of his men."

"Dr. Igor," Jose said. "Man had skills. He said something to Captain Masters that puzzles me. He said, 'My father would be proud.' Masters seemed to understand."

Moyer turned to J. J. "You ready for your new role?"

"Nope. Were you?"

"Never felt ready." Moyer looked at his wife, daughter, and son laughing. "I am, however, ready for what comes next."

He rose from the table and walked to his family.